FLIRTING WITH DANGER

I'm playing with fire. My decision to let Saylor travel with me is potentially life threatening not only to me, but to her too. She knows I'm a biker, but I don't think she understands what that actually means. She doesn't know my job or what it is I do when I'm on the road. I want to be honest with her, but I can't betray my club and I won't make her an accomplice to my crimes.

My answer to her question was all the reason she needed. She agreed almost immediately, trusting me with her life without any demand for further knowledge of anything. Moments after I told her, I received a text from Shady notifying me that she'd canceled her flight. She was canceling a trip she's always wanted to take, just to be with me. As I watch her pack a bag, the thought eats away at me and now I have to ask her why.

"Don't you want to know where we're going?"

"It doesn't matter. Anywhere but here is good enough for me." I grab her elbow, stopping her from shoving things into her backpack until her gaze reaches my eyes.

"I need more than that, Saylor. Why are you so willing to run away with a piece of shit like me?" She frowns at my words.

"I've been in this town my whole life. I have nothing. I know you are confused about why I chose you. I can see the uncertainty in your eyes every time I look at them. All I can tell you is that you inspire me. You make me want to live." Her eyes drop to her hands a moment before she looks back at me with sorrow and tears in those green pools I'm so obsessed with. "I just want to live."

SINNER'S CREED

KIM JONES

BERKLEY BOOKS, NEW YORK

BERKLEY

An imprint of Penguin Random House LLC
375 Hudson Street, New York, New York 10014

Copyright © 2016 by Kim Jones.
Penguin supports copyright. Copyright fuels creativity, encourages diverse voices,
promotes free speech, and creates a vibrant culture. Thank you for buying an authorized
edition of this book and for complying with copyright laws by not reproducing, scanning, or
distributing any part of it in any form without permission. You are supporting writers and
allowing Penguin to continue to publish books for every reader.

BERKLEY® and the "B" design are registered trademarks of Penguin Random House LLC.
For more information, visit penguin.com.

Library of Congress Cataloging-in-Publication Data

Jones, Kim.
Sinner's creed / Kim Jones.
p.   cm.
ISBN 978-1-101-98769-8
1. Motorcyclists—Fiction.   2. Man-woman relationships—Fiction.   I. Title.
PS3610.O6267S57 2016
813'.6—dc23
2015028334

PUBLISHING HISTORY
Berkley trade paperback edition / March 2016

PRINTED IN THE UNITED STATES OF AMERICA

10   9   8   7   6   5   4   3   2

Cover photo by Claudio Marinesco.
Cover design by George Long.
Text design by Kelly Lipovich.

Penguin
Random
House

For my beautiful Saylor Grace

ACKNOWLEDGMENTS

To God for giving me the gift of life, the courage to take a chance, and an eternal love.

My husband, Regg. You are by far the best husband I've ever had. And even though you're the only one I've ever had, it doesn't make me love you any less.

Amy—you're not just my best friend, mother of my godchild, or favorite girl. You're my inspiration—my rock. You're the one who helped make me who I am—which is a pretty damn good person if you ask me.

Mom and Dad—I know you'll love me no matter how successful I am. For that I thank you. But I'm still not cutting you any slack in Phase 10.

My sisters—eh . . . I don't really have anything special to say about the two of you. Kidding. I love you both very much. Not everyone can say that they have sisters as talented as mine. I mean, one runs ninety-nine Dollar Generals and the other has given me nineteen brothers-in-law.

Katy Evans—you helped make this book possible. Thanks for loving me and my stories. Your friendship, encouragement, and feedback played a HUGE part in this novel. You're sweet, genuine, and make me feel like a superstar—which I really am.

Joanna Wylde—thanks for helping me make the right decisions. You're my voice of reason. Your guidance and support are two of the greatest gifts you could ever give me. And a car . . . that would be a nice gift too.

To the girls who reassured me that *Sinner's Creed* was truly everything I thought it was. Chrisy Morris, Sali with an i, Benbow hyphen Powers, Danielle Kendall, Brooklyn Brown, Katelan Awesomeness, Kathi Pepper and the Pepper girls—you are amazing. I couldn't have done it without you. Or cigarettes. Definitely cigarettes.

My family—my aunts, uncles, cousins, stepcousins, half cousins, ex-cousins, in-laws . . . There are too many of you to list. But you know who you are. And you know how much I love you. If you don't, I'm telling you now.

To my HNDW family—it is because of you that I have an infatuation with the lifestyle. Not only are you sexy, badass, and . . . sexy. You're a true inspiration and your actions teach what true brotherhood is all about. A special shout-out to Jared . . . my Dirk.

My editor, Cindy Hwang. Thanks for enduring me and my antisocial, early-morning behavior. I have a feeling that was just the beginning of a long and fruitful relationship. There's no getting rid of me now. I'm like a fungus, baby—I grow on you.

Last and certainly least, I'd like to thank my agent. Even though you sometimes ignore me, I still couldn't have done this without you. Thanks for believing in me. And remember, I love you despite all your many, many flaws. Amy Tannenbaum—you're my horse; I don't care if you ever win a race.

PROLOGUE

I KNEW THE man in front of me was doomed.

This was a test. I had to prove my loyalty. The club had my pride, now they wanted my innocence.

The knife I held in my hand would be kept as proof that I was guilty of murder. It wouldn't help my case that the man was begging for his life, on his knees in front of me. We were the only two on the video. It was everything they needed. My fingerprints, my weapon, and my face. The club would use it against me if I ever turned on them.

I wasn't scared to take this man's life. I knew he deserved everything he got and so much more. What scared me was knowing that if I did this, there would be no saving me from the depths of hell, from the fiery roads of eternity or the haunting sounds of this man's screams, which I was sure would give me nightmares for the rest of my days.

But, this club is all I know. I'm out of options. Either I prove myself now, or I walk away and never look back. I look up at my grandfather, who gives me a nod of encouragement. His black eyes are full of hate. They have the same effect on me now as they did when I was seven. He is the only man I fear, and the only man I don't want to disappoint.

The club means something to me because it means something to him. He is all I have. He has molded me into the monster I've become. If I knew for sure that not becoming a killer would ensure me a spot in the afterlife away from him, I would take my life right now. But, I know there is no place for me but hell. With him. For eternity.

I can only hear the man's screams, but I see my grandfather mouth "pussy." He is growing impatient. I have to make a decision. So, I ask myself, *Is killing this man worth pacifying the demon-possessed grandfather who raised me? Is taking a life really worth seeing the small, temporary sparkle of pride in his eyes that I've never seen in my twenty-one years? Is it worth the small mustard seed of hope that this will make him love me?* You're fuckin' right it is.

I kill the man with the brutality that the club expects, stabbing him multiple times until his face is unrecognizable. I let the faith I have in my grandfather's love fuel me. I let images of him smiling and telling me he loves me fill my head, and block the sight of the face I am butchering.

When I am finished, I search for him in the crowd, but he isn't there. When I finally notice the men around me, the body is buried and the evidence has been collected. They all wear a look of pity on their faces. Their eyes apologize for what my grandfather is, and what I have become. They can keep their guilt. They can save their sorrow. My cold, dead heart is at the point of no return.

The hell I once feared is now a desire. Satan isn't there anyway. He is here. His eyes are black as night, his heart is cold as ice, and the words *Sinner's Creed* are tattooed on his back. The same poisonous blood that runs through his veins runs through mine.

Hell is my home and Satan is this man, the only father I know. And if evil is he, then evil am I. I don't need his pride. I don't need his love. He wanted a monster; he got one. I am the spawn of Satan. I am the son of Lucifer. I am Sinner's Creed.

1

INNOCENCE.

THAT'S THE FIRST thing I thought of the first time I laid eyes on Saylor Samson. Her eyes were wide. Her teeth were chattering, and her hair was stuck to her head as she stood in the rain, shaking at the sight of me. I was scaring her. It was pouring, dark, and a man she didn't know was approaching her.

I usually had women throwing themselves at me. Leather, rain, and sex seemed to go hand in hand with the women I knew. But, looking at her, I knew she was not like the women I knew. She was a girl, a young one. Maybe seventeen.

I stereotyped her instantly, figuring she was one of those little cheerleading bitches that was out past curfew. Or maybe she told Daddy she was studying with a friend when really she had been fucking some guy outside the club that wasn't too far from here.

My kind didn't visit her part of town much. It was probably the first time she had ever seen a biker face-to-face. But she was in my part of town now with a busted tire, no cell phone service, and completely at my mercy.

I reached my hand out and she flinched. I wouldn't hurt her, but she didn't know that and I didn't feel the need to reassure her. Instead, I kept my eyes on hers as I opened the car door and found the button to pop the trunk. I grabbed the spare and changed the tire, while she just stood in the pouring rain and watched me, her arms crossed tightly over her chest, probably to hide her tiny tits.

When I was finished, I threw the busted tire in the trunk before giving her a salute and heading back to my bike. She never spoke and neither did I. By the time I was straddled across the seat of my Harley, she was gone.

That was five years ago.

SEXINESS.

That's the first thing I saw the second time I laid eyes on Saylor Samson. I was in downtown, a part of Jackson, Mississippi, where I wasn't shunned and she wasn't too out of place. She was walking down the sidewalk with her head down, texting, dressed in white cutoff shorts and a tiny tank top with a bikini under it. Her legs were long and tan. Her hair was blond and curly, and her eyes were hid behind a pair of aviators.

When she crashed into me, I grabbed her arms to steady her when the impact of her small, soft body colliding with mine caused her to almost fall. When she looked at me, I knew she remembered who I was. Her mouth formed that small O that's so fucking sexy on a woman, and when she released a breath of air, it was warm against my chin. I just stared at her, my eyes looking for hers through my own dark glasses. When she took a step back, I dropped my hand, gave another salute, and walked past her. By the time I got to the corner and looked back, she was gone.

That was three years ago.

MUSIC.

That's the first thing I heard the third time I saw Saylor Samson. She sang a song that immediately got my attention. It was beautiful. Just like her. Her hair was straight, and she looked elegant. Her body was hidden behind a piano, but her eyes found mine as I took a seat at the table closest to her.

I twirled the beer bottle in my hand and watched as she sang to me. She was asking me to come away with her. I ignored the looks everyone in the restaurant gave me. I didn't belong there. It was a nice place. People were wearing suits and shit, but I didn't give a fuck. I didn't want to sit at the bar where I half-ass fit in. I wanted to sit at the table next to the Aphrodite with the beautiful voice, right in the middle of the tie-wearing CEOs and their overpriced escorts. And she wanted me there. She hadn't looked at me like I didn't belong. She looked at me like I was the only man in the room. When the song finished, she left. Maybe she went on break. Maybe it was her last song. I didn't know and never would. I left when she did.

That was two years ago.

PROTECTIVENESS.

That's what the fuck I felt the last time I laid eyes on Saylor Samson. I was in a bar, she was in a bar. I had a date, she had a date. My date was a smokin'-hot redhead I'd picked up on my way in that had already come on my knee twice. Her date was a fuckin' prick who had jealousy issues. Not that I could blame him.

Saylor wasn't a little girl anymore. She was a full-blown woman whose dance moves had every dick in the bar twitching. Her hair was long. Really fuckin' long. Down to her ass and thick and curly and crazy, kinda like she stuck her finger in a light socket. And it was sexy. Really fuckin' sexy. I felt my dick press harder against my jeans, and it had nothing to do with the red-head humping my knee and sucking my neck.

Saylor wore a skirt that looked like it was made out of glitter and was so short, the cheeks of her ass hung out every time Lil Jon demanded she get low. My eyes moved down her legs to her high heels that were so tall, it looked like she was walking on her toes. I don't know how in the hell women wear that shit, but it was hot. Especially on Saylor Samson.

She was dancing on a table with a group of her friends. Judging by the sash and tiara the girl next to her was wearing, they were celebrating something. It physically hurt when I had to drag my eyes from Saylor's legs to find her date yelling at her. He was demanding she get off the table, and I could make out the words "go fuck yourself" on her lips. When he reached up and grabbed for her leg, I was already on my way over. I wasn't pissed because it was Saylor who he was messing with, or at least that's what I told myself.

Usually, I didn't get involved with relationship drama. This guy could be her husband for all I knew, but she was a chick and he was a dude, and I wasn't gonna stand for that shit. I felt her eyes on me, and I didn't want to look, but I did. The fight seemed to die out of her, and I knew it was because she knew I was there. I don't know how she knew and I didn't care. All that mattered was that she needed me. She needed me and she knew I could protect her. I could help her. She knew this shit, and she didn't even know my fucking name.

Adrenaline shot through my body. I could feel my temples throbbing . . . my nostrils flaring . . . my teeth clenching . . . my hands balling into fists. I was gonna kill that motherfucker. She was telling me with her eyes she needed this. She wanted this. She wanted me.

I grabbed the prick by the throat and he grasped my hand in a shitty attempt to pry my fingers from around his neck. I carried him through the crowd of people with his feet kicking in the air, trying to find the floor. Once outside, I slammed him into the street. I felt that familiar feeling of power consume me as I watched him struggle to catch his breath. People around us were screaming and cheering, wanting more.

That feeling of power intensified as my fist met his bleeding flesh each time I landed a blow to his pathetic face. When I finally stopped, I stood over his body that lay unconscious on the crowded street. I turned to the cheering group of people, searching for only one face. When I found her, she was watching me.

Her eyes were slightly narrowed and her face turned to the side as she appraised me. I wanted to know what she was thinking. I wanted to know why she didn't look scared. I wanted to know why she was so calm, acting as if she already knew this was going to happen. But her friends were pulling her back into the building before I could speak to her. When she made it to the door, she turned back and before she disappeared inside, her left eye shut on a wink. And then she was gone.

That was last night.

Today, I can't get the images of Saylor over the past five years out of my head. It's stupid. I know that. I've seen hundreds of women. I've fucked just as many. This one I haven't even touched, but I can't shake her from my thoughts. Two years ago, I'd asked the man at the bar she was singing at what her name was. All this time, that's all I've ever known about her. But in just a few minutes I will know everything, or at least everything that has been documented on paper. I won't know her favorite color or what makes her laugh or what her favorite food is or any of that shit. I'm sure

I can find out if I really want to, and I wouldn't even have to talk to her, but for some reason, this is shit I want her to tell me.

I slam my fist on the table, squeezing my eyes shut in pure aggravation. Why the hell do I care? It isn't natural for me. I have brothers all over the world, but I don't want to know their favorite color or what the fuck makes them laugh. I respect them, but it pretty much ends there.

I have to stay the hell outta Jackson, Mississippi. It seems like every time I come here, I see her. And every time I see her, I dream of her. And every time I dream of her, I dream we are together, and she is smiling. I've never even seen her smile, but I dreamed it was something beautiful. Like a sunset or a rainbow or a clear blue sky the day after a storm.

I clench my fist until my knuckles are white and bring them to my head, letting out a growl of frustration. Words like *sunset*, *rainbow*, and *beautiful* aren't even in my vocabulary. My thoughts have me feeling weak. I need to kill. I need to hit someone. I need to control the crazy shit that's happening in my head. *Fucking sunshine and rainbows . . . What a pussy.*

"Bad time?" I move my hands from my face and find Shady staring at me with a piece of paper in one hand and the other one held up in surrender. Good. By his reaction, I know I haven't lost my touch. I like that men fear me, even if he is my own brother.

"You got my shit?" I growl, ignoring his question. This is one of the reasons I ride Nomad—alone. Stupid shit like unnecessary conversation.

"Yeah, man. I got it." I snatch the paper from his hand. It's not that I don't like Shady, or that I don't respect him. I'm just not much of a people person.

Everyone I come in contact with has strict orders from Nationals to give me anything I ask for and not to fuck with me. The results will be nasty and guaranteed. The warning from Nationals is the only one they get. Most of them respect it and leave me alone, but there were always those that pushed the limits just because they thought they could. The unlucky bastards that didn't heed the warning now have scars of repercussion.

I study the paper, pausing long enough to dismiss Shady with a look, and read the address until it is memorized. That's all I need for now. The rest I can read later. I shove the paper in my pocket on my way out, passing the guys in the clubhouse without even a look. I give them my two-fingered, half-ass signature salute and I'm gone.

2

SINNER'S CREED MOTORCYCLE Club's Jackson chapter club-house is located in the old part of downtown Jackson. The place where even the cops don't bother coming. We run the whole block, and if you somehow end up on this street you are either lost, a business associate, or looking for trouble. Saylor's apartment is only a few miles from here, somewhere between uptown Jackson, where the rich fuckers live, and old downtown, where the projects are, and the Sinner's Creed clubhouse.

I find her apartment building easily. It seems less than middle class, something maybe college kids would live in or single moms. I've imagined Saylor in something a little nicer than some shitty apartment. Something like a cottage on the lake, where she could watch the sunset every evening.

Sunset.

There's that fucking word again. Invading my thoughts and making me want to stick someone in the neck with my knife. I park across the street and pull out a smoke, inhaling deeply in hopes that the nicotine will calm my annoyance with my mind. I don't know why I'm here. I don't know what the hell I'm thinking. I'm confused, I'm out of my element, and I'm twisted the fuck up.

Saylor isn't home. I've been here over an hour, stalking her apartment like some kind of freak, and she has yet to show. I hate myself for missing her. I wish I could stay longer, but I have a job to do. My club comes first. And it always will.

I'm going too fast down the small road that leads me to the highway. I'm going so fast that I almost miss the tear-streaked face surrounded by a mass of blond hair that belongs to the body of the goddess who is walking down the sidewalk. I make an illegal U-turn in the middle of the street and race back toward her, stopping my bike several yards in front of where she is walking. When I get off and remove my helmet, I stand next to my bike, willing my legs to not walk up to her and take her in my arms and comfort her.

Comfort. Another word I'm not used to having in my head.

She walks closer, stopping a few feet from where I'm standing. Her eyes are sad, and I feel my heart speed up and my mind go into overdrive with all the forms of torture I can perform on the one who made her so sad.

"You're late," she says, and then I see it. It's not a sunset or a rainbow or a clear blue sky. It's something so much better. Even though her smile is sad and is only the one used when it's appropriate to be polite, it's the most beautiful fucking thing I have ever seen. And I've seen a lot.

I don't know what I'm late for. Was she expecting me? I want to ask, but I can barely make it through the introductions. I don't know how in the hell I'll ever have a conversation with this girl. Just her presence seems to overwhelm me.

"I'm Dirk." My tone is harsh—the result of my pissed-off state, which just accelerated because she deserves a tone that is soft and kind and pleasant to her ears.

"I'm Saylor."

"I know," I tell her, and the look on her face says she might have already known that I did my research.

"I know I don't know you, but I feel like I do." I know exactly what she means, but I don't tell her that. I just stare at her, willing her to speak again, so I can add that voice to my dreams. "I remember you." Her admission doesn't surprise me. But now I'm curious about how much she remembers and how much she knows.

As if she can see straight through me, she tells me exactly what I'm wanting to hear. "You helped me change my tire. I was scared of you that night. Just one look at your vest and I immediately stereotyped you." She motions toward my cut with her hand. As if I couldn't remember what it said, I look down at it. The *1%* patch over my heart glares back at me, reminding me of who I am. I wonder if Saylor has done her research on me like I did on her. If she has, then this won't go much further than it already has.

"Say my name," I demand, wanting to hear how it sounds on her lips before she realizes what a bad idea this is and runs off. My eyes move to her mouth. I want to memorize the way it looks when her full, pink lips poke out to pronounce my name.

"Dirk." And it's perfect. I want to tell her to say it again, but she does so without my command. It's like she can read my thoughts, and I immediately try to clear my head of anything that might offend her. "Is there room for two on that thing?" She's standing with her arms crossed over her chest and when she nods her head toward my bike, the never-ending strands of wild, curly hair move, and the wind catches the scent and carries it straight to my nostrils at the same moment I inhale.

Motherfucker.

Her hair smells fresh like citrus. Like oranges and lemons and shit. Not like hairspray and all those fucking hair care products, but natural and clean. I feel the saliva building in my mouth.

"There's room," I say shortly. I don't like to talk. I want to listen and I want her to tell me everything. And I want to smell her. I want to smell her hair and her neck and kiss the parts of her body other men didn't care about or appreciate. Like the crease at her elbow, or behind her knee. I watch her walk toward me until she is standing so close that I nearly take a step back out of habit.

"Dirk," she says, my name coming out of her mouth on a whisper, and I inhale her breath and let it coat the back of my throat. "I just need to get out of here." Her eyes are pleading. They search mine, and I watch as they move back and forth in her head, looking for something from me. They are incredible. She is so close that I can see the thin brown circles that outline her bright green eyes. *Green* seems too simple of a word to describe them. *Emerald* isn't much better, but the word suits not only the color, but the delicacy of them.

She notices my uneasiness. She can see the question in my eyes, the one that asks, *Why the hell do you want to get on the back of a bike with a guy like me?* Most women would do it because bad boys are appealing to them. It would be a thrill to throw all their inhibitions to the wind. But Saylor needs me for another reason.

"I'm not scared of you, Dirk. Even if there was something left in this life that could scare me, it wouldn't be you. You've always been my savior. You may not know it, but you always show up just when I need you most. You're like my angel. And right now, I need you."

"I'm no angel." The word seems to lose some of its meaning by just being spoken out loud by me. It would have an entirely different definition if it actually applied to me.

"Please." She's begging me for understanding. She's asking me for help. And I don't know why I'm still standing here trying to talk myself out of it. Isn't this more than I could have expected? More than a man like me deserves?

I hand her my helmet, which fits after all her hair is shoved inside it. To hell with the reasons. She told me she needed me, and right now, there is nothing else I'd rather do than give her whatever it is she needs.

The only seat I have is on the fender. My bike is not equipped for a passenger, but I make it work by wrapping her legs around my waist. The feel of her body is warm against mine, sending my senses into overdrive. Her scent, the feel of her wrapped around me . . . I've never experienced anything like it. And soon, I'm speeding off into the wind, letting it bear the weight of both our problems and letting the road lead us somewhere other than here.

There is a dock in Vicksburg that gives a great view of the Mississippi River. At night it is lit up with the lights of tugboats, and the only sound is the hum of the engines. It's peaceful and often where I stay when I have business in town. The club uses this dock to transport shit, and I use it as an escape.

Many nights I've sat here, and Saylor's latest mental image is what I've envisioned. It would be different having her here. Better. I hope. When I stop the bike, I can feel her shaking. I close my eyes and grip the handlebars, pissed at myself for letting her get cold. I'm a fucking idiot.

I step off and remove her helmet to find that it isn't the weather causing her to shake. If the eighty-degree temperature isn't enough to convince me, the sobs racking through her body and the tears falling out of her eyes are.

I'm not a sentimental guy. I've never consoled a woman or

held one while she cried. That's not my job. My job is to take what I need, give her something equal in return, and leave.

But this is Saylor. The girl who has consumed my mind for over five years. I've spoken less than ten words to her, and she's still the most important fucking woman in my life. I've never been able to find the logic, and even now, I'm dumbfounded as to why she is the one.

I stand here, watching her cry. Not sure of what to do. Her legs hang lifeless off the sides of my bike, a result of them being numb after the hour ride. Her arms dangle at her sides, and she doesn't bother wiping her face or pushing her hair out of the steady stream of tears.

I'm not good with words. I'm not good with crying. I don't know what she wants or what she needs, because her eyes have become just as lifeless as her legs, and there is no way she can speak through her sobs. I've watched movies and I've heard songs that tell you how to hold a woman. I'm sure I could do it, but I have this ache in my fucking chest that won't let me do anything but stand here.

Minutes pass and her tears are still flowing, but her sobs have died. When she speaks, the relief is so great that I feel my knees starting to buckle and I have to change my stance.

"Dirk," she says, and the ache in my chest vanishes. I wonder if it's heartburn. I've never felt it before. "Can I stay with you tonight?" Her eyes are on mine, and even in the darkness I can see how red and puffy they are. I can see the need and the desperation there too.

"Yes." It's simple. She asks, I give. She wants this and I want to give her whatever she wants.

I have a room at the warehouse. It's small and simple, but has a shower, a toilet, and a twin-sized bed. That's all I need. I have a room like this in every town we have a chapter. Most are in clubhouses, but sometimes I get lucky and can find a place to crash off-site, away from the constant drama that comes with being in a motorcycle club.

I help her off the bike, noticing how her body seems to tremble slightly. It might be the fear, or the adrenaline of doing something dangerous, but whatever it is has no effect on the determination on her face. She places her hand in mine, walking beside me as I lead her to the building.

I open the door to the room and it is black. There are no windows and only a single light bulb that hangs from the ceiling. I pull the string and the light comes on, revealing the room, and I gauge Saylor's reaction because I want to make sure it's good enough. If it's not, I can get a place at a nearby casino. She walks around the small space and she is still holding my hand. The room is so compact that my arm stretches everywhere she walks and I don't have to move my legs.

I'm pissed again. She has been holding my hand and I've been so deep in my own fucking thoughts that I haven't had a chance to memorize what her small, warm hand in mine feels like. I relax my face in an attempt to not be so intimidating, but I doubt it works.

"It's perfect. Can I use the bathroom?" The sound of her voice is soothing and calm. It prides me knowing that I'm the only one in the world who can hear it right now.

"Yes," I say and release her hand. She smiles at me and it's polite, but so fucking rewarding. There is only a curtain that separates the space between me and her, and when she steps behind it, the loss of her presence has me feeling lonely. This is something else I will process on my ride or in my sleep. Right now, I just want the moment. I don't want my mind clouded with thoughts of what is wrong with me. I just want to hear her voice and see her face and feel her touch.

When she steps from behind the curtain, I just stand there

and appraise her. Her hair is a beautiful mess. Her shorts are short enough to reveal almost all of her thighs and legs, and her white T-shirt is so tight, I can see the outline of her bra beneath it.

"Do you live here?" she asks, and her question should annoy me, but it doesn't, and I find myself answering her.

"When I'm in town, this is where I sleep." I don't know why she chose me to share it with, but I finally get that smile that I've dreamed of. It's not polite or expected. It's genuine and fucking breathtaking. It stretches across her face, and I can see the top row of her teeth that are just as perfect as her smile. It makes me want to smile, and I haven't smiled in a long time.

My face softens, but I hold on to my smile because I'm undeserving of taking any glory from her. Her smile lights up the whole world and mine is nothing in comparison. This is her moment, and I would kill any smiling motherfucker who walked in this room and tried to take it away.

"You scared my friends last night." She takes a seat on the bed, looking up at me through her long, mascara-covered lashes. "Well, if you want to call them my friends. They're more like acquaintances. I thought that guy deserved what he got. I'd just met him that night. He had no right to try to claim me as his. I can't even remember his name." She doesn't know me, but she knows what I'm capable of. Yet she never hesitated to come here with me. Hell, she practically begged for it.

I want to know her reasons. I want to know why she is putting such trust in a man that looks like me, acts like me, and has a reputation like mine. If just the sight of my patches scared her, then she was aware of the bad rep bikers had. It didn't matter if the stereotype proved to be true or not. As an outsider, she knew the risks. She knew the difference between us and our two worlds.

I was the predator and she was the prey. I was the shark and she was the bait. I was the demon-possessed monster and she was the innocent, naïve angel. I could almost envision the sight of her white feathered wings trapped by the large, sharp jaws of my mouth. Shit like this didn't happen. Nobody could be as perfect as she seemed to be and still want something to do with an imperfection like myself.

I watch her stand, crossing her arms over her chest while she walks around the small room, having nothing to look at but cinder block wall, white-tiled ceilings, and concrete floors. But she seems intrigued by them.

"Sometimes I dream of you, Dirk." I feel something shift inside me. "Sometimes I swear I can even feel you lying next to me at night." She runs her hand over the wall, looking up at the ceiling and avoiding my stare. I'd dreamed of her too. I've never had the feeling be strong enough that I could actually feel her, but I've imagined for years what it would be like to have her laying next to me. On the darkest nights, when sleep refused to take me, my mind would always drift to her. Those dreams I controlled, but even in my imagination, I never felt worthy enough to touch her.

"Do you remember the second time I saw you?"

"Yes." How could I forget? I remembered every time I saw her.

"I was beginning to think that maybe I'd imagined you. That the man in my dreams was a myth—something my subconscious created to help me forget what happened that night before I saw you." I want to know what happened, but I can tell that she's not going to tell me. Her eyes darken at just the memory, and my blood pumps faster at the thought of someone hurting her.

"It was like you knew that I was beginning to forget you, so you showed up to prove to me that you were real. Then . . ." She pauses, fidgeting with her shirt. It seems like forever passes before she speaks again. "You came to my job. They were firing me that night. They'd just told me to finish out my song requests and leave. I was crushed. My music career was over, just like that." She snaps her fingers and smiles. There is no look of defeat or failure on her face, only happiness. "You reminded me that I have a bigger purpose in this world, other than singing. So, believe what you want. But to me, you're an angel."

Pride swells in my chest, but I quickly push it back down. I couldn't be that for her. Her expectations were too high for a man like me. I was a murderer, a thief, and a liar. I didn't just kill, I tortured. I didn't steal from the rich and give to the poor, I took what I wanted and I kept it for myself. Little white lies were the same as big ones to me. The only people I'd never lied to were my brothers. And I'd never lied to her. But I would, if she ever fucked up and asked the wrong questions.

"I need something from you, Dirk. I need something that only you can give me." This time, her eyes meet mine and she is battling with her pride. She wants to ask, but either she's afraid of rejection, or she doesn't want to show any more weakness. I can't be her angel, but I can't deny her either. It doesn't matter what she asks, I'll do it.

"Anything." My voice is low and gruff, and can barely be heard over the screaming in my head. I'm fucking up. I shouldn't do this. But my want is too powerful to listen to rational thought. It overrides my mind, controls my actions, and beats the hell out of my better judgment. I want to give her this. And I will.

"This goes against everything I believe. My morals, my ethics, and my desire to uphold his will in who he wants me to be. Dirk, I want you to hold me tonight. I just want you to hold me and kiss me and help me forget everything. I know it's selfish, but is it too much to ask?" Her voice is thick and emotional. I know she's gonna break down again. I don't know what she wants to forget. But I'll make sure she does. I don't know who *he* is. I don't know what control he has over her life. But tonight, she doesn't want him. She wants me.

I should be pissed that she called herself selfish. I should be pissed at the one who treated her like he didn't need to hold her like he needed to breathe. I wouldn't be that motherfucker. I would be the one who would make her feel special, even if it's just for tonight. Even though I know I can feel shit inside me that makes me realize that this is bad for me. But, I will make her feel special, because she asked for it and it will make me the selfish one. Because I can't offer her anything other than tonight, and I will make it so amazing for her that no other man will ever be able to make her feel like I did.

"It's not too much to ask," I tell her and watch as her eyes widen and her nostrils flare slightly. She is fighting to hold back her tears. Relief is on her face and sags her shoulders. That ache is back in my chest and it's fighting against a feeling of elation that I have because I gave her that relief. I'm going to get to touch her and I waste no time.

There are two steps between us and I close the distance, never letting my eyes leave hers. Mine are willing her to trust me and hers are telling me she does. I slowly raise my hand and push her hair over her shoulder so that it falls down her back. My hand grazes her neck, and I feel my pulse quicken when her mouth falls open and her eyes close. She is doing something to me.

"Saylor." She sighs as I whisper her name. When I trail my finger slowly down her neck and between her tits, the slightest moan escapes her lips and I feel my dick swell in my jeans. When I reach the hem of her shirt, I slide both my hands beneath it and up her rib cage, feeling her hot skin tremble beneath my calloused hands. She is as soft as satin, and I don't want the fabric of her shirt between us anymore. I move my hands up her sides, forcing her arms to lift, pulling her shirt over her head. When it's off and her face comes back into view, her eyes are open and full of want. I leave her bra but notice how her nipples have hardened and are pushing against the fabric. I swallow and it's the first physical sign of weakness I've shown. I gauge her reaction, but she hasn't noticed my fault and if she has, it isn't registering on her face.

The small amount of fear in her eyes doesn't grow when my hands drift to the button on her shorts, so I remove them too. They fall to the floor and she is now standing before me in a pair of white panties and a white bra. She couldn't be more beautiful or vulnerable, and to keep from feeling like I'm taking advantage of her, I have to remind myself that she asked for this. Maybe not to this extent, but the hungry look she wears says that she doesn't mind.

I make her stand there, her body convulsing in light shakes, giving her plenty of time to change her mind while I strip down to my boxers. Her eyes appraise my body and she likes what she sees. I see her fingers flex, wanting to touch me. But I don't give her time to make a move. I lead her to the bed a few feet away and she climbs in without hesitation and, fuck me, but I take a moment to drink her in. She is about five seven and the sixty-seven inches of woman, half naked and lying in my bed, is enough to please me for the rest of my fucked-up life. She hasn't touched anything other than my hand, yet she is more pleasurable than any other woman I've ever been with.

I pull the string on the light and wish there was a window in the room. I want to see her in the moonlight. Even if it's just her silhouette. I hear her breathing accelerate and I know she is nervous. She can't see me, but the feeling will be more intense because of it. I slide between the covers, keeping my weight on my arms as I lean down into her hair and inhale. Her body is shaking with need, and the fear and excitement and trembling is so intense that I speak to her in hopes of calming her nerves. "I promise to give you what you asked for and nothing else. Trust me." My whisper of words works and I feel her body relax. I kiss down her neck and across her collarbone before making my way to her mouth. When my lips find hers, she opens to me and I slip my tongue inside and I feel her sink further into the mattress. Fuck she tastes amazing. Like citrus. Just like she smells.

I keep the kiss slow and deep, trying to calm the urge to ravish her. She moans in my mouth and I have to lift my hips to keep my hard cock from touching her. Reluctantly, I pull away from her mouth and kiss down her neck, paying attention to every place that is bared to me. Her arms, her hands, her stomach, and of course that little crease at her elbow. Her moans are louder and her hands have found my hair. She pulls and it feels so fucking good I'm afraid I don't have the willpower to stop.

I don't go below her stomach because there is no way I can kiss her without diving beneath her panties at the scent of her pussy. The smell of her arousal is mouthwatering and I know she is wet and ready for me. I find her mouth again and kiss her deep. I can't get enough of her. I feel her hands tracing the muscles of my shoulders and my back. Her nails are short but manage to find their way into my skin. I want her to mark me. I want to remember this night. I want her pleasure to scar me. But my wants are not important. Only hers.

"Dirk." At the sound of my name on her lips, the ache in my chest becomes heavier. She is desperate and begging for release.

"Tell me what you want," I whisper in her ear, kissing my way back down her neck as my hand rubs from her hip to breast and back down.

"Please," she begs, and I know she can't say it. She is ashamed and embarrassed to say what she really wants, and her words tell me she is not very experienced. My fingers trace across the hem of her panties and I hear her take a deep, staccato breath in anticipation. I slip my hand under the material to find her bare and wet.

A groan escapes me and it's my second show of weakness. I find her small clit that throbs between her wet lips, and I rub it softly.

She is shaved, her lips just as full as the ones that surround her mouth, and I can't imagine her feeling any different or any more perfect. A moan rips through her chest and I feel my own swell at her reaction. I shift my weight so I'm on my side and her legs open wide, inviting me in.

"Baby, you feel so fucking good," I whisper in her ear, and I'm rewarded with another moan of pleasure. She likes the way I compliment her. She likes that I called her baby. I like that she likes it. Her hands push her bra up, exposing her chest to the darkness, and I'm so fucking jealous of it I growl. My mouth finds her hard nipple easily, and when she says my name, I don't care if I ever see them. Kissing them is so much better. I want to kiss her pussy. I want to taste her wetness. I'm working hard to not let her come in hopes that she will ask me, but I know she won't.

I release her nipple from my mouth and whisper over it, my breath blowing against it, and although I can't see, I know it is puckering further in the darkness. "Can I kiss your pussy?" I ask. I've never said those words in all my fucking life. I've never had to.

"Please," she begs me, and I'm hesitant because I know I will never get to do this for the first time again. It will never be the same after I first taste her. I will never get that feeling of satisfaction again. I will chase this high for the rest of my life and nothing will ever compare. But I won't let it stop me. I can't. Now my dreams will be filled with her smile, her scent, and her fucking taste.

I slide between her legs and take her panties off, tossing them to the floor. I don't want to tease her any longer. I bury my nose in her sweet-scented pussy and inhale deeply. She is divine. When my tongue slides between her lips, her sound is more than a moan. It is a cry of passion that almost makes me lose it. My mouth consumes her pussy—drinking her and savoring her scent and taste. I kiss her with my lips, sliding my tongue over her again and again. I avoid applying too much pressure because I'm being an asshole and want to taste her longer, but she's not complaining.

She is writhing under me and crying out my name. I insert the tip of my finger inside her and she tenses, but she relaxes when I don't push further. Her reaction screams at me. It tells me this sexy goddess, that no other woman can compare to, hasn't been touched in a long time.

The thought of no one being inside her for so long has me consumed with a feral need so intense that I almost tell her that she is mine. It makes me fucking crazy and desperate to take her. I circle my tongue around her clit, giving her the pressure she needs to release. She screams and I feel her tighten. I push deeper into her, feeling her walls contract around my finger that is buried deep inside her. I continue to work her with my mouth and finger until she comes down from her orgasm. Then I remove my finger and replace it with my tongue, tasting her release, until she shivers from what I know now is the cold. I kiss my way back up her body, bringing the covers with me and pulling them over us before removing her bra completely. I want to feel her chest against mine, and I want her to be comfortable.

When I lay beside her, she turns in to me and I feel her arm snake around my waist. And I hold her. Like I've done it a million times. My head is swimming with thoughts of what just happened. The taste of her lingers in my mouth and on my chin. I'd just eaten the sweetest pussy of the sweetest girl that I didn't even know. And the only thing I got in return was the remnants of her release. And it was more than enough.

"I like when you call me 'baby,'" Saylor says while we lay next to each other, still trying to catch our breath. I could tell her I like it too, but I'll show her instead. I'll call her baby as much as this man of few words can. The silence stretches on until she interrupts it once again.

"It's been a while."

"I know," I say in response, trying to smooth her hair out of my face. I give up because I would rather have my arms around her. It just feels good.

"I had my heart broken when I was a teenager. At sixteen, I thought I was in love. After that, I made a promise to my mother that I wouldn't give myself to anyone else until I knew they were the right one for me. I always keep my promises." I think about this a minute and I remember that the information Shady gave me said her mother was deceased. I feel my body tense as I become angry at the thought of her mother leaving her, and the son of a bitch that broke her heart.

"Now she's gone. Cancer. She died during treatment." Saylor's voice is low and I feel her tears leak onto my chest. I hold her a little tighter, and I don't know if it is my hold that opens the floodgates or the reminder of her mother, but she starts sobbing again. "Dirk," she manages.

"Yeah?" I say through the twisting pain in my chest. It fucking hurts.

"Will you hold me and tell me everything will be okay?" At her words, I move our bodies so that I am completely entwined with her and my lips are at her ear.

"Everything will be okay. I'm here." When I reassure her, she completely loses it, and it scares me. I wonder who will do this for her when I am gone. My body rocks her and the movement surprises me. I'm holding a woman who is crying in my arms and rocking her. I hold her and rock her for what could have been hours until her breathing returns to normal, and she is in a deep sleep, with her arms wrapped tightly around me. And it's the best fucking feeling I've ever had.

3

SOMETHING IS TOUCHING me. I feel a hand stroking my two-day beard, a leg entwined with mine, and a soft, warm chest pressed up against my own. I open my eyes to find the light on and Saylor looking at me while her fingers stroke my face. She is more gorgeous in the morning than she is at night.

"I've been laying here waiting for you to open your eyes so I could stare at them." Her voice is strong, like she has been up for hours, and I wonder how long she has been watching me. I don't ask her, I just let her stroke my face, and try to ignore how good it feels to have her touching me.

"Your eyes are beautiful," she whispers, and I make a point not to blink so I don't fuck up her joy. "Hazel. It's such a mysterious color. I think if I studied them long enough, I could find every color of the rainbow in them." I doubted what she said, but if she thought she could, then I would let her test her theory all day.

"Are you leaving soon?" Her question reminds me of what I was dreading before I finally fell asleep last night. I know I have to leave and part of me can't fucking wait to get on my bike so I can process all this shit, but the other part wants to stay right here forever.

"Yes." I watch the sadness form in her eyes and that ache in my chest is back, and I have the feeling that it has nothing to do with heartburn.

"Where are you going?" I couldn't answer that. I should tell her it's none of her business, but I won't.

"West." My short answer appeases her and she doesn't push further. I'm glad she doesn't ask, but I wonder if her lack of interest is because she doesn't care to know or if she is scared to push me.

"I don't want you to leave." I don't want to leave. I want to stay here. With her. But I can't. This is my life as a Nomad and as much as I like her, I could never mentally handle being in one place for too long. Riding is my therapy and without it I would go to the deepest, darkest depths of hell where everyone is my enemy and life has no meaning.

I can't lay here with her any longer. I have to leave. I have to ride. I can't get soft. Nobody can do my job and have these feelings. I don't want to think of her when I do the shit I do. She is too precious to be surrounded with the violence and world of shit I face every day.

"I have to go," I say, moving over her and grabbing my bag. Once behind the curtain, I let the anger I feel rising consume me. I was stupid. So fucking stupid. I let her too close. I needed her to piss me off so I could hate her. She was a mistake. I never should have touched her, or tasted her, or let her say my fucking name.

I step in the shower and start scrubbing her scent from my body. I don't want to smell her. I don't need a reminder. I know she will still be here when I get out, but I'll force myself to avoid her. If I can just get away from her I will never come back to Jackson again. I will get Nationals to assign someone else for this part of the country.

I punch the cinder blocks in front of me, letting the pain in my hand numb the pain in my chest at the thought of forgetting her. I'll stop before I break any bones, but I want the blood on my knuckles to be a reminder that the hands that touched her were the hands of a killer not worthy of her.

"Dirk?" Fuck. So much for avoiding her. She just got her first taste of the fucked-up monster that I am. And it will be her last.

I hang my head in defeat and keep my fist pressed into the concrete, twisting it so the gravel digs deep into my opened wound. I need to hurt. I deserve it, but I don't feel anything. I tense when her soft hand touches my back, but she doesn't let it stop her from running her hands over me. There is soap in them, and I can feel her washing me with the gentleness that a mother uses to bathe a newborn baby.

She is too good for me. I should pull away, but I can't. I want her to touch me. Something inside me screams need, but this time it's me who requires it. Demands it. Must have it to breathe.

I feel her trying to turn my body toward her, and motherfuck me if I don't turn to face her. That wild hair sticks in every direction around her head and shoulders and halfway down her back. It makes her body look tiny in comparison. It's the first time I've seen her naked. And I'm not disappointed. Her tits are perfect— small, perky, round, and a few shades lighter than her stomach. Her nipples are a dark pink, hard and begging to be in my mouth. Her stomach is flat, but not toned to perfection. Natural and curvy, just like her tits. Only the top part of her pussy is bared to me and it's pale in comparison to her thighs.

"Hey," she says, her voice apologetic. I look at her face that is flushed red with embarrassment. At what, I don't know. She avoids my stare and fidgets before muttering, "I'm sorry." I feel a growl crawl up my throat and I want to roar.

"You are not fucking sorry," I snarl. My breathing is heavy

and deep and it takes everything inside me not to rip the whole room to shreds. This time I see the fear in her eyes. Good. I never want to hear her say those words again. But, just like everything else about her, those words are now embedded in my head.

We are trained in the MC never to say we are sorry. We apologize. *Sorry* emphasizes how bad or stupid something is. She is not stupid. Or bad. Or embarrassing.

I should tell her I'm poisonous. I should say that I'll ruin her if she stays around me. But I don't. Because this is over. "Get dressed." Those are the only words she needs to hear.

I don't speak to her again. There is no point. I've made up my mind. She will cease to exist from my life. I'll call Nationals once I'm in Texas and inform them that I won't be returning to Mississippi.

Saylor will fade from my thoughts eventually. It might take years. It might be when they put my cold, dead body in the ground, but she will one day be nothing. Not even a memory.

I pull up at her apartment and wait for her to get off the bike. I don't even want to look at her. She can keep the fucking helmet. I would cut my hand off before it went anywhere near her. I could do this. I could force myself to hate her. It would be easy. It had been so far. Keeping my mind trained on forgetting her was working. Just as long as she doesn't—

"Dirk?" Fucking words. I hated them. Why the hell couldn't everybody be mute? But I'm sure even if we were, Saylor's incoherent mumbles would be the most peaceful sound on earth. "I want you to take me with you." You have got to be kidding me. She did not just ask to go with me. I have to leave. I have to get away from her. Right. Now.

"Good-bye, Saylor." Good-byes are forever. At least for me they are. I never say good-bye to a brother. I always give them a salute. It's a show of respect that says I will see them at a later time. Even in death, I'm sure the majority of my brothers will see the same hell I will. Saylor will never see me again. Not even in the afterlife—if there is one. She will be somewhere much nicer. I'm sure of it.

"Dirk, please." Her pleading voice is powerful enough for me to turn my head and look at her. Those eyes. They are begging me. I want to ask her why she wants to go anywhere with a guy like me. I want to ask her what the fuck has stopped her from having a relationship with a normal, tie-wearing, stand-up guy who can take care of her. But I don't ask questions. Her answers wouldn't make a difference anyway.

I stare at her a little longer. This must be what crucifixion is like. No. It couldn't be. There is nothing as bad as this. It's fucking brutal. And it's not her fault. She is just the sacrificial lamb that is being dangled in the face of the lion. She has been a pawn in life's game and I have taken advantage of her.

I grab my helmet from her hands and place it on my head, torturing myself with her scent. I flip the visor up and look into her eyes. I'm glad that this is the last image I'll have of her.

The prayer I see in her eyes will haunt me. I tell her words that I have vowed to never say, because this time, they're the fucking truth. "I'm sorry."

Nationals are a group of highly respected men in the club that call the shots. They are the problem solvers, they handle the business, and they order the hits. With a club as big as Sinner's Creed, we have to have leaders to avoid problems between chapters. All chapters govern themselves and handle their own revenue. Nationals appoint the president, the president appoints his officers, and I'm the one who enforces them. My bottom rocker reads

National, but it isn't my rank. I reign over chapter members, but I'm not exempt from Nationals' orders. Although I have influence, where they're concerned.

Nationals are located in the small town of Jackpot, Nevada. The summers are smoldering, the winters are freezing, but the location is perfect for an MC like Sinner's Creed. The town consists of a casino, a restaurant, a couple of gas stations, and a post office. The population is small, but there is always a steady flow of traffic from the casino that draws people in from Idaho and Utah.

Gamblers pay little or no attention to what goes on around them, so we don't have the interest of anyone but the people that live here. Since this is where Sinner's Creed was born, the town has gotten used to the thought of us being here, and accepts us as one of them. We've never brought havoc to this town, and we never will.

Texas, on the other hand, is one of the most sought-after states. We own Texas, but we've had to fight for it many times. If you have business with Mexico, then Texas is the place you want to set up shop. So, we did. We have fourteen chapters there, but even that isn't enough to keep the wolves from knocking. And that is why my trip to Jackpot is so important.

I've been away from Saylor for two weeks and I still can't shake her from my system. I'm angrier, more anxious, high-strung, and violent than I've ever been. I've stopped at several clubhouses on my way to Jackpot and each time I left one, I left bad blood in my wake. The little shit that use to bother me, but not enough for me to act, has me breaking bones and severing ties with people who are a part of my world. And I'm drawing the attention of Nationals, which is never a good thing.

There are only a few things that can break me down, and getting a call from Shady notifying me that Nationals don't want to meet is one of those things. It's their way of telling me to calm the fuck down before I do something I might regret. If I have words with a patch holder or a club affiliate, that's one thing. If I have words with Nationals, that's another. Disrespect was unforgivable, and by refusing to see me, they were doing me a favor.

I'd known Shady for years. I was already a Nomad by the time he patched in, and for some reason, I could carry on a conversation with him when I couldn't with anyone else. He was always so fucking happy, but if shit got real, he was the one that could be trusted. He was the complete opposite of me, but somehow we got along. Because of my importance in the club and his ability to get information, we spent a lot of time together.

Shady could get intel on anyone. He was a beast with a computer. If we needed leverage, Shady arranged it. If we needed nonexistent knowledge, Shady found it. And if we needed a number, an address, or a name, Shady had it. I performed the job, and he supplied me with the information. We were a team. But today, my teammate was pissing me off.

"What the fuck you mean she's leavin'?" I bark into the phone. I'm in Utah, crashing at a clubhouse, three days from Jackson and he calls to hit me with this.

"I mean she just booked a one-way flight to Del Rio. And, Miss Saylor has also arranged to be picked up and transported across the border. She is going to Meh-he-co." He was enjoying this, but I didn't have time to be pissed at him. Saylor was leaving. Mexico wasn't a place for a girl like her. I don't know why she wants to go, all I know is that she can't.

"When does she leave?" This time, I'm not growling. I'm not barking or spitting or roaring. I'm whispering. It's all I can manage. His news has hit me so hard in the chest that I can't even catch my breath. Am I hyperventilating? No fucking way. I smoked too much. I knock the cherry from my cigarette and put it in my pocket. I had to quit.

"Because I knew you'd freak out and because my birthday is

coming up and I want a decent fucking present and a hug because I have mommy issues, I made sure the only available booking was for Friday. That gives you four days, in case you can't do the math." I should thank him. Hell, I want to. But that would only fuel his fire, and that fucking inferno doesn't need to get any bigger. He is already enjoying this too much.

"Watch her," I tell him, finding my voice and my bike.

It took three full days of hard riding, but I finally find myself standing outside Saylor's apartment door. I hope she is pissed. I hope she is so mad at me that she starts beating the shit outta me. I will gladly drop to my knees and let her pummel my face to her heart's content, then stitch up her hands before I leave. That is what I deserve. She needed me. She begged for me and I left her. I couldn't have taken her to Jackpot, but I could have figured something out.

I haven't slept in two days, but I'm not tired. My body is pumping with adrenaline at just the thought of seeing her. It's like I'm possessed. Like I have been put under a spell. I kept the images of Saylor outta my head when I left her, but on my way back, she was all I saw. It's noon here and Shady assures me she is home. I pound on the door and I hear her voice a few seconds later.

"Who is it?" She sounds hoarse, like she has been screaming. The thought of her screaming from pain has my blood boiling. The thought of her screaming from pleasure that someone else gave her has me wanting to kick the fucking door down and kill whoever is inside.

"Open the door," I spit through clenched teeth. I wait on the questions to begin: *Why? What do you want?* But, instead I hear the slide of the dead bolt before she opens the door wide. On the outside, I am stone-faced. I know I'm wearing that intimidating, murderous look I wear so well, but on the inside, I can't fucking breathe.

Her hair is piled on top of her head and sticking in every direction. She wears black, square-framed glasses, a blue, sleeveless T-shirt that is just long enough to cover her navel, and the sexiest little pink satin panties I have ever fucking seen. "You came back." She looks at me like I'm a ghost. Like the last person in the world she expected to see was me. "Sometimes all you need is a mustard seed of faith." She is talking to herself but her words hit home to me. I should tell her faith is a dangerous thing. I should tell her that it will make her weak. But I won't.

When she smiles at me, thoughts of my past disappear and I just want to touch her. "I can't believe you're here," she says, and even though her voice is dry and raspy, it's so soothing that I close my eyes.

I hear movement behind me and push inside and slam the door. I don't want anyone seeing this goddess but me. My eyes are not worthy of her, but the neighbor's sure as hell ain't. I can't help it. If I was a saint and was sentenced to hell for this one crime, then I would gladly do my time, but I can't go another minute without having her in my arms. I can sit here and process how stupid I am, or how this adds a new level of fucked-up to my life, but I don't.

I drop my bag to the floor, grab her around her waist, and lift her to me. She wraps her legs around my hips, her arms around my neck, and welcomes me into her embrace. She smells better than I remember. She looks better than I remember and I lick the shell of her ear and she fucking tastes better than I remember.

I know I smell. I haven't had a shower in days, but I don't care. I just need to hold her, touch her, and be near her. I'm not pissed and my mind is not racing with thoughts to kill. I'm content and it's never fucking happened before and I don't give a shit what my mind is telling me; that dead heart in my chest is telling me I like it.

As I hold her tight to me, I can feel my adrenaline draining and fatigue taking over my body. I can feel everything shutting down. I need sleep and I need her. I walk through the small, neat apartment and find a bedroom that I know is hers. It has to be. There is a picture above the bed of a sunset.

I try to lay her down, but she doesn't let go of me. Fuck yes. She wants me. She missed me. She isn't pissed at me and she doesn't hate me. She wants to stay in my arms and I'd sleep in a straitjacket if it meant that tight grip she has on my neck stays there.

I kick my boots off, unlock her legs from around my waist, and fall back on the bed with her on top of me. My feet are on the floor. I'm dressed in leather. There is no pillow under my head, but the weight of her body on mine is more than enough to make up for the discomfort.

"Please don't leave me like that again, Dirk," she whispers into my neck. I'm taken back to the last time I held Saylor this close in my arms. She was sated, sleepy, talkative, and vulnerable. She'd told me about her promise to her mother. Her words were fresh in my mind and still had the same effect on my cock.

I close my eyes and take a deep breath, tightening my hold on her. I will have to leave her again. I have a job. It's my life. But that's not what she meant. She wants me to give whatever this is a chance. I'm tired of waking up without her. So I tell her words I should have said the first time she asked me not to leave.

"I won't," I promise, and just like Saylor, I keep my fucking promises.

4

I WAKE UP what could be minutes or hours later and find that Saylor is still on my chest. She has scooted down my body and her grip has loosened around my neck. Her face is now in the center of my chest and her breathing tells me she is in a deep sleep. I cradle the back of her neck with one hand, grip her waist with the other, and stand. I lay her back down, and when I let go her eyes flutter open behind her glasses.

"Don't leave," she says to me, her voice barely a whisper.

"I'm not." I remove her glasses, and her eyes close again. It's two o'clock, which tells me we have been asleep for less than two hours. But I need a shower. There is dried blood on my cut, my hands need to be bandaged from the punching session with a wall I had after receiving Shady's call, and I need to shave.

I walk outside, surveying the apartment as I unstrap the waterproof bag that contains almost everything I own. I retrieve my other bag from the hall and find the bathroom connected to Saylor's bedroom. She is laying with her eyes open when I pass her.

"I thought you left," she says, and the fact that she didn't trust me when I said I wouldn't hurts.

"I didn't."

I shower, shave, and make my way back to the bedroom in nothing but my boxers. I want to lay with her. I want to hold her and kiss her and whisper to her like she'd asked me to a couple weeks ago. But she isn't here. She is gone. The bed is empty and I recognize the feeling welling in my chest. Panic. And then she walks in with a tray of food.

"Let's eat. Picnic-style in the bed." I'm starving, but even if I wasn't, I would eat whatever she gave me because it would make her happy. I want to make her happy.

She sits cross-legged on the bed and I look down at the tray she is holding. Pasta with Alfredo sauce, garlic bread, and tea. My mouth is watering and it's not for the food. It's for the lips that press against the fabric of her panties. I want to eat her, devour her. I could survive off of her release. I reluctantly pull my eyes away from her pussy and find her staring at me. She knows I was looking. She knows that I want her, and she is turned on by it. I sit on the bed, my back against the headboard so that I am facing her.

"You shaved. It looks good," she says, her cheeks reddening. She's not embarrassed for admitting it, only by how much it pleases her. "I'm not a real good cook."

I doubt that, but I just take the plate from her hands without comment. I'm sure it will be delicious, even if it is not. Just because her hands prepared it. I take a bite and she waits in anticipation for my reaction.

"It's good," I tell her and she relaxes—happy that it pleases me.

"Have you ever been to Mexico?"

"Yes," I answer simply, wondering where the hell this is going. Is she going to ask me to go with her? Is she going to tell me she's leaving? Small talk annoys me. When I'm with a woman, there is loud music because I don't like small talk. We fuck, I enjoy it, she enjoys it, and we go on about our business with nothing more than a good-bye. But with Saylor, it's different. I like to hear her talk.

"I've never been," she says, and I watch her mouth as she takes another bite before continuing. "I want to go to one of those outside bars and drink tequila in the rain. I want to dance under a strand of Christmas lights like in the movie *Mr. and Mrs. Smith*." I've never seen the movie, so I don't know the scene she is talking about, but I know a place that sounds a lot like it. "I want to wear a white dress with a flower in my hair." I picture it, and it's so beautiful that I'm talking before I can stop myself.

"I'll take you." I can't believe I just said that. But I did, and I meant it. I don't want her to go without me. I want to take her to Mexico. I want to watch her dance in the rain, in a white dress, with a flower in her hair while she is drunk off tequila. I watch her smile, and it is shy, and unbelieving.

I've lost my appetite. I don't make empty promises, but someone did. That's why she is so doubtful. I need to reassure her, but my words will fall on deaf ears. I will have to prove it with my actions.

Sleeping with Saylor feels good. I like the feeling of her body perfectly molded to mine so much, that even after I've completely rested, I lay here with her wrapped around me. I pull my eyes from the rise and fall of her chest and focus on the ceiling. I can't look at her and think clearly, and right now, I'm thinking hard.

I'm thinking that I have to leave very soon and that I want her to go with me. But I don't know how the club will respond to that. They will not like her being around. They don't trust women. They will be afraid she will say something and get us all in a world of shit. I know that my job makes me a target. I don't give a fuck if anyone comes for me, but she is a liability. I could keep her safe, but I would have to trust her.

My phone rings, pulling me from my thoughts. Nationals. I move from the bed, trying not to disturb her. "We need you in Amsterdam by tomorrow for a benefit. An old friend had a wreck and they don't think he is gonna make it. We need all the help we can get, brother."

"I'll be there." The call is disconnected and a sick feeling comes over me. To become a Nomad, I had to take a physical and written test. They wanted to know my body could endure long rides and extreme conditions.

The written part tested whether I would be able to decode messages like this one. Amsterdam was code for Alabama. A benefit was code for a funeral and a wreck told me that I needed to make my target's death a painful one. When I got to Alabama, I would decode a set of numbers disguised as a birthday and they would tell me the coordinates of where I needed to go. There, I would pick up the package that would contain all the information I needed on my target.

This kind of job was usually pretty easy for me, but now I had to make a choice. Either I left Saylor behind, or I made her an accomplice. I didn't want to do either, but I had to choose. The easy thing to do would be to just leave and not tell her. But I couldn't do that. Not to her. Not again. And there was no use in thinking any more about it. My mind was made up.

I look over at Saylor, who is now awake, smiling up at me sleepily. "I have to leave, Saylor." I watch her smile fade and her eyes drop to her fidgeting hands. My words have just crushed her. I don't like seeing her sad, but I like that my absence can be so upsetting. She wants to be with me. "I want you to come with me." Her head snaps up in shock. I wait for the questions of where and for how long to start. I search her face for the look of regret before she tells me she can't be away that long when I tell her I don't know when we're coming back.

"Why do you want me to go? Why now?" The doubt in her voice puts that ache back in my chest. She never thought I would ask, and the only explanation I have to give her is the honest truth.

"Because I don't want to be away from you anymore."

I'm playing with fire. My decision to let Saylor travel with me is potentially life threatening not only to me, but to her too. She knows I'm a biker, but I don't think she understands what that actually means. She doesn't know my job or what it is I do when I'm on the road. I want to be honest with her, but I can't betray my club and I won't make her an accomplice to my crimes.

My answer to her question was all the reason she needed. She agreed almost immediately, trusting me with her life without any demand for further knowledge of anything. Moments after I told her, I received a text from Shady notifying me that she'd canceled her flight. She was canceling a trip she's always wanted to take, just to be with me. As I watch her pack a bag, the thought eats away at me and now I have to ask her why.

"Don't you want to know where we're going?"

"It doesn't matter. Anywhere but here is good enough for me." I grab her elbow, stopping her from shoving things into her backpack until her gaze reaches my eyes.

"I need more than that, Saylor. Why are you so willing to run away with a piece of shit like me?" She frowns at my words.

"I've been in this town my whole life. I have nothing. I know you are confused about why I chose you. I can see the uncertainty in your eyes every time I look at them. All I can tell you is that you inspire me. You make me want to live." Her eyes drop to her hands a moment before she looks back at me with sorrow and tears in those green pools I'm so obsessed with. "I just want to live."

I'm trying to decipher her meaning. I'm trying to decode her words, but I come up with nothing. The only reasonable explanation is that she has been hurt. Someone here in this shitty town has hurt her and she just wants to get away. I'm her knight on a steel horse. Her genie in leather. Her dark Prince Fuckin' Charming. But she needs to know what she's agreeing to.

"Do you know who I am?" My voice is barely a whisper. I hope she doesn't ask, because I don't know if I could tell her. She smiles, and when she speaks, every doubt inside me vanishes.

"You're Dirk."

I managed to strap Saylor's backpack to the top of my bag, creating a backrest for her in hopes of making the trip a little more comfortable. Now I'm watching her in my mirror as she stretches her arms out and feels the wind. Riding makes you feel free, and for me, it's liberating. Judging by the smile on Saylor's face, she feels the same way.

We have traveled almost a hundred miles and she has yet to bitch or ask to stop. She has been shifting for the past fifteen minutes, probably because her ass is numb, but she doesn't complain. When I finally stop for fuel, it takes her a moment to get her legs moving again.

"Tell ya what," she says, smiling up at me as she takes off her helmet. "Let's not stop. You drive and when you get tired, I'll drive, but let's just keep riding."

I look to see if she is serious. She isn't. I take her hand and help her from the bike and she sashays away from me, still smiling. I fill up the tank, then stand by the pump waiting on her.

I hear bikes pull up and my eyes search their backs, looking for colors but finding none. They are independents. Just average Joes out for a ride. But when their conversation turns to the "hot piece of ass" walking across the parking lot, they become average Joes with a fucking death wish. They shout to her, but she has eyes only for me. And she is smiling.

"They bothering you?" I ask loud enough for the shitheads to hear. I'll kill them if they are. Right here in this fucking gas station parking lot. I'll rip their eyes out and make her a necklace with them if they offend her.

"Nope. They bothering you?" she asks, still smiling as she pops a piece of candy in her mouth. Skittles. I think.

"Yes." I growl. And they are. I'm waiting for her to tell me to calm down or ignore them, but she just keeps smiling.

"Well, let's get the hell outta here then." She grabs her helmet and I watch her put it on, her fingers pulling the strap tight under her chin. Then she stands there and waits for me. I'm still debating whether or not I should leave bodies in the parking lot. But she is ready to ride. I have a feeling there will be a lot more like them, and the thought makes me want to use these pricks as an example of what happens when people fuck with, look at, or even think about Saylor Samson. She knows I'm deliberating, so she waits.

This is why I like her. I'm sure if I did kill them, she would still be waiting for me, right here by my bike. Not theirs. I pull my helmet over my head and straddle my bike, standing it up and waiting for her to follow suit. She does and the feel of her weight on my shoulders as she uses me to balance makes all thoughts of independents with death wishes die. When we pull out, I watch her stick her middle finger in the air at the three men. She can't see it because it's hidden behind my full-face helmet, but the corner of my mouth turns up.

Several miles down the road, her hands are on the visor of my helmet. She is trying to lift it. I don't know why and I make no move to help her. My brain is too busy trying to process her actions. She gives up, then slips her fingers under the bottom and I feel them on my chin. I sit completely still, wondering why I haven't moved her hand away from my face. Then I feel something small and round between her fingers. She finds my bottom lip and slips it inside. It's a Skittle. A fucking Skittle. I hold it between my lips as she stares at me in the mirror, keeping her fingers wedged under my helmet and on my chin. When I began to chew, she smiles and gives me a thumbs-up and turns her head to the side, as if asking me if it's good. My thumb rises just an inch off the handlebar, and she beams.

For the next several miles, she feeds me Skittles. And I like it. And it's driving me insane. One minute I'm anticipating how I will kill someone and the next I'm being fed Skittles. By a woman. Who is on my bike. Riding with me to perform a hit for the MC.

When the Skittles are gone, she frowns at me and I feel my own frown forming. She won't touch me anymore. But Saylor doesn't disappoint. Her hands are no longer touching my mouth, but they are sliding over my arms, under the sleeves of my T-shirt, and across my shoulders.

She begins to massage her fingers into my tight muscles and I feel them relax under her touch. It feels . . . good. Women touch me when I fuck them, but it's always their long, fake nails that are raking down my back while I pound into them. This is intimate. She is getting nothing in return. She is doing this because she wants to. And she is singing. I can't hear her and there is no music, only the sound of my pipes, but I see her lips moving and I'm sure the sound is heavenly.

When we hit the Alabama state line, I pull over at the first gas station I see and message Nationals, asking them when Pete's birthday is 'cause the club doesn't have it written down. There is no Pete. He has no birthday. This is part of the code.

The coordinates tell me I'm going to Banks, Alabama. I know Banks. It's a small town of about two hundred people. I know who is in Banks, and the other 199 people there will be better off once he is gone. Saylor sits behind me, patiently waiting for me. When my work is finished, I get off the bike and hold my hand out to help her.

"I was thinking." So was I, but her thoughts have got to be more interesting than mine. "We should take a picture." I don't agree, and a small part of me wonders if she will be upset when I tell her this. But pictures leave a paper trail. Just like the credit card I use to get gas. The difference is this credit card isn't mine. It's a fake. A picture with my face in it with Alabama in the background links me too close to the crime scene. And that reminds me why this was a bad idea. If Saylor told anyone where she was going or who she was with, I would have to call this whole thing off. That would piss off the club, which in turn would piss me off. I slam my fist into the gas pump. I'm so fucking stupid.

"Who did you tell about me?" I ask, my eyes closed.

"Nobody." Her voice is small, but unafraid.

"Saylor." My tone is warning—warning her she better not be fucking lying to me. She says nothing and I turn, expecting that look of guilt liars wear. But she is sad. Sad because I don't believe her? Sad because I'm yelling? I don't fucking know, but she needs to tell me.

"I don't have anyone to tell, Dirk. It's just me." She is being honest, but I have to be sure.

"You have friends." She rolls her eyes at my words.

"Friends? Define 'friends.' I have two and they are in Europe. Nobody knows where I am, Dirk. Just me and you." My anger fades a little. Not enough for her to notice, but enough for me to not want to rip this pump out of the ground and throw it through the building.

"Where is your phone?" I demand, and she takes a step toward me. I don't move, but I should. I'm too mad for her to be close, but fuck she smells good.

"Do you know what would've happened if you hadn't come back when you did?" I search her face, wondering if she wants an answer or if she just wants to remind me what a fuckup I am. She wants neither.

"I would have left. You know I was planning on leaving that day. I had to get outta there, Dirk. I had to leave. Whether it was with you or on my own, I was gone. There are three people in this world that really mean something to me. The two that I really mean something to are in Europe for the summer. It's not their job to keep tabs on me; they've never been able to. It wouldn't be surprising to them to find me gone. I don't work, I'm not enrolled in classes right now, and there is nothing about me not being home that will throw up a red flag to anyone. Nobody is gonna miss me, Dirk. If that pathetic reason isn't enough to convince you why I thought this trip was a good idea, then nothing is. And to answer your question, my phone is at my house, on my dresser. Right where I left it." She walks past me toward the store, and the need for her to answer the question that is pounding in my head outweighs the need to remain myself—the man who never asks questions.

"What about the third?" I call out to her. "What about the third person who really means something to you?" She turns and her voice carries across the parking lot and flows through my ears like honey.

"I'm looking at him."

I'm putting my life and Saylor's on the line, and all I have to go on is her word. If she lied to me, I would be crushed. Her word means more to me than any man's. I trust her like I trust my brothers. Many of them have the power to put me behind bars for the rest of my life. She has the power to put me in the grave.

I made a decision long ago to trust my brothers. I knew it would be worth the risk because I couldn't live life without the Sinner's Creed MC. Today, right now, I make the same decision to trust Saylor, because I can't live life without her either. And I still don't know why.

The tank is full. I've smoked two cigarettes. I've done a pretty good job of sorting shit out in my head. It's been over twenty minutes and Saylor still hasn't returned. I'm getting worried. And I gotta piss. I scan the store and I don't see her. When I stop outside the women's bathroom, I hear her voice. She is whispering, and I make out my name in her hushed words. I see red. She lied. She is on the fucking phone. She is talking to someone about me. I should just leave, but the pain in my chest is knee weakening. And it makes me angry.

So fucking angry that I kick the door in. And then I see her. She is on her knees, in this shitty-ass bathroom, and she is . . . praying. Her face is panicked when she sees mine, not that I blame her.

I have to hold on to the doorjamb to keep from passing out. That's how relieved and ashamed I feel. I don't pray, but I respect people who do. I disrespected her. Shame is not something I have felt in a really long time, but it is here now and it's worse than I remember it.

"I was j-just . . ." She is stuttering. Not in an indignant way, but because she doesn't know what to say. But I do.

"I'll wait outside." I turn to leave and I see the clerk picking up the phone. She is going to call the cops. I could rip out the phone lines, but she has seen my face. I would have to kill her, and I don't want to. She is an older woman, and I'm sure she hasn't done anything that warrants death. Her life is more valuable than the one I will take tomorrow, but what about all the people that will suffer because I don't do my job?

There are no cameras. I knew that before I chose to stop. I'm looking at her, and her face is white. She looks like she is going to pass out.

"Dirk." I hear Saylor's pained voice from behind me and I see her on the floor. I forget the clerk and rush to her. She looks fine, other than the twisted look of agony on her face.

"Is something wrong?" the clerk asks, her voice shaky and cautious. She has made her way over to us with the phone still in her hand, but she hasn't dialed any numbers.

"I have low blood sugar. I almost passed out. That's why he kicked the door in; I wouldn't answer him." She is looking at me when she says this, and I know she is doing it to save my ass. What she doesn't realize is that it is the clerk's life she is really saving.

"Oh thank God!" I turn to see the clerk clutching her chest in relief. "I thought he was going to kill you or something!" I ignore her comment and look back at Saylor. "I almost called the cops!" This woman is getting on my fucking nerves, and Saylor notices.

"Will you help me up?" she asks, and she is trying to fight a smile. I haul her from the floor and when she is on her feet, I take her hand in mine. I survey the door, and it is still in one piece. The only damage is to the cheap eye hook that has been ripped from the doorjamb.

"Don't worry about that. I'll have someone fix it tomorrow," the woman says, as she eyes the two of us hand in hand. "You are a lucky girl to have a man that cares so much for you." She walks toward us and I stiffen. I don't want her to touch me and she looks like the hugging kind. Saylor intercepts and steps in front of me, sticking her free hand out to the lady.

"Thank you for your concern." Saylor's smile is genuine and

fucking remarkable. She renders the woman speechless and I know the feeling. She turns back to me and winks. I let her hand go, and disappear into the men's bathroom. Saylor's winks have power over every part of me, including my growing cock.

We are about three hours from Banks, Alabama, and I let Saylor feed me Skittles, compliments of the store clerk, for the first hour. She is singing again and I'm pissed again 'cause I can't fucking hear her, but I do enjoy her touch. I put my cut in my bag before we left the store. My fuckup with kicking the door down and the fact that we were nearing our destination has me taking precautions earlier than usual.

It wasn't out of the norm for me to not wear my cut on a run, but I try to wear it as much as possible. There are MCs all over this part of the country, and I need to represent as often as I can. We have charters in forty-seven states including Hawaii and Alaska. We are world-renowned, but the U.S. is our home. I've visited a few other countries here and there, but Mexico is the place I frequent more often than the others. I go there for business, but mostly just for pleasure.

I suck another Skittle into my mouth, making sure to touch Saylor's finger with my tongue. I've watched her more than the road and noticed that every time I licked her finger, she put it in her mouth before diving into the bag for another. I don't know if she knows I notice, but I won't tell her, because I don't want her to stop.

The sugary candy is good, but my stomach needs something a little more filling. If I'm hungry, she probably is too. I would have to get better at this shit. Usually, it was only my needs that mattered.

Troy, Alabama, is located about ten miles from Banks. It isn't a big town, but big enough that we won't draw any attention. I find an older motel where they accept cash and the rooms have doors that lead outside. I leave Saylor outside by the bike while I book the room in the same name that is listed on the credit card and license in my wallet. When I get back outside, I see Saylor taking a picture of herself with a Polaroid camera. I didn't even know they still made those things. But she was now holding the picture, fanning it in the air, waiting on the image to become clear. She sees me and smiles.

"I have helmet hair, but I don't care. I wanted to have a picture to help me remember my first ride."

"No pictures," I snap, feeling anger creeping back into my veins. Why in the hell had I not warned her of this? But if I did, what in the hell would I have said? "Do you have any more?"

"No. Just this one." I grab the picture from her fingers. There is nothing but a brick wall behind her. Her smile in the picture has an instant softening effect on me.

"I can't let people know where I am. So we can't leave anything behind that might put me in any of these places. Do you understand?" I ask, hoping like hell she does so I won't have to explain anything further.

"I do. I promise I won't take anything with you in it or leave any incriminating evidence behind." Her words are serious, but her smile is playful.

Our room has two beds. I didn't know if she wanted to sleep with me, so I made sure she had an option. I have my tank bag, my luggage bag, and her backpack in my hands, and I'm frozen in place at the door—watching her. She touches everything in the room, her eyes closed. She is breathing deep as if to memorize the smell of the room. I inhale and all I smell are stale cigarette smoke and that cleaner they use that has the same scent as the towels.

When she opens her eyes, she is looking at me and she smiles, revealing her teeth.

"It's perfect," she tells me, as if I had asked what she thought of the place. It's the same thing she said to me at the warehouse. It's nice to know she's not hard to impress.

"I have to go out." Her smile falls some, but I can tell she is trying to hide her disappointment. I would love to be in her head, but if I had to guess what she is thinking, it would be that she will do anything to prevent me from thinking bringing her was a mistake. My heart does that weird fluttering thing where you can feel it skip a beat.

"Stay inside. Don't leave. Don't answer the door. If the building catches on fire, get your shit and find the nearest bus station to take you back home." My voice is harsh when I speak to her, but it isn't to hurt her or scare her. She knows this, because she doesn't look offended. I remember she has to eat, and I know she won't tell me if she is hungry. I'll just bring her something back, but I don't know how long I'll be. Fuck.

I drop her bag and stomp out, loading my shit up and speeding off to the nearest burger joint, which is just around the corner. I nearly bite the man at the counter's head off when he asks me what I want, because I realize I don't fucking know.

She could be allergic to something or a vegan or some shit. One thing about the club, I knew all that shit about my brothers. But I don't know anything about Saylor.

Most girls eat salad because they're on a diet or care about the way they look. Judging by Saylor's body, she takes care of herself. But she isn't like most girls in any other aspect, and I wasn't gonna stereotype her just because she has a good body. So I order her the same thing I order for me—a cheeseburger and fries.

When I walk in, she is just how I left her except her boots are off. She is propped up against the headboard, her ankles crossed, writing in a leather-bound book. A diary? People still did that? Social media seemed like all the diary you would need, but here again, Saylor didn't seem like the type that would put her thoughts all over the Internet for the world to fucking see. Just seeing her with a diary had me liking her a little more, although I liked her enough just fine.

"Are you allergic to anything?" I snap, then mentally kick myself for being such an asshole.

"Yes," she says, closing her book and looking up at me. "Bullshit and politics." She smirks. I'm allergic to the same damn things. Her sarcasm lightens my mood considerably and I take a seat at the small table, waiting for her to join me.

"Something smells good." She takes the seat across from me and props her legs on the bed. She grabs a burger without complaint and dives right in. Not bothering to check it and make sure it's dressed the way she wants. She isn't picky. I like that.

"About earlier, ya know, at the store, I wasn't praying for myself." I stop eating, not wanting the sound of chewing to prevent me from hearing whatever she has to say.

"I prayed for you. For your safety and your understanding and your forgiveness."

I'm confused and the wrinkle in my brow shows it. Forgiveness from him or from her?

"I think you are a very special person. You deserve a life with someone that can give you far more than I can. I hope you will forgive me for not being what you need." Her eyes are full of sorrow and I wonder why she thinks so low of herself.

I'm already making plans to call Shady and get a list of every man she has ever had a relationship with. I will interrogate each and every one of them until I find the son of a bitch who has made her doubt herself. When I find him, I will rip his limbs off one by one and I will do it in a way that he will stay alive for the whole fucking procedure. I want him to suffer.

Before I let anger completely consume me and fuel my desire to kill, I leave a part of me open so I can provide comfort to her. I grab my bag and pause in front of the door.

"You are *all* I need." And I fucking mean it.

5

MARTIN WALTON'S GRAVE looks like it hasn't been visited in years, and at the bottom of the vase beside it, under the faded, artificial flowers, is a note attached to a prepaid cell.

There is an address on the note and a time. The address leads me to a trailer park, and I hide my bike off the road about a half a mile away. I walk the short distance to the run-down trailer located in the very back. There are no cars, no lights, and no sign that anyone has been here in months. The grass is tall, but there is a trail to the back door that tells me someone has been here recently. My target must be using it as a hideout and it thrills me that he thinks he is safe. Not a chance, motherfucker. I look at my watch and it's a little after midnight. This time tomorrow, he would be dead.

Travis Cool, or T-Man, had a problem with getting laid. Or maybe he just liked the thrill of fucking a comatose woman. Whatever his reason for using date-rape drugs for his pleasure was wrong. He hadn't been reported to the authorities as far as we knew, but I'm sure after he sees me, he is gonna wish he had. Prison would be a lot better than what I had in store for him.

He would likely have never been caught if he hadn't fucked up and messed with someone who had ties with the club. I don't know who she was or what her connection was, because it didn't matter. What mattered was that I was sent to do a job to avenge a woman who meant something to one of my brothers. Therefore, she meant something to me.

It happened a few months ago, but planning a hit on someone takes time. We had to make sure there was nothing that could be used to point the murder toward the club. Now that all the loose ends were tied up, it was time for T-Man to meet his maker.

This brought thoughts of Saylor's earlier confession to my mind. There is no way that she and T-Man shared the same maker. Saylor was pure, beautiful . . . flawless. T-Man was scum, ugly, and unworthy of breathing the same air as Saylor. I would have to find out her religion, and his. Maybe they had two different gods. That would explain it.

My mission tonight is to scope out the place and plan my entry. I crawl under the back of the trailer and begin to cut away the insulation and cheap particleboard flooring. Once inside, I do a sweep of the place, and am gone within five minutes.

I return to my bike in a hurry, ready to get the hell away from here and back to the woman I know is waiting for me. I try not to let what-ifs cloud my head, but it's pointless. What if she left? What if she decided I wasn't what she wanted after all? No. She would be there. I know it, or I keep trying to tell myself that.

By the time I make it back to the motel, my chest is tight and I'm finding it hard to breathe. I grab my bags and can't get the key in the lock fast enough. When the lock clicks, I take a deep breath and push open the door; expecting the worst is always best.

There is no denying that Saylor is here. Her scent fills the air and I can make out her silhouette, even in the darkness. She is sleeping. I close the door gently, cussing the fucker for being so loud. She is on her side, her hair unbraided. She has showered and the dampness of her hair has tamed it somewhat so that it lays across the pillow. Fucking beautiful.

I leave her to shower, and instead of cringing when I see all her female shit covering the counter, I welcome it. I like knowing her shit will be sitting next to mine tonight. It is a reminder that she is real.

I take the bed next to Saylor's because it's the right thing to do. I never was one to really follow the rules, but I want to try to do right by her. I watch her back, wishing she would turn over so I can see her face, but instead I memorize the curve of her body. Her hips are full compared to her waist, and the slope of her body reminds me of a half-moon. I reluctantly let my eyes close, but her face is still the only thing I see.

"Dirk?" I hear her voice in the darkness and open my eyes to find her propped up on an elbow, searching the room.

"I'm here," I say and it's soft, comforting. A tone used for soothing and reassuring—one I don't use very often. She turns so she is facing me and sits on the side of the bed.

"Can I sleep with you?" she asks, and she sounds so fucking lonely that I want to kill myself for leaving her.

"Yes." She doesn't hesitate and I see she is wearing a T-shirt and nothing else. I lift the covers, and she slides in, her back to my front. Her hair is everywhere and covers my face. She lifts her head and tries to smooth it down, but I stop her. "Leave it." I wrap my arm around her waist and she locks her fingers with mine. Her scent is all around me. Her body is warm and smooth and I feel myself harden against her.

"I tried to wait up for you, but I fell asleep." She waited for me. This means that she would deprive herself of sleep, just to be with me. There goes my heart again, doing that fucking thing. "Dirk?" I like it when she says my name and I think she knows it. That is why she says it all the time, or that's what I want to believe. "Yeah?" She is silent and the anticipation is fucking killing me. I will her to talk, and breathe a sigh of relief when she finally sheds mercy on me.

"You make me feel safe." I know this, but it still feels good to hear her say it.

"You are safe," I tell her. I would never let anyone touch her, and I mean it so much that I have reassured her when usually I wouldn't say anything.

"Not just from the world, but from my own thoughts." I'm a man who knows about thoughts, and I know how bad they can affect you. I feel my grip around her waist tighten. "And that's what I'm scared of most," she adds on a whisper. What haunting thoughts could Saylor possess? If her mind wasn't a part of her, I would steal it and trade my soul for one that brought her happy thoughts. I kiss her hair and she sighs. I think it makes her feel special. "Good night, Dirk."

"Good night, baby," I tell her, because I'm pretty fucking sure that makes her feel special too.

I feel Saylor crawl out from under my arm just as the sun is making its way through the crack in the curtains. The bottom of her ass is visible to me and either she isn't wearing panties, or she is wearing a thong. I will take her either way.

I watch as she searches the counter for something and I find her face in the mirror. Her brows are drawn together and I don't know if it's out of pain or because she can't see.

"What's wrong?" I ask. My chest is tight and my stomach knots with worry.

"Just looking for some headache meds," she answers, and I watch her squint at her own words as if it pains her to talk. My chest tightens further and so does that knot in my stomach. It's just a headache, but if she hurts, I hurt. It's that fucking simple.

She finds what she is looking for and I hear her tearing the plastic off a cup before filling it with water. She takes the meds and stands at the sink, her head down and her arms locked, holding herself up. She is sick and I don't want to lay here and do nothing.

I'm out of bed and standing behind her, looking at the two of us in the mirror. She doesn't look up, and I can't see her face because her hair is hiding it. My concerned face is very similar to my pissed-off one, and I make a note to work on that.

"Sometimes," she starts, then takes a deep breath. Her voice is low and I hold my breath because I don't want to make any noise to add to her discomfort. I hear a horn honk in the distance, and I'd kill that motherfucker if I thought I could get to him in time.

"I get really bad headaches. It's my eyes." I've heard of this. She wasn't wearing glasses yesterday, but judging from the contact solution and case on the counter, I'm pretty sure she was wearing those. "I'm fine." Her voice is stronger, reassuring, but when she looks up, her face is pale and her lips are white. She is sweating and this is not a headache, it's a migraine. I'm sure if I asked, she would say she was nauseous. But I won't. Nothing makes you more nauseous than when someone asks if you are.

I take her by her hand, my other going around her waist, and lead her back to the bed. Once she is under the covers, I go back to the sink to get a cold rag. By the time I make it back, she is turned on her stomach and the covers are off. I swallow hard at what I see.

It's not a thong she is wearing, and she's not naked. It's boy-shorts. The kind that a girl's ass cheeks hang out of. They are black and have lace around the edges. Fuck. I force my eyes from her ass and move her hair until her neck is bare. I place the cold rag on it and she mumbles something I think is a thank-you. I sit on the other bed and stare at her, unsure of what to do.

"Dirk." I'm not even sure it's my name she says, but I'm on my feet, leaning over her. "Hold me." There is no mistaking those words and I do as she says. I lay on my side and put my hand on her back. I stroke her because it seems like something I would like her to do to me. I'm not disappointed. Saylor is soon asleep and so am I.

Before I open my eyes, I can feel her looking at me. She is humming. I don't know the song, but I'm sure she hums it better than any Grammy winner could sing it. I open my eyes and she stops humming, so I close them again. I can hear the laughter in her voice as she starts humming again. For the split second my eyes were on her, she looked fine. Better than fine. There was no trace of this morning's migraine on her face. Maybe it was just a head-ache. I've never known a migraine to disappear within a few hours.

"Are we going to ride today?" She quits humming to speak to me and her voice is just as pleasing as her hums.

"I have to leave," I tell her and wonder if I will ever be able to share what I do, or what I will tell her when she finally asks. She knows I'm not leaving for good. The fact that we have crossed that bridge and she now trusts me, tells me that we are making progress. I look at the time and see I have two hours before I have to leave. I'm hungry, so I'm sure she is too. "Get dressed," I tell her and roll away from her and toward a cold shower.

Most men claim they can't live without pussy. I have been trained to live without food, water, and light. Pussy was the last fucking thing on my mind. But I now see why men say it. I've never had a woman like Saylor in my life. Hell, I've never had any woman in my life, but I see the impact she has on my self-control. I can feel it slipping, and soon, I'm gonna fucking lose it.

I'm washing my hair when I feel her behind me. I try to ignore her, but she puts her hands on me and they are full of soap, just like the last time we showered together. The cold water doesn't affect her in the least. I like how she washes me. I can't remember it ever being done before. And I really like that she expects nothing in return.

I'm clean enough and I step out without facing her. I have too much shit to do today to have visions of her naked under a cold stream of water in my head. It will be hard enough as it is.

I'm dressed before she is out, and now I'm rethinking taking her somewhere for lunch. I know it's shitty of me to keep her cooped up in here alone, but being around her softens me. I need to get into kill mode and she will fuck up my vibe.

"I'll be back," I yell through the door and leave before she has a chance to answer. This time I grab chicken sandwiches instead of burgers. I know it's not an equal exchange. I know it won't make up for it. But just the fact that I tried makes me feel better.

Saylor seems to sense when I'm going to fuck up because when I get back, she isn't dressed, ready for me to take her out. She is wearing another T-shirt and some shorts, sitting at the table waiting for me. She didn't wash her hair and I'm glad she chose to leave it like it was.

"I got chicken," I say as a form of greeting. She smiles and I'm forgiven, not that she was pissed in the first place. We eat in silence and I wait for her to break it. She lets me suffer until we are almost through, then she finally speaks.

"I like that you don't talk a lot. Have I told you that?" She looks at me and her face is confused. She is thinking hard, but there is no need for it. I know every line she has ever said to me, and that's not one of them.

"No."

"Well, I do," she says and continues eating. I want her to talk more. I only have forty-five more minutes before I leave, and I want to hear her talk the whole time. It's not good, I know that. I am contradicting myself. I didn't take her to eat because I needed space from her. Now I want anything but space, and I don't care that it will likely fuck up my game tonight. "Does my talking bother you?"

"No." Hell no. Fuck no. No.

"Riding is therapy for you, isn't it?" she asks me, and by the way she is looking at me, she wants an answer.

"Yes." I've forgotten my food. I've forgotten T-Man. I'm just sitting here waiting on her to finish whatever it is she wants to say. If there even is anything else she wants to add.

The next thirty-nine minutes are pure fucking turmoil. I have to leave and she hasn't said another word. We just sit in silence. She writes in her diary. I watch her write in her diary. When it's time for me to leave, I'm so anxious to hear her voice that I can't wait to tell her I'm leaving because I know she will say something.

"I'll be back later. Have your stuff packed and ready. But don't wait up. I don't know when I will be back. It might be late. But it shouldn't be too late." I'm rambling. I've never rambled in my entire fucking existence. What is it about her that makes me do crazy shit that's just not me? I'm pissed when I grab my bag and stomp toward the door. I'm dangling by a thin rope off the side of a mountain. I don't even want to hear her talk because I'm sure she will say something that will push me over the edge.

"Dirk?" She says my name like she wants to ask me something. She wants me to look at her. I don't want to, but I can't fucking help it. I turn to her and she is serious. There is no smile, just wide, honest, green eyes that suck me in with the force of a category-five hurricane. "You're my therapy." And just like that, I'm falling.

———

I'm in the woods waiting for T-Man to arrive at the place he thinks is a safe house. Strapped to my side is my Stroman miniature dirk that will take his life. It is only about three inches long, but the blade is sharp and effective when used in the right area.

I can't let thoughts of Saylor take over right now, because she makes me weak. Instead, I let the lyrics to Metallica's "Seek and Destroy" pound into my head. An hour later, I'm ready to kill. I have only one thought on my brain. Blood. Red blood that will seep out of T-Man, through the cheap particleboard of the trailer and onto the ground.

When I see him pulling in, I feel that familiar sense of power coursing through my veins. Tonight, I'm the reaper in black. I'm hell and I'm knocking on his front door. And he doesn't even fucking know it. When he is inside and alone, I wait. I wait for him to get comfortable. I see him look out of the window a few times, but he gives up all too soon.

I crawl out of the darkness and under the trailer to the back room where I cut a hole in the floor last night. I remove the carpet and now I'm in his house. He is on the phone, so I wait for him to end the call. He is promising dinner to someone on the other line. He laughs. He is happy. He sounds fucking ecstatic, but it won't last long. I know the conversation is winding down, so I advance. When he says good-bye, I'm standing behind him.

When your mind is made up to kill someone, never hesitate. Do your fucking job. But it needs to be painful. That was my order. I kneel behind him and slice his tibial tendon. When he falls to his knees, I wrap my arm around his throat and place my knife behind his ear. His screaming stops and his hands come to my arm. He is thrashing, breathing heavy. He is panicking, and

I think of all the women who panicked after waking up bruised and battered and not knowing what happened.

He is telling me he has money. He will pay me. I don't need his fucking money and because he insinuated that I do, I stab my knife into the cartilage of his shoulder. He screams louder. He should know why this is happening, but I want him to hear it from me.

"You fucked up. You drugged the wrong woman. You fucked with something that belongs to Sinner's Creed, and now you will die at the hands of a brother."

He is begging now, swearing that he doesn't know what I am talking about. He just wants to live. He is sorry. I've heard it all. There is nothing he could say that would ever make me change my mind. But, before I kill him, I have to know.

"What religion are you?" I ask, and my question catches him off guard.

"I-I'm an atheist." I knew it. And then, I cut his throat.

I hang around long enough for T-Man to choke to death on his own blood, then I leave the same way I came in. There will be no tracks, no fingerprints, and no evidence. A smooth kill, just how I like it.

I walk the mile to my bike with thoughts of Saylor praying in my head. I'm glad she and T-Man didn't share the same god. I would never be able to process how that shit worked.

I'm ready to get back to Saylor. I'm so ready, I'm practically running. When I get there, I will want to sleep with her, but I can't. We have to leave. We need to get as far away from here as possible. I'm sure the body won't be found for a couple of days. No one knew about T-Man's "safe house" but him. I plan to be long gone by then.

When I get to my bike, I remove my gloves and hoodie and stuff them in a plastic bag before putting them in my luggage. I grab a fresh shirt and my riding gloves and throw my helmet on. By my calculations, I should see Saylor in fourteen minutes.

It only takes me twelve, but there are people outside in the parking lot so I keep riding. I stop at a store down the street and fuel up. I go inside, get what I need, and park my bike behind the building. I walk back to the motel and wait for the men to go inside. I don't want any witnesses. Even though no one saw my bike within a mile of T-Man's house, I don't want to take any chances.

An hour passes before they leave and I should already be a hundred miles from here. I decide to leave the bike, and Saylor and I will just walk back to it.

I find her in the room, sound asleep. I hate to wake her, but we have to leave. She is in the bed we slept in together and she is hugging a pillow. My pillow. Her face is buried in it. She missed me.

I find her stuff packed in her bag and sitting at the foot of the bed. Her clothes are laid out and she is wearing nothing but her shirt and panties. If she has to wear clothes, I like these best. I sit down beside her and gently shake her shoulder.

"Hey," I say, barely above a whisper. I watch her eyes open and then close as she buries her face further in the pillow. It's cute.

Cute.

I don't like that word and I vow to never use it again.

"Saylor," I say a little louder this time, and I watch her take a deep breath. She is agitated.

"I'm up," she says and her tone is one I haven't heard. And that word I vow to never use keeps popping in my head. Her hair is already braided and I watch in amusement as she grumbles the entire time she puts her clothes on. "Two thirty in the morning. I swear. I've been asleep for five minutes. Just long enough to start a dream. Then I have to get up." I almost want to smile. Almost.

"What was your dream?" I ask, and my question surprises me. I know why I asked. I want her to tell me it was about me.

"Doesn't matter," she mumbles, and I like this side of her. It's different. It would annoy most men, but I like it. She is perfect enough that it's okay for her to be a little bitchy every now and then.

I'm in a good mood. I get like this every time justice is served. I'm still riding high on the horse of power and I don't see getting off of it anytime soon. She betters my already good mood, and I feel like laughing. But I don't, of course.

"It's always the good part." She is standing in front of me and she is no longer aggravated. She is curious. She is hoping that by explaining it to me, she will be able to find the answer for herself. "Right when you know it can't get any better, so it doesn't. It ends. Poof. Gone. Just like that," she says with a snap of her fingers. "I don't get it. Even if you didn't wake me up, something else would have. I'm destined to never complete a good dream. It's just not in the cards."

I don't want to leave. I want to sit here and let her lecture me on dreams and how they come to an abrupt stop just before the good shit happens. But we have to go.

"You ready?" I ask, knowing that she is. Her backpack is in her hands, her clothes are on, and she is standing, waiting on me.

"Yeah. I'm ready." I stand up and I am only a couple of inches from her. I dig in my pocket and hold out a pack of Skittles. My reward is a huge smile and a hug. I wrap my arms around her awkwardly, wondering why this is so easy when we are in bed and so weird when we are not.

"You, Dirk. Man of my dreams. Man who wakes me up before the good part in my dream. Man who brings me Skittles, are even more perfect than I thought."

I was in her dreams. She said so. She thinks I'm perfect. She said that too. I'm trading in my power horse for a kitten because now I feel all warm and fuzzy on the inside. And I'm gonna name that kitten Saylor. And I hate fucking kittens. And I hate this warm and fuzzy shit. And we need to leave before I get pissed because someone gave Saylor the wrong definition of *perfect*.

I take her hand and she walks beside me in silence back to the bike. I heard a quote once that said beauty was in the eyes of the beholder or some shit. Maybe perfection was the same way. Everything Saylor thinks is perfect is anything but. But, if she believes it, then maybe it's true. Who am I to judge her opinions?

When I'm a good hundred miles away, full of Skittles and low on energy, I pull over on the side of the interstate and make the call to Nationals on the prepaid that was left for me. When the call is connected, there is no greeting, only silence.

"I guess the benefit will go toward a funeral." I hang up without a response and smash the phone into the pavement with the heel of my boot. When it's completely crushed, I kick the bigger pieces into the grass and head to the next town.

I stop just south of Birmingham and fuel up. The gas station offers breakfast and I send Saylor inside to get us something. She returns with a bag of shit and I survey it while I smoke.

"I got two biscuits, three packs of Skittles, two OJs, a Mountain Dew, a Coke, a few granola bars, some M&M's, a pack of peanuts, and a bag of Flamin' Hot Cheetos." I just stare at her. Was I depriving her of food? Was she that fucking hungry to buy out a damn convenience store at five in the morning?

"A road trip ain't a road trip without junk food, and I get tired of sitting in a motel without anything to snack on. There is only so much sink water I can drink before I go crazy." I fed her. I start to tell her that, but she stops me when she pokes her lip out in an exaggerated pout. "I'm sorry, did *you* want something?" This is funny to her, and her comment is kinda funny to me. Kinda.

"I'm taking the Cheetos," I say, and my comment makes her laugh. It's a beautiful sound. And all I can think about is how perfect she is and how fucking lucky I am.

6

I FIND A motel similar to the one in Troy and go inside to pay, leaving Saylor with the bike and the twenty-pound bag of snacks. When I come out, she is taking a picture again. When we get to the room, she walks around with her eyes closed and inhales, again. Then she tells me it's perfect, again. I see a pattern forming and it is so intriguing, I want to know why she does this. I will ask her. Eventually.

We have two beds again and I will take the one unoccupied until she asks me to sleep with her, which I'm sure she will—if the pattern continues. I take a shower then join her for breakfast at the table.

"You know what I like about biscuits?" she says through a mouthful of food. I don't know, but I'm dying to hear. I want to know more about her. Even the simple shit. Like what she likes about biscuits. "Jelly. It's like dessert." I see her point. I wait for her to say something else. I've never hated the silence; I've always welcomed it. But when she is with me, all I want to hear is her.

We can talk about anything. Fucking female problems if she wants. I'm debating asking her a question. One that's simple, like her favorite color.

I shift in my seat, willing my mouth to speak. "What's your favorite color?" she asks, and I shoot her that looks that says, *Are you fucking kidding me?* but she is undeterred. "Mine is black. Is that weird?"

Her face is pinched in confusion. She wants an answer, but I can't speak. My brain is still processing how the hell she can read my thoughts. Maybe she is a witch. That would explain this crazy spell I seem to be under.

"Yellow. And it's not weird." I huff, and grab my bag before heading into the bathroom. Thoughts of the supernatural and witches and those people who can move shit with their eyes are pounding in my head.

Maybe I'm just that transparent. I light a smoke and then another one, trying to get my pulse to return to normal. When I feel half-ass like myself again, I return to the room.

She is in bed, writing in her diary. I strip down and she watches with lustful eyes. Then she licks her lips. And I go hard. I crawl into the bed she isn't in and roll onto my stomach, burying my face in the pillow. It has that motel smell, and I wish I had her pillow instead of this one.

I close my eyes, and before the darkness sets in, I feel her sitting on my ass. She is wearing my favorite outfit. I don't have to look at her to know it. I can feel the heat from her pussy through my boxers and her naked legs on either side of my hips.

"I've always been a dreamer," she says as her hands rub together and then stroke my back. They are wet with lotion. The pressure is intense, but feels so fucking good I almost moan. "I've wanted to be just about everything. It started with a lawyer when I was a kid. I didn't even know what they did, but I wanted to be one." She makes her way to my shoulders, then slides her hands down my spine, across to my hips, and back again to my shoulders.

"Then I wanted to be a teacher. I like kids, but twenty-four of them for eight hours a day is too much." I'm trying to concentrate on her words, but her hands are all over me and it's hard to focus. "Anyway, I aspired to be a singer and when that didn't work out, I chose massage therapy. I never made it through the whole class, but I did learn the basics." And it shows.

I feel myself relax under her touch, and eventually my body has the same consistency of the jelly we ate this morning.

"I love the way your muscles feel under my hands," she whispers, and I tense at her choice of words. Love. Not like, but love. "I want to rub you every day."

I want her to. And I want her to tell me she loves doing it. That word sounds perfect on her lips. She is humming. I don't know this song either, but it's beautiful. I don't know if it's her humming, her touching me, or the fact that I used up all my energy killing a man this morning, but I fall into the deepest most restful sleep I've had in years.

The next morning, we're up early and ride hard until I reach Oklahoma City. I check in at a motel, watch Saylor perform her ritual, and then hit her with the news of my leaving.

"I have some business I have to handle. I booked the room for two nights. It might be tomorrow before I'm back." I watch as she falls on the bed, clearly exhausted from the long ride.

"'K. I'm just gonna take a bubble bath and watch a few chick flicks." She doesn't seem bothered in the least about my leaving, and I wonder if she's thankful for some time alone. When I watch her drag herself back out of bed to retrieve her bag by the door, I know it's only the exhaustion talking. We rode too hard today.

I pull some twenties out of my wallet and lay them on the table by the window. "Order some takeout. I'll be back later." She stops long enough to look at me, then offers me a smile.

"Be careful." No one had ever told me to be careful. Shady had once said "don't die," but that was as close as I'd gotten to anyone caring.

"Will do." I leave, knowing I can't stay any longer. I need to put distance between us and the softening effect Saylor has on me. I need to get focused. I have a job.

Oklahoma City has a problem and I'm the solution. My orders today were to pull the president's patch and give it to the sergeant at arms, and eighty-six the current vice president. Eighty-sixing someone can involve a few different things, but the outcome is the same. He will never ride for an MC again. But this one deserves a visit to the hospital as his parting gift. And that's exactly what the fuck he is gonna get.

"Headstrong" by Trapt is blaring in my ears when my tires hit the pavement, and the song is so fitting I put it on repeat. This is who I am. This is what I do. I'm not the lust-struck, hand-holding, tear-wiping pussy I've been the past several days. Today, I'm Dirk—Sinner's Creed Nomad National.

It's late when I roll into the Sinner's Creed Oklahoma City chapter's clubhouse. They are all here waiting for me. They were informed I was coming and I know they are scared. Every fucking one of them.

This is a 1 percent MC. These are men who are trained to hurt, trained to endure hurt, and trained to kill. But only a few can compete with the best. And I'm the best. I'm the best at hurting, enduring, and killing. I'm the man they fear because I have nothing to lose, and they know that.

I have no home, no family, and nothing but this patch that keeps me alive and makes this life worth something. I'm the man they fear because I'm the one who puts them in their place when they fuck up. It's in my blood to be a member of Sinner's Creed. I'm third generation, and I'm old school.

I don't take shit, I don't give shit, and I don't give a fuck about the politics. I respect every man that wears the same patch as I do, but I only like a few of them. By *like* I mean I can be around them for an extended amount of time and not want to rip their fucking heads off.

I tried being a brother in a chapter. It wasn't for me. Nationals knew I belonged, they knew I was a soldier, and they knew I couldn't handle the brotherhood aspect of the club. I was valuable. Too valuable and too informed for them to let go. That's how I became the youngest Nomad in the history of the Sinner's Creed MC. I started when I was twenty-one, I was given my Nomad rocker at twenty-three, and I've been busting heads all over the U.S. and bordering countries ever since. Tonight would be no different. Almost a decade of experience was under my belt, and my skills showed it.

I push through the door of the clubhouse and make my way to the back, where church is being held. I stand by the door and respectfully wait for their invitation. Even I don't bust into someone's territory without asking. I never disrespected my brothers and I would break the knees of any man who did.

I am waiting for less than five minutes before I'm summoned into church. I usually hoped things would go smoothly. Tonight, I want shit to get out of control. I need to blow off some steam.

"Nationals have made a decision. I'm here to enforce their decision." I walk to the president first and pull my knife out of my cut. There is no fear in his eyes, only sorrow. He hates to lose the presidency and I hate to take it from him, but he had his chance and he failed. Pussy fell at his feet because of the *P* patch he wore, and it was his undoing. If you can't run your house, you can't run your club. He should have kept his dick in his pants and his ol' lady wouldn't be taking everything he fucking owned. I think of Saylor and how if she was my wife, I would never have any desire to touch another female. I don't have the desire now and I haven't even marked her as my property.

Fury. Rage. Hate. That's what I'm feeling this moment, and it's directed toward the motherfucker whose officer position I am fixing to take. Just the thought of some son of a bitch treating Saylor like this asshole treated his wife has me seeing red.

I cut the patch off his cut, close my knife, and deliver a right hook that breaks his jaw. I hear chairs slide across the floor and I know the others are fixing to challenge me.

The first is the sergeant at arms, who is soon to be the president. He yells something but all I can hear is the roaring in my ears. He hits me—hard, but I feel nothing. I don't want to hurt this man, my brother; he is just doing his job. So I hit him just above his eye, in his brow. Blood gushes from his head, and while he is wiping to get it out of his eye so he can see me better, I speak.

"SA, I don't want to hurt you, but I will." He acknowledges my words and although he is still pissed, he doesn't make any threatening moves toward me. Everyone is on their feet, even the VP, who is fixing to be in a world of pain. I go to him, and he knows what's coming. It would be stupid of him to fight back, but he will because he is a man.

I don't want to be here any longer than I have to. I have something to do, someone waiting for me, and the faster I handle him, the faster I can get back to her.

He throws his hands up, welcoming a fight. That's his first mistake. He thought we were gonna square up. I don't give him the chance for a fair fight. My job is to hurt him. Which I do. I break his nose, and the feeling of bone crushing beneath my fist is so fucking satisfying that I don't stop hitting him until he is unconscious. I pull his cut from his back and hand it to the secretary. He takes it with a nod of understanding.

"He is out bad. He was warned. Drop him off at his house and keep his bike." I turn to the SA, who is still trying to stop the bleeding in his brow. Fear registers on his face when I pull out my knife. It isn't me he fears, but losing his cut. That is one of the aspects that make him a good brother.

I cut the SA patch from him roughly and watch his eyes close. I put my hand on his shoulder, which is a show of high respect coming from me. I usually don't touch anyone unless it is to hurt them. "Brother." He opens his eyes at my words. "You are the new president of this chapter. You earned it. Don't disappoint us." I hand him the president patch and step away. "Appoint your officers. I will be outside."

I send the two Prospects at the door inside to take care of the unconscious body of an ex-brother. It should have been a dead body. He told the club he handled something when he didn't. The result cost the club money, time, and favors to the wrong people. The money, time, and favors were forgivable, the lie was not. A lie is a lie, no matter how big or small, and you don't lie to your fucking brothers.

I prop up against the wall outside and pull a cigarette from the pack, noticing the blood covering my hands. I should wash it off, but I'll keep it a little longer as a reminder.

Church is over before I finish my cigarette, and the new president of the Oklahoma City chapter joins me and hands me a beer. His brow has finally stopped bleeding. A piece of bloody gauze now covers the wound.

"Officers," he says, handing me a piece of paper.

I finish my beer with him before calling Nationals and informing them of the new officers of the Oklahoma City chapter. Now my business is done.

As I mount my bike, I get a weird feeling inside of me. One that makes me wonder what has happened to the man I was only fifteen minutes ago. Right now, I no longer want to be that man. I'm ready to be that lust-struck puppet I was this morning when I woke up. The reality should be sickening but it's not. Because right now, I just don't give a damn.

We're at a gas station, two days from Jackpot, when I get a call from Shady. I can tell by the gravity in his tone that his news is bad.

"We got a problem. Remember Chester?" Chester, a member of some riding club who I'd beat to death a few months back. The guy had it coming for disrespecting one of our Nationals repeatedly, but I knew there would eventually be blowback from it.

"What about him?"

"We discussed his brothers wanting revenge, so I've been keeping an eye out. One of them spotted you. He sent a message out on an unsecure line. They're planning an ambush."

I replace the nozzle on the pump, wondering why Shady was so worked up about this. It wasn't the first time someone had threatened me.

"I'll deal with it," I say, doubting anything would happen anyway.

"Um, Dirk?"

"What?"

"What about Saylor?" Shit. Of course Shady knew she was with me. The little fucker knew everything. But his reminder has the hair on the back of my neck standing up. I had put Saylor's life on the line. There was always a target on my back, and as long as she was with me, there was a target on hers too.

"Let me know as soon as you find something out. I'll keep my phone in my helmet." I hang up, watching Saylor as her smile fades when she notices the look on my face. We'd been talking more. I'd even explained my patches to her, and she had read me a poem from her diary. Two steps forward, three steps back.

"Something wrong?" I don't want to lie to her, but I know she needs reassuring. I tuck a strand of hair behind her ear, leaning down to kiss the crease between her eyes. It's the most intimate gesture I've given to her when we weren't in bed. I feel her body melt and hear her sigh. She likes it and I know that my touch was all the reassurance she needed. And her smile was mine.

We're on the interstate, rolling at a leisurely pace of ninety-five when I hear them. Seconds before I see them, my phone rings loudly in my ear. I flip up my visor, reaching in to open the phone. Shady's voice can be heard loud and clear, even before I shut the visor to block out the sound of the wind.

"I just got confirmation, but I think some are already on you."

"Some? How many are there?"

"More are coming, but I don't know how many." I pull the throttle back on my back, hitting a hundred on the speedometer within seconds. I grab Saylor's arm, pulling it tighter around my waist, hoping she gets the message. When her fingers lock and I feel her press up against me, I know she does.

"I see three in my rearview. I'm gonna try to lose them, but I'm on the interstate. Got an exit coming up—fifty-six off of I-40 west."

"I'm pulling it up now." I ride faster, hoping Saylor doesn't freak out as I split two eighteen-wheelers. She tightens her hold and despite the situation, I want to smile. I wonder if she is getting the same adrenaline high I am right now. "Take the exit, then go left." I wait until the last minute before taking the exit, cutting off a car in my path. Before I'm at the intersection, I can see the three bikes exiting the interstate right behind me.

"We got anybody around here?" Sinner's Creed had support clubs in every state, but having one in this area would be sheer luck.

"Nope." I guess it isn't my lucky day. I stay straight, running red lights and passing cars through the small town.

"Got another problem, Dirk." Of course he does. "You're probably about to lose reception." How the fuck Shady knows that I don't have a clue. I guess that's part of the "mad skills" he always claims to have.

"If I lose you, keep trying me. I'm passing Lott Drive on highway 564." The three bikes in my mirror are now only two. If I can find somewhere secluded and put enough distance between us, I can stop and shoot them. I don't want to, but it isn't only my life that's at risk . . .

"There's a house for sale ten miles from you. It should be vacant. Try to make it there. Follow the signs. It will be on the le—" Shit.

I see the sign up ahead and start to slow. Pulling my gun from my cut, I check my mirror for any other cars and thankfully there are none. As I'm turning, I extend my arm beside Saylor, shooting aimlessly beside me. The bikes slow and I speed up, using the distraction to put as much distance between us and them as possible. Saylor's screams can be heard over the sound of the gun, and the feeling is sickening.

I replace my gun then rub my hand over hers, trying to calm her. Noticing the sign, I speed up, waiting until the last minute to turn, and I have to put my foot down to keep from dropping us. Saylor rides it out, not panicking and leaning away, but leaning with me. Her trust fuels me and I pull back on the throttle again, determined to not let her down.

The road leads us deeper into the country until the houses

become further apart. The bikes are far enough behind me that I should be able to turn into the driveway and pull around back before they see us. The small sign ahead sits next to a driveway that is thankfully paved. I pull onto it, flying over the small hill with no knowledge of what's on the other side, but I have no choice. The hill leads into a curve that I know I won't make.

My bike leaves the driveway, bouncing through the yard. I manage to come to a stop at an old shed without killing us both. I climb off, breaking the lock with the butt of my gun before opening the door and pulling inside. Saylor is off the bike and standing in shock beside it. Once it's hidden, I listen for the sound of pipes, but they are long gone. I'm pretty sure they didn't see us, but I won't take any chances.

I grab our bags and Saylor's hand, pulling her behind me as I run to the back door of the old house. The door is made of wood and I easily pry it open with my pocketknife. I walk inside, breathing in the scent of mold and staleness. Locking the door behind us, I pull Saylor into my arms. Her heart beats heavy and hard against my chest.

"You okay?" That's a stupid question. Of course she isn't. She nods into my chest, and I know she's lying. "Look at me." She looks up, and I see the fear in her eyes. She isn't afraid of me, only the situation.

"What did those men want, Dirk?" I look away, knowing the time has finally come for me to make a decision. I have to be honest with her. There is no half in or half out in this life. Either she knows everything or nothing at all. I would prefer nothing, but knowing Saylor, she wants everything. And I'm afraid it still won't be enough to make her leave.

"They wanted me. Revenge." I see the question in her eyes. Just as I expected, she wants more.

"Are we safe?"

"I won't let anything happen to you." My words are determined. I speak the truth and she believes it.

"What about you?"

"I can take care of myself." My phone rings and I've never been more thankful for Shady's interruption.

"Shady," I say, never letting my eyes leave Saylor's as I hold her in my arms.

"He's alive!" he says, in a very dramatic voice. It's loud enough for Saylor to hear and she smiles.

"What do you want?"

"To make sure you aren't dead, of course. Got big plans tonight?" I can almost see the prick wiggling his eyebrows. "Don't forget my bir—" I hang up, not giving a shit about his birthday and wondering how a thirty-year-old man could still expect presents and well wishes—especially from someone like me.

I follow Saylor into one of the back bedrooms that has a window seat. She sits, looking out across the yard, then up at the darkening sky. I'm content with just standing here and staring at her, but I'm sure she is fixing to start asking questions. I just hope they are ones I can answer.

"You said those men wanted revenge. What did you do?" I walk up behind her, standing close but not allowing our bodies to touch.

"I handled business."

She lets out a small laugh and shakes her head. "Let me guess, it's confidential." I let my silence answer for me. She doesn't push further and I start to relax, knowing she won't always be this easy to pacify, but thankful that she is right now.

"You should sleep. I have some calls to make." I don't wait for an answer as I leave her and walk around the house, then through the yard to familiarize myself with the place. After I'm comfortable with my knowledge of the layout, I return to the shed, where my bike is hidden.

In my saddlebag, everything is a weapon. From a tool to a gun, I have it all. Today, one of my homemade creations will serve a better purpose than just a weapon. I pull out the lock that is tied inside of a bandana and replace the broken lock on the shed door. Now that my loose ends are tied up, there is only one thing left to do. I light a smoke, lean against the shed, and call Nationals.

"I see you're still alive." What the hell was it with the doubt?

"I see you and Shady think alike."

"I need you here by Friday."

"I'll be there."

The line disconnects and the conversation is over before half of my cigarette has been smoked. It took less than a minute for my club to do nothing more than give me another job. Some days I can't help but feel like just a number. But as I look down at the 1% patch on my cut, I know that it doesn't matter how I feel. It only matters who I am. And tonight, just like every other night of my life, I am only one thing. Sinner's Creed.

The only piece of furniture in the house is an old couch that sits in the living room. I'd returned to find Saylor sitting there writing in her diary. She was so absorbed by what she was writing that it took her a while to notice me. Even then, it's like she could sense me before she saw me.

She asked me to lay with her on the couch, so I did. Now I lay here in the darkness with nothing but the sound of her breathing filling the room. Until I hear the growing sound of pipes.

Blood runs cold through my veins as I strain to hear what direction they are coming from. I know they are coming back to find me. They likely had people at each end of the road, waiting to see what direction I went. Since I never left, they know I'm here somewhere, and if they're smart, this will be the first place they look.

The sound grows louder as headlights dance across the wall in front of me. There is no time to call for backup. Even if there was, there isn't anyone within a hundred-mile radius. All I can do now is hide and hope that they leave. I place my hand over Saylor's mouth. I feel her tense beneath me then immediately relax at the sound of my voice.

"It's me. I want you to crawl to the hallway. Don't make a sound." She nods and slips off the couch, crawling in the direction of the hallway. I grab our bags and follow her, then stand and grab her hand before leading her into the back room we were in earlier.

I pull open the closet door and usher her into the tiny space. I place her directly behind me, pull both my guns from my cut and wait. I can feel Saylor's hands gripping the back of my cut, hanging on for dear life. I let her touch power my need to protect her and fuel my anger. I'll kill any motherfucker that I see, just to keep her safe.

I close my eyes and concentrate on the sounds around me. The only thing I hear is the steady beat of my heart and the hammering of hers until the back window on the door is busted open. They're in the kitchen. Footsteps . . . three sets. The voices are hushed at first, and then become louder. They are amateurs, likely men who have no direct ties to the man I killed. If they were personally affected, they would know me. And they would know to treat each step they take as if it were their last.

"Nobody's here, man. The shed is locked up tight, no sign of forced entry on the house. Let's just get the hell outta here."

Fear. If I couldn't hear it in his voice, I could smell it on him the moment he stepped into the room. I keep my guns trained on the center of the door, ready for them to open it. But footsteps descend and soon, the sound of three bikes leaving is echoing through the night.

I turn my head, burying my face into Saylor's hair. "Stay here.

No matter what, you stay in this closet. You understand?" She nods into my back, and I start to walk away but her tight grip on my cut holds me to her. "I won't let anything happen to you," I say, reassuring her. I wish I could touch her, but there is no time for that.

She lets out an exasperated sigh, and I'm unsure why until the moment she speaks. "It's not me I'm worried about. It's you."

I've made my rounds. I've cleared our hideout. I've followed protocol and done everything I'm supposed to do. But the only thing I can focus on is Saylor's words. No one has ever said something like that to me. Not even my own brothers. My club cares about me; they have to. I'm valuable to them. But, if I died today, someone else would only take my place.

But Saylor, she makes me feel like I'm the only man on the planet. Like if my life was lost, hers might as well be too. I know my thoughts are pretty fucking extreme, but I can't help how she makes me feel.

I take time to get my shit together before going back to her. What I find when I open the closet door is not what I expect. I'm expecting her to be curled into the fetal position, bawling her eyes out and begging me to take her home. That would be a normal reaction for someone who just had a near-death experience. But Saylor is on her feet, until she launches herself at me.

"What took you so long?" she asks me between kisses. She is breathless, and her words are angry. My hands are on her ass, holding her around my waist. She slaps me, then grabs my face between her hands, forcing me to look at her. "I thought you were dead!"

Tears of anger are flooding from her eyes. She kisses me again and I can taste her salty tears on my lips. I don't want to be anywhere in the world but right here. With her. And I don't care if this is dangerous for her.

I should be taking her home. I should let the anger I feel toward myself for putting her in this shit in the first place push me to do the right thing. But I can't. And by the way she is attacking me, she sure as fuck don't want to leave me.

My heart is nearly beating out of my chest, for her. I don't care if she reads my thoughts. I don't care if she is in my head. She can have me. All of me. She can have the bad and the good and I will give her everything I've got.

She is ripping my clothes from me. I lay her on the floor so that I am on top of her. And I remember her promise. I remember she promised her dying mother that she wouldn't give herself to anyone unless they meant something to her. I won't make her break her promise.

I pin her arms above her head and slow the kiss down. I hold her there until I feel her submit to me. When I pull away from her mouth, she has calmed down. Her breathing is almost normal, but the hollow of her throat is moving rapidly with her pulse. I kiss it then slide my tongue across her collarbone. I raise my head and look into her eyes. She wants me. She needs me.

"I'm here," I tell her, and she closes her eyes at my words. "Look at me, Saylor." She does and when her eyes are locked on mine, I tell her the words that she needs to hear. "I'm here. And I'm not fucking leaving." She searches my face, looking for any uncertainty or doubt. She won't find any.

"I want you to make love to me, Dirk." Her words are my sunset. They are my rainbow, my clear blue sky, and my complete undoing. Every man has a purpose. I always thought mine was with the MC. Now I know the real purpose of my existence. To be anything Saylor Samson wants me to be.

I remove my torn shirt and then hers, watching as her body shakes in anticipation and excitement. I keep my lips on her body as I remove her clothes until she is naked beneath me. I pull her to a sitting position and push my hands into her hair, letting it knot around my fingers. She moans softly into my mouth, and I want to take her now, but I have to remind myself to take it slow.

I'm on my knees between her legs, and I gently push her away from my mouth until she is lying on her back. I watch the outline of her ribs come into view as she takes a deep breath, trying to calm herself. I place my hands on her knees and spread her wide before me. Her pussy is slick and wet. Her scent is intoxicating. She is beautiful, even here.

"Fuckin' perfect," I say, and when my breath blows across her, her back arches off the floor. I kiss the insides of her thighs, then work my way down her legs, all the way to her pink-painted toes. I want to kiss her everywhere. So I do. I kiss down one leg and then up the other until she is shaking with need.

I part her lips with my fingers, my eyes delighting in the soft, pink flesh between her legs. It makes me want to beat my chest and announce to the world that once I take her, she will be mine.

But she already is mine. She has been mine for a long time. This feeling is more powerful than knowing I can take a life. It's more powerful than knowing I can cause fear and pain. It's the power of bringing her pleasure. And other moments of my life when I thought I was powerful don't even compare.

I slide my tongue across her pussy and she is so hot for me that even the heat of my mouth is cool in comparison. I let my tongue swirl over her, making sure to not miss one inch of the sweetness that is her arousal. I slowly insert a finger inside her and soon she is bucking her hips to meet the thick, callused knuckle that is caressing her. I push further and then add another, circling her and stroking her walls—widening her in preparation for me. I continue the slow, torturous strokes until I feel her relax completely—ready for release, but I deny her.

I climb over her, kissing my way up her body, letting her pleas for release fuel my desire to make this perfect for her. Her knees are open and welcoming. I kiss her mouth and let her taste herself while I pull my jeans and boxers off. Now my naked body is covering hers and it's a perfect fucking fit.

I leave her mouth and pull one of her nipples between my lips, sucking hard then soothing her with my tongue. Her hands are in my hair. Her head is pressed into the carpet and her eyes are closed. Her mouth is open and mine finds it once again.

My cock is hard and throbbing, begging to be inside her. I kiss her softly on the corners of her lips then find her bright green eyes, open and willing me to take her. She is nervous. She is scared. But her desire for me outweighs her fear.

"Please, Dirk." She can see the uncertainty in my eyes. She can read my thoughts. She knows I'm just as nervous as she is. I don't want to hurt her, but I know I will. I have to tell myself that eventually, the pain will subside and I will be able to bring her to levels of pleasure she never thought possible.

"I'm here, baby. I'm here." She likes when I call her baby. I like how her body seems less tense now that I've told her I'm here. And I've called her the endearment she says she likes. I'm not gonna use a condom. I'm clean and I know she is too. She is on the pill. I saw it on the counter along with her other female shit that I like so much, especially when it's sitting next to mine. I'm gonna take her bareback and just the thought of how she will feel when I'm inside her, skin on skin, has me breaking out into a sweat.

I place the tip of my cock at her entrance and watch her take a deep, steadying breath. Her eyes are open and they never leave mine as I push slowly inside her. The head is in and I haven't hurt her yet. I'm not deep enough for that. I'm trying not to concentrate on how good she feels. I'm trying to focus on bringing her the least bit of discomfort I can. I could probably just thrust into her and shed a little mercy on both of us, but that seems brutal.

I push a little further until I feel her tightening around me. I take a deep breath, preparing to advance. There is no way this pain could be worse for her than it is for me.

"Kiss me," she says, her eyes on my lips. I oblige and while I'm distracting her with my mouth, I push through her tight walls until I am completely inside her. She is tight. So fucking tight that the grip her pussy has on me is almost painful.

"Okay?" I ask, breathy and nervous. She nods before taking my mouth again. When I feel her contract around me, I pull back, then thrust into her slowly.

This time, her ragged breath is not from nerves or pain or discomfort—it's from pleasure. I fuck her slowly, burying myself completely. Widening her to accommodate all of me. I shift myself so that I'm hitting that spot inside her sweet pussy that causes her eyes to roll in the back of her head. I drive faster into her, filling her.

I want to suck her nipples. I want to kiss her lips. I want to lick her neck. But I can't take my eyes off of her face. She is experiencing sex with me for the first time and she fucking loves it. Her moans are loud. Her hips are thrusting, urgent and impatient. I can't pull too far out of her because she likes the way it feels when I'm buried deep inside.

Her fingers are in my hair, on my shoulders, clawing my back. Doing everything in their power to force me further into her. She wants it harder, but I don't want to hurt her. I don't want her to get lost in the moment and then be in pain tomorrow. I want to fuck her slow, and work her up to the hard fucking that she desires. But she's not having it.

"Harder, Dirk. Fuck me harder." I'm battling one head with the other. My cock wins and I sit up on my knees and wrap my arms under her thighs. Her back is arched off the floor and I pull her to me, slamming into her, and her breath catches in her throat. I'm worried I've hurt her, but when I slow down, she demands more.

"Again. Do that again." I grip her thighs and drive back into her, pulling out slowly, before delivering another powerful thrust. "Yes, just like that. Please, don't stop." Nothing could make me stop right now. If the house was on fire, we would go up in flames before I deprived this lovely creature of what she wants.

I watch as her tits bounce with each thrust, and I have to fight my own release. Her hands are fisted in her hair. Her moans are loud and guttural. I'm working her sensitive spot with practiced perfection. I'm thanking all the women I have ever made come because it has made me the expert I am at pleasing her. When her body stills and I feel her pulsating around me, I coat her release with my own. And this time the moans that fill the room belong to me.

I ease out of Saylor, then cover her body with mine. I kiss her face—her eyes, her nose, the corners of her mouth, and her pink cheeks that are damp with sweat. I want to hold her and tell her how perfect she was. I want to tell her how amazing she felt and how special she is to me. But her arms are around my back and she is clinging tight to me, her head buried in my neck. She wants me to hold her.

I know she is exhausted. I know her release was so intense that she will just want to sleep. And she will. In my arms. I flip us so that I am on my back and she is on top of me. She moves down my body until her head is on my chest. She is shivering and I'm sure her postorgasmic state and hypersensitive flesh is what is causing it.

I feel around on the floor, and the first thing my hand lands on is leather. Without a second thought, I cover the woman that means so much to me with the colors that reflect who I am. The only two things important in my life are now one and the same. My arms go around her and I hold her tight, letting my body heat warm her.

"Dirk?" Her voice is sleepy, and I can't see them, but I know her eyes are closed. She is moments away from sleep and I wish she wasn't so drained. I want to ask her if she is okay and if she enjoyed it. Although, I already know the answer to one of them.

"Yeah?" I'm doubting myself. I'm afraid she is going to tell me it wasn't what she wanted. I'm scared she is going to tell me she made a mistake. I fear that after what she witnessed tonight, she will want to leave me. I'm panicking. I don't want her to leave. But if she wants to, I will have to let her go.

"I'm glad you came back." The reminder of what happened earlier—how many close encounters she'd had with death because of me—has me so pissed at myself. I want to hit something. "You really are the one for me."

Saylor's words are being tossed around in my head. I don't know what to make of them. I thought we had already established that I was the one for her. That's why she is with me. That's why she is laying across my chest, thoroughly fucked and sated.

I think back to our first night together. Her words are just as clear now as they were then. She said she wouldn't give herself to someone until she knew they were right for her. Herself. Was she implying more than just sex? Did that involve her heart too? I'm panicking again. There is no life in my own heart. How would I ever be able to handle hers?

I'm overthinking this shit. I need that therapy I can only get at a hundred miles an hour. But, I'm Saylor's therapy. She said so. I don't know what all that entails, but I do know that it includes holding her to my chest while she sleeps. So I don't ride. I don't abandon her and leave her here to fend for herself. I hold her and listen to her breathe, because now I know that she is my therapy too.

7

IT'S EIGHT IN the morning. I'm functioning on two hours of sleep. I want to lay on this floor with Saylor and forget about the constant fucking ringing in my ears. I know it's Shady because he personalized his ringtone to "Twinkle, Twinkle, Little Star," just to piss me off. But I can't ignore him. If I don't answer, he might think I'm dead.

Saylor is awake and she is staring at me. I'm starting to believe she sleeps in thirty-minute intervals. Not only is she awake, she is bright eyed and bushy tailed—or whatever the fuck they call it. She is wearing that "just fucked" smile, and it suits her. I'm just waiting for her to say something because I know she will. And it will be totally off the wall.

"I like this tattoo," she says as she traces her fingers across the red star at the hollow of my throat. It's a reminder of my first kill. My brother was murdered, I avenged his death. A throat for a throat.

"I like this one too." I feel her finger trail down my chest to the number *13* that is over my heart. It's a reminder too. One that tells me to never lie to my brothers. "How many do you have?"

"Twenty-seven." My voice is thick-laced with sleep. Her green eyes grow at my words. I like that I have the ability to shock her.

"I want a tattoo." Her lips poke out and her voice is whiny. I can see the laughter in her eyes and I know she is only kidding, but there is some seriousness there too. "I want a tramp stamp."

I don't know what that is. But just her use of the word *tramp* has me angry. That's not as bad as pissed, but a little worse than mad, and not how I wanted to start my day.

For some reason, Shady decides to take this moment to call again. I'm just before smashing the damn thing when she pulls it from the pocket of my cut and hands it to me. And then I see what she is wearing—my shirt. And I didn't fucking notice. I feel something in me. I know this feeling. I know it better than any other. Pride. Just the sight of her in my shirt makes my dick stand at attention.

Shady is talking in my ear, but I can't make out his words. All I can think about is how good she looks in my shirt as she stands to walk over to the window. And how fucking good it makes me feel. And how the more I think about it, the more a feeling I don't know keeps creeping up inside me. She is walking back toward me, and her hair is everywhere. The sleeves of my shirt are at her elbows and the bottom stops midthigh. Even against the black material, her skin is tan and flawless. I want to fuck her.

I tell Shady I'll call him back and hang up, not bothering to answer his question of "What the fuck happened last night?"

"Come here," I tell Saylor, and I watch her bite the corner of her bottom lip. Her face flushes red and she has a hunger in her eyes. A hunger for me. She walks to where I'm still laying and wastes no time straddling my hips. And she's not wearing panties. And I can feel the wetness of her arousal and the sticky remnants of mine between her legs. Fuck.

I see her arms cross, grabbing the hem of my shirt to remove it. "Leave it," I command. And she does. Her hands fall to her waist and I sit up, taking her face between my hands. Her lips are pink and full. Her small, perfect nose is dotted with just a few tiny freckles. Her eyes are wide and yesterday's mascara still sits on them.

She is, without question, the sexiest fucking thing I have ever seen. And I remind myself to thank her one day for teaching me the real definition of sexy. It isn't long legs, high heels, fake tits, red lips, and flawless hair. It's tanned legs with scars, bare feet, tits that fit perfectly in my hand and mouth, lips that have been kissed too hard, and hair that is a perfect mess—all the time.

Everything seems average compared to Saylor, because she is anything but. I kiss her lips, softly. I taste the morning on her breath, and it's delicious just because it's hers. I kiss her slow, taking my time running my tongue through her mouth because I want her to taste just like me. Just like she smells. I know she is sore. I know I'm an asshole. And I don't care about either. I want her, and by the way her hands are knotted in my hair, she wants me too.

I feel her hand between us, looking for what she wants. When she finds it, I'm hard and thick in her hand. She lifts her body and centers the head of my cock against her slick pussy. It's hot and inviting, and I feel her heat sucking me in. I watch as she lowers herself onto me, taking me inch by inch. I'm saying something, a string of cuss words, maybe. I don't fucking know. All I know is that she feels good. Great. Fucking amazing. And she looks just like she feels.

I see her eyebrows come together. I see her nose scrunch up slightly. I see her mouth gaped open and I feel her heavy breathing across my face. She is pushing through the pain, and my mind fucking thanks her. And so does my cock.

"Just give me a minute." That's my girl. Yeah, I fucking said it. My girl. I kiss her. I concentrate on fucking her mouth with mine so my hips don't jerk and hurt her. Or make her feel rushed. Or show her my weakness of impatience.

I slide my hands under the shirt she is wearing. My shirt. And I find her tits that were molded for my hands. I rub them, squeezing them gently, rubbing my thumbs over her nipples—and it's just what she needed.

I feel her relax and when she does, she moves. Only a little at first, and then faster. She is inexperienced and I don't care. I feel her tensing and I think she is uncomfortable doing this. Maybe she doesn't want to disappoint me. But there is no way she can. I slide my hands to her waist and hold her still, then pull away from her mouth.

"Just rock your hips. Like you're dancing." My voice is soft, and I like that I get to use it on her. She does as I say, and it's better, but she still hasn't relaxed. She is forcing this and I want her to like this as much as I do. I tighten my hold on her waist and she stops. She is avoiding my eyes and I know she is embarrassed, so I bury my face in her hair and whisper to her.

"Think of a song, baby. A slow song. Move to that rhythm. Don't worry about what will make me feel good. Do what makes that sweet pussy feel good." I keep my face buried in her hair, noticing how she sighed when I called her baby. She really likes that. I kinda like it too.

She sits on me, unmoving—thinking I suppose. She can take all the time she wants. As long as I am inside her, she doesn't even have to move. I push her hair away from her neck and lick the soft flesh. It's tender and smooth just like her pussy. I continue to lick up her neck, across her jaw and to her ear.

By the time I make it there, she is moving. And I know it's to the beat of a song. She is working my cock with the perfection of a stripper—but better. Any man who has ever had a lap dance has dreamed of what it would feel like if she rode his cock while she danced. I'm one of those men, but I'm no longer dreaming. Saylor Samson is dancing on my cock that is buried inside her while the lyrics of some song are in her head.

I feel my balls tighten and I'm hoping she releases soon, or I'm going to explode. My thumb finds her clit and it moves in time with her. She works me faster, and I know she is close. I pull my head out of her neck so I can watch her face. Her eyes are closed and she is moaning, her mouth hanging open. She has to look at me.

I'm fixing to tell her to open her eyes, but she reads my mind, like the fucking witch she is. Her eyes open wide and I'm lost in a deep sea of green as she comes around me. That's all I need.

I'm pulsing inside of her, and her moans are so pleasing to my ears that I bite my lip to keep my own from interrupting. Her head falls to my shoulder as we both try to catch our breath. Fucking feels good. Coming feels better. But this is a different feeling. It's more. I don't know what that more is, but I like it.

We need food, a shower, and I need coffee, but I have a job. So, we head out toward Nevada, where a bigger problem than last night awaits. Like what in the hell I'll do with Saylor when I get there. I glance at her in my mirror and she is looking to the left. I wish I could read her thoughts.

Suddenly I can't wait any longer to hear her voice. I've only heard her talk a few times today but it wasn't enough. And we need to discuss what happened last night.

I'm exiting and we haven't been riding an hour. Waffle House seems like a good place to eat, and I tell myself it has nothing to do with the fact that it is the closest restaurant to us.

I find us a booth in the back where I can see my bike, and she sits across from me. I like this because I can look at her. Like I always do. Or stare. Whatever the hell you want to call it.

When the waitress comes, she ignores Saylor and looks at me. I find her unappealing, but I see the look of lust in her eyes. I can read her just like I can read Saylor. The only difference is when I see it on Saylor, my dick gets hard. When I see it on the waitress, it's fucking annoying.

"Coffee and water," I grumble, and she hasn't even asked. But she is a waitress. What the fuck else does she want? When she turns to Saylor, her look of lust turns to distaste. If I hit women, I would slap her. Saylor just smiles and orders chocolate milk. It's not surprising.

I watch Saylor look over the menu, and I try to figure out what she would want. My best guess is a chocolate chip waffle, or an egg-white omelet. I don't know why these two things pop in my head, but they do. She likes chocolate, and even though she has proven to not be a health nut, I'm sure at some point she does eat healthy.

I'm still looking at her, trying to burn a hole into her mind, when the waitress returns. She is looking at me again and it pisses me off. Everyone knows, ladies first. What a fucking idiot. But we need to get on the road and I don't want her to spit in my food.

"Steak and eggs. Medium on the steak, over-medium on the eggs." I'm telling her this while I'm looking at Saylor. Her head is cocked to the side and she is eyeing me.

"Are you in my head?" she asks with a curious smile. *I wish Saylor, I fucking wish.* "Same for me," she tells the waitress, and she doesn't look at her either. I'm glad she can't take her eyes off me.

"When I was little, my mom had this boyfriend and he would never let me order for myself. Even when I was old enough to know what I wanted, he would always order for me."

I watch as she takes a sip of her milk, and I'm so happy she is talking that the waitress could shit in my food at this point and I wouldn't care. "He always made me get a waffle. Just because

I was a kid doesn't mean I had a bad taste in food. So my mom and I went out once without him and she told me to get whatever I wanted, so I ordered what he always had. Steak. And I loved it."

She laughs at the memory, but even her laughter can't help this feeling that I am just like her mom's boyfriend. Not that I would ever make her get a fucking waffle, but I did think that was what she wanted. Do I label her as an immature adult? Do I consider her childish? I mean, she did order chocolate milk.

"Why did you order that drink?" I really need to work on my tone.

"Because it's chocolate milk." I'm confused by her answer. She said it like her reason was obvious, and I don't know what the fuck that means, and I don't like her being so damn evasive. It's a first for her.

"Try it." I look down at the milk. Does she think I've never had it? "Some things in life you just can't pass up. Chocolate milk is one of them."

I look at her and I see a sadness in her eyes. I don't know if it's because I'm an asshole and I hurt her feelings or because some old memory is triggered, but I'm drinking because I'm hoping it will take her sadness away. When I drain half of her glass without realizing it, I finally understand her answer. And I don't know why in the hell I ever passed it up.

We've eaten and are now just staring across the table at each other when I finally address the big-ass elephant in the room. "About this morning," I say, hoping she will take the conversation from there. I watch her face flush and I wonder if she had already forgotten about nearly dying this morning. "Before that." Her cheeks darken further and she drops her head.

"What about it?" She is way too nonchalant.

"You could have been killed, Saylor." My emphasis on the word *kill* does little to scare her.

"But I wasn't." I stare at her, wondering if I should lean over and shake her. Does she not realize the danger she is in as long as she is with me? "I was scared. Hell, I was terrified. But for some reason, it was kind of exciting."

I watch her eyes grow at the memory and it makes me want to hit something. I don't know what I'm more pissed at. Her for being so fearless, or me at being so proud that she is an adrenaline junkie—just like me.

"You're fuckin' crazy," I say, more to myself than to her. She snaps her head up, then throws her straw at me. I'm starting to think she's serious, when she smiles.

"I prefer the term 'fucked up.'" She smiles wider and I just shake my head. I turn away from her and can't help but smirk. Saylor Samson may very well be fucked up. But she's my kind of fucked up, and I wouldn't have her any other way.

8

WE'RE IN COLORADO, it's four in the morning, and Saylor is not in bed. I'm scanning the room, willing my eyes to adjust to the darkness, trying to find her. She is not in my bed, not in the other bed, and not sitting at the table. But the bathroom door is shut and I know it was open when I went to sleep. I should wait five minutes, figuring she is probably just pissing, but only two pass before I am on my feet. I knock on the door, but there is no answer. I try again and still, no answer. The door is unlocked, and when I push it, something is lying against it. I feel myself panicking. I know it's her.

"Saylor!" I yell, beating on the door like a maniac, because I am one. Because I don't know what the fuck is wrong.

I push against the door gently, until there is enough room for me to stick my head in. And there she is. Curled in a ball on the floor, in the dark with her hands over her ears. I push further, watching her tiny, still body slide across the tile, and finally there is enough room for me to walk in. I'm on my knees in front of her and now that I'm here, I don't know what the fuck to do.

"Please don't yell," she whispers, and it is a plea that is barely audible.

"What's wrong?" I try to whisper, but my heart is racing, along with my mind and adrenaline, so my voice is harsh and way above a whisper. I see her flinch, and I swear I'll cut my fucking tongue out if I speak too loud again.

I put my hand on her shoulder and bring my face closer to hers. Her breathing is steady, like she has been asleep. I know the motel ain't the Roosevelt, but the beds aren't that uncomfortable. I would prefer them over the floor. And then I smell it. The sickening sweet and sour odor of vomit, and I still. "My head. It hurts. I need my medicine."

I reluctantly leave her and sort through the shit on the counter to try and find some Tylenol. When I grab Saylor's bag, what I find is a prescription for Imitrex. I ignore the fact that Saylor has an issue with migraines that is severe enough that she has to take prescription meds, and return to her with water and the pill bottle.

"How many?" I whisper successfully.

"Just one." I help her sit up and place the pill on her tongue then lift the glass to her lips. When she is finished, I hold her in my arms, allowing all of her weight to be on me. I will sit like this for the rest of the day, as long as she is comfortable and in my arms.

"Will you help me back to bed?" I gather her in my arms and carry her back to our bed, but when I try to lay her down she clings tighter. So, I lay on my back and put her on top of me. Her head is on my chest, her hair in my face, and I'm rubbing her back because it seems like that's what I'm supposed to do.

"Thank you, Dirk," she says to me and when she speaks my name, a greedy part of me thanks her aching head for giving me this moment to take care of her. I should say something. *Good night* and *sweet dreams* don't seem appropriate, but since I'm enjoying her need for me much more than I should, I reward her with that word of endearment that is growing on me.

"Anytime, baby."

There is no sign of what happened this morning registering on Saylor's beautiful face when I wake up to find it looking at me. I won't bring it up unless she does, and by the way she looks, she isn't going to. I don't blame her either. If I woke up wearing a radiant smile and feeling as good as she looks, I wouldn't want the reminder either.

"Okay, don't be mad." I immediately tense at her words as she sits on her knees in the bed next to me. She is dressed, her hair braided, and she has makeup on. I couldn't be mad at her no matter what she did. She could have shaved my head. Masturbated without me. Ate all the Skittles. I don't care if she painted my fucking toenails. Anything.

"I went next door and did laundry." Except that. I've had people in the past tell me to count to ten when I became angry. I'm at five and I can't last any longer. My temples are throbbing and I feel my whole body get hot. I'm fucking pissed because she left the room. Without me. When she was under strict instructions to never leave.

"I told you to not fucking leave this room." I'm growling. I'm growling through clenched teeth, and it is at the infuriating woman that I thought could do nothing to piss me off. When her smile widens, I become more pissed.

"Wait!" she says, holding her hands out to me, as if I'm fixing to bolt. Which is exactly what I want to do. She clumsily gets off the bed while I just lay here, watching her every move. "Look! I did your laundry too!" She is still smiling. I'm still pissed. And her attempts at pleading her case are pissing me off further.

Then her smile dies and she bites her lip. "On a scale of one to ten, how mad are you?" she asks cautiously. And I know there is more. "Okayyyy, a ten it is."

Now she looks nervous. Really fucking nervous. She is fidgeting and biting her lip and looking at everything but me. Maybe it's because she was sick last night. Maybe it's because she looks so fucking good this morning. Or maybe it's just that I'm losing my edge, but I feel my anger dissipate just a little. A fraction. A fraction of a fraction. But I feel it. So she did our laundry. She fucked up and left the room, but she had good intentions.

"Um," she starts, and my face has softened, I can feel it. I'm willing her to go on, and I almost want to smirk at her. Then, I see my cell phone in her hand. And my eyes lock on it. When they do, she notices and the fight dies from her as she sighs and decides to tell me everything that is on her mind.

"Your phone rang, and I answered it." She doesn't have to say any more. I'm on my feet and over to her, snatching the phone from her trembling fingers before I can stop myself. I flip open the screen and find Nationals as the last received call. I'm shaking. I can feel the angry tremors all over my body. I glare at her and she speaks, without having to be told. She is scared, frightened, terrified, and she damn well should be.

"I just said hello and this man asked who I was and I told him Saylor and he asked why I was answering your phone and I said you were asleep and he said not to interrupt you and then he asked where I was from and I told him 'cause I knew y'all must have been friends and . . ."

I'm not listening anymore. I'm in the bathroom away from her and her motherfucking rambling. I'm still pissing when I hear her voice through the door. "Dirk, I'm sorry. I didn't know. I shouldn't have answered it."

It's not that she answered it. It's that Nationals knows she is with me. And they know her fucking name. And where she lives. And if anything goes wrong, they will eliminate her because that's how the game is played.

She is not innocent in this. They don't know what all she knows and they don't care. All they care about is protecting the club. Which is what their job is. It's what my job is. Until I let a woman into my life and took her around the country with me while I took care of club problems. I did this. I couldn't be pissed at Nationals—I couldn't be pissed at her. But I am.

Her life is now in danger because she made it that way. I tried to protect her, but now there is no protecting her. She belongs to the club. They will take no chances, and they shouldn't.

"Get your shit," I snap at Saylor, even though she is standing by the door with her backpack on, ready to go. I throw on some clothes, and stomp out the door with her on my heels. I should take her to the nearest airport and send her ass home, but now I can't. Now she will make that journey to Nevada with me, and she won't be just some girl like I planned to introduce her as. She will be exactly what she told them, which is exactly who she is—Saylor Samson, a threat to Sinner's Creed.

I don't know what is gonna happen when we get to Nevada. The worst keeps popping in my head. Worst as in they tell me to get rid of her. Make her disappear, or they tell me they are gonna get rid of her and make her disappear. Who did I want more? Her or the club? I couldn't live a life where they both existed. It wasn't possible.

I expected Saylor to perform her normal ritual when I finally decided to stop for the night—six hundred miles later. But she didn't. She went straight to the bathroom, took a shower, and when she came out, she kept her head down and her eyes out of sight. I decided then that I needed a drink.

So now I'm sitting in a bar, less than a mile from where she is probably sleeping, attempting to drown myself in a bottle of whiskey that I can't bring myself to touch. I've been sitting here looking at this fucking glass for almost an hour, and all I can see in the amber liquid is her face. This must be what depression feels like.

I put the glass to my lips, but before I can take a sip, I'm greeted by a woman who is anything but Saylor. A month ago, I would be banging her in the bathroom in a matter of minutes, but now all I can think about is how her perfume doesn't smell like citrus. How her eyes are not that breathtaking shade of green. How she doesn't have a heart-stopping smile and how her hair is perfectly straight and there isn't a light socket in sight.

She is rubbing on me, wrapping her arms around my neck and shoving her big fake tits in my chest. She is telling me that she will suck my cock and how she knows I'm big, but that's okay because she doesn't have a gag reflex. She is grinding her hips in a way that lets me know she is good at what she does.

But she isn't my kind of good. My kind of good is awkward, inexperienced, and perfectly imperfect. My good is in a T-shirt and panties that cover a set of tits that are small and natural, and the sweetest pussy I have ever tasted. And my good is alone. And I am here. And she is guilty of nothing but being the best thing that has ever happened to me. And I'm a fucking fool if I sit here one second longer.

I slide the woman the whiskey, lift her from my lap, and head back to the one thing that can save me from this drowning pool of depression. My life vest. My rescue. My Saylor.

Saylor is in the bed farthest from the door when I come in. She is on her side, facing away from me, and she is asleep. I sleep in the bed closest to the door, and tonight, she will sleep with me.

I kick off my boots, and gather her in my arms. Hers instinctively go to my neck and I don't know if it's her or her subconscious that wants me, but some part of her wants me and that's all that matters. Saylor is not asleep, though.

"I'm sorry, Dirk. I'm so sorry." I could correct her and chew her ass for saying it, but there is no need. Right now, she really feels that way. And I haven't given her any reason to feel different.

"I don't know what I was thinking. I'm so stupid!" She is disappointed, sad, hurt, angry, and regretful. And each one of these emotions is directed at herself. I would feel much better if they were directed at me.

Now, Dirk. Now is the time to say something. I'm opening my mouth to speak. I might even be preparing to make those *shhh*ing sounds that you use to calm women and babies, but Saylor is sniffing me and she doesn't like what she smells.

"You've been with someone." Her tone is not accusatory. She is saying it like this is her punishment, and she is willing to accept it. "I can't believe I've done this. I've ruined us. I've ruined you. I've ruined everything."

She sounds so defeated that I can literally feel my heart breaking. I pull her closer to me and she doesn't pull away. She holds tighter, touching every part of my cut as if to mask the woman's scent with her own.

"I haven't been with anyone. Not since I've been with you." I could elaborate. I could become that poor, desperate motherfucker who tries to make his woman understand that it wasn't his fault. But with Saylor, there is no need for elaboration. She believes me and I know this by her cry of relief that soon turns to a guttural sob of reprieve.

I want to show her there is no one else. I need to show her how much I worship her. I never want her to doubt me. I never want her to regret who she is, no matter what the cost might be.

I roll her to her back and climb between her legs. She is sobbing in my perfumed neck, and I have to pry her hands from around me.

"I need to kiss you, baby." And that's all she needs. Her hands stop fighting. Her body relaxes and she makes an attempt to stifle her cries so I can kiss her mouth. But I don't want the set of tear-stained lips on her face. I want the smooth, wet lips of her pussy.

When my head is between her thighs, her legs are open—inviting me in, and there is dampness on her panties where she is wet for me. I want her taste so fucking bad that it takes every ounce of my willpower not to shred through the material with my teeth. I'm so impatient that I don't bother to remove them, I just pull them to the side and slide my tongue between her slick lips.

My moans mirror hers as I devour every drop of her arousal, kiss every inch of perfection, and fill her with my fingers. I let her come and I continue. I kiss her, lick her, overwhelm her with my mouth until she is breathlessly begging me to stop. I've lost count of how many times I've tasted her release, how many hours have passed and how long I have been in the heaven that's between her thighs. But, when I come up to kiss her mouth, she is without energy, without thought, and without a tear. And just like every other way, I like her just like this.

9

THE NEXT MORNING, I find Saylor writing in her diary at the small table across the room. She doesn't know that I'm awake, and I take this time to study her. Her hand is moving fast across the pages of her diary, and her face tells me she is in deep concentration. I know if she is writing about yesterday, they are definitely words I don't want to see. And I don't want her to think about it. I want her to forget it ever happened.

"Do you believe in God, Dirk?" she asks without looking up. How the hell did she know I was awake? I shouldn't even ask myself that. I already know the answer. It's because she is in my head. And if she is, then she should know the answer to her question. But I tell her anyway.

"Yes." She turns to look at me and she is surprised. Shocked. Unbelieving. Maybe I should elaborate. I don't want to, but I will because I owe it to her. "I believe there is a God, I just don't believe that he created me." That probably sounds crazy to her ears, but it makes sense to me.

"Why would you think that?"

I clear my throat and continue. Even though this shit is too deep to talk about when I first wake up. "There is no way the same creator of someone as perfect as you, is responsible for creating someone as fucked up as me." She still doesn't get it. I can tell this by the incredulous look on her face.

"Do you really believe that?"

"I don't want to talk about this anymore," I tell her, and I wait for the whining to start. I wait for her to tell me how important it is that I change my ways. I wait for her to bitch at me for not taking this serious. I wait for her to quote scripture and start singing hymns. I wait for that look of pity or disappointment. And I wait. And wait. And wait. And it never comes.

The subject is dropped. That look of happiness that covered her face when she first mentioned her god is still in place. But now, it's directed toward me. I'm glad. I'm a jealous man. I hate to be jealous of the creator of the universe, but I would be lying if I said I wasn't glad that I am back at the forefront of her thoughts.

"I'm really, really hungry." Saylor's words along with her growling stomach are music to my ears. Now she needs me. It may just be to feed her, but it's good having her back at my mercy.

I stand, ignoring thoughts of what I want to eat this morning, and grab a pair of clean jeans, thanks to Saylor. She runs around the room gathering her shit while I watch. But when she takes her shirt off, I can't watch any longer. My willpower isn't strong enough. I have to walk out.

The Colorado air is clear and cool. I almost feel guilty for lighting a cigarette, but when I inhale the smoke into my lungs, I no longer care. It's Saturday and we will be in Jackpot by nightfall. There is a mandatory meeting, and someone from each chapter is required to be there. I'm not part of a chapter so the responsibility falls on me.

I get that sick feeling in my gut when I think about what will happen when I get there. Saylor will be the topic of conversation, and I will have to keep my shit in check. I can't lose it on my brothers. If I do, then I will be dealt with, which means Saylor will be dealt with too.

I take a deep breath and vow to myself to not fucking think about it anymore. I'll handle it when I get there. But, when Saylor walks outside with her bag slung over her shoulder, thoughts of the club and what might happen to her hit me full force. The innocent look she wears reminds me of how much I might've fucked up her life. I grab her bag, packing the bike with more force than necessary.

"Dirk? You okay?" Her sweet, cautious voice is laced with concern.

"Let's go," I snap, immediately regretting it. I'm not pissed at her, but the hatred I feel for myself right now is too strong for me to attempt to not sound like a dick. When she makes no move to get on, I chance a look at her. She looks annoyed.

"Dirk," she says to me, her hands fidgeting nervously with the hem of her shirt. "You are the only reason I smile. You are the only person I want to be with. You are my reason for everything. Don't shut me out any longer." She doesn't wait for my answer. She just climbs on the bike and waits for me to mount so we can leave. But I have another plan.

I lift her from the bike and carry her back into the room. I slam the door behind us and sit her on one bed, then take a seat on the other.

"Ask me anything," I say, hoping like hell that she doesn't ask just anything. But it's time I'm honest with her. Might as well clear the air before we get the wrath from Nationals.

"Tell me about your parents." Shit.

"I didn't know my mother, but my father was a shithead." That's a good way to start. "My grandfather wasn't a very good role model, but he was all I had. He raised me. He was a member of Sinner's Creed. I was brought up in the life of an MC. It's all I knew. All I know. What I am. And all I'll ever be."

I watch the sadness build in her eyes before she hides it. I don't want her feeling sorry for me. I'm just before telling her that when she asks another question.

"Tell me something about you. Something that has nothing to do with the club." Her smile is encouraging and I find myself wanting to tell her shit that some know, but not because they ever asked. Just because they'd known me all of my life and it's how I'd always been.

"I don't like people touching me and I don't like conversation." I'm not sure what else to say. But, as I sit here and stare at Saylor, whose eyes light up every time I share a little more about myself, I can't help but feel like there is something else she needs to know.

I should rehearse my next lines in my head, but I'm just gonna say it as it comes to me, which I'm sure I'll regret. "The only time I like being with women is when I'm buried balls deep inside them, but I like being with you all the time."

I watch the jealously flare in her eyes when I tell her about fucking women—a line I could have worded differently. Then I watch it melt when I mention I like being with her. I'm sure her stomach is doing that flipping shit mine's been doing here lately.

Now it's time for me to ask some questions. "What triggers your migraines?" I watch her tense and I know that either I'm not gonna like her answer or she isn't gonna tell me the whole truth. I'm betting on the latter.

"I think it's the high pressure." I'm calling bullshit and when she continues on a ramble, I know my instincts are right. "I've had them for years. I don't take medicine to prevent them, I can only take it once it happens. And it always happens in my sleep. Usually after a really long day." Her voice drops several octaves when she tells me the last part, and now my mission is to do what I can to prevent it.

"We won't ride so hard anymore," I tell her. I'm not growling, but that calm tone I've been working on ain't nowhere in sight either.

"I don't want to slow you down," she says, and does so in a way that is pleading. She is hoping, or probably praying, that I don't leave her behind or change my mind about bringing her with me. I concentrate on that soft tone I know I'm capable of and force myself to use it.

"You won't. I'll make it work."

"Will you tell me why you got so mad at me when I answered your phone?"

"Because they know who you are and, because of who I am, the club will stop at nothing to ensure their safety." It's evasive, but it pacifies her. And I'm sure she already knew what the answer would be before I told her.

"Did I get you in trouble?" *No, baby. You got yourself in trouble.* But that's not information she needs to know. And once again, she isn't worried about herself, only me.

"I stay in trouble." My words are funny to her. And I think I just made a joke. Or something like it.

We stop on the road later that evening and I order us a pizza from a gas station. We take a seat in the small dining area, and I watch as Saylor scarfs it down like she hasn't eaten all day. Then I remember she hasn't. I'm not even sure she ate any of the Skittles that we bought along the way. Since I'm not that hungry, I'm guessing she fed them all to me.

"When you're fucking hungry, you need to tell me," I snap, and when her frightened, innocent eyes land on me, I wish I wasn't such an asshole. I could sit here and wonder why she looks scared, but I know it's because I just bit her head off. She is still looking at me, unsure of what to say. That's a first.

I take a deep breath and I can't even look at her when I speak. "I want you to tell me if you're hungry. I've rode by myself for so long that sometimes I forget about your . . . needs." My voice is calmer, but I want to hit something. I hate apologies and even though I didn't give her one, it was something like it, and I hate those too.

"Okay, Dirk. It won't happen again." Her voice is so full of regret that I have to punish myself by looking at her. But she is lost in her own thoughts. And I want to know what they are. And when she repositions and faces me, I know she is fixing to tell me.

"I'm gonna try to say this without scaring you. I don't want you running for the hills." I want to laugh at her words. She doesn't scare me and I wouldn't run from her no matter what she said.

"When people have feelings for one another, sometimes all they can think about is them. Not eating or sleeping or . . . well, really they don't think about anything. It's like the excitement they have for one another outweighs their body's need for the basic essentials. That's how I feel. The high I get from being with you has me for-getting to eat, sleep, or even think. Then, when I do eat, I realize I'm starving. When I do sleep, I find myself crashing with so much fatigue, I don't even move in my sleep. And when my thoughts are somehow not centered on you, that's when reality steps in and I have one of my crazy episodes." My mind is running a hundred miles an hour. And there is only one thing I want to do: scream and run for the hills.

"I'm going to smoke," I huff, hearing her laughter as I walk out.

If I had Oprah's number, I'd call her right now and give her my left nut for some advice. I heard every word that Saylor said. I've run the lines in my head over and over, and they still have me all twisted up on the inside. But what's more fucked up is that I feel just the way she does.

I try to remember what life was like before she slept with me every night, and what I recall is a little disturbing. In five years, there has never been a woman who I didn't compare to Saylor. There has never been a night when I didn't see her face in my dreams. And the more I remember, the more I realize these feelings aren't as foreign as I thought—now they are just real.

I don't know how long I've been outside, but when I come back in Saylor is sitting at the table, writing in her diary. We'll be in Jackpot soon and there are some things we need to discuss before we get there.

"We will be meeting up with the club tonight." I guess that's a good way to start. When I don't get a reaction out of her, I continue. "Don't ask questions, and if you are asked any questions don't lie, but be as evasive as possible. I don't want them knowing any more about you than they already do." Saylor finally looks at me. By the way she is fidgeting, I know she is nervous.

"I really messed up when I told them who I was, didn't I?" Saylor is smart. I never had to confirm her fuckup; she knew the moment she answered the phone that it was a mistake. But she needs to know the truth and I now know that she can handle it.

"Nationals are a group of higher-ups in the club. They call the shots and they are the ones who give me my orders. By having you with me while I'm working, it makes you a liability. Nationals will stop at nothing to ensure club business stays club business. My word should be enough to convince them that you don't know anything, but I don't know how this will be handled." I wait for her reaction to my words and get exactly what I expect: nothing.

"So, are you in trouble?" she asks, and the nervousness is back. Maybe she doesn't understand the severity of the situation.

"This isn't about me. It's about you and your safety." I'm growing impatient, and the tone of my voice shows it. She needs to have a better regard for her own well-being and stop fucking worrying about me. When she speaks, it's clear she is exasperated.

"Just tell me, Dirk. Are you in danger with the club?" I take a deep breath and sit up, trying to find the right words. Maybe I need to scream at her to get her to understand. Maybe I need to shake the shit out of her. Or maybe I just need to answer her infuriating fucking questions.

"No." That's all she is getting. I can take care of myself. The only way I would be in danger is if Saylor did something stupid, which I know she wouldn't. Or if they ordered me to do away with her, then I would have to fight a losing battle with them, or do as they said—which would never fucking happen.

Saylor doesn't seem nervous anymore, just complacent. And I'm not sure how that makes me feel. "I got this, Dirk. I won't disappoint you, I promise."

I watch as she walks away, her ass swaying with every step until she disappears into the bathroom. She could never disappoint me. But I can't dwell on that heart-swelling feeling I have about her trying to make me proud, because another feeling is overpowering it. Curiosity. Because I know my beautiful mess of a goddess has a plan forming in her head.

We arrive in Jackpot, Nevada, just as the sun is setting. Go fucking figure. When we pull up outside the run-down bar where the annual party is being held, I feel the sickness setting in. Saylor has been all smiles, shits and giggles the whole ride, and I don't understand it.

A line is forming outside to greet us. I'm so busy searching the faces of my brothers, trying to read their reaction, that Saylor has to call my name to get my attention.

"Dirk." I get off the bike and look at her, the smile she wears calms me instantly.

"Everything is going to be fine." I can't believe that this woman is bringing me comfort and reassurance when it should be the other way around. And that sickness in my stomach is replaced with something different. A feeling I'm still trying to process.

I help her off the bike, wishing I could kiss her, but this is my club. My brothers. My life. I won't look like a pussy in my world. I'll reserve that side of me for when I am alone with Saylor. Which is exactly where I want to be right now. Everyone gives me space, waiting for me to acknowledge them before they say anything.

"Just stay close to me. I'll handle everything," I tell her before walking toward the crowd. My body is stiff, my muscles are tight, and I can feel the vein in my neck throbbing with each heavy beat of my heart. I'm in kill mode. It's just a precaution, but it's the best defense I have.

I don't hold Saylor's hand. I don't have to. The fact that she rode here with me should let everyone know who she is with. I don't tell them her name because it is none of their business. I give them my salute, shaking hands with a few of the older ones that have been around the longest, and walk inside with Saylor on my heels.

I know they are looking. I know what they're thinking. I just hope nobody does anything stupid. I would hate for Saylor to witness what I am capable of.

Once inside, Shady is the first face I notice. He smiles and I glare. He sees Saylor, smiles wider, and I feel the hair on the back of my neck stand up. My face must tell him how bad I want to rip his fucking head off, because his smile dies and he gets right to business.

"'Sup, Dirk?" Shady asks, shoving his tattooed hands into his pockets. I give him a nod before walking through the bar and out the back door to a private porch guarded by SAs and enforcers. They move when they see me, and I notice all six Nationals are here. Good. I can get this shit over with and not have to repeat myself. Each one stands and greets me. I shake their hands and even hug the National president, who has a Prospect help him stand. This man is the reason I'm still alive.

"Dirk, my brother," he says, and even after all these years, his raspy voice still slows the heart in my chest back to its normal rhythm.

"Roach." I don't say any more because he isn't listening anyway. His eyes are on the woman who is standing behind me. I watch as they widen slightly at the sight of her. Not that I can blame him. His head turns from side to side as if he can't believe she is real. I turn my body so that I can see them both, and when my eyes land on Saylor, I realize I haven't even noticed that her hair is down. Or what she is wearing. Her hair is everywhere, which is nothing unusual, but the wind has added to its unruly nature. She is wearing ripped jeans that sit low on her waist, a white T-shirt that fits tight to her tits, and a silver necklace I have never seen before that says the word *faith*.

But it's not her hair or her clothes that have the attention of everyone around me; it's her smile. It's not that breathtaking, teeth-baring smile she gives me, and it's not a small polite smile. It's a smile that is full of kindness and warmth and makes you feel at peace when you look at it. I'm so caught up in the feeling of ease that has consumed me that it doesn't bother me when she speaks. The sound is so welcoming that I don't want her to stop.

"Hi, Roach. I'm Saylor Samson." I stand in a trance as she takes a few steps forward and leans in to give Roach a kiss on the cheek. And even that doesn't bother me. I pull my eyes from

Saylor to gauge Roach's reaction. He seems as possessed as me. Then, this man who wears a patch labeled *funeral director* surprises us all when he smiles.

After Saylor has been introduced to everyone outside, they ask her to sit. I feel my uneasiness growing again and I will Saylor to smile at me. But she doesn't even look my way. Her focus is solely on the six men seated around her. I stand to the side, within arm's reach of her, and get a quick count of weapons. Surprisingly, there are only two. I know I can get to them before they draw them.

"Well, tell us about yourself," Jimbo, the national VP, says. I stare at him as he takes a deep pull from his pipe, then blows his smoke out on a cough before passing it.

"There really isn't much to tell. I'm in between jobs and using this time to study and explore possible career opportunities in the medical field." Saylor's words are as smooth as silk to every ear but mine. I feel my face frowning when I realize that this is something I didn't even know.

"The club could use a good nurse," someone adds, but I'm too busy with my own thoughts to figure out who said it. I should have asked her these things. I don't like that they know more about her than I do.

"I'd be happy to lend a hand anytime." I notice a nervous tone in Saylor's voice that wasn't there moments ago. I look down at her and she looks to me with pleading eyes, but someone is demanding her attention before I can decipher what she wants.

"What I want to know is about your time with Dirk." My eyes go to a voice I know all too well. Chaps, the national enforcer who helped train me. He was a retired Navy SEAL and believed that a man who governed himself should be able to prove his physical and emotional ability to handle any job.

Chapters had each other to lean on. When one couldn't perform a task, another stepped in. When the club gave me an order, I had no choice but to execute it myself. No matter the conditions.

But Chaps's idea of training consisted of leaving me in the dark for a week with a gallon of water and only my thoughts to keep me company. He said mental endurance was more powerful than physical. When they let me out, I proved my strength by breaking his nose as soon as he opened the door. We haven't got along since then. I can feel Saylor's eyes on me, but I keep my focus on Chaps. He is too unpredictable.

"I've known Dirk for years," Saylor starts, and her voice is back to normal. "He has always been there when I needed him. When life got tough, it was like he just magically appeared. A week ago, I asked him to take me away with him. The anniversary of my mother's death hits me hard every year and I just needed to get away. He agreed, although I think my large appetite and unpredictable, untamable hair gets on his nerves sometimes." She adds the last part on a laugh and I know it's to let me know she is joking. I hear Roach's raspy laugh that turns into a cough, giving me the distraction I need to check on her. She shoots me a wink, and it's all the confirmation I need. I turn back to Chaps, who is wearing that fucking smart-ass smirk while he looks at my girl.

"I bet I could tame your appetite and your hair."

"Dirk, where is the bathroom?" Saylor is at my side with her hand on my arm before I can react to Chaps's comment. Jimbo stands between me and Chaps with his back to me, blocking my view of the motherfucker I want to hurt. Bad.

"Dirk?" Saylor's pleading voice is more powerful than any thought or feeling inside me. I turn to look at her and she shakes her head, begging me to keep my cool. "Please show me to the bathroom."

I look back at Chaps, but all I see is the back of Jimbo's cut.

He is saying something to Chaps, and if any of them are smart, they will put him in his place before I do.

I grab Saylor's hand in mine, letting every-fucking-body know that she is with me, and lead her inside. When she goes to piss, I walk in with her. She stands at the sink, taking deep breaths and playing with the necklace at her throat. "Dirk, I really need you to keep your shit together." Her choice of words are not very wise.

"Nobody talks to what's mine like that. Nobody. I don't give a fuck who it is. He'll be lucky if he walks out of here." I'm growling and I don't want to. I'm in her face and I shouldn't be. Her flinch is the only thing that makes me realize my actions.

"Dirk, I'm trying really hard here to make this right. You have no idea what I've sacrificed to fix my mistake. All I'm asking is that you try and control your temper. They're just words." Her breathing is fast and she looks like she wants to cry. She knows nothing about sacrifice. I was willing to give up everything I've ever known for her. The last person she wants to talk to about sacrifice is me.

"This is my club. You are my problem. If you make a mistake, I'll fix it. Words will get you hurt just as fast as actions with me. Don't act like you know them, Saylor, because you fucking don't." I spit my words at her. There is so much malice and force behind them that I find myself taking a step back to keep them from physically hurting her. But Saylor doesn't want space between us. She closes the distance and I feel her finger in my chest as she speaks.

"Don't you yell at me," she says, her voice quiet but shaky with anger. "I know you're mad about what he said. I know you're mad because you can't control the situation. I know it drives you crazy to know that I might be in danger. But have you ever thought about how I feel? If I lose you, then I lose everything. Do you have any idea how infuriating it is to know that you could be taken from me, all because you're a jealous asshole and can't keep your temper in check?" She stares at me and I wonder if she wants an answer. But I'm too angry to say anything else. If I do, she might just get her feelings hurt, and I know better than anyone that words are something you can't take back.

She takes a deep breath and releases it, trying to calm her temper, I think. But when she grits her teeth before she speaks, and pokes me hard in my sternum, I know it didn't work.

"Now, I'm going to have a drink at the bar. And if you really want to protect me, then be smart and protect yourself. Because if they hurt you, then I'll give them no choice but to hurt me too."

Saylor storms out of the bathroom, leaving me so fucking confused and horny that I'm tempted to go to the bar and drag her back in here just so I can fuck her.

I light a cigarette and close my eyes, willing my mind to slow down and process her words. It's never occurred to me until this moment that she cares for me just as much as I care for her. She doesn't want to lose me. She doesn't want me to do anything stupid because she doesn't want to lose everything. That everything is me.

From what I know of Saylor, she is fully capable of doing something crazy to protect me. She already has. It wasn't as extreme as this, but it kept me from killing a gas station attendant and some horny independents.

Images of Saylor waving a gun around and bashing heads with a beer bottle are not something I want to see in real life. Chaps was testing me. Pushing me to my limits. He knows he struck a nerve and he is likely to try it again. As much as I would like to kill him for his comment, I want Saylor more. So much more that I am willing to swallow my pride and give Chaps a warning, which is all I need to do. If he fucks up after that, the club will know he was given a chance and will back me if it gets physical.

I look at myself in the mirror, and the man looking back at me isn't the same man he once was. I open the bathroom door and scan the room, spotting Saylor's curls immediately. She is sitting with the ol' ladies at the bar, drinking and laughing. She is happy. She is safe. She is mine. And nothing else really matters.

Chaps is pissed when I walk back outside. I notice the amount of people have doubled while I've been gone. They are expecting me to retaliate. I look into every set of eyes around me. The men sent to stop me glare at me murderously, and I'm sure they are pumping themselves up in their heads.

Roach sits expressionless, waiting for me to strike. Once it is stopped, he will confront me, but even he knows not to step in now.

Jimbo looks pissed. By the way his nostrils flare each time he looks at Chaps, I know his anger isn't directed at me. This could happen how they all expect it to. If it did, I would walk up to Chaps and immediately throw the first punch.

Since he is on his feet, I know it's what he's predicting and maybe even what he wants. If this was a regular chapter member, there wouldn't be an issue. But, this is a National. A man who worked hard to get where he is and is one of the most respected men in the club. And because it's me who he is up against, everyone knows shit can get bad really fast. They know I couldn't give a fuck less about his title, and we have history. I won't do what I'm known for; I'll do what is right by Saylor. Then Chaps calls me out.

"You got something you wanna say, Dirk? You brought this threat into our world, and I think it's time you answer for it. So, do what you do. You don't fucking scare me."

I'm just about to take a step toward him when I hear Saylor's laugh carry through the bar. There is no doubt she knew I was fixing to fuck up; she always does. That laugh gives me the strength I need to do what I know is right.

"Saylor is mine. Don't talk to her. Don't look at her, and don't fucking test my patience where she is concerned again. I believe I've proved my loyalty to this club, and my word should be enough to stand up for any transgressions you try and accuse me of. She rode with me. She knows nothing. She is not a threat, will never be a threat, and don't refer to her as a threat again. I've never given this club reason to doubt me. And if I remember correctly, I've pulled the trigger for you more than once, Enforcer. This is your last warning. You won't ever get the chance to fuck up a third time with me."

I don't know how long I stand there, staring into the eyes of the first man who has challenged me and didn't get a fight. But it's long enough to force him to shift on his feet. A patch holder I don't know assists Roach until he is standing between us. He first looks at Chaps, and when he speaks, there is no denying the warning in his voice.

"I won't stand behind you if you pursue this." Jimbo seconds his motion, and soon all the Nationals agree that Chaps should stand down. While they wait for his decision, Roach turns to me, and I find that sparkle of pride I longed for from my grandfather in the eyes of my brother.

"There is no problem here, Dirk. The club trusts you will handle yourself and your property, like you always have." I feel my chest swell with pride at the thought of making Saylor my property. Branding her with my patch, my name, and my club would be the equivalent of marriage for people unrelated to an MC. It would show everyone in my world that she was mine, not that anyone would have any doubts after today.

Chaps steps up next to Roach, and my feelings shift immediately, as do my eyes. And what I see is not defeat, but respect, not that I need it from him.

"You're a good brother, Dirk. I never should have doubted you. It won't happen again." When he sticks his hand out to me,

I know that even Saylor's laughter couldn't persuade me to shake it. I give him a nod, and pull a cigarette from my cut. Ignoring his outstretched hand.

"We need some beers," I tell one of the patch holders who was sent in for reinforcements.

"Sure thing, Dirk," he says, and disappears inside. Conversation starts and the whole ordeal is squashed and forgotten, just like that. Not another word will be spoken about it. Beers are passed around and a toast is made in honor of the anniversary of our club. We pour some out on the ground in honor of fallen brothers and drink in honor of our patch.

Chaps tips his beer bottle toward me and tells me, "One day, Dirk. One day you will shake my hand." I take a pull from my beer, knowing that will never happen, but keeping the thought to myself. Then, I hear Saylor's laughter again, and now I'm not sure it won't.

10

"DIRK, DON'T LET me fall off," Saylor slurs as I practically carry her to the bike. While I'd been on the porch with Nationals, she had been taking shots with the ol' ladies at the bar. Three hours and a fifth of liquor later, she was finally ready to call it a night.

"I won't, baby." I help her with her helmet, and then on the bike, pulling her arms around my waist and locking her fingers together. The place we are staying is only a few minutes from here, and I take my time getting there. The last thing I need is for her sexy little ass to fall off. I turn down the gravel drive, unable to keep the memories of my childhood from flooding back.

This is not my home and never was. My bike is my home, and it has been since I was old enough to ride. This is just a place that reminds me of who I am and what made me that way.

The white, wood-framed house hasn't changed a bit. If the Prospects from a nearby chapter didn't keep the yard cut, you would think it was abandoned. I can't remember the shape I left it in the last time I was here, but I'm sure Saylor won't complain.

It's probably better than most of the cheap-ass motels we have stayed in. And she thinks they are perfect. I really need to get her a dictionary.

I pull the bike under the old carport, next to all the other shit that hasn't been touched in the last ten years, and cut the engine. Saylor is laying on my back and if she is passed out, I don't know how in the hell she stayed on. I unlock her fingers and hold her hands in mine, mentally preparing myself for what lies inside the house.

"I'm comfortable. Let's just sleep out here." Saylor's words are slow and slurred. I like getting to know all the different sides of her.

"Deal." I don't want to go in any more than she does. I hate this place, but it's my responsibility, and since I have to be here a few days anyway, I might as well get it over with.

"Whose house is this?" she asks, her head still on my back. I don't know why I feel the need to tell her, but I do.

"Mine." I feel Saylor's head lift, and watch her in my mirrors as she looks around the dark carport.

"I didn't know you lived here." I can tell by her body language that she is ready to get off the bike and explore the place. Nosy little shit.

"I don't live here. I just own this place. Let's sleep." The need to share shit with her vanishes just as suddenly as it appeared. I should have known better than to expect her questions would stop.

"Does anyone live here?" she asks, moving to get off the bike. I stand and help her, ignoring her question, thinking maybe she will just let it go. When I don't answer her, she asks a different question. Fucking conversation. "Did you grow up here?" I grab our shit from the bike and move through the carport easily, despite the shit strewn everywhere. I know this place better than any, and it hasn't changed in years. "It's quiet here." Saylor says, and before I can process that her words are a simple observation, I'm lashing out.

"I don't wanna talk about it, so stop asking so many fucking questions." I kick the shit outta something, an old carburetor, I think, and the noise causes Saylor to yelp. Now I want to kick the shit outta myself. I should apologize, but I can't bring myself to speak.

The padlock on the door is rusted and I'm struggling to get it open. What I really want to do is kick it down, but I've done a good enough job at scaring the shit outta Saylor. No need to fuck things up worse. I hear shit being moved behind me and turn to find Saylor half sitting and half laying on an old lawn-mower. I can't make out her face, but it's bright enough I can see her body is limp, and I'm hoping like hell it's from exhaustion and not from me. "You okay?" I ask, my voice low and hoarse.

"I would be if you would hurry the fuck up and get me to bed," she huffs, and suddenly, I'm not angry anymore. I'm not pissed at myself, her questions, or this rusty-ass lock. I'm just happy that she is making an effort to be bitchy and isn't sad. I manage to get the door unlocked and push it open. The smell of stale cigarette smoke and rat piss fills my nostrils, and I know I'm home. My stomach turns at the thought of referring to this place as home, and the fight to not retrigger old memories is won. And it's not in my favor.

"Dirk! Get your wormy little ass in here and get us a beer!" *Black yells, and I'm on my feet at the sound of his voice. I know I won't get to it fast enough. I know that no matter how I bring it to him it won't be good enough. Just like I'm not good enough. I know this because he reminds me of it every day. "Damn, boy. You ain't worth the shit paper I wipe my ass on. Your daddy should have shot his wad in an ant bed instead of in your whore of a mama."*

I grab the beer out of the fridge, making sure not to drop one or shake them up, and pass them around the table. The smoke in the room is thick, and I know it's drugs and not cigarettes. And it's not the kind of drugs that looks like cigarettes either. Black calls it dope. I don't know what that is, but I do know not to ask. I wait to see if he wants me to do something else. "What the fuck you want, a hug? A cookie? Get the fuck outta here!" He is yelling, but it is at my back. At the sound of his voice, I'm moving. This time, I'm glad it's away from him. I leave my door open, afraid he might holler for me and I won't hear him, then I disappear into my hiding place to re-lace my shoes for the twentieth time today.

I listen to the voice I've feared my whole life, and it is as loud in my head as it was in real life. I can still see everything. I can still smell everything, and I can still feel the same chills rolling through my body as I did when I was a kid. Not that I ever was. I sure as hell wasn't ever treated like one or got the opportunity to act like one.

I shake my head, physically trying to remove the memories. I turn around and Saylor's sleeping form is all I need. I scoop her up in my arms and carry her inside, kicking the door shut behind me. The sound doesn't even wake her.

There isn't a bed in this house I want to sleep in, or couch I want to sit on, but the furniture shouldn't bother Saylor. She doesn't have the memories that I do. I lay her down on the couch before pulling the air mattress from the large tote that still sits in the middle of the living room floor. I plug in the pump and stand there in the dark, waiting for it to inflate, and dread checking the house. That would mean I had to turn the lights on. And tonight, I really didn't want to see this place in color. But I haven't been here in months, and it is very possible that there are snakes or raccoons or some shit that have somehow made their way inside.

I leave Saylor, dragging my feet down the hall to the small bedroom, and stop. Might as well get the worst over with first. Fuck. I turn the light on, and the room comes into view, the sight drying my mouth and quickening my heartbeat.

"Pussies cry, Dirk. Are you a pussy?" I shake my head, furiously wiping the tears from my face. Black charges across the room toward me. I'm so scared I stop breathing. I know he is going to hit me. I could try to run, but that will just make him even angrier.

He uses the back of his hand to slap me across my face, the force of his swing throwing me to the floor. I feel the blood running down my cheek from the gash in my face caused by the big skull ring he always wore. "Don't you ever shake your head at me. If you got something to say, fucking say it. You're not a mute, you little bastard. Do you hear me?" I try to talk, but I have no air in my lungs. I draw in a deep breath, but before I can speak, he is kicking me. I curl into a ball, holding my stomach. I'm coughing, struggling to breathe. My brain ignores the pain and focuses on his words. I have to answer him. I have to.

"I'm not a pussy," I say, forcing my eyes to look up at him. My tears have died, but the reason for them is still very much alive in my head. The nightmare. The one that kept coming back.

"Good. Be a man, Dirk. Don't ever let me see you cry again." And he never did.

The old, stained mattress still sits in the corner of the room. A pillow and an old blanket lay on top of it. I walk to the closet and look in. The light from the room is enough for me to see inside. An old suitcase, a pair of shoes, and poster of a motorcycle lay on the floor covered in dust and cobwebs. The hiding spot that protected me all those years was still there, covered with a piece of paneling. It was the one place Black didn't know existed.

He bought the house before I came along, but never had use for the room. I'm not sure he had even been in it until I moved in.

I had a mattress and clothes. He said that was all I needed, so that's all I got. I look around the room at the white, wooden walls that need to be repainted. The original hardwood floors are dusty and worn, and the bedroom window is covered in cobwebs. The silence is the best thing about the house. It always was.

I cross the hall and turn on the light in what was once Black's room. His bed is just like he left it—half unmade with his welder's cap hanging on the post. His boots sit in the same place they did every night when he took them off, right by the door. The top of his dresser is an inch thick in dust and covers his loose change, spare keys, and an empty pack of Camel cigarettes. The black and white blanket over his window reads *Harley-Davidson* with the emblem printed in the middle.

I don't step inside. I wasn't allowed in there before, and as far as I'm concerned, nothing has changed. I check the bathroom, flushing the toilet and running the tub and faucet to get the rust out of the lines before turning out the lights and walking back to the kitchen. The lighting is dim; only one bulb illuminates the whole front of the house. I will need to swap out the blown ones before I leave. The refrigerator is empty, and the only things in the cabinets are a few cleaning supplies and some old dishes. I turn the water on in the sink, waiting for it to clear before washing my face.

I fucking hate this place. I don't know why I torture myself by coming back here. I should have burned it down a long time ago. I grab my bags from outside and when the cool night air hits me, it helps to release some of the pressure in my chest. When I walk back in, it returns.

I lock the door, then pull two pillows and a blanket from the tote and throw them on the now fully inflated mattress. The house is cool, even without air-conditioning. The weather has been in the fifties at night, and the large trees that surround the house help to shade it from the sun. Tomorrow, I will probably have to plug in a window unit. The lack of insulation keeps the house about the same temperature as it is outside.

I'm undressed and just before climbing under the covers when I notice Saylor laying on the couch, sound asleep. How the fuck did I forget she was here? When my eyes land on her face, everything else disappears. My memories don't matter. This house don't matter. Black . . . He don't fucking matter either. Only her. Saylor Samson.

I walk over to her, looking down at the beauty her god created. One arm hangs off the couch, the other is above her head. Her nipples are hard under her shirt that is stretched tight across her chest. I wonder if it's because she is cold or because she is dreaming of me.

Her shirt is raised, making the lower part of her stomach visible, including her belly button that I have an urge to kiss. So I do. I place my lips on her stomach, the heat of her flesh burning them. I turn to look down her crossed legs, all the way to the tip of her boots that are covered in dust. I don't know what I want more—to stand here and just stare at her fully clothed, or get her naked and hold her in my arms.

The battle is quickly won and I start by taking off her boots, then remove her socks and kiss her pink-painted toes one by one. I pull her jeans down her legs, kissing every inch of skin bared to me. She hasn't stirred, and I know she can't enjoy this while she is sleeping, but that's not why I'm doing it. I'm doing it because I like the way her skin feels on my lips. I want to cherish every part of her, and I know it's not just because I care about her. It's more, but I still can't make out the word in my head.

I kiss her hands, up her arms, across her collarbone, up her throat, her chin, her cheeks, her eyes, her nose, and then her parted lips. I carry her to the mattress, folding her into my chest and inhale her hair that still smells like her. Not a smoky bar, not perfume or hairspray, just her. I'm almost asleep. I'm in the hell hole I grew up in, and there isn't a bad thought around. My mind is peaceful, my arms are full, and my heart is filled with something. That nameless emotion that I've never felt.

"Dirk?"

"Yes." My voice is a hoarse whisper, and I feel her shiver when I place my lips on her head. What seems like forever passes before she answers. When she does, her voice is the same whisper, but this time it's filled with conviction.

"I think I'm falling in love with you." And just like that, my nameless emotion finally has a name.

I'm wondering why I'm not bolting. I don't know why I'm laying here and although my heart has swelled, it's not beating out of my chest. For some reason, her words just feel . . . right. Like I've heard her tell me a million times.

Maybe it's because she said she *thinks* she is falling in love. Maybe it's because I don't really know what love is. Or maybe it's because I've known it all along. If love is accepting me, caring for me, trusting me, and allows me to accept, care for, and trust her, then she loves me.

And then I feel it.

My heart beats heavy against my chest. My head is swimming with ideas of what to do. The word *love* is pounding in my head. It's in black and white and written on every surface my eyes land on. Love. Love. Love. Love.

It's too foreign to me. It's out of my element. I've heard the word because my brothers throw it around all the time. But it's not the word that bothers me. It's the emotion.

Saylor is stroking my back. And she is humming. I stay frozen beside her. I don't want to move and I have to remind myself to breathe. The walls are closing in on me. Then she sings. I don't know the song. I can't make out all the words, but her voice is calming and I let it steady my heart, ease my mind, and relax me. She sings the song over and over. I'm not listening to the words, just the melody of her sweet voice. And I'm drifting with her voice in my ears and one question in my mind.

Do I love her?

The feel of the hard floor I'm laying on wakes me. My trusty fucking air mattress has leaked to nothing more than a piece of flat material separating me and the dirty boards beneath it. Saylor isn't beside me, not surprising.

I stretch, my eyes focusing on the yellow-stained ceiling that reminds me of where I am. I take a deep breath through my nose, letting the smell of the house I hate so much reopen my wounds. When the scent fills me, I freeze. It doesn't smell like old memories. It doesn't smell like Saylor either. It smells like pine.

I sit up to see Saylor sweeping the floor. She is wearing my earbuds, with my iPod stuck in the pocket of my shirt. And she looks beautiful. She hasn't noticed me, and whatever song is playing has her in a good mood. I watch her while she nods her head, occasionally singing a line. Her voice is so low, I can't make out the lyrics, and I'm sure she is doing that to keep from waking me. And she doesn't want to wake me because she thinks she loves me. Love.

Thoughts of last night resurface and I'm on my feet in search of something that will take them out of my head. She sees me and smiles. I stare at her until I disappear down the hall. When I catch a glimpse of myself in the cloudy mirror, I wonder why I always have to look so damn pissed. I try to relax my face, but I still look pissed. Fuck it.

Saylor is still dancing and singing in the kitchen, not bothered by my facial expression. I guess if it don't bother her, it shouldn't bother me. I snatch the earbuds from her ears and she beams up at me. Damn, she's beautiful.

"What are you doing?" I ask, or growl, or snap. I can't be fucking normal. I can't look normal and I can't speak normal—obviously.

"I'm cleaning." I look around the room, and the kitchen counters are clean. The walls are clean. The baseboards are clean. The refrigerator looks brand new and the sink is filled with dark brown water. A pine-scented bottle of cleaner sits on the floor. The clean floor.

"Why?" I ask, moving my eyes around the dining room that we are standing in. Everything is clean here too. Even the window. I can actually see out of it.

"Well, if it isn't obvious enough, this place was a mess. And it smelled funny. Like varmint shit . . . or something. And everything was sticky." I watch her look around the room, her nose scrunched up and her eyes narrowed at the reminder. When she looks up at me, her face relaxes and her eyes widen. "Shit, baby. I apologize. I shouldn't have said that." She called me baby. She didn't say sorry. "I like your house," she adds. Her words are genuine and I believe her—not that I gave a shit in the first place.

I like *baby*, but I think I like her saying my name more than I like the endearment. I like that she apologized, although one wasn't needed.

"I don't want you cleaning my house. I never stay here anyway," I say, ignoring my thoughts and focusing on the topic.

"I don't mind. I like your house. Really." Her hand reaches out to touch my arm, reassuring me that her words are true. It wasn't that she was cleaning my house, it was that she was cleaning a mess that wasn't hers. "Will you give me a tour?" Her sweet question is accompanied by her sweet smile that is irresistible to me.

I agree to the tour, then grab my bag from the couch, pulling my eyes away from her spellbinding smile, and throw some jeans on. I avoid looking at her bare legs and where my shirt stops on her thighs. If I looked, my semihard cock wouldn't be semihard for long.

I look around the old house that is only about a thousand square feet. There isn't much to show. You can see the kitchen, dining room, and living room from anywhere you stand. The hallway leads to the bathroom and two bedrooms. It was simple. But it's the story she wants.

I debate about how much I actually want her to know for about two seconds before I decide that nothing I say would bother Saylor or make her think less of me. I just didn't want her pity. If she started getting teary eyed or any of that shit, I would just shut up.

"I don't remember much about my life before I moved here. I remember being on the road a lot and staying with people I didn't know. I'm not sure who took care of me before I was capable of taking care of myself, but someone must have because I'm here." Black never told me about my mother. He never spoke of my father much either unless it was derogatory. I often wondered who fed me when I cried and changed me when I shit, but I didn't know and never would, so it was a waste of time thinking about it. But I still did.

"I was seven years old when a man, who I was told was my father, dropped me off here. My grandfather didn't want me anymore than my ol' man did, but he didn't have a choice. I guess he could have dropped me off somewhere too, but he didn't. I reckon that's why I put up with his shit for so long. He must have cared about me to keep me around."

Thoughts of a life without Black were just as unpleasant as the memories of life with him. "Even though my life here was shit, it was life, and that was better than the alternative. Or so I thought." I tense at my words, wishing I had kept them to myself. I look at Saylor, searching her eyes for the pity I hope is there so I can shut up, but her eyes are void of emotion, and her kind smile urges me to continue. Well, fuck.

I grab a cigarette and have half of it smoked before I continue. "I never had a chance to be a kid. My grandfather, Black, had me doing club shit before I was old enough to know what I was doing. When I finally figured it out, I was so good at it that I didn't want to stop. It helped me keep my mind occupied, out of Black's way and in his good graces."

"What did you have to do?" I shouldn't tell her. But I do.

"When a shipment of drugs came, I prepared it for individual distribution." I stare at the Formica dining table and matching chair where I spent endless hours cutting, weighing, and bagging cocaine.

Mindlessly, my hand went to my ear, rubbing the permanent grooves caused from the mask I wore for so long. Sometimes days at a time. "I handled the money, making sure Black got a bigger cut, and figuring out a way to hide it. That's how I got so good with numbers."

"Fifty-fifty is a deal made between fools. Sixty-forty is a silent deal for the man who no longer wants to be a fool."

"By the time I was twelve, I knew as much about the business as Black. At fourteen I was dealing. And at sixteen I had more respect than any man around these parts. Other than Black."

I look at Saylor's face. It's impassive. I wonder what she is thinking, but I don't ask. I light another smoke, letting my eyes land on everything and letting everything trigger a memory.

Kitchen floor: where I witnessed Black murder a man by

strangulation. Refrigerator: the first time Black hit me. Couch: the orgy Black had with two women and three brothers. Living room window: the hours I spent looking out of it, waiting for Black to return. Front door: the hours I spent listening for it to open, waiting for Black to leave. The hallway: the last time Black hit me and the first time I hit him.

I swallow hard, remembering that feeling of power I got when I realized I finally had control of my own life. I want to relive it like I have done many times, but I want to tell it more.

"I was fifteen." I stare down the hall, my eyes focusing on the closet door at the end of it. I feel Saylor's eyes on me. At some point, she had climbed on the counter that separated the kitchen from the dining room. I clear my throat and start again.

"I was fifteen when I transitioned from a boy to a man. I'd been gone all day, delivering shit to clients that had midmonth orders. It was July and unusually hot. I was so fucking tired. I'd sold out, which wasn't unusual for me. But this time, Black didn't have any for himself and was pissed when I showed up with a pocket full of cash and not a single bag of coke. I never argued with him. I just let him cuss me until that wasn't enough, then I let him hit me until he was satisfied that I understood why he was right and why I was wrong. He started in, calling me every motherfucker in the book while he sat on his ass in the living room. When he didn't get a response, he stood up and yelled louder. I walked down the hall away from him. Just like the coward he was, he pushed me from behind. I lost my balance and fell against the hall door."

I reach my hand up, fingering the scar in my brow. My eyes fall on the hinge at the bottom of the door, and I stare at it just like I did years ago. "I hurt him that night. I hurt him so bad that I spent the next three days nursing him back to health because I couldn't bring myself to let him die. We never spoke of it and he never put his hands on me again. I just wish I had that strength when I was seven." I'm staring at the hinge, replaying the scene again. Saylor's voice cuts through my thoughts.

"Where is he now?" I turn to see Saylor still on the counter, her hands fisted in her lap. Her expression is a mixture of anger and pride. But still, there is no pity. I think about her question before I answer. I could tell her simply, or I could tell her the whole truth. She didn't tell me she was proud of me for standing up to him, and she doesn't have to. It's written on her face. I did everything in my power to put that look on Black's face and I never saw it. Yet this woman that I've spent less than two weeks with wears it. That in itself deserves the whole truth.

"I killed him."

11

I WATCH SAYLOR closely, waiting for her reaction, and I don't expect any less than what she tells me.

"Good." She gives me a nod of approval, burning her eyes into mine like she wants me to feel the hate she has for this man that she doesn't know. I could tell her how. I could tell her why, but I won't. She doesn't need the details. I'm sure she thinks it's because of what he did to me, but it's not. When I became a Nomad, I took a job. One that I did without question no matter the target.

When I came to Nevada and my mission was to kill a man who stole from the club, I was more than happy to oblige. When I found out he was a brother, I was even happier. I would make him suffer longer because I expected more of him. I had trusted this man, as had my brothers. But, when I found out it was Black, my anger was replaced with guilt.

I knew what Black had done all those years because I helped him do it. I stopped working for Black the day I almost killed him. It had been years since I'd been involved in the business, but I was still guilty. Telling the club was easy. I was ready to accept my fate because I deserved it. But, when I told them, they excused it without question. I knew they just wanted him dead, and they knew if any man should kill him, it should be me.

"Tell me how you killed him." I look at Saylor, wondering what she could ever get out of this. She reads my unspoken question. *Witch.*

"I want to know so I can visualize it. I need that imagery to help me process everything you've told me. I want a happy ending to this story and that will give it to me."

Every man dies. Every man has done something in his life to warrant him of it, but hearing those words come from the mouth of Saylor sends chills down my spine. I can't imagine her wishing death on anyone, no matter their transgressions.

"I can read your body language. I know you're pissed. I know you have hate for this man because of what he did to me, but he was all I had. He took me in when he didn't have to. Even though he didn't want to, he let me stay. He gave me what I needed to survive. He made me a man and I'm not proud of the man I am, but I still owe that to him. Right or wrong, good or bad, at least he did what no other motherfucker on this planet wanted to step up and do. I killed him, Saylor, but it wasn't like what you think."

I watch her process my words and can see the disappointment she has in herself. Even from the grave, Black had the power to corrupt the purest of minds. Because it's Saylor's he's fucking with, I want to resurrect him and kill him all over again. And this time, I want him to die the horrible death Saylor was hoping for.

"The last high of his life he didn't get from coke. I sat at the table with him while he snorted line after line of raw opium and heroin. By the time he realized something was wrong, he was already dead. Black, the only father I knew, the evilest man I know, the one son of a bitch who deserved to die a horrible death, went out the way we all want to. He went to sleep and never woke up." I watch sadness form in Saylor's eyes and I wonder why she pities him. "Don't feel sorry for him."

"I don't," she tells me, and by the way she is glaring at me, she means it. "I don't. I just hate that he didn't suffer more for everything he put you through." Her words are heartwarming. Even though they pertain to the murder of a man, she says them in a way that makes me feel special.

Just before I melt into a pool of mushy vagina on the floor, she changes the subject. "Give me the tour."

Saylor jumps down from the counter and walks up to me, looping her arm through mine like I'm fixing to take her on a fucking stroll instead of a showing her a shitty little house that smells like varmint shit, or so she said.

"This was my room," I say, watching as she walks around the room with her eyes closed. If she says it's perfect, I'm gonna lose it. But she doesn't say anything. I see her poke her head in the closet and then disappear.

"Where does this lead to?" she asks, and by the echo in her voice I know she is already halfway inside the hole in the wall. I walk in to see her on her knees with her ass in the air. Thank fuck my shirt covers her. "Dirk." She calls to the darkness and I ignore the thoughts of what panties she is wearing and focus on her question.

"Nowhere. It was once a closet off the bathroom, and some-one must have remodeled and just walled it up. I found it by accident." Flashbacks of days I spent inside the dark hole fill me. It was an escape from Black when I knew he was angry enough to kill me. It was a refuge for me and provided the only sense of security I had my entire childhood.

Saylor backs out of the hole, brushing the dirt from her knees, and smiles at me. "I like it. I wish I'd had a secret room growing up." I'm glad Saylor didn't have to endure the shit I did. The thought of her growing up in a house with a man like Black makes me sick. If she'd had a hidden room, she would have used it to escape her parents when she didn't get her way. Mine was used to save my life.

"I'll build you one if you want," I tell her, wondering how in the hell I could do that at her apartment.

"Nah, I'll just use yours." Saylor walks out of the room and before I can stop her, she is over the threshold and standing next to Black's bed. "This was his room, huh?" she asks, looking at me from across the hall.

"Yes. But I've never been in there." And he has been dead for years.

"I think you should," Saylor says, walking to me and wrapping her arms around my waist. I just stand there, letting her hug me without touching her. It doesn't feel right—not in this room. "Hey," she says, squeezing me tight.

"Hey." Saylor's hair is dirty. Cobwebs and paint chips are scattered throughout the tangled curls, and I stand there wondering what in the hell she will do to get it out.

"This is your house, Dirk. It doesn't have to be full of bad memories. We can make new ones." She pulls back, looking up at me, but she must feel like she isn't close enough. She wraps her arms around my neck and lifts herself. I grab her hips and hold her around my waist, feeling the heat of her pussy even through my jeans.

"Will you let me help you change this place up a little?" I don't know what she means by *change*, but I like the word when it refers to this house.

Before I can respond, she is telling me all the ideas she has.

"Just cleaning it up and painting it will make a world of difference. We can even get new furniture. And I'd love to cook you dinner."

She looks at me, her eyes wide and pleading. "Please? It will give me something to do."

I have plenty she can do and it doesn't involve cleaning or painting. It consists of my cock and all the places she can put it. I don't give a fuck about the house. If she wanted to burn it, paint it, or blow the motherfucker up, I'd let her. If it made her happy.

"I have somewhere I need to go today. I won't be back till late, but there's a truck out back. You can do what you want." I'm not happy about Saylor spending her time cleaning and doing shit for a place I don't care for, and she knows it.

"I like it here. I'd like to come back or stay a little longer if you will let me." I look around, surprised at her admission.

"Here?" My bewilderment amuses her.

"Yes. Here. It's quiet. And it's just us." I like it being just us. I like the quiet. I like that she likes this place.

"We can stay until I have to go on another run. And you can come back anytime you want." She likes my answer.

"Thank you, Dirk." My name rolls off her tongue and instantly hardens me. "Kiss me," she demands, in a whisper.

I kiss her slow, working her mouth with my tongue. I grab her hips, pulling her closer to me until my cock is centered between her legs. She breaks the kiss, unlocking her legs and sliding down my body until she is on her knees in front of me. "I want to taste you." Motherfuck me. My cock is in Saylor's hands. My fingers are in her hair and when she takes me all the way in her mouth, my knees go weak.

I gently guide her head, looking down at her while she looks up at me. Her eyes are wide and watery, her moans are loud and desperate and her mouth is filled with cock. My cock. The sight of her is as big of a turn-on as the feeling of being inside her. I tighten my grip on her hair and pull her head back until she reluctantly releases me.

"You're fucking perfect," I tell her, fighting the urge to come by just seeing her like this. The hunger in her eyes almost makes me want to let her continue, but she deserves more. "I want to fuck you." She whimpers at my words.

"Please," she begs and I feel my cock twitch. I lift her from the floor and wrap her legs around my waist, carrying her into the living room. I eye the couch, then change my mind and take her to the deflated mattress on the floor.

I look down at her while I take off my jeans and watch as she pulls her shirt over her head and lays back. Wearing nothing but a pair of satin panties that are soaking wet. For me.

I'm naked, on my knees and inside her before I can stop myself. I wanted to taste her. I wanted to tease her. I wanted to take my time. But what she wants always overrules what I want. I fuck her hard because I know it's what she wants. She is screaming for more and I'm giving her all I've got. I push her legs up until her ankles are at her ears and watch as her eyes roll back in her head when I hit deeper than I ever have.

"Too much," she manages and I can't help my smirk. I let her legs down and fall between them, taking her mouth with mine and giving her slow, measured strokes that fall short of that sweet spot she loves, and don't reach too deep.

"Not enough," she says into my mouth. I ignore her, fucking her just enough to keep her wanting more. She is trying to pull me deeper. She is begging me to give it to her harder, but the torture will be worth it when I do finally let her come.

"You want on top?" I ask her, knowing what she is going to say.

"Yes!" Her answer is a half sob, half scream, and I know

when I flip us she is going to fuck me half to death. I roll to my side, pulling her on top of me. When she sits up, her eyes close when I sink all the way inside her.

"Oh, fuck," she whispers, and then she starts to move. Ten seconds in and I'm fighting to keep from losing it. Just when I think I can't hold out, she stops. Her eyes are closed but there is a hint of a smile on her face. I jerk every time her pussy squeezes me, and I want to scream at her because she knows good and fucking well what she's doing.

"Saylor," I say in frustration. I've never had a woman control me like this and I'm not going to start now.

"Is it too much?" she asks, her eyes still closed, but her face breaks out into a smile.

"You know I can force you," I warn her, feeling my hands twitch to grab her waist and move her myself.

"But you won't." And she's right. "I think we should stop now and then later we will want it more." No fucking way.

"Move, baby, or I'll move you." Orgasm denial is a powerful thing. And I'm not fucking into it. At least not when it's me that's being denied. Her eyes open to that sexy half-mast that has my cock jumping inside her.

"You don't play fair," she says, but it's breathy and I know she wants me to fuck her as bad as I want to. I grab her ass and lift her, and she doesn't fight it. I raise my hips to meet her and watch as she plays with her tits—alternating pinching her nipples and palming them with her hands. Her body stiffens and she's coming around me.

My arms are burning in protest, but I keep lifting her up and down on top of me until I reach that feeling of euphoria that has me exploding inside her sweet pussy. When I stop, she falls on my chest, exhausted, and I'm not sure from what. I did all the fucking work—not that I minded.

I like that Saylor's orgasms are so powerful that they leave her drained. It must mean I'm doing something right. "It's hot," she says, breathing heavy. I roll her off me, give her a quick kiss on the cheek, then head to the shower to cool off myself before finding some way to cool the house.

"Where you going?" she calls after me.

"Cold shower," I say over my shoulder, and she is running toward me before I'm in the bathroom.

The shop outside is filled with shit from one end of the eighteen-by-twenty-four-foot building to the other. It takes me ten minutes to find the two old window units I knew were out there, but I finally do.

"So, who takes care of this place when you are gone?" Saylor asks from the door. She is showered and standing there looking dangerously sexy in cutoffs and a white wifebeater with no bra.

"We have a chapter here. They cover the pipes and cut the yard." I take care of the inside, which hasn't really been taken care of.

"Well, that's nice of them," she offers, and I have a feeling Saylor is looking for conversation.

"If you say so." I haul one of the units out, and head inside with Saylor on my heels. I put the unit in the living room, figuring it will cool the front of the house, which is where we will spend the majority of our time. Once it's plugged in and running, I turn to find her fanning herself, covered in a sheen of sweat, and I contemplate turning it back off. She's sexy when she's sweaty.

"I'll get the truck running, and you can go to town and get whatever you want. You may want to go by the grocery store since we are gonna be here awhile." There is no reason to shield her in my hometown. She is safer here than anywhere else. Now that the club knows about her, have met her and approve of her, no harm could come her way. Not that there was much trouble she could get into in this town anyway.

When she jumps up from the arm of the couch, my eyes land on her chest. "But first you need to put a fucking shirt on." I stomp out of the house, fighting like hell to avoid thoughts of men looking at her. I would rather go with her so everyone knows she's mine, but I have other shit to do.

Surprisingly, the truck cranks with no problem. It's rusty and old, but the air works and it's full of gas. The Prospects were trying like hell to make an impression. By the look of the manicured lawn, the fact that the pipes in the house weren't busted and the truck was running, they were doing a pretty good job.

Saylor walks out of the house, now fully dressed. I'm sure people will still look at her, but maybe their thoughts will be a little more G-rated.

"If you take a left out of the driveway, it will take you right into town. It's small, but it has a hardware store and a grocery store. You should be able to find whatever you need." I pull my wallet out and hand her my credit card, wondering why men bitched about giving it to their women. What the fuck was money when it was compared to making their woman happy?

Saylor frowns and I wonder what I've done to fuck up. "I don't mind using some of my own money." I know she is just being kind, but it pisses me off.

"My house. My woman. My money." She isn't worried about my threatening tone or the fact that I'm trying to control my anger.

"But it was my idea and it's only fair for me to help out. I didn't expect you to take care of me all this time. I can help pay my own way." Her innocence makes her ignorant. The fact that she has clearly never had a man take care of her doesn't make the situation better either, and because of this, I should show some mercy. But I don't.

"I don't give a fuck about what you think is fair. You'll spend my money or you won't spend anything at all. Take the damn card, Saylor. You're pissing me off." My words seem to shock her just as much as they shock me. I'm not pissed at her. I'm pissed at the situation, but that's not what I said. And I've hurt her feelings. Motherfucker. I'm such a dick.

But, instead of apologizing, I stomp inside like the asshole I am. I hear the truck crank up a few minutes later, and the urge to chase it down and tell her what a fuckup I am consumes me. By the time I get the door open, she is already at the end of the driveway. Words. They can make a day go from perfect to screwed up in a matter of seconds.

I ride back to the bar, wishing I wasn't in such a shitty mood, and find Nationals in the same place as I'd seen them last night. By the looks of them, I'm sure they haven't even been to bed. Beer bottles, ashtrays, pipes, and shot glasses cover the patio.

Two naked bitches are laid out on one of the tables, and Jimbo is getting his dick sucked by another. When I walk up, she never stops, not that I expected her to. In this town, sucking the dick of the National VP of Sinner's Creed MC is equivalent to being crowned homecoming queen. You make the local headlines, and every bitch in the area envies you.

"Dirk." Roach nods and I walk over and shake his hand so he doesn't have to stand.

"Roach," I say before yelling for a Prospect. Two appear in the door, looking just as nervous and out of place as we all did when we heard a patch holder yell for us. "Clean this shit up," I growl, pointing to the shit that lay scattered around the patio.

I say hey to Jimbo, not interrupting his blow job, and the other three Nationals including Chaps and the two patch holders who look like they could die from exhaustion. To most they probably look normal, but not much gets past me. "You got something for me?" I ask Roach, hoping like hell he don't.

"Shit's pretty quiet right now. I may need you down in Texas in a couple weeks, but there ain't no hurry. I'm trying to figure out how we can handle some shit without getting someone hurt. I'm hoping we can calm the waters with another one percent club, without going to war. It's our territory, and we don't want 'em there, but sometimes you gotta make sacrifices for the greater good. I just want you to let 'em know where we stand. They went down there 'cause we let 'em, not for 'em to show their teeth. We all know whose is bigger."

Roach gives me a toothless smile and I can't help but smile back. Even when I was a kid, he always seemed to pull it out of me. It's sad knowing that a man who has taken more lives than any infamous serial killer gave you the only warmth in your life. Until Saylor, of course.

"Just let me know," I tell him, forcing thoughts of my dark days with Black from my mind. Not too long ago, he was one of the ones sitting on this slab in the back of a shitty bar getting high and calling shots.

"So, Saylor." Roach doesn't say any more, he waits for my reaction. When he sees me tense, he smiles. "Tell me about her. I never thought I'd live to see the day you let a woman into your life. I'm glad I did."

The kindness in his eyes is the same I'd seen for years when he looked at me, but this time it's a little softer. I guess Saylor has that effect on people.

"I'd rather not," I tell him. I don't like sharing shit with anyone. Roach is the closest brother I have, other than Shady.

"Jimbo, I hate to fuck up what you got going there, but I need a minute." I look over to Jimbo, who mutters something under his breath but pulls the woman's mouth off his cock and stands up. Not surprising me in the least, I find that it's the pass-around I've had more than once. She doesn't pay attention to me though; it's all about rank to her, and Jimbo is higher than I am, therefore his dick is more important than mine. Thank fuck.

Her makeup is smeared all over her face. Her nose is red and raw from the amount of shit she has snorted, and her eyes are wet and bloodshot from taking Jimbo all the way to the back of her throat for so long. And she loves every fucking minute of it. He never lets go of her hair and I watch as she slides her hands between her legs, horny as hell at being treated like the dirty slut she is.

For the first time in my life, I find it repulsive. The other bitches are woke up, transforming them from innocent sleeping forms to ready-to-fuck prostitutes in a matter of seconds. I'm sure a train on both of them is already in the works.

When we are finally alone, I take a seat next to Roach, avoiding his eyes for as long as I can. When I finally look at them, they are expectant. "Tell me."

I don't tell Roach because he wants me to. I tell him because it would be disrespectful for me not to.

"I've seen her a few times over the past several years. Just in passing. She lives down in Jackson." Roach nods in acknowledgment, but he wants more. Him and Saylor have a lot in common when it comes to me. They can get shit outta me when no one else can. "I think she might have had a nasty breakup or some shit. She begged me to take her with me. Said she wanted to get outta town. I felt sorry for her."

For some reason, it makes me feel like shit not telling him the whole truth. I guess it's written on my face too 'cause Roach raises his eyebrows, letting me know he thinks I'm full of shit. I sigh, shift in my seat, and figure *fuck it*.

I light a smoke, passing it to him, then light me another one before continuing. "There's something about her." I look out at the clear blue sky and feel myself getting lost in my own words. "It's like she has known me forever. She don't get pissed at me or bitchy. She's not like any woman I've ever met. I feel like she is in my head, reading my thoughts, and even though I know what she sees is sometimes scary, she never runs from me and I never see judgment in her eyes. It's almost like she's some sort of angel, or some shit. I haven't figured her out yet, but I'm trying. Each day I learn something new about her. And every time I do, I like her a little bit more."

I sit there, staring at my boots, wondering why the fuck I'm even talking. Roach is silent and when I look over at him, his eyes are distant and for a minute, I think he's dead. I'm just before calling his name and shaking him when he speaks.

"I had a woman like that once. Paulette. Remember her?" I remember, but I don't say anything. He isn't paying attention to me anyway. He is lost in some memory.

What I remember of Paulette is that she was a nice woman. I'd only seen her a few times because Roach didn't bring her around a lot. She was different from the other women. Quiet and kept to herself. "She's married now. Got about ten grandkids and lives over in Montana. I thought about killing her ol' man, then showing up at the funeral and taking advantage of her vulnerability. But she's happy. I reckon I can't kill a man for doing something for her that I never did."

Roach grabs his pipe, taking a hit then offering it to me, knowing I'll decline. "I reckon what I'm trying to say is this. You ain't had a good upbringin'. Black didn't deserve a kid no more than I did. But, he got you and he did what he thought he had to, to make you a man. He did and you owe him that. I know sometimes you hate yourself, Dirk. I know you hate Black just as much. But Black's dead. He's gone.

"The only reason I let you do it was because I knew that was the only way you could get closure—move on from the past and start a future. I know you hate him for the things he did to ya. Hell, I hate him for the shit he did to ya. I hate I couldn't do more to stop him. But you can't blame the man for the rest of your life. We got one shot, Dirk. One fucking shot in this life. Make it count. Don't be like me and die an old man all alone 'cause ya think Black beatin' on ya fucked you up too much to be loved. Let that woman love you. And if you smart, you'll love her back."

Roach's eyes are pleading. They are begging me to take his advice. I don't know if I will. I don't know if I won't. In this moment, all I know is that if I choose not to, looking at Roach is like looking in the mirror at the man I'm destined to become.

12

I'M SITTING OUT back, and my conversation with Roach is back to what it's always been: business. We're discussing the chapters, the problems with other clubs, and finances, when a patch holder comes barreling out the door. When he doesn't look the least bit sorry or concerned about busting up our meeting, I know something is wrong.

"Dirk, you got a call." I'm on my feet, knowing that whoever is calling doesn't have my cell. Which means that it has to be someone that I know isn't connected to the club. I'm hoping like hell it's some bitch wondering if I'm in town, but my gut tells me it's Saylor. That she needs me and got the number for the bar where she hopes I'm at.

Maybe she wants to know a paint color. Maybe she's having issues with my card. Maybe the truck broke down. I'm playing every scenario imaginable in my head, but in the few seconds it takes for me to get to the phone, I know it's nothing like that. If she's calling here, it's important. I snatch the phone off the counter and bark into it.

"Yeah?" I say, waiting for it to be any voice other than hers.

"Um, Dirk?" It's a man. A young one. Maybe even a teenager.

"Who the fuck is this?" I ask, not confirming who I am.

"Yeah, um, my name is Nate, I work over at Greer's Grocery, and this lady told me to call and see if I could get you on the phone." He pauses and I want to kill.

"What lady?" I growl, wishing he would just tell me what the fuck is going on.

"Sir, I'm not sure. She just fainted and . . ." I drop the phone and run to my bike, passing a nervous Shady on the way. I throw my helmet to the ground, knowing the second it takes for me to put it on is too long.

Fainted? Is she hurt? Is she okay? She had to be conscious to tell them to call me, but how bad was it? I pull the throttle back on my bike, going as fast as possible without killing myself on the curvy road that leads to town. It doesn't take me long to get there, and my heart sinks when I see an ambulance parked outside the front door.

I push through the crowd of people roughly, my feet taking me to the group huddled in a circle by the frozen food aisle. I push a medic to the side and look down to see Saylor taking deep breaths through her white lips. I drop to my knees beside her and take her hand in mine. Her other hand is on her forehead, holding an ice pack to it.

"What happened?" I ask. When she hears my voice, her neck cranes to see me.

"I fell," she says noncommittally. I'm calling bullshit, not that I have to. The nervous voice that called me tells all.

"No sir, she passed out. I watched her." I look up at him and his cheeks turn red with embarrassment. I'm sure he was watching her. I never thought I would be grateful for someone ogling my woman.

"I just got a little dizzy. It's the weather." Saylor is grasping at straws to try to hide the obvious reason she is laying here on the floor. And I don't know why. I suddenly get the feeling she is hiding something from me, but before I can ask what it is, the horny bag boy tells his side of the story.

"She was fine one second, then I saw her swaying. The next, she went down like the *Titanic*. Bam! Her head hit the handle on the freezer door, and it hit pretty hard when she landed too." His theatrics piss me off. I don't like him trying to make a huge spectacle of Saylor.

"Sir, she needs to go to the hospital and get a CAT scan, but she is refusing. I've been trying to convince her, but she won't even let us put her in the ambulance." The medic's concerned face worries me and I look down at Saylor, hoping I can talk her into going. Or I can just force her to go. Either is fine with me.

She is shaking her head, and tears are brimming in her eyes. "Dirk, I don't want to go to the hospital." The determination in her voice makes me feel like shit for even trying to talk her into it.

"You need to go get checked out," I try, and my shitty attempt falls on deaf ears.

"I'm asking you, Dirk. I'm begging you. Please, don't let them take me. I'm fine." By the look on her face and the desperation in her voice, I know this is a battle I need to let her win. But I have to try.

"Please, baby. Something could be wrong." I've pulled out all stops. I even try to make my eyes do that puppy-dog shit, but it doesn't faze her. It only pisses her off.

"Dammit, Dirk. I said no. Have I ever lied to you? No, so take me home. I'm not going to the hospital. I'm not out of my head.

I know who I am, I know where I am, and no one here is authorized to make decisions on my behalf." She turns to look at the medic, and I can't help feeling a little sorry for him.

"Now get that damn blood pressure cuff off of me so I can get the hell outta here." The medic begins releasing the cuff immediately. I help Saylor up and surprisingly she is steady on her feet, despite the huge goose-egg knot that has formed on her head. I want to carry her, but she glares at me, so I settle for my hand around her waist—not that she needs it. Determination alone could let her walk out of here unassisted.

The store manager appears, wearing a shirt that's too small and a badge that states his title. He is holding a clipboard in his hand and looks almost pissed when he sticks it out to Saylor. "You need to sign this. If you are refusing medical attention, then we ain't liable for anything that happens down the road." I'm two seconds from grabbing the clipboard and smashing his nose with it when Saylor gladly signs it and thrusts it back in his hands. She walks out and I have to practically jog to keep up with her.

When we get outside, Shady is there with two other patch holders and I tell him to take my bike back to the house. He nods without any questions, giving Saylor and me a once-over before leaving. I help Saylor in the truck before getting in and pulling out of the lot. When we are almost home, I chance a look at her, and her anger has faded. She just looks tired.

"You okay?" I ask, wondering why I'm treading so lightly. I feel like I'm walking on eggshells. I haven't felt like that in years.

"I'm fine. I don't like hospitals," she mumbles, and I don't push further. She has her reasons and I'm sure they're good ones. I pull up at the house, jumping out to help her, but she is already out and moving to the bed of the truck. I see bags of groceries and things from the hardware store and give her a quizzical look. "I told the bag boy to go ahead and check me out. No need in all that shopping going to waste because my stupid head don't wanna act right." She doesn't notice her slipup, but I do.

"You do that a lot?" I ask, referring to her head that is anything but stupid.

"What? Pass out? No. It's happened before but not often. It's part of the reason I have migraines too." She doesn't elaborate and I don't ask any more questions. I don't want to admit it, but the truth is I'm afraid of the answer.

She grabs a bag and I take it from her, then take her hand and lead her inside. The house still smells good and I'm thankful that she got a notion to clean today, although I'm sure that cleaning is as far as it's gonna go for now.

"You wanna lay down?" I ask, while she fishes receipts and my card from her pocket.

"No, I wanna stay up for the furniture." That gets my attention, and, as if she summoned them, a truck pulls up the driveway with the town furniture store's logo on the side. "I was mad at you when I left. I might have spent too much money trying to get back at you. We can take it back if you want." I shake my head at her words.

"Money means nothing to me. If you try to piss me off by spending it, never gonna happen. Even if you managed to clean me out, I can always make more." She smiles knowingly, as if she figured as much even before she spent it. I meet the two men at the door, noticing another truck pulling up. The man gets out, asking where I want everything, and I point to the clean side of the carport. "Just put it out here. I'll move it in later." I look at a frowning Saylor in the doorway and raise my eyebrows in question at her.

"I paid them to move the old out too," she says, and even though I told her she could redo everything, a piece of me isn't quite ready to let the past go. She knows this and fixes the problem, like she always seems to do.

"Just push the couch into the dining room and put everything in the living room. We'll set it up when we're ready." The man nods his head, avoiding even looking at Saylor. I'm sure it's 'cause he won't be able to focus on anything but her chest. Although she changed her shirt, this one is just as tight as the other. At least she put a bra on. Looking at her legs, perhaps I should have told her she needed to put some pants on too. Her cutoff shorts are so short, the pockets hang out the bottom of them. I like the way she looks, but I don't want anyone else liking it.

While the furniture is being unloaded, I unload the truck—taking everything to the kitchen while Saylor puts it away. I would rather she just sit down, but I'd be fighting a losing battle. When the movers are gone and everything is inside, I survey the damage.

Saylor has more stuff than I thought she was capable of buying in such a short time. Paint, groceries, decorative shit, bedding, dishes, two sets of mattresses, two bedroom suites, a couch, a love seat, a table with chairs, two end tables, a bookshelf, and six lamps. My house looks like a fucking furniture store threw up in it.

"You like it?" she asks, standing beside me. I want to answer, but I need to sort my words so I sound appreciative. Because I am. It's just a little overwhelming. "I got rugs and stuff too. I even bought some pictures and stuff to do the bathroom. It'll be perfect when I'm finished."

These material items mean nothing. The fact that she is standing here next to me makes this godforsaken place perfect. Something I never thought possible.

"I like it. Thank you." My words aren't much, but she smiles.

"I'll cook for you tomorrow. Tonight, I'll make us a sandwich, but I want to set up a real bed first." She grabs a bag of stuff and heads down the hall. She is acting as if she didn't just collapse in a grocery store and has a big bump on her head. I'm not sure what to think of it, but if she wants to act like nothing's wrong, then I guess I should too.

I'm standing in the middle of what was once my old bedroom. Saylor never asked my opinion, she just did what she wanted and I did what I was told. I thought it would take longer to have the room ready, but Saylor surprised me with her ability to get shit done.

It's late, maybe even after midnight, but my old bedroom has been transformed into a new bedroom in less than a day. The room is now a bright yellow and the queen-sized bed we just set up takes up the majority of the small space. The floors still look old and worn, but they are clean and Saylor has a few rugs laying around the room. Two nightstands, two lamps, three candles, curtains, a white comforter, and twenty fucking pillows later, the room is complete.

"Now it feels a little more like a home. I can't wait to sleep in this bed!" Saylor is excited and I don't know what over. It's a damn house. But whatever.

"I'm hungry," I mumble because I'm an ass, I'm tired, I'm hot as hell, and I haven't eaten all day.

"Me too." Saylor finally drags her eyes away from the room and to me. Her smile outshines the bright yellow of the walls, and I don't think even the sun could outshine her in this moment.

I follow her to the kitchen and watch as she makes us a sandwich, just like she promised hours ago. I lean up against the counter, listening to her meaningless talk that I love so fucking much. Love. Shit.

"Tomorrow, we'll do the living room and kitchen and dining room. It won't take us long. The painting is the worst part and even that wasn't so bad. I've already cleaned everything anyway.

After I eat, I'm gonna work on the bathroom. I figure we can work on the other room last, or whenever you're ready." I know she is referring to Black's room. I'm still not sure how I feel about that, but at least I have a couple of days to think on it.

Saylor's head has a nasty bruise, but the swelling has gone down and she hasn't complained about it all day. I wonder if it hurts her.

"What happened in the store?" My words catch her off guard and she stops midchew, her happiness fading.

"If the obvious isn't enough, I guess I'll tell you again. I fainted." She continues eating, avoiding my eyes. I need more and she knows it, but she isn't giving in that easy.

"You got something you want to tell me?" I ask, knowing good and damn well what her answer will be.

"When the time is right." Well, that was an answer I wasn't expecting. I'm beginning to wonder if she gets off on tormenting me.

"The time is right." And it is. Nothing she tells me is gonna make me push her away. I don't care if she has head issues that make her faint and give her migraines. I'm a walking fuckup. Just because I don't fall out in grocery stores or wake up vomiting doesn't mean I don't have my own issues. I'm almost convinced that she is gonna argue or just not answer me, when she speaks.

"When I was a kid, I was in a bad wreck." She has my undivided attention. I watch as she busies herself around the kitchen while she finds the right words to say. I pull out a smoke and lean back, waiting patiently for her to continue.

"I had a pretty serious head injury. Migraines and fainting are a part of my life. I'll have them as long as I live. I don't take meds daily because I don't like how they make me feel. I've had the fainting spells for so long that I've grown accustomed to them." She stops and points to the fading knot on her head, but never looks at me.

"This is nothing. I've had worse. It's the first time I've fainted in a long time." She avoids my eyes and I'm sure it's because she is afraid of what she will find. She knows I'm a busy man. She knows her issues could potentially make me look at her differently. All I can think is that if she really knows me, then she knows I couldn't give a shit less about her issues. I could tell her this. I could reassure her that it doesn't bother me. But who needs words when you have a mouth like mine.

I grab her arm, pulling her away from the counter that she has mindlessly been cleaning, and into my chest. And I kiss her. It's my thank-you because she told me. It's my reassurance because she needs it. And it's my promise that I still want her. When she melts into me, I know she gets it.

I break the kiss, just so I can look at her. Precious. Pretty. Cute. Beautiful. All those words that were once so foreign to me are now words that frequent my mind, and they are all directed toward her. I'm looking in her eyes, and guilt is swimming in them. I don't know why. Maybe it's because she feels guilty for placing this burden on me. Maybe she feels guilty because she can't offer me a life without worry. Maybe if I open my mouth and speak to her, her guilt will vanish.

"You're perfect." I want to tell her that I think I might love her. I want her to know how much. I want her to tell me back, but I'm too scared to say the words. I don't know what it will mean if I do because I've never said them in all of my life.

"Do you love me, Dirk?" Fucking mind reader.

Now or never, Dirk. Redeem yourself now or never. I'm trying to speak, but my mouth just opens and closes over and over. I look like a fucking idiot—much like I feel.

"You don't have to tell me." Her voice is low. Her eyes are pleading. She needs this and I need to get my shit together and give it to her. Straight.

"I don't really know what love is because I've never felt it."

Her face falls and I know they're not the words she wanted to hear. But I don't want to lie to her. I can't give her something that I don't have. Then I see the pity in her eyes.

"You've felt it; you have just chosen to ignore it. There are people in this world that love you, Dirk, you just have to let them." She smiles sadly at me before pulling out of my arms and heading to the bathroom.

I should probably help her. I should probably just say those three fucking words that will make her smile and put her in a better mood. But I don't think those are words you can just say. They're something you have to feel, which I do, and something you have to prove, which I haven't. And something I don't want to think about right now.

I walk outside, knowing my bike in the wind will give me the answers I need. I'm not even out of the driveway before I realize that answers are not something I want. What I want is to forget. I want to forget about her questions, her assumptions, love, and every fucking thing it entails, so I ride. And forget is exactly what I do.

13

SAYLOR HAS FUCKED me in every room of my newly renovated house, in every position, on every piece of furniture, every day since she asked me if I loved her. That was a week ago. I'm wondering if she is trying to fuck the words out of me. If she keeps it up, it might even work.

Every room in my house is a different color. Every room looks totally different, and every day I find the old memories fading and being replaced with new ones of me and her.

Black's room wasn't as hard to go through as I thought it would be. Lucky for me, he didn't have very much shit in there. His personal items like his clothes, hats, and shoes were all burned. Even his furniture and linens. The closet held two boxes full of shit. One was full of patches, pictures with the club, and a few corny-ass letters from some bitches while he was in the army. The other box was filled with his father's things.

There were some old pictures of Black and his dad, two American flags, his parents' death certificates, and a box of old jewelry—probably his mom's. In the back corner of his closet, I found a safe. I couldn't figure out the combination to save my life. When Saylor suggested I try my birthday, I did just to humor her. Surprisingly, it worked. My heart did some funny shit and I thought of love. If using my birthday as a combination to a safe was the only love he could ever show me though, he could keep it. But what I found inside changed my perspective on Black— slightly.

While Saylor ogled the hundred-dollar bills I pulled out, acting as if she had never seen so much money, I focused on the letter with my name on it. I opened it up, fighting the shaking in my hand, and saw that it was dated just days before he died.

Dirk,

If you're reading this I'm dead. The club knows about the money I've been taking and I'm sure they're gonna kill me. I hope it's you that does it. At least it'd be well deserved. I didn't know your mama. Hell, I barely knew your daddy. I didn't want you, but I didn't have much of a choice. I owed a favor to someone and that someone told me we would be square if I took you in. Much like you I've never had a family other than the club. A biker is what I am and what I'll die as. I ain't no daddy. Never claimed to be. But I want you to know that I did what I did because that's the only way I knew to teach you. I never told you before because I didn't know how. But I'm proud of you, Dirk. I always have been. From the very first day you came into my life, I was proud to call you mine. You're a better man than I ever was. A better brother too. If I got to live my life over, I'd want

*another shot at being a daddy. And I'd want my son to be
just like you.*

Black

In two days, I bet I've read the letter a hundred times. I kept
trying to find closure in it, but I never did. I finally burned it
yesterday. The words were now permanently imprinted in my
memory. I couldn't figure out if it made me hate him more, or
like him less. Each outcome was just as negative as the other.

Who in the fuck did Black owe a favor to? And why the fuck
would that someone trust him to raise a kid? If I knew, I'd kill them
myself. They deserved to pay. They are responsible for a monster
that was created over something as simple as a favor. If Black hadn't
raised me, I might have had a shot at a decent fucking life. But he
poisoned me and I have, in turn, poisoned so many others. He was
proud of me. He said so in a fucking letter. Had I known then what
I know now, I never would have killed that man all those years ago.
I would have taken my life in a different direction.

But because I wanted his love and pride so much, I was willing to take a life to earn it. That was the beginning of the train
ride I would take to the deepest depths of hell. If he got a chance
to live life over, I'd kill him before he had a chance to ruin anyone
by turning them into me. Nobody wants their son to be like me.
Nobody.

Today, I'm just sitting on my new couch, while Saylor writes in
her diary, debating on whether or not I should go dig up his body,
just so I can watch it burn. Maybe that would make me feel better.

Tomorrow, Saylor has to go home while I go to Texas. I don't
know how it will be without her, but I know I'm already dreading it. By the sad look on her face, she is too.

Something happened and Nationals decided that I need to get there as quickly as possible. So Saylor and I will be flying to Houston in the morning. It's a layover for her, but a drop-off point for me. My brothers from a chapter there will pick me up. I'll get a bike from the shop and hopefully only go about three days without seeing her. Tonight, I just want to hold her, but the hungry look in her eyes tells me I'll be fucking her first. That's fine too.

Saylor has a sad look in her eyes as we pack up to leave. Just as we are about to head out, she asks me to wait a minute. I watch as she stands in the kitchen, closes her eyes, and inhales deeply. Long gone is the scent I'm so familiar with. It is now replaced with something that smells like pomegranate or some shit.

She touches everything, memorizing it as if she might not ever see it again. I want to reassure her that she will, but I don't. I'm too caught up in how sorrowful her face is. I don't follow her down the hall because I feel like this is a moment she needs to herself. And then I hear her voice. She is singing. I've never heard the song, but she is telling me she came to my house and asking me if I would forgive her for doing it. Her voice is haunted. I've never heard Saylor sing with such emotion.

I cautiously walk down the hall to where she is. She is looking out the window of my bedroom, staring blankly into the backyard, her voice even more pained. I don't understand what's happening. I don't know what's triggered her song or her actions. But, as I listen to the words, I feel her painful emotions and they're like a knife through my heart. When she is finished singing, I stand for an eternity waiting for her to say something. Do something. Fucking something.

"When I was a little girl, I imagined living in a house like this.

With a husband and a family." She is whispering and I have to strain to hear her. When she turns from the window, a distant look is in her eyes.

"You told me that you didn't know what love really was." She looks up at me, and the sadness in her eyes is so intense that I'm forced to look away. But when she speaks again, I'm drawn back to her. This time I focus on her mouth rather than her eyes.

"Real love is wanting someone to experience the same, deeply powerful feeling that you do. The one that takes your breath at certain moments and speeds your heart at others. And it's wanting it without any regard to who that person chooses to share it with. That's the love I have for you, Dirk. And I would give anything in the world for you to feel what I feel. Even if it isn't for me."

She leaves me alone and I know she is letting me process her words. There is no need. I know what she feels, because I feel it too. I don't need a definition. I don't need to think about why I've never felt it before. Because it doesn't fucking matter.

It's taken me thirty years to have a feeling like this, and it's been worth every second. If I could do it all over again, I wouldn't change a thing. Because what I have shouldn't be wasted on anyone but her. She deserves it all and she has it. It's not just a four-letter word. It's not just a feeling or an emotion. It's not just something you say. It's a necessity. A vitality. A need that can't be filled. A reason. A purpose. It's a sunset. A clear blue sky. A rainbow. It's everything that's anything that makes you happy. Everything that's anything that makes you whole. It's the only thing that can save my soul, and the only thing I've ever wanted.

Love.

I'm tripping over my feet trying to get to her. I don't want another second to pass in this life without telling her how I feel. She already knows it, but I want to say it. I want the words to sound as beautiful to her ears as hers did to mine. I find her in the living room, touching the furniture and memorizing a place that I won't let her forget.

"You once said you would give anything for me to feel what you feel." She opens her eyes to look at me, and I can see everything she told me, spelled out in the sparkling green pools.

"I feel what you feel. I have no pride when it comes to you. You have everything. I love you, Saylor. And the only reason I'm telling you those words is because I want you to have it in every way I'm capable of giving it to you. But they're just words. I'll show you I love you and I'll spend every fucking day of the rest of my life convincing you that what I have is just for you. You'll never have to worry about me feeling like this for anybody else, because there will never be anybody else. If what I feel for you is love, then you are what love is. And it doesn't exist if you don't."

I stand there, waiting for a reaction. In movies, I'm sure this is the part where she runs and jumps in my arms and we kiss. In a book, this is where she gets teary eyed and says *Oh, Dirk*, in that way that makes women swoon and men want to vomit. But, in real life, her reaction is only a knowing smile, then a sigh, a lip bite, a sadness that pools in her eyes and a wrinkle in her forehead.

"I am not love," she says, and I notice she is getting fidgety. Her arms are crossed over her chest, her bottom lip tucked in her mouth, and she is staring down at the floor, shifting her weight from one leg to the other.

"What you feel for me is love. What you felt for Black, that's love. Your brothers, you love them. Love is all around you, Dirk. It always has been. What you think is respect and loyalty and all that shit—that's love. Maybe not the way you feel it for me, but you have it for them too. If I don't exist, love will still be here. And you will find it in the family around you." She looks determined. Like she wants me to believe in love more than anything. Yet she hasn't actually ever said the words to me. Only in a roundabout way.

Her words are pounding in my head. They demand attention and I know my brain won't sleep until I process what she said. I think of Black and I wonder if I ever loved him. I did. It wasn't like this, but it was an intense feeling that I've never felt for another man. He was the only parent I had and I wanted his love more than anything. Maybe more than Saylor's.

I think of my club. Roach, Jimbo, even Shady means something to me. It goes beyond the patch and the respect I have for them. I never wanted their love because they never denied me of it. They love me because I'm their brother. All this time, I've loved them too. I love.

I'm not awestruck by the fact; I guess I've always known. Saylor has that look in her eyes and I know she is aware of my revelation. She could probably recite my unspoken words verbatim. When her eyes become watery and a smile spreads across her face, she doesn't have to tell me, but I know she will.

"I love you, Dirk." And it's perfect.

Saylor seems shocked when she looks at her ticket and sees we are flying first class. I'm beginning to think that she thinks I'm poor. Not that I care either way.

I like how fascinated she is with all the extra shit that comes with flying first class. I like how she has a sparkle in her eyes and kisses me in thanks and ignores the stares of people around us. I like how she asks the flight attendant if the drinks are free, then tells her to keep 'em comin' when she finds out they are.

By the time we land, she is buzzing and happy and has that sexy, dreamy look in her eye, and I find myself smiling down at her. A real smile.

I love her.

I find the gate that will connect her flight from Houston to Jackson, and for the first time in my life, I wish I wasn't in the club. I want to stay with her. Just the thought of not being with her for three days has my stomach knotting and my mind searching for a way to stay. But it comes up empty-handed, just as I suspected.

"I don't want you to go. I want you to fly with me to Jackson and fuck me in the bathroom at thirty thousand feet." Saylor's pout turns into an eyebrow-jumping suggestive attempt at sexy. It works, until she hiccups. Shit. That's sexy too.

"I have to. I'll be back on Monday." It was Thursday. That was three days, seventy-two hours, and too damn long to not see her face . . . smell her hair . . . feel her body . . . It's official. I'm a pussy.

"Well, don't tell me good-bye. Just leave," Saylor says, turning her back, hitting me in the face with her hair in the process. I smirk at her, even though she can't see me.

I grab her shoulders and turn her to face me. It's an easy task considering she doesn't fight me. I knew it was exactly what she expected me to do. I have only a few minutes left, and in the time it takes me to walk to my waiting car, I have to transform from a pussy to the Nomad for Sinner's Creed I was before I met her.

I lift her chin with my finger and look down at her green, watery eyes. "Three days, baby." She blinks up at me and gives me a sad smile.

"I like when you call me baby." I lean down and kiss her softly, wondering how the fuck I'm gonna survive without tasting her. "I love you."

"I love you," I say without hesitation. It's natural. And I like the way it sounds on my lips. And I like the way she smiles when I say it. And I have to leave so my nuts have time to drop before I get to the clubhouse.

I hand her her backpack, then pull a phone from mine. "My number is the only contact in here. If you need me, call me. If you just want to talk, text. If I don't answer you back right away, I'm working, but if you call, I'll always answer. Let me know when you land." She takes the old flip phone and laughs. This time I know what she's thinking. And she is right.

"Let me guess, untraceable prepaid?" She shakes her head and puts the phone in her back pocket. "I'd be lying if I said it wasn't exciting dating a criminal." I smirk at her comment, then give her my own before turning and leaving her.

"I'd be lying if I said you make me not want to be one."

I'm not surprised to find Shady behind the wheel of the black sedan that is waiting outside for me. His computer skills and ability to find out information on anyone is just as important on this mission as my muscle and power of enforcement is. I'm glad he's here, because if anyone can put me in a shit mood, and pull me out of this Saylor trance I'm in, he can with his corny-ass jokes and goofy-ass personality.

"Lover boy!" is the greeting I get, and a death glare is his. "Right." He closes his mouth and pulls out into traffic, passing me an envelope in the process. I open it to find pictures of men that I've never seen wearing a cut I'm very familiar with.

"Death Mob is making a move. They're trying to set a chapter up just north of Houston." Shady's information doesn't come as a surprise to me.

Death Mob is the second-largest 1 percent MC in the states. Sinner's Creed is the first. They have their territory that mostly covers the northeast part of the U.S., where we cover the majority of the south and the southwest. Including Texas.

"I've done some diggin'," Shady starts, and from the way he

says it, I know what he found isn't gonna be something I like. "They're handing out patches like they're fucking candy. They're taking MCs and turning them into one-percenters overnight. My best guess is they're preparing for a war. Roach don't want 'em in Houston 'cause of the business we got with the border, he don't want to start a war, but my guess is they do." My jaw clenches at the news. I can feel the blood moving through my veins as time stands still. Motherfuckers like me and Shady earned our shit. It wasn't given to us.

Being a one-percenter is about more than numbers. Quality over quantity and all that shit. We hung around for five years, prospected for one, and some probated for two. It took a lot to earn the trust that was given and the respect that was needed. I'd give my life for a brother I've never met because I know he's had to prove himself. And he'd give his life for me—no questions asked.

Our patch united us because we all sacrificed something to get it. Our pride, our freedom, and our lives. Even though one-percenters were their own government, we all had to answer to someone. And that someone was Dorian, the infamous don for the Underground Mafia. We actually worked for Dorian, as did Death Mob. While we handled the majority of the transfer and did all the illegal dirty work, it was Dorian who handled the distribution—which was considered to be the most important and riskiest part of the illegal operations. Therefore, they got the biggest cut and they called the shots.

Sinner's Creed and the Underground had been in business together for a long time. History had proven our loyalty to them, but at the end of the day it was all about business. And engaging in a war with Death Mob was bad business. Dorian had the power to pull the strings on all of us. If Sinner's Creed lost their position with the Underground, then the club would fold.

"We can't do shit about how they run things. All we can do is keep an eye on them and let them know where we stand. I'm here for the paperwork; you're here for the dirty work." Shady sticks out his lower lip. "You get to have all the fun."

"You sound like a fag." He laughs at my response. Nothing against men who like men, but I can't stand a man that acts all prissy-fied. Shady couldn't be more gay in this moment if he wore a dress and lipstick. Considering he is still laughing, I know he did it on purpose. Glad he can prove my theory. The best way to go from pussy to Nomad in less than five minutes was to be in an enclosed space with Shady. I guess that's why I love him. Fuck.

14

THE CLUBHOUSE IN Houston doubles as a honky-tonk that is open to the public on Friday and Saturday nights. Today, it's only filled with patches, and they all belong to Sinner's Creed. A black Harley Street Glide is parked at the door and I know it's there for me. A Prospect that goes by the name of Rookie is wiping the saddlebags when I walk up.

I've met Rookie a few times, and I know by the determination on his face and the fearless look in his eyes that he is gonna be a good brother. I'm pretty intimidating, and if a man can look at me and not show fear, he has my respect. If I don't scare him, nothing will.

It's hard to prospect without the help of narcotics. It makes for a long year of minimal sleep and food, and a fuck of a lot of tongue biting. By the calmness in his demeanor, the exhaustion in his face, and the deep circles under his eyes, I can tell that Rookie is proving himself to this club and he's doing it without drugs. That earns him more than respect from me.

"Rookie." I give him my salute and he nods in return, knowing better than to offer his hand.

"Dirk." He doesn't bow before me or throw himself at my feet, but to him I'm worthy of it. Because I'm the man to impress. "Can I get you a beer?"

"Yeah. Bring two." He disappears inside and I prop up against the building and light a smoke. My phone buzzes in my pocket and I know it's Saylor.

Delay. They say they are working on the engine. My luck. Because I'm a nervous wreck and I miss you, I'm getting drunk.

I smirk at the screen before realizing that Saylor is getting drunk and I'm not there to warn off any men who think they can fuck with what's mine.

Anybody fucking with you?

She answers almost immediately.

No, Mr. Overprotective. No one is fucking with me. I miss you.

Because she makes me soft, and Shady is nowhere in sight, I ignore her comment and end the conversation.

Text me when you land.

I shove the phone back in my pocket, but it vibrates again.

"Fuck," I mutter, pulling it back out and thinking that maybe giving Saylor a phone wasn't such a good idea. Especially since she's drinking.

You are the biggest, baddest, meanest motherfucker I know.
Go get 'em baby.

I'm smiling at the screen. And I don't know why. Even from a distance, she can see right through me. I look up to find Rookie staring at me like I'm crazy. My smile dies and I snatch the beer from his hand.

"Don't ask," I mutter, shoving the phone in my pocket. Rookie drops his eyes to his boots, but his hat can't cover his smirk. By the sissy bar on the back of my bike and the passenger floorboards that have been installed, I'm pretty sure the news of Saylor has reached Houston. "You got a girlfriend?" I ask, and his confused look tells me that he is wondering why in the fuck I'm striking up a conversation.

"I do," he says, and for some reason, it makes me like him more.

"What's her name?" I ask, motioning for him to drink with me. He tilts the bottle to me in thanks and takes a long pull before answering.

"Carrie. She's great." He smiles and it's not at me. It's at the thought of her.

"What she do?" He gives me a nervous look and I know what he is thinking. "It ain't like that, Rookie. I'm just making conversation." The truth is there are a lot of assholes in this life. Some that would use women to see how big of a weakness they are for a Prospect. Seeking out girlfriends, lovers, or even wives, then taking pictures of them together and showing it to a Prospect to see what reaction they get isn't unheard of. It's actually pretty common. It never bothered me until now.

"She's a nurse over at the Texas Children's Hospital. I love 'er." There is conviction in his voice, and he is making his point loud and clear. He don't want her fucked with. I can see the dare in his eyes and I know he'll kill for that woman. Kill even me.

"How does she feel about the club?" I know I'm not having this conversation because I'm a changed man. I'm having it because I'm hoping his answers can shed some light on some of my own questions regarding me and Saylor's relationship.

"This club is what I want. She respects that." I know Rookie's background. The club had saved his life when his daddy about beat him half to death. It was a coincidence that we were in the same place at the same time, but Rookie thought it was destiny. Hell, maybe it was. He is twenty-four. By twenty-five he will be a patch holder, and Carrie will spend the rest of her life coming in second place.

"What about what she wants?" I ask, and the question is not for him. It's for me. I'd never even asked Saylor what she wanted. I've just assumed what she wants is me.

"She's a good woman, Dirk. She has a good heart and she's smart as hell. But she can't fix me. And this club can. She loves me hard. So hard that she's willing to give up part of me, just to have a piece of me. She gets it. And I love her more because of it." He looks away, the demons of his past coming back to haunt him, and they are fighting with the angel that protects him. Rookie has a Saylor.

"You'll make a good brother one day, Rookie. But in my eyes, you're already one. Gimme your card." His body sags at my words and he's on the verge of tears. I know the feeling. My signature will get him a patch no matter how long he has left prospecting.

I see the relief in his face and it reminds me of the man I was before I became the man I am. Rookie won't be forced to do the things that I did. My signature is enough. He won't have to give his innocence, because I say he's loyal enough without it. As I sign my name to his card, I feel a weight being lifted off my own shoulders. Today, Carrie is saved from the monster that could have been created. I just wish Saylor was as fortunate.

I lead the pack to Juke's Joint, where members of Death Mob are known to hang out. Bikes line the front of the bar located in a shitty little building just off the interstate. We pull in, blocking their exit, and before I can light a smoke, they crowd around the door, watching us.

We stand our ground, demanding they make the first move. I could stand here all night, and it looks like I'm going to have to. It feels like Death Mob has something to prove. It is a show of respect to greet your superiors, and since Texas is our home state and we gave them permission to be here, we are superior.

While we wait, I take the opportunity to size up the men who could quickly become my potential enemies. They are big, dirty, and stand in a line of twelve. Their stances tell me they are ready for a fight, if that's what we're bringing to the table. That wasn't the plan, but I'm always down for a good ass kicking.

Their size doesn't intimidate me. Neither does the 1% patch they wear. Hell, I wear the same fucking one. Where we are grouped, talking and bullshitting like they don't exist, they stand silent. That is a show of weakness to me. If they don't have shit to prove, then they shouldn't act like they do. They look like they're in a pissing contest over a piece of cheap pussy rather than a mutual show of respect between two MCs.

When Shady sends Rookie in to get some beers, shit begins to happen. When a man wears Sinner's Creed colors, other MCs better show him some respect. It doesn't matter if the word

Prospect is on his patch or not. He may not be a patch holder, but he is sponsored by one. And Rookie's sponsor was Shady. In all my years, I have only seen Shady lose his shit twice, and both times it was over someone disrespecting our patch.

When the men at the bar refuse to let Rookie pass, I know my count for Shady's loss of control is about to change. I watch Rookie as he stands his ground. I know he is doing everything in his power to persuade the men that this isn't what they want. He never looks over his shoulder at us for help because he doesn't have to. He can fight his own battles—another reason he would make a good brother. But he won't have to fight it alone for long. By the signature neck roll Shady performs when he's ready to bust some heads, I know things are fixing to get bad.

I am two steps behind him when he makes his move toward the door. The rest of the club stays put when I shoot them a look. We have this. I don't want a bar brawl right now, and Death Mob would be stupid to start one.

When we reach the porch where they are standing, Shady puts his hand on Rookie's shoulder, pushing him back a step. When he is nose to nose with the sergeant at arms, he gives him that goofy grin that I fucking hate. Or love. Or hate. Again, Shady has the ability to put me in a pissy mood without even knowing it. Now I want them to initiate a fight so I can hit something.

Shady's motives are simple. Instead of going to the president, he goes to the SA. It saves time. If he had confronted the president, he would have had to deal with the SA anyway because that's an SA's job: protect the president.

"What the fuck's the problem?" Shady asks, his voice sickeningly sweet. I keep my eyes on the VP, warning him to keep his mouth shut.

"This bar is for patch holders only. Y'all can come in, but ya Prospect needs to stay outside. Maybe pick up some cigarette butts or something." The president takes that moment to thump a cigarette into the gravel. Shady laughs, and I know better, but it almost sounds like he finds the SA's remark humorous.

"Yeah, we gotta keep them Prospects on their toes," Shady mumbles, and then I watch his expression change out of the corner of my eye. His lips curl into a snarl and his eyebrows draw together. This hundred-and-ninety-pound man just transformed into kill mode. He glares into the eyes of the SA and I can see the fear forming in the eyes of the VP I'm staring at.

"The thing is, that's *my* Prospect. Those colors he wears belong to Sinner's Creed. He goes where *I* tell him to go. This is my fucking town, my fucking bar, and my fucking parking lot your leader is throwing shit in."

My eyes go to the president, who is fighting an internal battle. Does he look like a pussy or does he die? He just needs to look like a pussy.

Shady spits over his shoulder and sniffs several times. This is his way of trying to calm down and still look intimidating. "Now, two things are gonna happen next. One, you're gonna move the fuck outta the way so my guy can get us some beers. Two, one of you is gonna pick up that fucking cigarette butt. And both of those things are gonna happen in the next thirty seconds."

I challenge the VP with my eyes, knowing he is about to break if someone else don't. I see movement to my right and watch a man walking toward us out of my peripheral. He is several yards away, and he is taking his time getting here.

"Or?" the SA asks. What a fucking idiot. Shady's smile is back, and when he looks at me, he is fucking beaming—not a hint of worry or hostility in his face.

"Or my man Dirk here is gonna demonstrate how he got his name." The SA looks at me, but I ignore him. Shady is full of shit and I make a mental note to slap the fuck outta him when this is over. I had my name long before I even knew it was a knife. Payback would be hell.

"The infamous Dirk," the man approaching says, and I'm sure it's a distraction, so I don't look away. "I don't think we have a problem here. Let the young man through."

The VP steps back and I finally get the chance to see who this peacekeeper is and what rank he has to override the president. An older man with a long white beard and a limp stops a few feet from me.

"Son," he says, addressing a young patch holder next to him. Whoever this motherfucker is must be somebody, because the look on the guy's face shows that he is honored to be addressed by him. "Do me a favor and grab that cigarette. Your president accidentally dropped it."

He looks at me, expecting a nod of acceptance from his explanation of the president's behavior. He won't get one. The patch holder disappears from my view, and the old man smiles at my unchanging expression. When he steps forward and sticks his hand out for me to shake, I take it. Because this man is owed my respect. Whoever he is. "Cyrus, Death Mob Nomad, southeast region."

"Dirk, Sinner's Creed," I respond, his introduction answering all my questions. He was an old-timer with the power to overrule just about anyone because of his position and seniority in the club.

"These young cats these days. President ain't but about thirty. Sometimes that patch can make you forget what's more important." He is talking about respect, but I don't give him the verbal confirmation he wants. "We appreciate y'all lettin' us set up camp here. I can assure you what just happened won't happen again."

"It would be for the best," I tell him, not as a threat, just as a fact.

"There ain't no problem here, Dirk, but we need a mutual

understanding." His seriousness is evident, but his face still holds a smile.

"We don't tolerate disrespect. If you say it won't happen again, then I'll take your word. The only understanding we need is that we reign superior here. We've earned the respect of this town, and just because Death Mob wears a one percent patch, don't mean they are exempt from showing it."

"Agreed. Nice to officially meet you, Dirk. I hope next time is on better terms." He waits for my response. He needs to hear me say there aren't any problems, because if I don't, they will assume this isn't over.

"It's all good," I tell him, and when I feel my phone buzz in my pocket, I know for sure it is. I watch Cyrus until he disappears inside, then check my message. It's from Saylor.

I've landed. I'm taking a cab home. I hope everything is good with you.

Glad you're home. It's all good. It really is. But I miss her. I'm calculating the hours it would take me to get to her, fuck her, then be back here before noon. It's not possible.

I miss you. A lot. How will I sleep tonight? Shit. How will I sleep tonight? The thought of having another woman sleep with me crosses my mind, but disappears almost immediately.

In your bed. Alone. Just the last word has me thinking of what I would do if I caught her with someone else. I'd kill him. Simple.

I love you. As I'm rereading the message, Shady decides to show up, and I shut the phone and glare at him.

"Something wrong?" he asks, and I think he thinks the look I wear is for someone other than him.

"How's shit inside?" I dig my cigarettes out, avoiding his question.

"Introductions were made. No apologies, but I expected that. What did Cyrus say to you?" Shady hands me a beer and takes my pack of smokes, getting one out for himself without asking. Not that it matters, what's mine is his. Except for Saylor, of course.

"What happened today won't happen again. We won't have any problems. If we do, we'll go to him first. Sinner's don't need the heat right now." Shady agrees and we take a seat on the steps, letting the noise from inside replace our conversation. Until Shady talks.

"So, you gave Rookie a signature. Kid must be doing something right." I don't answer him; I just stare out into the lot at the bikes. "You never gave me a signature. What the fuck's up with that?" He is only joking, but I can hear the hurt in his voice. I don't know why, probably because of this whole love revelation that I've had, but I feel like I owe him an explanation.

"I didn't have as much pull then as I do now. I'd only been a Nomad for a couple of years when you came along." I look at him when I say this. The nod of his head tells me he understands, but the question in his eyes tells me he wants a conversation and he used that line as an opening. I should have known. He got his name because of his ability to do shady shit to get what he wanted. Which is what he is doing to me.

"We're brothers, Dirk. But it goes beyond the patch. You know I'm here if you ever need anything." I almost want to laugh at the sincerity in his voice. What I manage is a smile. I turn my bottle up, take a pull from my cigarette, and thump the butt in the gravel. When I look at him, he is looking at the glow of the red cherry from my cigarette. I know what he's thinking. A war almost broke out over something as simple as a cigarette, and here I was throwing one down. It made my smile widen. I put my hand on his shoulder and give it a squeeze. When he looks at me, I'm smiling and he looks like he wants to punch me.

"I didn't get my name from a knife, and I don't like people thinking that I did." He shakes his head in aggravation, taking his eyes off of me and back to the still-burning cherry. He wants to say something but knows that this is an argument he can't win. I squeeze his shoulder again and he looks back at me.

"Our brotherhood does go beyond the patch. And I appreciate your offer. Same goes for you." He smiles and you would think I've just made his whole fucking day. Dumb-ass.

I leave him processing my words, but turn back when I get to the door. "Hey, Shady," I call, and he turns, his goofy-ass smile still in place. "Pick up that cigarette butt."

I walk inside, leaving an officer for the Sinner's Creed MC picking up my trash in the parking lot, and having only one thought in my mind—payback is hell.

Nationals knows about the situation with Death Mob, and even though my work was done, they wanted me to stay in town a couple more days to make sure Cyrus stayed good on his word. He did.

The next night we pulled into Juke's Joint, Death Mob was waiting to shake our hands. I just gave them a salute and kept walking. Now that I'm almost back to Mississippi, Nationals wants me back in Texas. Just fucking great. But at least I'll have one night at home.

Saylor and I have kept in contact the three days I had been gone. She always tells me she loves me and I never respond. I don't think it's necessary. She knows it and I shouldn't have to send it in a message to confirm it. Although, I like when she says it to me.

I didn't tell her when I was leaving, and now that I'm outside her apartment, I wonder if I should have. When I hear voices inside, my first reaction is to kick down the door. When I hear male laughter, my second reaction is to set the building on fire. But, today, there is another issue at the complex, and two patrol cars linger at the end of the parking lot. So, instead, I decide to text her. I'm so pissed I can barely punch in the letters on my phone.

Who the fuck is here?

I wait several minutes and get no response. I light a cigarette, trying to calm my growing temper. It helps clear my head and I decide to give her a call. From outside the door, I can hear her telling them to be quiet because it's him. That's me. That means she is hiding me from them.

I'm flooded with all sorts of emotions; betrayal, hurt, sadness . . . but above all, fury. I close the phone just as she says hello and knock on the door, willing my hand to not knock a hole through the wood. When a man with blond hair wearing a V-neck answers, I lose it.

I grab his shirt, lifting him off his feet and pushing him inside, then closing the door with my foot. I don't need any witnesses. He looks like he is about to shit his pants, or throw up. I'm not sure which one.

When I break his nose with my fist, he screams like a girl. I crack my neck, flex my fingers, and take a deep breath, letting my plan of torture run through my mind again and again. I'll break all his bones first, then I'll cut him in places where he will slowly bleed out. I want him to feel the pain for as long as possible.

As I reach down to pull him from the floor, I'm blinded by a mass of curly blond hair. Arms are around my neck, legs around my waist, and I fall to my knees with the impact. I start to pry her off of me when her mouth connects with mine. She isn't asking me to stop. She isn't begging me to spare his life. She is kissing me like I'm the only man in the world.

Everything around me dies and I am consumed only by her. My Saylor. My hands fist in her hair and I kiss her back with ten times the passion she is showing me. Her taste, smell, and body fuse with mine, and everything about the two of us becomes one. From our rapid heartbeats, to our perfectly molded bodies, to our tongues that fight to get more from the other.

I feel like her blood is my blood, her touch is my touch and her mind is my mind, and it is saying I miss you and I love you. Nothing can break us away from this moment of euphoria. Nothing but high-pitched screams, two men crying and banging on the door. Saylor pulls away and she is smiling. If her kiss didn't have me breathless, her beauty would.

"You broke my friend's nose," she says, and looks like she couldn't give a shit less. "I missed you so much."

I start to tell her I miss her, but the word *police* and banging on the front door has me snapping out of the moment. I stand up, pulling her with me, and wonder what in the hell I'm gonna say. My mind is clouded with her, and I can't think rationally to save my fucking life.

"I got it." She looks at the man holding a towel to his nose and says, "Go along with the story." He shoots her the finger and when I take a step toward him, he hides in the chest of another man who looks just as terrified as him. Confusion has me cemented to the floor. "Come in!" Saylor's voice is excited, and I know it's not because the cops are here, it's because I am.

"There a problem here?" the first officer asks, his hands resting on his gun and his eyes on me. Before I can answer, Saylor intervenes.

"No. This is my boyfriend, and these are my friends," she says, cheerful as ever.

"Then why is he bleeding?" he asks, jutting his thumb toward the crybaby in the corner that has the hair on the back of my neck standing up. Before any of us can say anything, crybaby intervenes.

"I didn't know he had a key to get in. When I went to open the door, he pushed it and it broke my nose. Now I'm gonna have a big hump in it." He cries out the last part, and the man next to him starts making *shhh*ing noises and rubbing his back. Motherfucker. They're gay.

I look to the officer, and apparently the relief in my face has softened it and our story is believed. He nods his head, says a few words to Saylor, and leaves with his partner in tow. Saylor slips her hand around my waist and makes the introductions, still acting as if nothing is wrong.

"Dirk, Donnawayne and Jeffery. Guys, this is my Dirk." Her Dirk. Only hers. She looks up at me, eyes filled with love and I cup her cheek, loving how she closes her eyes and turns her face into my hand so she can kiss my palm.

"Well, in case you didn't know, mean ass, we're gay," Donnawayne says, removing the towel from his face so I can hear him. I just stare at them, not knowing what in the hell to say. It doesn't bother me that they are gay, it just isn't something I'm used to. I'm also still reeling from the fact that these men have no desire whatsoever for Saylor.

Jeffery keeps an arm around his lover and extends the other toward me. "Nice to meet you, Dirk. I just hate it had to be like this." He smiles and there is no hostility in his voice. He isn't pissed that I broke his boyfriend's nose, not that I'd care too much if he was.

I don't take his hand and he closes his eyes and snaps his fingers. "Right. Not a toucher. It's fine. We will excuse just about anything for the man who has made our girl so happy."

My girl. Not his. But his words were genuine and I now know that these are the other two people that are important in Saylor's life.

"No, we will not!" Donnawayne says, shrugging Jeffery off and lightly slapping his chest. "Saylor, he broke my nose. I think he owes me an apology." I move my focus to Saylor and I'm glad I did. She is beautiful.

"I love you," she says, ignoring her friends and searching my face as if she is trying to make sure her memory of me didn't deceive her.

"I love you too, baby," I tell her, because she wants it. She wants the words, she wants the endearment, and it's been too damn long since I've given it to her. I want to tell her again and again, but the other couple is arguing and fucking up my concentration.

"Will you apologize? Please?" Saylor asks, her lip poking out. I'd kiss him if she asked me to right now.

I turn to Donnawayne and give him the most sincere look I can manage. "I apologize. You caught me off guard." Not that I owed him an explanation, but I thought it might help calm the waters. It doesn't.

"Yeah, well what about my nose? It was once my best feature." He is crying again and I look to Saylor for help. She just gives me an evil grin. I look at Jeffery, who is looking back at me, unsure of what to say. Yeah, well, that makes two of us. I shift, already regretting the words I'm fixing to say.

"I can reset it for you," I offer, and a look of hope fills his eyes. Fuck.

"You can? You will?" If he hugs me, I'll kill him. Saylor laughs and I know she knows exactly what I'm thinking.

"Come on. I'll get some ice," she says, and I follow her into the kitchen with the two men on my ass . . . I can only shake my head.

15

DONNAWAYNE'S NOSE WAS reset, Jeffery's hand was numb from Donnawayne squeezing the shit out of it every time I came close to him, and my discomfort was at a max by the time Saylor and I were finally alone. When I asked her why she chose two gay men to be her only friends, she responded with a shrug and "at least I know they won't take you." Her answer was good enough for me. But, even if her friends were female, there was no one I wanted other than her.

"Will you sleep with me tonight?" Saylor asks, between yawns.

"Yes," I tell her, thinking of how I want to make up for the days I missed.

"'K, I just need to take my contacts out." I wait for her in bed, ready to feel her body against mine. I haven't had a decent night's sleep since I was with her.

When she climbs in, she is naked and my cock stands at attention at the feel of her silky skin against mine. "I haven't slept hardly any since you left," she says, and I feel the weight of her body on me as she starts to relax. Her head is on my shoulder, her arm around my neck, one leg thrown over mine and her bare chest against my side. I like her like this. Just the feel of her next to me has my own body relaxing. We don't tell each other good night because words aren't needed. We both know this moment is as good as it gets.

Saylor is out for doughnuts when I wake up. I know this because the room is covered in Post-it notes, telling me. There are at least twenty of them, and I know she did it so that as soon as I opened my eyes, no matter where I looked I would know where she was.

I shower and am forced to wear a towel because all of my clothes are missing. My bag is empty and inside of it is a note that tells me she is doing my laundry. I find some milk in the fridge, and drink it while I check out her apartment. It's still pretty bare, but some of the boxes in the spare room look like they have been somewhat unpacked. I want her to pack them back up and ship them to my place. Which is where I'm gonna ask her to move when she gets back.

I hear the door open and close and I freeze, wondering if there is any way possible that it's not Saylor. I use the small island in the kitchen to cover as much of me as possible, and let out a breath when Saylor emerges. Her bright pink T-shirt is so long it almost covers her shorts, her hair is wild around her head, and she has on a pair of neon yellow running shoes. I take it Saylor likes bright colors.

She smiles when she sees me, then her eyes fall to the towel around my waist. "Why didn't I think to hide the towels?" she asks, and in one swift movement, I'm standing completely naked in her kitchen. Her eyes travel the length of my body as I walk toward her, already imagining what she will feel like when I'm buried inside her. I want her on the kitchen table. I want her on the counter. I want her on the floor, against the wall, in the air, and everywhere in between. But the noise coming from the laundry room tells me the best place to have her is on the washing machine.

I could grab her hand and lead her there. I could tell her to follow me. But both of those will take away more time than what I'm willing to give. So I scoop her in my arms and carry her, making sure to step over the box of doughnuts that are now on the floor.

The machine is on the wash cycle, and the gentle back and forth movement is just enough to make her tits dance for me. I strip off her shirt and bra, anxious to have her in my mouth. When I gently bite down on her nipple, she moans deep in her throat and pulls me closer to her.

She's naked and I'm inside her before my mind slows down enough for me to think. I'm buried deep, letting her squeeze me with her pussy and pull my hair with her hands while she kisses me almost desperately. Fuck I've missed her. I move inside her, long, deep thrusts that are slow at first, then hard as I drive home that last inch. Her body jerks and she moans each time I pound into her. I love watching her—the way she squeezes her eyes shut, the way she throws her head back, the way she leans back on one hand while the other pulls at her nipples. She is a beautiful sight.

When her body tenses and she comes, the feeling she has can't be anything close to the feeling I get each time I look at her like this. My own release isn't as powerful as this feeling in my chest. Feeling my dick jerk inside her, flooding her, filling her . . . is pretty fucking intense.

But nothing can compare to what I feel for her in my heart. That mind-blowing, forget-everything, all-I-can-concentrate-on-is-this-moment sensation. This feeling you get when you reach that orgasmic high is what I feel every time I look at her. When she opens her eyes to look at me, I can see all the way to her soul. I can feel it. And I can feel her searching for mine. Playing games with the devil isn't smart. I sold my soul to him a long time ago, and Saylor Samson wants to possess what doesn't even belong to me. But I believe she is powerful enough to give the devil a run for his money.

"You were thinking about something earlier. Something deep. Tell me about it." Saylor is laying next to me on the living room floor, naked except for her socks. I can't even remember how we got here, but we've been here awhile.

"I was thinking about how much I love you." I answer honestly, staring up at the ceiling, holding her hand in mine.

"There was something else. I could see it in your eyes. Tell me." I stroke the back of her hand with my thumb, wondering how in the hell I am going to answer her question.

"I can feel you inside me. In places I haven't had feeling in a long time." That sounded stupid, but I hope she got it.

"You're talking about your soul, aren't you?" I don't answer her because she already knows what I mean. Plus, I don't like saying shit when I'm not sure it's what I want to say. "Just because you think you're not good enough, doesn't make it true. That's not your decision. It's God's."

I don't like this conversation and I don't want to talk about it anymore. I'm hoping by ignoring her, the subject will be dropped. I'd rather talk about anything than this.

"I'm sick, Dirk," she says, and my head jerks toward her. Maybe she has a headache. Maybe a stomach virus. I don't know and I can't tell because she won't look at me. She keeps her eyes on the ceiling. I stare at her, silently begging her for more information so I can fix her, and wondering if I need to go ahead and inform Nationals that I won't be leaving today.

"Saylor." I squeeze her hand and she finally looks at me, her eyes shining with unshed tears. When she blinks, I follow one until it rolls off her cheek and onto the carpet. "What's wrong?" I ask, and if it wasn't for the flood of tears, I wouldn't know she was crying. She doesn't sob, or make a sad face. She looks almost relieved.

I turn on my side, propping myself on my elbow so I can look down at her, but she pushes me away. She stands and I follow her to her room. She grabs a robe from the bed and puts it on, disappearing out the door. I'm trying not to get mad, but her nonchalance about the situation is driving me insane. If she is sick, then why don't she tell me what's wrong? Why the fuck is she crying? Why can't we just stay naked?

She walks back in, holding a basket of clean laundry, and I grab my one and only pair of sweats off the top. My mind takes a break from the turmoil I feel in my chest and silently thanks Saylor for throwing the clothes in the dryer before leaving the laundry room.

When my junk is covered, I feel marginally better about chewing Saylor's ass for not giving me any info other than "I'm sick." But, when I turn to find her, she is looking at me—her face and neck wet with tears.

"I'm not just sick, Dirk. I'm dying." Her eyes are begging me to understand what she said, but I can't. We're all dying. Every day on this earth puts us one day closer to that inevitable day we will all face. But that's not what's she's saying. She is saying she is dying like she knows when that inevitable day is.

I feel my heart leap to my throat, then fall to my knees as her words sink in. The emptiness in my chest is almost too much, and I know if I wasn't looking dead at her, it would be as if she were already gone. Because she is telling me she is leaving.

"Those headaches I have are caused from an inoperable, malignant brain tumor." She pauses as if she is waiting for her words to fully register. They don't. All I'm hearing is *I'm dying* and all I can think is *She can't.*

"My mother died from the same thing. After she passed, they removed the tumor and did some research. They found it was hereditary. I've been going for routine CT scans since. At first I hoped it might have somehow skipped me, but they found it about six months ago when I went for my checkup."

Brain tumor? Couldn't they just take it out? She said inoperable, but she didn't say incurable.

"They can fix it," I inform her, because these days, chemo and radiation and all that shit cured these types of things. She would lose her hair, but it would grow back. Technology was amazing. There were smart people all over the world, finding cures for cancer right now. Little lab geeks in white coats with glasses and all that shit.

"There's no fixing it, Dirk. It's gonna happen. Maybe not today or tomorrow, but six months from now I won't be here."

How could she be so calm? How could she not care? Why the fuck has she been keeping this from me?

"I'm at peace with this, Dirk, and it's taken me a long time to get where I am."

I'm still shaking my head, telling her this isn't real in a way that I've been taught not to. I don't nod, or shake my head. I speak when I have something to say, but I can't find the words. She puts her hands on either side of my face and I still. I'm frantically searching her eyes for any sign of hope, but there isn't any.

"How can you say you are at peace with this?" I whisper the words, afraid if I say them too loud that the part of my brain that can fully process what I'm asking will hear and make this all true.

"God has decided that I'm not needed in this life anymore."

"I need you," I say through my teeth, fighting back the burning that is going on behind my eyes. I know what it is, and because I haven't felt it in so long, it hurts more. Saylor's thick walls and peace with the situation are failing. The small amount of sadness I saw in her eyes isn't so small anymore.

"And you have me." She is smiling. It's sad, but it resembles happiness and I don't see the happiness in this moment. Not one fucking bit.

"You lied to me." The words hurt more when I say them out loud, and I'm searching for anger to replace pain, but it's not working. She's shaking her head, panic welling in her eyes.

"I didn't know how to tell you. I could never find the right time." Her words help me find the anger I've been searching for. I grab her wrists, pulling her hands from my face and pushing her away. She reaches for me and I step back. I don't want her touching me. I don't want to look at her. All her actions make sense now. She isn't a heartbroken woman with a broken past; she is a dying woman that wanted to live on the wild side and mark *biker* off her bucket list before it was too late.

"You used me." I'm whispering. The realization of being a pawn in her fucking sick game of limited life did more than slap me in the face. It ripped out my fucking heart. Maybe the next time she prays, she should ask God to shed some mercy on her soul. Because it's gotta be pretty twisted to allow her to do what she's done to me.

"I never used you, Dirk! I love you!" Her desperate cries would hurt me, if she hadn't made me so numb.

"You love me?" I can't hide the shock in my voice. I should have known love was a fucked-up thing. Black actually did do something for me. He shielded me from the one thing that could hurt me more than anything else. Fucking heartbreak.

"Dirk, please don't hate me. I need you." Hate her? I could never hate her. But I had to leave. She knew that.

I find my voice, laced with as much malice and ice I can find.

I'm digging into the deepest, darkest, most tainted part of my soul to tell her the last words I ever want her to hear me say.

"Out of all the endless hours I've spent with you. All that fucking time and not once you could tell me? You should have told me before I ever let you into my life. I gave you everything and what are you giving me? A six-month notice that what I thought I'd waited my whole life for was going to die?"

I'm not angry at Saylor, but I know I'm taking my frustration out on her. It's not her fault this is happening. But who else can I blame?

"I need you, Dirk." I shake my head at her words, wishing I could forget everything.

"I have to go, Saylor. I have a job to do." I grab my bag and turn to leave. I was a fool. A fuckup. I knew she was too good to be true. I don't deserve her. I never did and now the universe is proving it. So I do the only thing I know how to do. I run.

"Will you be back?" Her sweet voice hits me right in the chest.

"I just need some time."

I chance a look back at her, wanting nothing more than to hold her in my arms. I step closer, allowing her scent to engulf me. When I'm close enough, I lean down and kiss her head. I'm giving her the only thing I have left. A good-bye and words that I've vowed never to say, but have spoken twice to her. "I'm sorry, Saylor." Because that doesn't seem to be enough, I wait until I'm on my bike before I whisper the words she will never hear. "Good-bye."

"Whiskey," I snap to the Prospect whose lack of eye contact and silence are the only things keeping him alive. For some reason, they put this new blood behind the bar in Houston. I guess they thought it was a good way to break him in. If he could survive me after the shit mood I've been in the past week, he could survive anything.

Roach called yesterday telling me that we needed to make a move on Death Mob. It seemed they wanted more of Texas than what we were willing to give. My job was to ask them to leave. I knew it wouldn't turn out good and Roach did too, but he considered me trained enough to handle it. And I would. Alone. I dared a motherfucker to try and take me out. If I went, I'd take a hell of a lot of 'em with me. Life wasn't that great these days anyway.

Death Mob didn't have the relationship with Dorian that Sinner's Creed did, but Cyrus had a lot of reach. He had several connections in his pocket, and word on the street was that he was sniffing around about our business with Mexico. That wasn't good for us, but it sure as hell wasn't good for him.

I finished off the bottle of whiskey, letting it numb the pain I still had in my chest over her—the one whose name we don't speak. My anger turned to resentment, my resentment turned back to anger, and when I couldn't find things to get pissed off at anymore, I became sad. That's where I am now. Fucking sad. Heartbroken. Crushed. Devastated. All those fucking words that express that dying feeling inside of you. It's more painful than being shot, stabbed, and beaten to a pulp. I've experienced all three and none of them can compare to this.

When I walk outside, silence descends and it is a sure giveaway that I am the topic of conversation. But nobody attempts to stop me or say anything. Roach had given them strict orders to let me handle shit. He had put his faith in me this long; there was no sense in doubting me now. When I mount my bike, I look over to find Shady sitting on his, putting his helmet on. I just glare at him. My look speaks more volume than my words.

"Brothers for life. Ride or die. I'm ya boy blue. All that shit," he says, slapping his chest and throwing up what I'm guessing are gang signs. I don't need his help, or his love and loyalty. I need his respect. And right now, he needs to respectfully stay the fuck outta my way.

"Don't." My one-word warning does nothing. I'm gonna have to fight this asshole.

"Look, man, I push papers. Let me do something," he says, his voice exasperated. He knew this fight was coming. Paper pusher my ass. Shady has fought plenty of battles. He is sick with a gun. But, if he thinks he is gonna make me feel like shit and I'm gonna cave, he's wrong. I'm much better at fucking with people's heads than he is.

"Just what I need. Some-fucking-body else using me to get their thrills." He knows what I mean and the remorse is on his face. Good. I'll guilt his ass into staying and save my strength for Death Mob.

I close my shield and tear out, leaving a cloud of dust behind me. When it clears, Shady's bike comes into view in my mirror. I should have fucking known.

16

IT'S SATURDAY NIGHT at Juke's Joint and the bar is crowded with Death Mob. More members are pouring in from other states and like Roach said, they're showing their teeth. And of course, ours are bigger. Only a few cars are out front, which tells me that the only citizens are the people working. They know enough by now to keep their mouth shut. If they don't, I'll remind them.

Shady pulls in next to me and I'm sure he is gonna say something stupid to really piss me off. I'm surprised when he doesn't. I look over at him and his face says he's ready. Kill-mode ready.

Inside, it's the typical late-night pool hall. A heavy cloud of smoke hangs in the air, the lighting is dim, and the place smells like beer and piss. I do a quick count and I see seventeen patches. That's two more than the bikes outside. So either someone is riding bitch or one of the three cars in the parking lot belong to Death Mob.

Behind the bar, a young girl and an older man are working.

The owner and a barmaid. That accounts for the other two vehicles. Shady goes to the bar and orders a beer, then says something to the owner, who looks over at me, then nods and steps in the back, taking the barmaid with him.

Only a few noticed when we walked in, but we now have everyone's attention. Metallica's "Sad But True" is the only sound, and I can't keep thoughts of her out of my head. I walk to the jukebox and unplug it from the wall, thinking that it would probably make me feel better if I just smashed the fucking thing in.

The crowd has gathered closer to me, hovering around a pool table, almost closing me in a corner. Good. I like fighting my way out. I put eyes on Shady, who is still at the bar, drinking his beer as if it's just another Saturday night. He is watching, but doesn't look the least bit worried. The SA steps forward. I should have known his big ass would be the first one to say something. I'm glad. I like him least anyway.

"I like that song." *Really, motherfucker? That's the best intimidating line you got?* Idiot.

"We think it's about time y'all get outta Texas," I tell him, hoping like hell that he takes another step so I can break his fucking legs.

"We?" I hate when they try to play calm. What I want to say is, *Control your fucking breathing, dick, then you might actually convince me that you ain't scared.* But I don't. I let him know so that there is no misunderstanding.

"Sinner's Creed Nationals. They've sent me to ask you nicely to leave. You have your territory and we have ours. We don't fuck with the northeast and y'all don't fuck with the southwest. That's the rules. If you want to expand your business in Arkansas or Louisiana, we can negotiate that territory. But Texas is covered." That's how you play calm, and my words are as smooth as satin. I promised to be nice, but only once.

"Sent you to ask us nicely, huh?" He nods his head, looking around the room at his brothers, who all stand stock-still. They're glaring at me with their arms crossed over their chests. It looks like a scene in an action movie. If I were a laugher, this would be one of my shining moments. When I look over at Shady, he is smiling, fighting hard not to laugh. He sees it too. "So we can stay in the northeast, and we can negotiate for Arkansas and Louisiana, just not Texas." *That's what I said, dipshit.*

"That's right." *There's your confirmation, motherfucker. Now, start swingin' or get the hell out.*

"I've heard about you, Dirk, but you don't know shit about me. So, let me enlighten you on something. I don't just tuck my tail between my legs and run. Regardless of what y'all think, Sinner's Creed don't run shit. Now, why don't you turn around and walk outta here, before your little brother over there has to spend the next few weeks spoon-feeding you."

I'm ready to put his head through the pool table when I'm caught off guard by Shady's commotion. When I see him make a dramatic scene trying to get over to me, I know his sarcastic, smart-ass, goofy fucking tactics are fixing to have us brawling. And I can't fucking wait.

"Dirk! Dirk!" Shady is serious as fuck, pushing his way through the crowd toward me. He's made a huge circle through all of them, shouting my name and mumbling *excuse me*s like he is trying to prevent me from doing something stupid.

"One minute," he mouths to the SA, who looks just as confused as everyone else. Shady grabs my arm and turns me so that my back is to the group. I fight hard not to push him away, but I know there is an underlying meaning to his ridiculous fucking behavior.

"Six are packing heat, others just knives and wrenches. Dude in the back, far left, has a couple of broken beer bottles. I don't know about SA, couldn't get my hands on 'em. I got one in the chamber, ten in the clip and a .380 on my ankle."

He pauses long enough to look at me, and the excitement dancing in his eyes has me smirking for the first time in days. "If it turns into a gunfight, I can get us out the door, but we gotta leave on foot. That's plan A." He looks back and I glance over my shoulder, watching as he holds his finger up before turning back around.

"Plan B, we leave alive and come back later. Do it the smart way where the odds aren't so against us. Your call, brother. I'm down for whatever." And he is.

If there was a shoot-out tonight, chances were two of the bodies on the floor would be ours. I'd let my personal shit interfere with my club life, and now a brother's life was at risk. So was my club. If a war broke out between Sinner's Creed and Death Mob, Dorian would come knocking on our door. We couldn't afford the heat with the Underground. I couldn't disrespect my patch. I couldn't shame my club. And I couldn't bury Shady with his blood on my hands.

"Plan B," I say, and no sooner than the words are outta my mouth, the SA is talking. By the time he speaks the first word, I know our plans are about to change.

"Saylor Samson. Maybe you should just run on home to her. From what I hear, she needs you right about now. She sure is sweet too. She tastes just like oranges."

I'm still turning around when Shady makes his first move and puts a bullet right between the eyes of the SA. Guns are drawn and shots are fired in a matter of seconds. I duck behind the jukebox, using it as my shield as Shady finds cover behind the pool table across from me.

When I hear the first click of an empty clip, I nod and Shady fires over his head while I stick mine out and focus on the remaining targets. I pump two shots into one of them while Shady's reckless aim, used only for a distraction, drops three and has the remaining diving for cover. He keeps shooting while I reload, then stand, exposing myself, dropping two more while making my way to where Shady is.

The sound of Velcro while Shady unstraps the gun from his ankle is the only noise in the room. I only have a few rounds left, but I slide out the clip and push it back, making it sound like a full reload.

"Ready?" I ask Shady, my hushed word barely audible over the pounding of my heart in my ears.

"Yeah."

I nod and we stand together, guns drawn, and face a room with several sets of hands in the air.

"Stand up," I command, and they do without hesitation. They look like they are ready to die, their chins held high in the air with pride written on their faces. Shady scans the bodies on the floor, looking for signs of life and not finding any. I see legs moving behind a table and jerk my head for Shady to check it out.

"Gut shot. He might live." For the first time, I realize the president and vice president are not here. And four of the five standing are Prospects. I look around the room and find that almost all the bodies on the floor are wearing brand-new patches. Their leather isn't worn, their threads aren't dirty, and none of their faces match the ones from the other night—other than the SA.

"What's his rank?" I ask Shady, who pushes the man to his side despite his painful cries.

"Patch holder."

"What's his chances?" I hear the man yell in protest as Shady checks him out.

"Aw shit, he's good. Lost some blood, but it didn't hit nothing important. You want me to finish him?" Shady's nonchalance shouldn't be comforting, but it is.

"Nah," I say before turning my gun on the only patch holder standing and put a bullet through his skull. The pride the Prospects once wore is diminishing now that they are looking at what could be their final moment. I should fuck with them, but I won't. They're almost innocent. It pisses me off that none of them were packing. Their sponsor probably told them they couldn't carry.

"Turn around," I demand, and the lip of one begins to quiver as he obeys. I walk around them so I can look into the face of the wounded man on the floor. "Why are they prospecting when you have been handing out patches to everyone else?" He hesitates to answer and Shady puts the toe of his boot in his side. He yells and when Shady releases it, he starts talking.

"They didn't come from an MC. The only way you can roll up without prospecting is if you came from a three-patch MC." His information isn't enough to betray his club, but if he answers my next question, that information will.

"Why are you building an army?" Silence. Just as I had predicted. He was loyal to a degree, at least. When Shady pushes against his side again, he talks but it's not what I want to hear. I predicted that too.

"Fuck you! I ain't saying shit!" he screams at Shady, who looks at me. I shake my head, a move I've grown accustomed to here lately.

"You're gonna talk, but it ain't gonna be to us. You seem like a smart man, so I'm only gonna say this once. If you fuck it up, your wife and kids will be getting a visit from us. If you don't have a wife and kids, we'll get your mother, your father, your grandma, your exes, fucking mailman . . . something. We will find your weakness and we will torture them in front of you. If y'all been talking about me like I think you have, then you know I don't make idle threats. Your SA made this shit personal. And he fucking paid for it. This wasn't an act of Sinner's Creed. It was an act of Dirk. You tell them that. If you wage a war with our club, you will lose. If the club wants to retaliate, tell them to bring all they got to me, I'll be waiting."

I turn back to the Prospects, who wear a look that tells me they are fixing to puke or cry. "When they ask you, and they will, you better let them know what that motherfucker said to me about my ol' lady. Remind them of the uninvited visit they paid to property of Sinner's Creed. If you don't, it'll be your door I'm knocking on."

I gauge their reactions and find the one that looks the most guilty. I put my gun behind my back and step up to him, his forehead only a couple of inches from my nose.

"Saylor," I say, the name burning the back of my throat like a fucking torch. His eyes widen and I know he knows something. "How do you know her?"

The man on the floor starts to say something, but Shady silences him. "Don't lie to me. I really don't want to kill you."

He looks nervously over at the pool table, knowing that although he can't see the man, he will know him by his voice. "Shady, explain to our friend over there what's gonna happen if he or any of his brothers puts a hand on one of these Prospects." I can hear Shady's muffled voice and the man's low cries. He won't touch him. "Talk."

"I don't. I was told to follow her and I have been. She goes to this clinic and the club found out she was sick." He pauses and I know it pains him to say it, but not as much as it's gonna pain me to hear it. "She's dying." The sadness in his eyes is real. And I wonder if he has ever encountered Saylor, or if he is affected by her from a distance.

"How do they know that? Did she tell you?"

"No! Tick, the SA, he talked to her but all he said was that he was your friend. They were in the lobby at the hospital. He never went back . . ." He trails off and I pull my gun from behind my back. I place the barrel right between his eyes, scared that even though this isn't his fault, his answer might make me angry enough to kill this innocent kid.

"Did he touch her?" I snarl, feeling a mixture of panic and anger forming inside of me.

"He just kissed her hand." I lower my gun, the relief that he only saw her in a public place and that she wasn't harmed, almost bringing me to my knees. The anger inside me dies. The panic dies. Saylor will soon die. My sadness is back.

"Get him to a hospital." I sidestep the Prospects, and Shady is beside me as we jog to our bikes. Sirens are in the distance and I'm sure they're not for us. Nothing neighbors the building, and the traffic from the interstate is loud enough to drown out any sound that might reach a passing car. But the noise is enough to have me distancing myself from the scene as fast as possible.

And there isn't a sound loud enough to drown out the Prospect's words that are screaming in my head. "She's dying."

As soon as we returned to the clubhouse, Shady put a call in to Jackson, ordering the chapter to keep eyes on Saylor 24-7. If any member of Death Mob came within a five-mile radius of her, they would handle it. It should be me protecting her, but I'm still battling with my pride, and my pride is still winning.

Other than a flesh wound on my arm, which I'm just now feeling, and a small cut on Shady's cheek from a shattered window, we returned unscathed. Shady, sensing my need to calm my nerves, fires up a blunt outside and passes it to me. The familiar burn in my lungs is enough to calm my racing heart and bring me off of my adrenaline high. And enough to put me on one that will have me not giving a shit about what's gonna happen when other Death Mob chapters find out that we just killed twelve of their men.

"This might create a shit storm and I'm good with that, but we need to talk," Shady says, interrupting the silence and the smoke haven I'm in. I'll never understand why people feel the need to fuck up a perfectly good moment with conversation. I ignore him, hoping it will work but knowing good and damn well it won't. "You need to go back to her." Her. The one that is dying.

"Not another word, Shady." It's my final warning. I take another drag, breathing the smoke deep into my lungs, and hold it, letting this burn replace the one at the mention of her.

"You're a fucking idiot, Dirk." Maybe I didn't hear him right. Shady has never been this ballsy around me. I'm about to ask him to repeat himself just so I can be sure I heard him right, when he starts again.

"The girl is dying, Dirk. She's dying." I'm on my feet and so is he. I'm going to shut him up since he lacks the capability of doing it himself. But there is a gun pointed at my head.

"Just as sure as God made little green apples and I'm standing here, I'll take your fucking ear off if you don't hear me out." He is telling the truth, but I'd rather have my ear shot off than have to listen to him.

Before I can take a full step, I feel the skin on my arm shred just below the other flesh wound. "The next one will be your dick." The sound of the gunshot drew a crowd, but I tell them to leave us alone. Reluctantly, they do.

"Okay motherfucker, you got my attention," I spit through my teeth. My arm is fucking killing me, but I won't let him know that.

"She loves you. I don't know why, but she does. People like me and you, Dirk, we don't get women like her. For some reason, you got lucky. So she's sick and she didn't tell you. Did you tell her what you did? Did she know that the man she was sleeping with every night had killed more people than Hitler's fucking army? Man, you're so fucking blessed and you don't even see it."

Shady puts his gun away. Either he is tired of fighting or he thinks I'll stay here and listen. He's wrong. I walk away, but even though I can't see his face, it doesn't stop me from hearing his voice.

"We all gotta die, Dirk. And we never know when. We take each day for granted. But you know exactly how long you have to make this life mean something. Don't fuck it up, Dirk." I'm searching for a comeback. I'm digging for an excuse. But the truth is, Shady's right, and I got nothing.

The last person I expected to see walk through the door of the Houston clubhouse was Roach. But here he was, in old, gray flesh. It's been two days since the shoot-out and we'd heard nothing. For Roach to be showing up less than forty-eight hours after couldn't be good. I stand to hug him, but we make no pleasantries. I follow him out back, where I find Shady and Jimbo waiting. Shit. This is bad.

"Turner and Hooch. Dillon and Festus. Fucking Bonnie and Clyde." Roach is pissed. Jimbo is pissed. I'm anxious. Shady looks confused. He mouths "I'm not Bonnie" to me and I want to slap him. This shit is serious. And I sure as fuck ain't Bonnie.

"I said handle it. Not shoot up a whole fucking chapter. Do you have any idea the heat I'm getting? Dorian is gonna have my balls once he catches wind of this." He's right. It was handled wrong. It doesn't matter that if Shady hadn't pulled the trigger first, I would have done it. But I did make sure to let them know this was on me. Not the club. And I'm pretty sure Roach already knows that and it probably pissed him off more. We are a club. A family. A brotherhood. We stand behind each other right or wrong. No *I* in team and all that shit.

"Roach," Shady starts and I wish he would just keep his

mouth shut. "The motherfucker made it personal." I know the hell that is coming next.

"You think I give a shit about your fucking personal lives?" He turns to me and I know he is about to make this shit real personal. "You're a fucking idiot, Dirk." I've been called that a lot here lately, but it hurts more coming from him. And because it's true.

"If you ain't there to take care of your ol' lady then she ain't your fuckin' ol' lady. If you would've been there, then they never would have showed up. You left her, dumb-ass. You been walking around here for two weeks with your little pink panties in a twist. Man the fuck up. If you want her, go get her. If you don't, then quit putting the whole club at risk because of her."

Roach takes a deep breath, trying to calm down. He looks like death, and if I already didn't feel like shit, this moment would make me. I've disappointed him. It's a shitty feeling.

"Disappear for a while. Both of you. At least until I can get this shit cleaned up."

They leave, and Shady and I are left feeling like kids who just got sent to their room. I don't know what his plans are, but mine are forming in my head. Fast.

"I'm heading down to Mexico. See ya around, Dirk." Shady's leaving and I wonder if it's the last time I'll ever see him. We don't know what tomorrow holds. But, if I knew he only had six months to live, I know what I would tell him.

"Thanks, Shady. For everything." I walk away before he wants a hug or some shit. Shady's destination is Mexico. So is mine, but I have a stop to make first.

17

I'VE BEEN SITTIN' at the airport in Jackson for hours. I can't find the balls to leave. I don't know what she will say or if she will say anything. She may not forgive me for what I did, but my heart, the one that I managed to piece back together on the flight over, tells me she will.

When my phone rings, it's a number I don't recognize. I'm hesitant, but I answer because only a few people even have this number.

"Yeah." I hear noise in the background like two people are arguing. Then, I hear the familiar voice of Saylor's friend. It's Jeffery.

"Dirk?" I stay silent, trying to figure out who the other voice in the background is. Jeffery is obviously covering the phone. "Shut up!" he yells and I have to pull my head away from the phone. "Dirk? It's Jeffery."

"What do you want, Jeffery?" To castrate me?

"We have a little problem." Alarm bells are going off inside my head. Something is wrong.

"What? What's wrong?" I'm shouting, drawing stares from people in the small airport.

"Don't tell him shit!" This time, Donnawayne's voice can be heard clearly through the phone. He is pissed. I hear a struggle and then a door slam before Jeffery starts rapidly speaking.

"She's gone, Dirk." My heart sinks. My world stills. But Jeffery is still speaking. I catch a few words here and there, but I just want to hang up. I want to die. I want to torture myself for wasting the past two weeks being selfish when I should have been with her. "Dirk?"

"Do you know where she is or not?!" Donnawayne's scream cuts through my thoughts. *What?*

"What?" I find my voice, it's weak but it's there.

"Saylor. Do you know where she could be?" I hit my knees in relief. I need to puke. Or faint. Or laugh. My reprieve is almost too much.

"She isn't dead." I say the words out loud and I find myself laughing.

"What? No! Oh, shit! I'm sorry. I meant she is gone, as in we woke up this morning and she had left. Her coffee can of cash, her diary, and her backpack are missing. We don't know where she is."

I pull my shit together and stand. I find my way outside into the fresh air, then light a smoke. I must have told them to give me a minute at some point, because they are still on the phone with me when I use the cherry from my first cigarette to light my second. Now maybe I can be of some use.

"Okay, when's the last time you saw her?"

"Last night. She fell asleep on the couch and we stayed there with her. Then this morning, I thought she just went out to get coffee, but it's after two and she's not here. And her stuff is missing." Jeffery calms a crying Donnawayne while I think, but he didn't give me much to go on.

"Did she say anything? I mean the smallest thing could mean something."

"No. Nothing."

"We didn't even get to talk because of that damn movie." I hear Donnawayne's voice in the background and something triggers in my memory.

"What movie?" I ask, already knowing what the answer is.

"*Mr. and Mrs. Smith.*" And just like that, I'm booking a flight to Del Rio.

In the town of Ciudad Acuña, there is a bar called La Dama, meaning "the lady." It's just across the Mexican border and a place I've visited many times. The *damas* are plentiful there too. But I'm not going for them. I'm going for the white lights that hang on the patio, the endless tequila, and my *dama*, who will be waiting for me.

Call it coincidence, fate, or divine intervention, but a black van was in the border line next to the cab Saylor took. And in that black van was Shady, who led her to the place she was searching for, after he called to tell me where she was. She never asked him to not tell me. I guess she assumed I was either coming or I didn't give a shit. She probably thought the latter.

I'm ruling out coincidence and narrowing down the battle between fate and divine intervention when I find exactly what I'm looking for in an airport gift shop. Shit like this don't just happen.

It's dark, I'm standing outside La Dama, and I'm holding in my hands everything I need to make Saylor's vision come true. When lightning strikes in the distance and I smell rain in the air, in the middle of a fucking drought, I know that fate has nothing to do with this moment either. This is divine intervention. Her god didn't let her down, and it may be unintentional, but he's helping me out too.

Saylor is sitting at a table on the outside patio, running her finger across the glass of tequila that sits next to a bottle that's just over half full. She hasn't been here long and her mission is to get drunk, obviously. I'm not breathless at the sight of her. I'm not excited or joyful either. I'm heartbroken, again, and I'm on the verge of doing something I haven't done in years.

Cry.

She's lost weight. There are dark circles under her eyes, and her face is sad. Her hair is wild and crazy, just how it always is, and it's the only thing that hasn't changed about her. There is no happiness in her eyes. There is no smile on her lips. The light that comes from her and illuminates everything around her is dim and depressed. And all I can think in this moment is that it is my fault.

I've taken everything good about her and destroyed it. I've sucked the joy and will to live right out of her and for what? Because I'm selfish. I've spent the past two weeks annihilating everything good about her because I was too selfish to appreciate what I had. No matter how long I had it.

The truth is, that even if the only time I ever had with Saylor came from those few encounters before I even knew her name, then I was luckier than the people who went a lifetime never being graced with her presence. I was an idiot, but I was fortunate. Some people only get one second chance. Now I have two.

My hands are shaking when I lay the black box in front of Saylor, who doesn't even look up to see who it's from. When she whispers my name, I finally get that breathless, excited feeling of joy I should have had when I first saw her sitting here.

"You're late." I watch her lips as they struggle to turn up to form a smile. I wonder if the memory of the first time we officially met is playing in her head like it is in mine. "I was beginning to think you were not going to make good on your promise." She stares at her glass, never looking at me.

I promised to bring her here, not show up later because I'm so fucked up that I left her when she needed me most.

"I'm here now," I tell her, and my voice causes her to look at me for the first time. Even tired, sad, and heartbroken, she is still the most beautiful sight I've ever seen. Cliché, but so fucking true.

"Yes, you are. Will you sit with me?" When I do, she grabs my hand and holds it. My eyes lock on hers and I can see the dull pools of green slowly coming back to life.

"I know why you left. This isn't easy for you. I know that now. I knew that then. But there is nothing we can say to fix what is wrong, so let's not waste time with apologies or what-ifs or who was right and who was wrong. Let's just live this moment. I want it to be as special as I've always imagined it would be."

I want to tell her I'm sorry. I want to tell her nothing is her fault and I shouldn't have left. I want to tell her I was wrong and she was right and all the shit that men say when they fuck up. But she wants none of that. And it's not that important that I tell her because she already knows.

She's proven time and again that she has the ability to read my mind, and this time is no different. I'll make this night perfect for her. Better than she imagined.

"I bought you something," I say, motioning to the untouched box in front of her.

"And I'm pretty sure I already know what it is." And I'm pretty sure she does too.

Saylor emerges minutes later from the bathroom, wearing the white, floor-length dress I bought her. In her hair, I place the flower I picked from the tropical plant growing outside, and it completes the picture.

I pull her into my lap and we drink cheap tequila from a bottle, while traditional Mexican instrumental music plays in the background. By the time the rain starts, she is buzzing, I'm intoxicated more by her than the liquor, and not a word has been spoken between us.

I sit her in the seat across from me before standing and making the final arrangement to make her night special. I make my request, pass a twenty to the bartender, then make my way back to Saylor, who is still watching me from across the room.

"Mondo Bongo" plays through the speakers and I hold my hand out for hers. She takes it with a smile and I pull her into the rain. Saylor dances with her eyes closed, while I hold her hips and move with her. The rain drenches us both, but we dance on. I hold her in my arms, kiss her with my lips, and tell her everything I haven't said in this one moment. She feels it. And I feel her. I feel her love piecing my heart back together. I feel her body that moves in sexy sways in my arms. And I feel her soul. A soul that God didn't need to shine any mercy on. Because this one, this one was made perfect.

I get us a room next door. This time when we shower together, she bathes me and I don't leave when she's finished. I return the favor. Before, she used the time to memorize everything about me. Now it's me memorizing everything about her.

I memorize the shape of her collarbone and how the hollow of her throat is deep and holds water when she leans her head back and takes a breath. How the weight of the water makes her hair perfectly straight, forcing it to brush the top of her ass. How the swoop of her back curves inward and when she moves just right, two dimples form on the lower part of it. How her thighs thicken, then narrow at her knees, then thicken at her calves. The small arch in her feet and the descending order of size in her toes. Her full, pink lips that have been kissed too much. Her small, narrow nose that is dotted with freckles. The wrinkle in her forehead and the laugh lines at the corners of her mouth.

Everything about her is now permanently etched in my brain, but I plan to focus on these parts every day, just to be sure I don't forget. We're in bed and I want to make love to her. So I do. And she wants it. It's intimate. It's long. And it's amazing. I kiss all the parts I memorized. I lick every piece of flesh exposed to me, and let her fall to pieces in my arms every time she comes. Over and over again. Then I bury myself inside of her, memorizing the way her walls contract around my cock as I fill her.

I know everything about her body. I know the goodness of her heart. I know the destiny of her soul. And I know she loves me. Because she's told me over and over tonight. I guess that's the only thing I needed to hear, and I can only hope that her love is something I can memorize too.

The sun rose long ago and we're still in bed. And I'm still holding her. And today my will to stay is not as strong as it was yesterday. I can't keep thoughts of the future out of my head. How many times will I get to hold her before she is gone? How am I here when all I really want to do is run?

I have an answer, but only to that last question. I can't run because she needs me. And I promised her I would never leave her again. But I've already broken that promise once, and I'm a coward.

"Don't run from me, Dirk." Maybe it's because I started to pull away. Maybe it's because of her ability to read my mind or maybe it's because she knows me well enough to know what my plan of action is. Whatever the reason for her words, they are what I need to hear.

When she tries to pull away, I hold her closer. And I let Shady's words cut through my brain. It shouldn't take this kind of news for me to want to hold on to her. She could have died in a car wreck, or from an aneurism or a fucking kidney infection. Does it really take her saying the words *I'm dying* for me to realize our time together is limited? Even after I'd heard them, I ran. What about all the time I've wasted? What about all the nights I left her? What the fuck was I thinking? I should have held her this tight and kept her this close from the moment I knew she owned my heart.

We all have to die, but it's one of those things we choose to ignore because we don't want to imagine life without the people that mean the most to us. But, the truth is, no matter if it's in six months or sixty years, Saylor is going to die. So am I.

One day, I will wake up and she won't be here, or she will wake up and I won't be here. Knowing that I only have at most six months makes me want to give her what she desires even more. And that's me. Because I am all she wants. I can feel it every time I touch her. I can hear it in every word she speaks and I can see it every time I look in her eyes.

If Saylor only has six months, then I will give her six months of my undivided attention. I won't waste my time with fighting or ignoring her. I will make each moment count, just like I should have done weeks ago. I won't be selfish. I'll devote all my time to her and what she desires. Today we are alive, and I'm no longer afraid of losing her. I won't have to live long without her anyway. Because when she dies, I know beyond a shadow of a doubt that I'll die too.

We flew back to Jackson today, because Saylor has a doctor's appointment tomorrow. She told me this morning and she said it as if she didn't care much either way. She then told me that she wasn't planning on going, but now that things have changed, she needs to be there.

I know what changed, and the thought puts me back in my self-hating shitty mood, and that's not a place I want to be. So I ignored her words and booked us on the first flight out.

I don't want to hear the doctors remind her of what she already knows, but I'll go because she asked me to, and every moment I'm with her counts. Even the bad ones.

I could tell she was nervous and when I asked her what was wrong, other than the obvious, she said this appointment would tell her how much the tumor had grown in the past thirty days. I could read between the lines. I knew that this would determine if the six-month mark would increase or decrease.

Saylor was devout in her faith, but she was also human. Knowing she was near death was good for me because I could make her life on earth whatever she wanted. But, for her, it was one step closer to the unknown. We could say we believe all day, but faith can only take us so far. At some point, our human brain tells us we are leaving the only thing we've ever known and it is up to a supernatural being to determine our afterlife. It's not logical.

My best advice to Saylor when the time neared would be to not overthink it. It wasn't original or inspiring, but it was the best I had.

I try to be in a good mood the next morning, but I fail. I do manage to make her smile when I bring her doughnuts, but even that isn't enough to make this sick feeling in my gut go away.

Donnawayne and Jeffery wanted to go, but she asked them to stay behind. They respected her wishes and promised to be at her apartment when we got back, but Donnawayne's hatred for me grew when he found out I was going. Oh well, he would have to get used to me or get the fuck over it. I wasn't going anywhere.

When we are finally called into the doctor's office, Saylor is placed into a CAT scan machine, and then we are ushered into a room to wait for the doctor. I thought it took days to get results back, but it seemed they didn't want to waste any time. The thought was unsettling. But now, here we are, at the oncology clinic in a private room, and Saylor is performing her eye-closing, hand-touching, nose-sniffing ritual. When she is finished, she looks at me and smiles, and I smile back. I've gotten better at it and she likes it, so I'm sure I'll be a professional at it in no time.

When the doctor knocks on the door, I stand next to Saylor and hold her hand, noticing the tension leave her shoulders at my touch.

"Miss Samson!" the doctor sings, and he is the happiest bastard I've ever met in my life. I wonder if he is putting on a good show or just a sick fuck who gets pleasure out of telling people they are dying. If it's the latter, I'll kill him.

"This must be Dirk." He beams at me and sticks out his hand. Not wanting to be rude to the man that could potentially save the love of my life, I shake it. "Saylor has told me a lot about you over the years. I'm glad to finally see the two of you together."

My eyes go to Saylor but she is avoiding my stare. Years? We'd been together weeks, not years. "I'm Dr. Beasley, the patient counselor." His badge read *clinic psychiatrist*, but I guess that was more intimidating than *counselor*.

"I've known Saylor a long time." He smiles fondly at Saylor, and I shift. I don't like how he looks at her. Even though he is old enough to be her grandfather.

"What you got for me, Doc? I know they didn't send you in here to say hello." Saylor cuts right through the bullshit and I feel pride swell in my chest.

"No, they didn't." His smile doesn't reach his eyes and I know the news isn't good. "Saylor, they want you to try chemo. Now, you know that won't stop this, but they would like to see if it slows it down. It's more advanced than what your mama had, but it still has some pretty intense side effects. The team is pretty sure you're strong enough to handle it, but we understand if you don't want to do it."

"Why? How much more time would I actually get out of doing this?" Saylor seems almost angry at the thought of going through this, and I move my thumb over her hand. When she looks up at me, I smile. She returns it, but it's weak.

The doctor takes off his glasses and rubs the bridge of his nose. I know he is debating on telling the whole truth or just what she needs to hear. When he sighs and takes a deep breath, I'm pretty sure what we are fixing to get is the truth, no matter how much it's gonna kill him to say it.

"For you? Maybe a month or two longer. According to your CT results, the tumor hasn't changed in size, so we're pretty sure the treatment will help to shrink it, giving you the month or two longer I mentioned. But, as you already know, the quality of life is gonna go down drastically. The drug is powerful. You'll lose your hair, be sick quite often, and possibly hospitalized for days at a time. You can stop whenever you want, but if you decide to do this, we are gonna need at least six weeks of treatment to make it worth doing." He pauses to take a breath and Saylor finds her opening to ask what's on both of our minds.

"So, you're telling me my quality of life will go down. Even if it does prolong my life it wouldn't be worth it. Why would I do that?"

"Another benefit is research. If we test it on you and see the tumor shrinks in size, we can get funded for more research on cases like yours. It's very rare, but the number of patients diagnosed with your type of tumor has increased significantly over the past few years, and we want to find something to treat it or slow it down."

"You want to try this on me, in hopes that it will shrink it so you can get funded to hopefully invent something that can prevent this in other families in the future?" Saylor is waiting for his confirmation that they're using her as their fucking guinea pig. The last six months of her life won't be spent in a hospital, while she withers away and dies. It will be spent doing things she's never done, seeing places she's never seen and spending time with me . . . Those were her words. Not mine.

"Advances have been made in being able to diagnose these tumors and differentiate them from other brain tumors. What I'm asking you to do may just offer these people some hope, treatment to prolong their lives, and possibly even a cure." I've heard enough. I'm ready to get Saylor the hell outta here. I hoped they found a cure, just not at the expense of my girl. I stand, reaching my hand out to hers. But, before I can move, Saylor is speaking, and her words paralyze me.

"I'll do it."

18

"**WE NEED A** minute," I tell the doctor when he starts to talk.

"No, we don't," Saylor says, refusing to look at me. I stand in front of her, placing my hands on either side of the exam table, and lower my head so she is forced to meet my eyes.

"I can show you the world, Saylor. I can make all of your dreams come true. Don't do this. Don't spend your last days sick and in a hospital. Enjoy life." I'm grasping at straws, trying to convince her. I'm panicking, doing everything but begging her, which I'm not above doing.

"You have an advantage. You won't take another day for granted because you know how limited they are. I'll leave the club. I'll stay with you. We can do anything you want, just please don't do this." Her eyes are filled with tears, and she is smiling. I think she enjoys me begging her, but I don't care. Whatever it takes.

"What about all those other people? I agree I have an advantage, but what about a child? What kind of advantage do they have? Knowing they will never get old, or drive a car, or a motorcycle." She throws the last part in with a smile and I know her mind is made up. "I have the chance to potentially save lives. Why wouldn't I do that?"

Because I'm a selfish bastard that wants you all to myself. I want to tell her that. I want to scream it at her, but I don't. I just look at her in defeat. She really is incredible.

"How long we got before she has to start, Doc?" I ask, pressing my forehead against Saylor's.

"No longer than a month, if possible." That was too soon.

"I want to wait until after Christmas. It's my favorite holiday and I don't want to spend it in and out of hospitals." Saylor's demands are easily accepted. After all, they were at her mercy.

"I'll set it up." The doctor leaves, neither of us bothering to acknowledge him. I keep my head against hers, staring at the backs of my eyelids. Just being in her presence makes the world okay. When I feel her fidgeting, I know she is going to say something, but I have no idea what it will be.

"So are you breaking up with me?" Saylor asks, the smile on her face telling me she already knows the answer.

"I'm here until the end. I promise." And if death came calling for me before her, then I'd fight him and I'd win, because this time, I was keeping my promise.

"Now, I don't have time for all that damn crying. Y'all gonna have to get your shit together or get the hell out. Think happy thoughts and all that shit." Saylor's words were falling on deaf ears. I'm watching the scene unfold from my position in the kitchen. I'm propped against the counter, eating an apple, trying not to find too much humor in Donnawayne and Jeffery falling on the floor and rolling around like fish outta water.

They took the news of Saylor's decision for treatment about as well as I did. Minus the whole rolling-around-on-the-floor thing. Apparently, they knew about the tumor and had made a pact to not mention it when they were together. Now that the timeline was confirmed and Saylor was starting treatment in just under two months, their pact had gone to shit.

Saylor looked to me for help and I answered her with my signature don't-fucking-think-about-it look.

"Hey!" The crying ceased at her demand and she even had my attention. "Who is dying here, huh? Who is gonna be laying up praying for death in a couple months? Not either one of you. So don't expect me to show you any pity. Stop acting like a couple of fuckin' drama queens."

When she stomped out of the room, I heard her door slam and I was ready to kill them for upsetting her, but Saylor wouldn't want that. I figured I should say something, but decided against it.

I let Saylor fume and watched as the guys hugged, then made their way to the kitchen. They were comfortable here, making themselves at home. I wondered how they would feel if I told them I wanted to take Saylor back to Nevada. Since they were important to her, I guess their opinion mattered.

"I want to take Saylor back to my place in Nevada. She likes it there." They both turn to look at me, surprised to find me addressing them. Or I guess that's why they were looking around the room to see if there was someone else here.

"Isn't that romantic?" Jeffery asked, just before Donnawayne decided to speak.

"That's the most selfish thing I've ever heard. Why you wanna take her away from two of the three people in her life that she cares about?" I saw his point, and I wanted to tell his boyfriend the frown wasn't necessary, but it was too late. I would regret my next words, but for Saylor, I would say them.

"Y'all are welcome to come up anytime. We have plenty of room." Jeffery beamed. Donnawayne rolled his eyes. I'm beginning to think he is holding a grudge because of the whole nose-breaking ordeal.

"Well, I think we all need to let Saylor decide what is best. And whatever she decides is fine with us," Jeffery says, throwing daggers at Donnawayne, who surprisingly agrees. He sighs dramatically, of course, and nods his head.

"I guess I need to go apologize to my girl. No reason in her being pissed at her favorite." He saunters out of the room and I want to correct him on *my girl* and *favorite*, but it will just start an argument that will lead to me breaking his neck instead of his nose.

We fly to Nevada the next morning and aren't out of the airport before my phone goes off. Nationals.

"Come to the bar. Bring Saylor." That's all that is said before Jimbo hangs up. I don't know what this is about, but I don't like that they just assume I'm gonna bring her because they told me to.

Roach was pissed at me the last time I saw him, and I don't need him taking his anger out on Saylor. If I don't go, they will come to me, and I don't want our house plagued with anything that doesn't bring Saylor happiness. A bunch of bikers showing up and beating my ass because I disobeyed a direct order would definitely not make for a happy experience.

"Who was that?" Saylor asks, as we make our way hand in hand to the exit.

"Jimbo."

"Oh." The defeat in her voice has me stopping and grabbing her chin, lifting her head to look at me.

"I'm not leaving you. They just want to talk. I want you to come with me." The fact that it is them that want her there is irrelevant.

"Okay." She forces a smile and I know she's worried. Not because she thinks I'm lying, but because of what they might ask me to do and what will happen if I refuse them.

"There is nothing to worry about," I reassure her, and she sees something convincing in my face because she now seems at ease with the situation. I just wish I was.

I don't have to get a taxi because Shady is waiting for us when we walk out. I hate asking questions, but there is just something I have to know.

"Why the fuck do you always just magically appear wherever I am?" He laughs, Saylor chastises me with her eyes, and I ignore both of them. I want an answer.

"Well, Dirk. There ain't very many people in the club you actually talk to. Since I'm one of the chosen few, the club deems it necessary that where you go, I go. With the exception of some places."

He is talking about when I go on runs, but there is an underlying meaning to his words that he finds funny. I choose to ignore that too. If I think too much on it, it'll just piss me off. But I'm already pissed, so I reach over the seat and slap him upside his head. He laughs and says he is kidding, but I know it hurt.

Next time, if he's brave enough to do it again, I'll cave in the side of his face with my boot. He will live, but he will look even more fucked up than he already does.

Saylor is looking at me like she can't believe I just did that. I shrug and rake my eyes down her body. She is wearing leggings and an oversized sweater. Her boots have some kind of fur sticking out the top of them, and even though her feet have to be warm, I see she has her hand stuck down in the side of one, rubbing the bottom of her foot.

"It's cold up here," she says, and shivers again as she says it. I pull her legs into my lap and take her boots off, checking the inside of them to see that the fur is only on the top. Well that's pointless. "They're cheap. They look warm, but the air gets through them."

"I'll buy you more," I say, while rubbing the life back into her feet.

"I'm on Coumadin. It's a blood thinner. It's supposed to help prevent clots, which apparently I'm more prone to, due to my fragile condition." She dramatizes the last part and laughs. I smile at her. Saylor's laughter is a beautiful thing. "Look, you can't joke with me about buying me new boots. I kinda got a thing for them," she says, pointing her finger at me. Good thing I was serious.

"Shady," I call to the oblivious idiot driving us. I don't look at him because I can't pull my eyes off of Saylor, who is smiling with her eyes closed and enjoying the heated foot massage.

"Dirk." Smart-ass.

"We need a mall," I tell him and Saylor's eyes open.

"A mall? What the fuck we gonna do at a mall?" I like that Shady is aggravated. I bet he has plans. I hope I fuck them up.

"Dirk is gonna buy me boots." Saylor is talking to Shady, but she is looking at me, full of love and appreciation, and awe.

"Well, Dirk is gonna have to buy you some boots later 'cause it's after nine and the mall is closed." Saylor frowns, but I know she is only joking. "Now, I'm sure we can break in, but you are gonna have to be really quiet and do exactly as we say." Shady acts as if he is talking to a child instead of a grown woman. He's done it before and I've found it comical. Now not so much.

"Now I see why he doesn't have any friends," Saylor whispers, but it's loud enough for Shady to hear. When he starts to protest she laughs, he smiles, and I'm so caught up in this moment that all I can do is what I do best these days, memorize. And the sound of her laughter is stored in that part of my brain I've reserved only for her.

Nationals are sitting outside, where it's forty degrees, when we arrive. I guess they like the peace and quiet more than the warmth. I want to tell Saylor to stay in where it is warm, but she is latched onto my arm. I shake Jimbo's hand, salute a few patch holders, then wait until Roach is finished talking with someone before I go to him. I'm not nervous, but I've got my guard up considering the last time I saw him he was chewing my ass.

We hug and there is no recognition of my fuckup on his face. He all but pushes me aside to greet Saylor, who takes his hand in hers and kisses his cheek. He offers up his seat under the heat lamp, and my worry about her getting too cold somewhat fades.

Small talk is made and I'm sitting on pins and needles waiting for him to get to the reason for our visit. He finally motions for me to walk to the other end of the outside patio with him. I look back at Saylor, who is being offered a cup of coffee by Shady. He sits down next to her and even though I don't like it, I'm glad he is there to warn off any men with death wishes.

After about fifteen minutes of bullshitting, Roach leads me over to the other side of the patio, away from everyone else. "We got a problem, Dirk." I freeze at his words. Not because of the weather, but because for the first time in my life, I'm not gonna be around to handle the club's problems. I'm going to have to say no to him. To the club. I'm not torn about deciding between the club and Saylor; I've made up my mind. I choose her.

"Death Mob set us up, Dirk. They baited us and you took it." Roach seems to age a year every second that passes. He's scared. And because he's scared, I'm scared too.

"What do you mean they baited us?"

"They ain't building no army. They rolled up a few guys just to send them to Texas to die. The plan was for them to find your weakness. They found it when they found Saylor. They knew you would retaliate if they fucked with her. They didn't do enough to warrant death though, Dirk. All they did was speak to her. It wasn't bad enough for twelve brothers to die. They knew that. Now they have the ammunition they need to start a war."

If Death Mob was willing to kill twelve of their own, then I know their reasons have to be good. I can't imagine what could be worth so many lives. "What do they want?" I ask, already dreading the answer.

"They want Texas." Roach's words are whispered, but there is no denying the powerful impact they have. Texas couldn't be traded. Sinner's Creed needed it to survive. Death Mob knew there was no way Dorian would just take it from us without probable cause. But to prevent a war, they would.

It was all about the business with them, and business couldn't be conducted if we were too busy killing one another. So they forced me to kill, and were going to take it to Dorian if we didn't hand them Texas. They would simply tell him of my transgressions, prove they have every right to retaliate, and inform him of a brewing war. To prevent it, Dorian would simply pull the plug on Sinner's Creed, and Death Mob would take over our entire territory. We would become nothing. Our patches would burn, our brothers would be out of work, and our legacy would die.

"Put in a call to Dorian. Beat them to the punch. Tell him what happened. Don't give them any names, just let them know that there was an altercation and one of your men took it too far. See what their solution is." I can see the wheels turning as Roach contemplates my advice. It might not be the smartest move, but it's the only one we have.

Roach starts to shake his head, already weighing the options and not liking the outcome. "I'm afraid that when this news hits the Underground, they're gonna make Sinner's Creed pay for it."

"It's the only shot we have. If we don't give Death Mob what they want, then a war starts. More lives will be lost and Sinner's Creed will still bleed, if not fold altogether." I place my hand on

Roach's shoulder. "It's our only hope. Maybe they have a solution. If we can stay whole, keep Texas, and get Death Mob off our asses, then it's worth whatever price we have to pay."

It takes a few minutes, but Roach finally agrees. "I'll make the call."

Shady took me and Saylor home and is staying for supper—Saylor's request, not mine. They laughed the whole way here. It's innocent and doesn't piss me off. I like that they get along, and it gives me time to deal with what's weighing heavy on my heart—Sinner's Creed.

I leave them, mumbling some excuse for going out to the garage. In the cold night air, I try again to process everything I'd learned only hours ago. I didn't know what the outcome would be once Roach notified the Underground of my transgressions, but what I did know was that it wouldn't be something we liked. Being an outlaw came with a price. And I had a feeling we were fixing to pay for it.

"Dirk?" Shady's voice cuts through my dark thoughts. Shit. From the look on his face, I can tell he has no clue. "You okay, man?" He knows something is wrong, but he is probably thinking of anything other than the truth.

"I need to do something. I'll be back in about an hour. I need you to stay with her." He nods his head, and I avoid his stare. I'm not one that is easy to read, but I don't want to take any chances.

I take Shady's car to the bar, where I find Roach along with all the other Nationals, still seated outside. An uneasiness begins to settle over me at the sight of all of them together. If they'd called a Nationals meeting, then I should have been invited.

Roach asks everyone to leave us, and they do. On their way out, not one of them can meet my eyes. When it's only the two of us, Roach gestures to the chair next to him. "We need to talk." His voice is weak and it's like he isn't here. He is only the shell of the man I once knew. He shifts, flinching as he does. When I lean in, he waves me away. I can't make out much in the darkness, other than his face. It's illuminated by a fluorescent beer light that hangs on the wall next to him.

"My days are limited, ya know?" I know, but it's not something I want to think about. He has been old since I've known him. That's been for over twenty years.

"There's so much I wanna tell ya, Dirk. So much you need to know." For some reason, I get the feeling he isn't talking about the shit with Death Mob or Dorian. "I know you found that letter Black left you. I know because I went to your house and found the safe there empty." I'm not angry Roach was in my house, if it's mine, it's his, but I am bothered by the fact he knew there was a letter.

"When you were born, I was told your life was destined to receive greatness. But the world you would've grown up in didn't want you. I don't know who your parents are. The man who took you to Black wasn't even your daddy. He was just some guy who was supposed to watch over you. He got into some trouble and needed a place for you to stay. So he came to me. He wanted Sinner's Creed to take you on as one of our own. Black owed me a favor. A big one. Life or death. So I made him a deal. If he took you on, raised you like his grandson, then I would forgive his debt to me. I've regretted it every day since. 'Cause ya see, Dirk. I owed some favors too." I've never known Roach to apologize to anyone. And I'm sure this is as close to it as he will ever get.

"When I agreed that Sinner's Creed would take care of you, my debt was forgiven. But instead of keeping you for myself, I threw you off on Black. I never should have done that to you. The only man who knows who your real parents are is dead. I can't even offer you the peace of knowing." It didn't matter who my real parents were. Hell, they didn't want me, so they hadn't earned that title—or my respect. Roach was the closest thing I'd ever come to having a parent. And Black might have been evil, but at least he kept me alive—that was more than anyone else had ever given me.

I wait patiently for Roach to continue. I see him fumbling for something and pull my smokes out, lighting one and passing it to him before lighting one for myself. He coughs, which seems to cause him great pain, then wipes his mouth with a black bandana. If it were white, it would be stained in red with blood from his throat. This, I've seen for years. I've always ignored it because he did. No man wants to be pitied. Especially a man like Roach.

Once his breathing is under control, I brace myself. "I thought by giving Black a chance to raise you, it would change him. It didn't. It made him worse. I'm not gonna apologize for that because I think your life with Black was better than the alternative. I knew Black was taking money for years, and I kept his secret. Because of you. I knew if they killed him my efforts would've been for nothing. If they put him out bad, I was afraid he would take his anger out on you. This club life ain't for everyone, Dirk. It's for sorry sons of bitches like me and Black. And troubled souls like you. But Saylor has changed you. You ain't the soldier you once were."

When Roach puts his hand on my shoulder and looks me in my eye, I feel a piece of me die at the desperate man looking back at me. "I didn't talk to Dorian. I talked to Cyrus." My heart stills. My breathing stops. My blood turns to ice in my veins. All because I know what's coming next.

I'd given my whole life for Sinner's Creed. My loyalty to the club was my greatest achievement. The MC was my world. It was all I had ever been good at. I'd never experienced anything outside of the club. Saylor was the closest thing I'd ever gotten to freedom from it. And she was the closest thing I'd ever get.

When my heart begins to beat again, when my breathing becomes regular and my blood warms, I know that I'm okay with this. I'm at peace with my decisions in this life, and I'm at peace with the decision that will take me from it.

I place my hand on my brother's, trying to offer him some sort of comfort. Tears flow from his eyes moments before he breaks. I love this man. And I know that he's loved me like I was his own flesh and blood.

"It's okay, Roach," I say, meeting his dead, lifeless eyes. The look in my own tells him that I can handle this. Once he composes himself, I light us a cigarette and lean back in my chair. "So, what was Cyrus's counteroffer?"

"You already know that answer," Roach says, the gravel back in his voice. This is the man I know. The one-percenter who trained me. The man who puts the club first—always, because that's what a real soldier does.

"And you know I have to ask."

If it weren't for the regret in his eyes, I might think he didn't care. But I know better. With a coolness only Roach is capable of, he delivers my answer in true Sinner's Creed fashion—no bullshit, no reservations.

"You, Dirk. They want you."

19

I ALREADY KNEW it, but now the reason behind the Nationals meeting without me was confirmed. They had to vote on Death Mob's offer. With something as extreme as a brother's life, the vote had to be unanimous. If anyone at the meeting tonight had voted differently, then Roach and I wouldn't be having this conversation. This tells me that everyone agreed to Death Mob's demands. But there was still a National that had a decision to make. The patch I wear below my bottom rocker allows me to have a say. My vote was always the deciding factor because I showed no partiality, not even to myself. Sinner's Creed was a brotherhood that went far beyond just one patch. It wasn't worth losing over one man—even if that one man was me.

Silence surrounds us as I wait for Roach to make the final move. After what seems like forever, he finally does. Without meeting my eyes, he gives me the order in the most grief-stricken voice I've ever heard. "I need your vote, Dirk."

I am a Nomad National for the Sinner's Creed Motorcycle

Club. And I will be until the day I die—no matter how soon that is. So I treat this time as if it were any other. As if my life isn't the one at stake. Because I am a soldier, and I will fight to the death for my club. And I will do it with the same honor and respect it has shown me all of my life.

With my head held high, the weight of my leather on my back, and determination in my voice, I cast my vote and issue the verdict. "I vote yes."

And just like that, the sacrifice is given—my life for Sinner's Creed.

Two blunts and a bottle of whiskey later, we're still sitting in silence. I'd asked about Shady, and Roach had assured me that he was safe. There was no mention of him even being there. Good. The Prospects had listened; so had the patch holder. My life would be taken, but it would be the only one. I wouldn't let another brother take the fall.

Time seemed to stand still on the back of the patio, in an old bar, in Jackpot, Nevada. But the real world was still happening outside this place. And in that world was Saylor. Roach needed my company. He needed my reassurance that I had no hard feelings against him or any of my brothers. But I'd given him all I could. Now I needed to devote the time I had left to the other most important thing in my life—Saylor Samson.

"Thank you, Roach. And I don't just mean for telling me this. For everything," I say as I stand to leave. He stands with me and I embrace him in a hug.

"I love you, Dirk. Love you like you're my own. 'Cause you are."

"I love you too, brother." And the words feel right. And I see peace in the eyes of the man before me. When I leave, my last image of Roach tells me this is our good-bye. But it's not me who will die first. Roach is knocking at death's door, and my life is just getting started.

I've made a promise to a woman and I don't plan on breaking it. I also made a promise to myself that if death came for me, I would fight him. I'm not scared to die, but now I have something to live for. And I'm not scared of Death Mob. I know that once they get the okay from Nationals, they'll come looking for me. I sent the message that I wanted all those motherfuckers to come, and I meant it. I've got something for them. And it sure as fuck ain't my life.

I get back to the house to find Shady and Saylor watching TV and eating ice cream. Saylor smiles when I come in, and I wonder what lie Shady told her to keep her calm. I lean down and kiss her, give her a smile, then tell her I need to holler at Shady a minute. I see the question in her eyes, but I shoot her a wink and it's reassurance enough that everything is okay.

Shady follows me out back and I fill him in on what I was told. It goes about as well as I expected.

"Are you fucking kidding me?" I *shhh* him, then stop and replay the moment in my head. I've never *shhh*ed someone in my life. What the fuck was wrong with me? But Shady didn't notice because he is still ranting.

"Calm the fuck down before Saylor hears you." He bites his lip, then kicks the dirt, runs his hands through his hair, then makes a grunting noise before finally calming down and turning his attention back to me. "It's my decision. I won't let the club take the hit for what I did. It's my fuckup, my responsibility. This one is on me. It's protocol, Shady. Don't act so surprised."

"Well, I am fucking surprised. I'm surprised that the club you've devoted your whole life to isn't ready to go to battle for you. Instead, they just want to turn you over to the wolves with a pat on the back and a 'thank you very much, have a nice fucking day.' You may have a say, but you are not the deciding factor. I don't care how important you think you are."

He's right, but my only other option is to run, and I refuse to put Saylor through that—not that I would even if she wasn't in my life. I'd rather stay and die than to go out like a coward.

"Fuck, Dirk. I can't sit back and let these motherfuckers just take you out." Shady kicks at the dirt again and mumbles a string of *fucks*, using the word every way imaginable. His behavior isn't unusual, but tonight I find it more comical than I normally do. So much so that I smirk at him. "What's so fucking funny?"

"You. I don't know if I should be offended or honored."

"Offended? How is that offensive? And what am I doing in this moment that is so honorable?" Shady looks like a whiny-ass teenager, and I find it so funny that my smirk forms into a smile that soon turns into me laughing. He looks at me like I'm crazy. Hell, maybe I am.

"I'm honored that you think so highly of me as your brother to be bothered by this." He nods in understanding, and when I don't continue, he throws his hand out and looks at me expectantly.

"And?" My laughter is short lived, but I'm still smiling.

"And I'm offended that you think I'm actually gonna let these motherfuckers get to me. When have you ever seen me lose, Shady?" He shakes his head, his own shit-eating smile replacing the look of confusion on his face.

"Never, Dirk. Never." Losing was something I didn't know how to do. And it was something I refused to learn.

I woke up the next day to find an army of men in my front yard. My first thought was would they wait until I finished eating? I didn't like to fight on an empty stomach. My second thought was how would I convince Saylor to stay inside while I dealt with this?

I knew Death Mob wasn't going to come shoot up my house—it wasn't their style. And it wouldn't give them the satisfaction they wanted. I figured they would try to catch me off guard, then capture me before taking me to an undisclosed location where they would remind me of why I was dying and then torture me until I finally did.

I wasn't worried about that either. I wasn't caught off guard very often, and never when someone said they wanted me dead. This wasn't my first rodeo with a bunch of pissed-off people looking for revenge. I'd dealt with it many times before.

I put some pants on, trying not to wake Saylor. I pause, forgetting the men in the yard and just stare at her sleeping form. It wasn't often I had the opportunity to watch Saylor sleep. She usually beat me up every morning. Laughter outside reminds me of who's waiting for me, and I look out the blinds in Black's room to get a better count of them. But counting wasn't necessary. The more the merrier. Because these men aren't Death Mob. They are Sinner's Creed.

I open the front door and am greeted by Chaps, who looks pissed off at the world. Like he always does.

"Got some bad news, Dirk." There was no need for any more words, but I knew they were coming. "Roach is dead."

It's tradition with our MC that chapters gather when a brother dies. All states meet at a neutral spot and spend the next few days remembering the one who died. The ones who didn't know him well listen and learn. We aren't a group that mourns—we celebrate. I guess my house was the meeting point. And I knew why.

The club might have followed protocol, but they damn sure

didn't want to. I could see it in all of their eyes when they spoke to me. Having the gathering here gave them an opportunity to get to know my house, familiarize themselves with my surroundings, and offer their protection to me and to Saylor, as long as they could. This was family. This was love. I still wasn't comfortable with saying it, but it is what it is.

Over forty members fill my house and yard, and more are pouring in by the minute. There will be close to a hundred by the time they all arrive. Saylor emerges from the bedroom and into the chaos. She looks nervous, then confused, then excited when she realizes it's an opportunity to show off our newly renovated home. She's dressed in a thick jogging suit and I notice layers underneath. Her rosy cheeks alarm me and when I press my lips to her forehead, fever burns them.

"You're sick," I tell her and she shakes her head at me.

"Don't. I really need the company." Her serious look morphs back into a smile when she greets someone else. I am forgotten as she busies herself in the kitchen making coffee. She still doesn't know the reason for everyone being here. When she asks Shady, he looks at me. I nod to him and he tells her. She covers her mouth, shakes her head, and I read her lips when she says, "He was such a nice man."

The commotion and attention is enough for her to forget the sadness of Roach's loss and maybe even enough to not remind her of what she's going through.

Even though I knew Roach was dying, it still didn't make today any easier. But knowing that he wasn't suffering anymore made it a little more tolerable. I'm just glad he went out before he had to depend on someone to feed and bathe him. His pride didn't matter to us. I'd have stood in line to do my share of taking care of him just as everyone else in this room would have. But that's not what Roach would have wanted. It damn sure wasn't what I wanted. I wondered if Saylor felt the same way.

Jimbo comes up to me, breaking my concentration, and it's a relief to see his face. It's an even greater relief to see the regret in his eyes. At least I know he is feeling some remorse about the deal with Death Mob.

"You got some big shoes to fill," I tell him and he manages a smile.

"Yeah, yeah I do."

"Nah! That fucker had the littlest feet. You remember how tiny they were?" someone says, and everyone laughs at the memory of Roach's size-eight boots he sported so proudly. I can't help but smile at the memory myself. He did have some little-ass feet.

I look over at Saylor, who is ever the hostess, laying all our damn groceries out on the counter. She is offering an endless buffet of shit that I know they will eat just 'cause it's there.

I follow Nationals outside, thinking how that word will never have the same meaning now that Roach is gone. They tell me that they are gonna cremate him and I agree with the arrangement. I know it's what he wanted.

There is no mention of Death Mob, but when conversation dies and everyone starts looking around avoiding the topic, I know it's on their minds. I guess they want me to say something.

"I'm not worried about Death Mob." The sound of my voice has every set of eyes in the yard turning on me. Eventually, the crowd around me grows and I have everyone's attention. I'm glad Saylor is still inside, where I hope she'll stay. The last thing I want is for her to be worried about me.

"I'm gonna reach out to them. Tell them what happened and give them an opportunity to stand down. If they don't, then I'll handle it. Roach said they only want me, and that's all they are gonna get." I light a cigarette, using the distraction to make sure I don't choke up or get pissed at my next announcement. It's an important one.

I take a deep breath, making sure to meet the eyes of all my brothers so they know my next words are for them. "I've never asked the club for anything. I've earned everything I've ever gotten and then some. I've devoted my whole life to this club. It's always been my reason. But now, I have another reason." I pause, waiting for that feeling of weakness to hit me. And I wait, but nothing is there. There is nothing undignified about my confession of love for Saylor. And by the looks on the faces of the men before me, they don't take my news as a show of weakness, but more as a show of strength and trust. Trust in them. Something not many of them feel when it comes to me.

"It's no secret that Saylor is sick." *Dying.* "I plan to spend every day she has left by her side. So, I'm asking you, brothers, to do me a favor. I would never ask the club to suffer for my mistake, but I will ask that you help me where she is concerned. I want to keep her safe, and with the heat that I have, I don't know if I can do it alone. I need your word."

I know what their answer will be. There is not a man standing before me that will deny my request. But club comes first, and that's something I have to respect. I'm not asking for an army, I just need a few soldiers.

Chaps, who was standing near the back of the crowd of men, is now making his way forward. When he is in front of me, I feel my uneasiness grow. I can read just about anyone, but today, this man is unreadable and I don't know what he is fixing to say. I'm beginning to prepare my counter speech to his "club comes first" reminder, when he speaks.

"It's a sad day when we are forced to sacrifice one of our own because of business. But we all know that with this patch, there is a chance that we are gonna have to prove that club comes first. That being said, I don't see any reason why we can't do something to hold them off until this is over." By *over*, I know Chaps is referring to Saylor's life. I don't like how he said it, but the shadow of sorrow in his eyes says that her death will be a great loss. And that it's something he doesn't wish on her. Or on me.

"I'm sure we can come up with something," Jimbo, the new national president, says. "Shady." Shady, who has been standing beside me, closes the distance between him and Jimbo. By the way his fingers are already twitching, I know he is ready to work at Jimbo's command. "Find a way to buy us some time."

I stand around, listening to everyone bullshit, and feel more like myself now that the intense conversation is over. I catch Chaps before he walks away and do something I never thought I'd do. I stick my hand out to his, and when he grabs it, I pull him in for a hug.

I owe this man more than my respect and should have given it to him long ago. Where Black is responsible for making me the monster, Chaps is responsible for teaching me how to survive like one. Even though this is enough, I give him more. Maybe it's because of our loss of Roach. Maybe it's because Saylor has taught me how short life is, or maybe it's because I now know that words aren't always a bad thing. Whatever the reason doesn't matter. There is something I need to say and something he needs to hear.

"Thank you, Chaps. For everything." My words are repetitive. I've said the same to Shady and to Roach. But each man deserves to hear them and each time I say them, they have a different meaning.

"You've earned it, Dirk. Every bit of it." I watch Chaps walk away to join the cloud of smoke coming from the end of the porch. Then I look out at my yard full of brothers that are owed so much more than what I've given them. I've spent my whole life living inside the walls I've built around myself. Who knew someone as fragile as Saylor would be the one capable of knocking them down.

I walk inside and find Saylor in the kitchen, trying to clean up the mess the club has created. When she turns so I can see her face, I know she's overdone herself. Her cheeks are red, her eyes heavy, and her movements slow.

"Hey, baby," I say to her, placing my hands on the side of her face. She looks exhausted.

"I just need to lay down a little while. I'll be fine." I walk with her to our room and watch as she climbs under the covers. Leaning down to kiss her head, I tell her I love her. But she is already asleep.

"Everything's taken care of, brother. You don't have anything to worry about for a while," Jimbo informs me once I'm back outside. I look at him, and he knows I want answers. But, he don't want to give me any. "It's not for you to worry about. It's handled and that's all you need to know."

I didn't like being on a need-to-know basis, but if Jimbo thought it was best, then I guess it was. He was the man now and I had to respect that. It would take some getting used to, but eventually I would.

"Thank you, Jimbo." He waves off my words and we drink in silence. Rookie comes to the porch to grab a handful of beers out of the ice chest, and when he leaves I know our silence won't last long.

"Looks like we are gonna be getting a new brother down in Houston sooner than we thought. Rookie must have made a hell of an impression," Jimbo says, opening the door for conversation. I just sit there, hoping he won't ask too many questions. Roach and I had the type of relationship where questions weren't necessary. If I said something, he believed it, respected it, and upheld it. No questions asked. Jimbo wasn't quite that easy. "Is there something special about him that maybe I should know?"

"Do you doubt my judgment?" I ask, wanting to know the truth and hoping he tells me.

"Not at all." I look at him and he is telling the truth, but his curiosity is what gets the better of him.

"Then there is nothing you need to know." I walk away from him but not before he smirks and shakes his head. Rookie would have his patch, and he would have his innocence. Carrie would have a good man and the club would have a good brother. And my word in the club was still influential. I missed Roach, but Jimbo would do just fine in his place.

"Dirk," Jimbo calls out, and I turn to find him pulling something from his vest. I walk back and take the black bag from his hand. "Ain't a man here that loves this club more than you. I brought these with me, figured today was just as good a day as any." I look down at the bag, knowing what is on the inside of it. I remember the feeling of completion the day this bag was handed to me. This isn't just fabric. It's not just thread woven together to create a design. It's not something you wear on weekends or something you do for fun. It's a lifestyle. A passion. A love for something bigger than yourself. It's proof that you are a part of that 1 percent that differs from everyone else.

"Rookie!" The thunder from my voice is loud and carries across the yard. Silence descends, and I stuff the bag in my cut before turning to find a wide-eyed Rookie staring at me. I could give him a hard time. I could drag this out. I could make him do stupid shit to prove that his pride still belongs to the club. But my emotions aren't where they usually are. And I'm pretty sure the woman laying in my bed is responsible for that. I'll have to remember to tell Rookie to thank her.

The crowd has gathered and word has already spread. Everyone here knows what's fixing to happen. Everyone but Rookie.

"There are three things a patch holder doesn't do. What are they?" I ask, my death glare on him making his hands shake and his brain kick into overdrive, trying like hell to remember anything he might have done to fuck up. Okay, so maybe my emotions aren't that fucked up. I could still be a dick.

"Lie to a brother. Steal from a brother. Disrespect a brother."

"What is Sinner's Creed?"

"It's the life of a man willing to sacrifice himself for his club. It's the blood that flows through my veins, the steady beat of my heart, and the reassurance that I'm never alone. It's loyalty at any cost, love in all forms, and respect in the highest. It's what I was born for. What I'll die for and what I want to be." His lines are rehearsed, but they are sincere.

"It's not what you want to be." I let the confusion sit on his face for a minute before throwing him the bag beneath my cut. "Sinner's Creed is who you are." And just like that, a soldier is born.

20

LATER THAT NIGHT, after everyone leaves, I'm just before dozing off on the couch when I hear the bedroom door open. Moments later, Saylor appears looking well rested and fucking breathtaking wearing my shirt.

"Are we alone?"

"Finally," I answer, and she walks over to where I am on the couch and curls up in my lap. "Feel better?" I ask, running my hand under her shirt and panties so I can grab her ass.

"Yes. I'm starving and thirsty and stinky, but I feel better," she says, her face buried in the crook of my neck. I put my nose to her shoulder and breathe in, thinking she is anything but stinky. "Well, don't sniff me!" She laughs, and I realize it's the first time I've heard it today.

"I like when you laugh," I tell her, thinking of all the things I could do to make her not stop. I've never tickled anyone, but I'm sure I could.

"I like when you laugh," she says, mirroring my words. I fake a laugh, and she laughs again. "A real laugh."

"That was real," I lie, and she laughs again. Hell, maybe I should lie more too.

"I want to go riding tomorrow and have a picnic," she tells me, sitting up and straddling my waist so I can look at her. I smile at her. It's real and easy and it feels good. I move an unruly curl of hair that hangs over her eye, before telling her words that I will be saying a lot for the next six months.

"Whatever you want."

Thanksgiving morning I wake up to the realization that time is flying by. It's been two weeks since Roach's passing, yet it seems like it was only yesterday. Saylor is already in the kitchen, preparing a feast for the club. I told her we could just invite a few people, but she insisted that we invite our whole family. I like that she sees my club as her family too.

Saylor has managed to make connections with a few of the ones I am closest to, who visit most often. Jimbo comes every Sunday, and he and Saylor play cards before he and I sit down to discuss club business, which there isn't a whole lot of. Or maybe he doesn't want me informed, considering, right now, I'm inactive.

Shady comes over almost every day and eats at least one of Saylor's meals. Sometimes he stays for two. The club has him here working, so he can keep Nationals more informed of the Death Mob situation. I know the real reason is because I'm here and they think I need him right now. Hell, maybe I do.

The club has kept me in the dark about everything where Death Mob is concerned. But Shady gave me his word that if they made a move, he would be two steps ahead of them. He seemed confident that whatever they offered them to keep me around a little longer was working. I just hoped it wasn't something that could come back and hurt the club after my time was up.

Rookie's been transferred up here temporarily. I know that's because of me too. When I asked him what Carrie thought about it, he said she flies up to spend her days off with him. Saylor overheard the conversation and got her feelings hurt that she hadn't met her. This, in turn, had me pissed at Rookie. I didn't like Saylor getting upset.

He promised to make it up to her and has. Now, one of the days Carrie is here, she makes sure to spend with Saylor. I know it's not out of pity. I can't think of anyone who doesn't want to spend time with Saylor, and considering Carrie blew off Rookie for a "girls' day" two days in a row, I know she is one of those people. Rookie and Shady thought we should make a guys' night, but to me, it sounded kinda lame.

Donnawayne and Jeffery have spent every weekend here since we left. This weekend, they would be with Donnawayne's family and I would be lying if I said I wasn't relieved. It would be awkward having everyone in the same place at the same time. Jimbo had yet to run into them, but Shady and Rookie were unaffected by their homosexuality. Maybe the club wouldn't be bothered, but it wasn't a risk I was willing to take.

Saylor's health is better than ever. She hasn't had a cold, a migraine, or even a bad day since she had the fever. Looking at her, you couldn't tell anything was wrong. But there wasn't a night I didn't go to sleep or a morning I didn't wake up when I wondered if it would be my last with her. Some days we ride, some nights we go to the bar, and sometimes we don't do anything. But everything we do makes her happy, and every time she smiles, I find myself smiling too.

Saylor yells for me and I drag myself out of bed and throw on some sweats before meeting her in the kitchen. I know she has plenty of shit she wants me to do. She went over the list about ten times last night, until I dove between her legs and made her forget everything that wasn't me. After she came in my mouth, I made love to her until we both fell asleep from exhaustion. It was the only way to shut her up, and I hoped that she went to bed tonight as chatty as she did last night so I could do it all over again.

Saylor asked me where everyone would sit and when I told her "wherever," she frowned at the thought. Her frown led me to asking what she wanted. Which was for everyone to sit down at a table and eat together. Now my living room furniture is under the carport, and in its place sits a table that can seat twelve—which sits next to another table that can seat twelve. We pushed them together, made room for twenty, and now Saylor is happy. And so am I.

I bring in the turkeys that have been on the smoker since yesterday, load, unload, and reload the oven racks at Saylor's demand and help her set the table with real, matching dishes I was sent to buy last week, before I'm instructed to go get a shower.

As I let the water beat down on me, I wonder how in the hell I got here. My morning has flown by and Saylor has been so busy trying to make today perfect that I haven't even gotten a chance to kiss her and tell her good morning. When she slips in behind me and wraps her arms around my waist, I know my little mind-reading witch is finally gonna shed some mercy on her man.

"Thank you for helping me make this happen, baby. You'll never know how much it means to me." Her words are forced and I know she is struggling to keep it together. It is no secret that this is the last Thanksgiving Saylor will ever have. I turn in her arms and wrap her in mine.

"You don't have to thank me. It should be me thanking you for giving me my first ever real Thanksgiving dinner." She knows it's my first because we talked about it. But she also knows that this one would mean more even if there'd been years of them before it. I grab her hair in my hand and gently pull until she is looking up at me. "Don't be sad. Today is gonna be perfect. Just like you."

And then I kiss her. I kiss away her doubt and her thoughts and her worries. Because that's what I do. I'm the man of Saylor Samson. And I will be for the rest of my life. No matter how long that is and no matter how long she's in it.

My house is full, everyone is hungry, and Saylor is the most beautiful hostess I have ever seen. She wanted us to dress up so we could take a picture. My look told her I wasn't. But her frown told me I was. She wanted me to wear something bright because she had never seen me in anything but black. So, I'm standing in the kitchen, daring someone to say something about the bright yellow collared shirt I'm wearing. I even tucked it in. And wore the new jeans Saylor bought me.

I look like an idiot, but nobody is noticing what I'm wearing 'cause they're all looking at her. Saylor is wearing a yellow dress that wraps across her chest, showing perfect cleavage, and belts at her waist. The sleeves are long but the dress stops just above her knees. On her feet is a pair of shoes that she calls "wedges," and they're yellow too. She said we look like Skittles. Which reminded her to get onto me about leaving the empty packs on the nightstand by our bed.

When everyone is seated, ready to dive in, Saylor grabs my hand with one of hers, then offers the other to Carrie, who sits on the right of her and asks if anyone wants to say grace. My eyes dart around the room, wondering how the club would react to her request. I don't know if this isn't uncommon or if they're so hungry they'll do just about anything to eat, but they all hold hands and take off their hats. Rookie agrees to bless the food, and I watch as all my brothers bow their heads while he gives thanks. When the prayer is over, I realize I'm the only man who didn't bow, and the only man who didn't say amen.

Everyone eats, complimenting Saylor on how good everything is, and she smiles then tells them that I helped too. I'm trying to force myself to eat, but my appetite is gone. Here, in my house and at my table, are the men I call family and the woman I love. I look at each of them smiling, eating, and acting as if it's just another Thanksgiving Day. But it's not. It's Saylor's last Thanksgiving Day. And right now, I feel like I'm the only motherfucker who cares about that.

I've tuned out their laughter, their talk, and their indifference to the turmoil that is happening in our lives. I'm ignoring everything they say and do. I'm wanting nothing more than to flip this table over and shatter every fucking dish in this house, and then dare them to ask me what's wrong. Someone is telling a story and when laughter erupts so loudly that it breaks through the silence I've created, I'm on my feet and out the front door.

At the sound of my chair hitting the floor, their laughter silences. And now, the only noise I hear is the heavy beat of my heart. When the door opens then closes behind me, I'm expecting Shady or Jimbo. What I don't expect is to see the face of my love. I've ruined her perfect Thanksgiving, but the look in her eyes isn't disappointment, it's understanding.

"I know it's hard, Dirk. I know every day I smile and act like nothing's wrong, but I feel what you feel too. I'm worried about what tomorrow will hold. I'm nervous about next month. I'm terrified of the unknown. But, more than that, I'm scared of what

I'll do when I don't have you." I light a cigarette, knowing if I continue to look at her that I'll break.

"I'm trying, Saylor," I tell her, but I can't even meet her eyes. I'm staring out into the yard, searching for something to focus my wandering eyes on so they don't land on hers.

"You're more than trying. You're making me happy." She wraps her arm around my waist and tucks into my side. I put my arm around her shoulders and hold her closer, wishing like hell I had the strength she did. "Some people say tomorrow everything will be better. I don't think that."

I find the courage to look down at her, and I'm expecting tears, but what I find is a beautiful smile on the face of a beautiful girl. My girl. My happy girl. "I think that today is great, and yesterday was even better." Saylor isn't living for the future; she's living for the present, and it's the past that makes her feel alive.

Time seems to fly by. Before I know it, it's Christmas Eve and I'm helping Saylor wrap all five thousand presents we bought at the Black Friday sale. It was a fucking disaster and if I lived another hundred years, I would never want to put myself through that again. Even Saylor said that that was a day she could have lived without.

I told her it wasn't necessary for us to shop on sale and she said it was the experience she wanted. I'm glad she got it. I just hate I had to be there. So did the little smart-ass working at Target. After he got smart with Saylor, twice, I snatched him up from behind his register then shoved him to the ground. I didn't hit him but my mug shot was now on the corkboard when you walked in, listed under "Barred for Life." Not that I give a shit. Plus, it made Saylor horny as hell and we had a chance to christen our new SUV—the one I bought because she said it would be nice to have one. When I took her to pick one out she was skeptical, but when I informed her the heat in the old truck was going out, she became excited. Saylor isn't very fond of the cold.

I tried to convince Saylor that Christmas wasn't about presents, and she agreed. When I got comfortable with the fact that we wouldn't have to do any shopping, she came back at me with "it's about giving, not receiving." So I tried to convince her that I should give her something, because she'd already given me herself. That didn't work either. She said we should spend a day doing something the other one loved most, and not buy each other gifts. But we should buy Donnawayne, Jeffery, Rookie, Carrie, Shady, Jimbo and every-fucking-body else in the club a gift too. So we did. Because Saylor always wins.

I've wrapped the last pocketknife, the last pair of leather gloves, and the last fucking V-neck of my life. Never again will I do this. Which reminds me that Saylor never will either, and it brings me back down to earth. I shouldn't bitch about these kinds of things because Saylor would probably give anything to do it again. When I told her this minutes ago, she never answered. When she pauses her wrapping and looks at me across the mountain of shit scattered in our living room, I know she is finally gonna respond.

"No, I wouldn't."

"You wouldn't?" I ask, the disbelief evident in my voice.

"No." She is sure of her answer, but she needs to say more to convince me. When she sighs, I know she's in my head. Good. She'll give me what I want.

"You know all that talk you have about selling your soul to the devil? How you're convinced that there is a god, but you aren't worthy of his love?" Here we go. I'm taken back to Thanksgiving, where I told Saylor the devil had possession of my soul. It derived from our conversation about praying before we ate. She said that if I believed in God like I said I did, then I shouldn't have a problem with prayer. When I told her I wasn't worthy of his time, she told me for thanks, he would make time. Now she thanked him every time we sat down to eat. I still didn't bow. Or say thanks. Or amen. Prayer was her thing, not mine.

"Well, what if I told you, that I had the same bargain, but it was with God. What if I had a choice to live out a long and fruitful life here on earth, or one that was short, but actually meant something? Would you still think I would do anything to prolong my days here?" It's just a metaphor. That really didn't happen. It couldn't have. But I don't want to discuss this anymore.

"I think we need fewer friends and shorter Christmas lists." She laughs and the subject is dropped, and I almost want to thank God for that. Almost.

Christmas morning at our house is not what I had planned. Saylor wanted a sleepover. And that's what she got. So instead of me waking up early to give her breakfast in bed, I'm up helping her cook pancakes for all the pajama-wearing hard legs that are asleep in my house. They include Shady, Donnawayne, and Jeffery. Rookie and Carrie were invited, but they were spending Christmas with her family. Jimbo was invited, but after running into Donnawayne and Jeffery one Sunday evening when they decided to stay over, he said he wouldn't be able to make it. I didn't blame him—I couldn't really imagine them having much to bond over. Their candy cane–foot pajamas made me want to puke. When Saylor said she'd order them in my size, I had to take my bike out—alone. When I returned several hours later, I found her still laughing. It made me forget her appalling suggestion and fall in love with her a little more. I loved seeing her so happy.

When we were all in the living room, piled on top of each

other because of the mountain of presents and enormous fucking tree that took up half the house, Saylor stood in the middle of the room, ready to hand out gifts. But first she took the time to close her eyes, hold out her arms, and breathe in the scent of pine and maple syrup and someone's, probably Shady's, rotten-ass feet.

I didn't pay much attention because I'd seen her do it so many times before, but everyone else in the room watched her with curious faces. When she was finished, the excitement in her eyes was so much that I found myself smiling at her, even as she took my picture. Today really would be a great day, and tomorrow, we would say yesterday was better.

Shady is pumped about all the cool new shit he has, and I realize that this might have been his first real Christmas too. Most of the men in our club come from broken homes and fucked-up lives. That's what drove us to be a part of Sinner's Creed. Here, we mattered.

I assisted in all the shopping, but when it came to Shady, I made sure it was things he could actually use. Like new leathers, a breather kit for his bike, and a set of Vance & Hines pipes. Saylor picked out a shave kit, socks, some black hoodies, and an iTunes gift card.

Donnawayne and Jeffery squeal and hug Saylor every time they unwrap a new present. It's only clothing, but apparently its nice shit 'cause they "just can't believe she got this." When they announce that they want to try everything on, I decide I need a smoke. Shady agrees and joins me on the porch.

"Saylor seems happy," Shady tells me once we are away from the chaos happening in my house.

"She is happy." As I'm saying this, I hear Saylor laugh.

"When y'all heading back?" Leave it to Shady to ruin a perfect Christmas. I refused to think about what would happen in just a few days, but now that he had brought it to my attention, there was no escaping the reality of what was fixing to happen.

"Friday." That was the day after tomorrow. Too soon. I knew life was about to get hard. I knew it would be hard for Saylor to endure, and hard for me to watch. I wanted to be selfish and ask her again to not do this. But I wouldn't. This was Saylor's decision, one she was hell-bent on keeping, regardless of the consequences.

Shady says something, but I'm more interested in looking at Saylor through the window than listening to him. She's wearing her hideous Christmas pajamas and her glasses and has her hair on top of her head. But what's so stunning is the smile she has on her face. Her laughter fills the room and I close my eyes, memorizing the sound and putting this image with it. This will be her last Christmas, her last time in Nevada, and the last day of life as we know it. Tomorrow we will step back into reality, and it's the last place I want to go.

It's early, maybe four in the morning, when I feel Saylor sit up in bed. So I sit up too.

"What's wrong?" Because something has to be. But Saylor doesn't answer me, she just stares straight ahead. I turn the lamp on and ask again. "What's wrong?"

"Do you know who Samson is?" Her voice is calm, sweet, and melodic. She isn't sick and I'm glad she isn't crying. And the only Samson I know is Saylor Samson. "He was a man who was given supernatural strength. He had lots of hair, tons of it. That was his source of power."

I'm not following. Saylor puts her hands into the thick, unruly curls of her own hair and pulls it around to her face to examine it. "I don't believe that my hair is the key to my power or strengthens my relationship with God, but I don't want to wake up to find clumps of my best asset on my pillow. My hair makes me who I am."

She looks at me and is just as confused as I am. I want to give her words of wisdom, but I just woke up and I don't know what in the hell to say. But I better say something because she is staring expectantly at me as if I can give her some insight into her epiphany.

"Your hair is beautiful. It's fucking amazing and it's one of the things I love most about you. But it's not why I love you, and it doesn't make you who you are." That sounds pretty convincing to me, but Saylor frowns and is now even more confused.

"Then what does?" This time, I don't have to think about what to say, because the words are spewing from my mouth before I can stop them.

"I don't know what that special thing is. I don't have a name for it. All I know is that you are you, and that's everything I need. Your good outweighs my evil and your love overpowers my hate. Whatever makes you you, gives me something that I never knew existed . . ." I can't name it because I'm too caught up in the realization and truth in my words.

"What?" But Saylor already knows the answer.

"Hope."

21

NOT TWO HOURS later, Saylor is straddling me in the bed, holding a pair of scissors in one hand and some clippers in the other.

"What are you doing?" I still haven't mastered the art of not sounding like a dick, but it doesn't faze Saylor anymore.

"I want you to cut my hair." No. Hell no. I haven't said anything because the look I'm giving her should say it for me. "Please?" Her begging will get her nowhere.

"Saylor, no." She pokes her lip out, but she has already accepted defeat.

"Dirk, yes." She is persistent, even when she knows she will lose. "If I cry, will that help?"

"Yes." I can't lie to her. She smiles, and I'm thankful that she would never guilt me with tears.

"Well, will you make love to me at least?" That, I can do. I grab the scissors and clippers from her hands before she hurts herself, and throw her on her back. The passion for me in her eyes will never get old, but will it be the last time I see it?

I kiss her, letting thoughts of this being the last time we make love run through my head. If this is it, then how does she want it? Slow and sensual lovemaking so I can cherish her? Or fast, hard-core fucking just the way she likes it?

"Dirk," she whispers, and I don't know if she is begging or wants my attention. When she breaks our kiss and pulls away from me, I have my answer.

"Stop overthinking this. I know things are fixing to change, and when they do we will take it one day at a time. Right now, we have to live for the moment. That doesn't mean it is or it isn't the last one we will have."

I decide that from now on, I will do what makes both of us happy. So I make love to her. I love her slow, taking time to kiss her and taste her. Then, I fuck her hard. I drown her screams with my mouth when she is beneath me, and then let them rattle the windows when she is on her knees in front of me. By the time she is spent and I am too, we both have what we want, and if it's the last time, it was the greatest. If it's not, then I'll make sure next time is even better.

It's Friday, and I'm feeling an emotion I'm not familiar with and I don't like. Nervousness. We are sitting in a little room, waiting on a doctor to come back with Saylor's blood test results. The nurse already came in and drew samples, took her vitals, and complimented her wild and untamed hair about ten times. This makes Saylor smile, or should I say smile more. She has been happy all morning.

I think she doesn't want to show how nervous she is because she doesn't want to upset me, but it isn't because I've seen any sign of wariness from her. She looks genuinely happy. And regardless of the situation, I can't help but be driven by her happiness too.

Now I'm taking pictures of her with big ass Q-tips up her nose. Photography is something I've gotten pretty good at, considering Saylor has done nothing but take pictures and "capture moments" for the past two months. Every picture she is in, I have taken. Except for the ones where she is with me, or where we are posing with our closest friends. Another brother assumed the responsibility then. Friends. I have friends. I've yet to fully grasp that concept, but it's growing on me.

A knock sounds at the door and before we can get the tongue depressors and cotton balls off our faces, two doctors walk in.

"Miss Samson. Good to see you haven't lost your sense of humor," a young man with a foreign accent says. He can't be much older than Saylor, but the title on his name tag clearly states that he is indeed a doctor. A specialist at that.

I shake their hands, something else I'm getting pretty good at, and introduce myself just as Dirk. I don't need a title. The love that sparkles in Saylor's eyes couldn't make our relationship more obvious than if I wore a name tag that said *I'm her man* with a big arrow pointing at her.

The doctor introduces himself as Dr. Zi, and then his colleague Dr. Marks, who is a little older, but not by much. I'm guessing he is about my age. I wish they were uglier.

Saylor is talking and I snap myself back to the present, wanting to slap myself for even noticing their good looks when a woman as beautiful as her is so much better to look at. She is telling them she feels good, is ready to begin, and is aware of the side effects. She says this like she doesn't want them to confirm it. In front of me. They look back and forth between us, and I grab Saylor's hand, bringing it to my lips and kissing it with a reassuring smile. I can handle it.

The doctor is saying something about him needing to inform her of what's going on, for legal purposes and all that shit, but neither of us are listening. When he clears his throat, Saylor pulls her eyes from me and nods her head at him, giving him the okay to start the process of ruining our lives. I shouldn't think like that, but I can't fucking help it.

"Your blood work is good. I'm going to administer some fluids to help prevent dehydration, and some steroids to help your body endure the impact of the chemo." He takes a deep breath and I just wish he would get on with it. Thankfully, he does.

"What we are giving you is a liquid form of chemo that will be administered intravenously. You'll lose your hair, your blood counts will likely bottom out, and you will experience extreme fatigue, nausea, and vomiting. These are just some of the side effects. But they are the most common."

He clips a picture of Saylor's brain to a board, and turns a light on, illuminating the image. "This is the tumor." He points to a dark spot the size of a golf ball on the right side of Saylor's brain. "Usually, the problem with treating a brain tumor with chemo is that most chemo drugs don't have the ability to cross the blood-brain barrier, but this chemo is stronger. Radiation is capable of penetrating the body externally. But, in your case, it won't work. This particular chemo is too strong to be used with radiation.

"So, what we have here is a type of chemo that can pass the blood-brain barrier, but will still affect the rest of your body, where radiation would only effect the area being treated. Most of the time, both chemo and radiation are used together, but we are hoping with the success of this drug that we will be able to eliminate the malignant cells with only one form of treatment. Again, this is something new. We don't know if it will work, but right now, we don't have anything to lose."

I start to say something, when Saylor squeezes my hand. By the look on the doctor's face, I'm sure he knows he just fucked up. We have a lot to lose. We have months of good, quality life to lose. We have memories and dreams and Saylor's ridiculous fucking bucket list to lose. She is doing this as a favor. And in doing that favor, she is losing the only thing she has—her life.

"My apologies. I didn't mean to sound so insincere. What I mean is, there is no medicine available to treat Saylor's condition. This is the only thing that could possibly work." Now he has my attention.

"Work? You mean cure?" My heart is beating out of my chest and the hope in my voice is evident. Even the doctor's hand in the air and shake of his head telling me to hang the fuck on a minute aren't enough to kill my mood of elation.

"No, sir, I mean work as in the treatment will reduce the size of the tumor and possibly give her a little more time. Saylor's condition is too far advanced to cure. But, if it works, it could possibly cure cases like hers if caught in time." I feel my heartbeat slowing, and look down into Saylor's face. She isn't defeated. She gives me a wink before turning back to the doctor.

"Okay, enough with the lesson. I've done my research, Doc. I'm familiar with what's happening. Say what you gotta say and let's get on with it." I didn't know it was possible, but I fall in love with her just a little bit more. She's the strongest person I know. Stronger than me.

"Well, okay then." The doctor smiles and I can't figure out what in the hell he is so happy about. "We are going to do this in six different treatments. Due to the power of the drug, each dose will be a little stronger as your body becomes accustomed to the impact. I know there isn't much happiness to be found right now, but hopefully this will brighten the mood a little."

He pulls six clear bags filled with colored liquid from his pocket. "This isn't the actual medicine, of course, but I wanted you to see what it looks like."

The colors are yellow, green, blue, purple, orange, and red. It reminds me of something, and I feel myself smiling.

"There is a long name even I have trouble pronouncing that we use to refer to this medicine. When explaining it to patients, we like to use something with a simple name that resembles what the drug looks like or how strong its effects are. Like Red Devil that is red in color and gives your throat the sensation of being on fire due to the sores that form in the back of your mouth and down your esophagus. Or Purple Haze that is purple in color and clouds your memory. This particular one doesn't have a name yet. I was hoping you would do the honors."

Saylor sits for a second, staring at the bags, and then looks at me—her smile matching my own. When she answers the doctor, I mouth her answer as she speaks it out loud.

"Skittles."

I was informed that I could visit Saylor during her chemotherapy but I couldn't stay. I didn't like being told that, but then Saylor said that if she was going to be absorbing Skittles through an IV, it was only fair that she eat some too. So, on my ride to the store, I take the time to go over everything the doctor said.

She would receive one treatment a week. Every Friday. There would be six cycles before they did another CT scan to see if the medicine had worked. A port was placed in her arm to prevent damage to her veins and to make her visits less painful. They weren't sure when or how often the side effects would take place. They didn't know to what extent they would be either. She would more than likely have nausea, vomiting, diarrhea, mouth sores, weakness, fatigue, hair loss, weight loss, and a lot of fucking discomfort. But the talk of blood transfusions and low immune system was what concerned me most.

She would be more prone to infection, which could result in her being hospitalized. Dehydration was another potential side effect, which would also cause her to be hospitalized. My job was to try and make sure none of these things happened. I couldn't prevent all of it, but I could keep her eating, drinking, and away from any sneezing, sniffling motherfucker within a hundred-mile radius.

When I'm back at the clinic, I'm led to a room where the brightest thing inside of it is Saylor and her yellow, stage-one bag of Skittles. The room doesn't offer any privacy. A dozen reclining chairs are arranged in a semicircle with a big nurse's desk that sits centered in front of them. All the chairs are occupied, with Saylor sitting in the one third from the end.

There are people ranging in age from teenagers to senior citizens. Saylor seems to be having a conversation with the two old men sitting next to her. The doctor warned her that these people would likely be the same people she saw every week. He also told her that it was very common to come in and find that someone has passed. His suggestion was to not mention it or discuss it with other patients, because studies showed that it caused a decline in people's health when they experienced the loss of someone fighting the same battle they were.

I don't see why in the hell they would make you sit in a room full of people fighting for their lives anyway. It's fucking depressing. Couldn't they put them in a cubicle or something?

When Saylor's laugh fills the room, I'm drawn to her, and I notice everyone else is too. I wonder if this place has ever been graced with someone like Saylor. Even though these people are sick and possibly dying, they should be happy they are getting the gift of Saylor Samson. I'm sure she will win them all over and, judging by their smiles, she already has.

"Dirk!" Saylor calls, motioning with her hand for me to come over. She is the happiest I've seen her all day. I make my way over, and am introduced to the two old men beside her. "This is Hershel and Ralph. Guys, this is my Dirk." I like how she says *my*

Dirk. I shake hands with the men, whose grips are strong even though their bodies look tired and weak.

I pull a chair up next to Saylor and present her with a bag of Skittles. Lucky for everyone else in the room, I bought several bags. After Saylor orders me to get some medicine cups from the nurse's desk, we begin filling them with candy and then I'm instructed to pass them out. An hour later, I'm asked to step out while they begin unhooking some of the patients, and I leave to a chorus of "bye, Dirk" and "thanks for the Skittles."

I call Shady once I'm in the waiting room with the other chemo patients' families, who all look like they've done this a few times before.

"Yeah." The distress in Shady's voice has me turning my back to the unmindful people in the room.

"What's wrong?" I bark, trying to keep my voice down.

"Nothing that you need to worry about. I'll be there in the morning." I don't like Shady's attempt at blowing me off, and I'm thinking that he isn't alone.

"Who is with you?" I ask, this time making sure to lower my voice as much as possible. It's not the people in this room I'm worried about; it's the ones in the room with him.

"Nobody. I'm just having a bad day. How's Saylor?"

"She's fine. Stop trying to change the topic. What the fuck's wrong?" This time I growl, and the lady sitting closest to me frowns, but doesn't look up from her crossword puzzle.

"We bought you the six months you needed with cash. But I've been doing some digging and it looks like they're planning an attack. They're gonna go back on their word, Dirk. Or either they're fixing to demand more. The club can't afford to give them any more." Fuck. I drop my head and walk out, knowing I'll have to walk a block to smoke a cigarette and knowing it will be worth every step. Fucking smoke-free environment.

But when I'm outside, I light up immediately, needing the nicotine more than I care about the ticket I'll get if I'm caught.

"How much more you need? I've got about half a mil. I can probably get that much more." Just the thought of paying those assholes any amount of money pisses me off, and I'm sure there will be indentions in the concrete with every stomp of my foot.

"We're already giving them five, Dirk. Something tells me an extra million isn't going to make much of a difference." His words shatter me. My club was giving up a lot just to spare me six months. I guess they thought it was the least they could do considering I was preventing them from losing the club altogether.

This was my family. And they were willing to lose every dime we had just to grant me my dying wish—to live long enough to take care of Saylor.

"Shady, I don't know what to do here." I'm the epitome of the phrase *stuck between a rock and a hard place*. For the first time in my life, I am lost.

"I'll find something, Dirk. I swear. I'll find something more important to them than money, more than Texas, and more than you."

I hang up the phone and make my way back to Saylor. I have a woman who needs me. I've made a promise to her. She trusted me when I gave her my word that I would be there until the end. But I'm terrified that death is knocking on my door.

I finally have a real purpose in this life. I can't be defeated. I can't give up. I know Shady will do everything he can, but I'm afraid it might not be enough. Before I'm opening the door to the small chapel provided at the clinic, I've got a plan forming for death if he comes. And I'm calling in a favor.

22

I MAKE IT back to Saylor just as they are unhooking her. She is all smiles until she sees my face. When her brow wrinkles, I force the corner of my lip to turn up, and diminish all thoughts but her from my mind.

She looks fine. Great. Better even, but I know all that can change in a matter of minutes. I ask her how it went and she tells me all about the new people she met. Apparently, she is now on a first-name basis with everyone she will be sharing a room with every Friday.

She talks animatedly about her plans to brighten up the room, and has already talked to the doctor and gotten his approval. She even contacted the art department at Jackson State University, and they promised to have her request filled by Thursday of next week. The local Home Depot would be donating the supplies, and she asks me to forgive her for using up some of her charm to convince the manager to do it. I do, of course, and then wonder if the manager was a man and if she was using the word *charm* instead of *flirt* to keep me from paying him a visit. I decide that the excitement Saylor has about her project is more important. At least the "charming" was done over the phone.

She wants ice cream, and I drive through Dairy Queen and am introduced to the Peanut Buster Parfait. It's the most delicious fucking thing I've ever tasted, other than Saylor, and we agree to make it part of our Friday post-treatment routine.

When we get back to Saylor's apartment, Donnawayne and Jeffery are there waiting. Because we flew home and Saylor doesn't have a car here, we borrowed theirs for the day. Shady was driving ours back from Nevada. He claimed he would be here in the morning. I sure as hell hope so. Driving a hybrid was sucking all the masculinity out of me.

While Saylor told Donnawayne and Jeffery about her visit, I stepped outside to call Shady back. But not before kissing Saylor's lips and telling her to holler if she needed me. This earned me a sigh from Jeffery and an eye roll from Donnawayne. Even after everything, he still didn't like me. I started to tell him that the fucking shirt he was wearing so proudly was bought with the money someone paid me to kill a man that looked similar to him, but then thought better of it. I didn't want to upset Saylor.

"What was wrong today?" Saylor asks while we are lying in bed. I'm rubbing her naked thigh, staring at the ceiling while she writes in her diary. I want to tell her the truth, but I can't.

"How do you feel?" I ask, avoiding her question. She gets it and doesn't push the issue.

"I feel great. I have tons of energy." We both know that this won't last long. The doctor warned us that the steroids would give her a false sense of well-being and to not overdo it just because she felt good.

"You still drinking?" I ask, catching a peek of her bare ass as she leans over and grabs her half-empty bottle of Gatorade off the nightstand.

"Yep." She turns the bottle up and drains it. Glad I have something to do, I get up to get her another one out of the fridge. My job as a Nomad was to always pay attention to my surroundings. I heard things and noticed things that wouldn't attract most people's attention. So when I hear the sound of muffled voices outside the kitchen window, I know they are not the voices of Saylor's neighbors.

Even though the next-door neighbors often hang out on their back patio this time of night, and their sound often travels through our kitchen, I can decipher between what is and isn't familiar to me. And these are the voices of people I'm not familiar with.

I walk casually back to the bedroom and stand in the door, waiting for Saylor to notice me. Within seconds she looks up and smiles, then I watch her face fall and head nod when I put my finger over my lips. I walk to the bed, making sure to put my body between her and the window, and take her hand, leading her into the bathroom, where there are no windows.

"I need you to lay down in the tub. Don't make a sound. There are some men here and I don't know what they want." I turn to leave and she grabs my hand, panic filling her eyes. "I'm coming right back. I promise." I kiss her softly on her lips and leave, hoping like hell she listens to me.

I pull my gun from my bag at the foot of the bed, then poke my head back into the bathroom to find Saylor laying in the tub. Her eyes are wide and scared, so I shoot her a wink. She offers me a small smile, but my wink does nothing to ease her worry.

I close the door, and when I'm out of her sight, I put my gun up and make my way down the hall. I'm sure nobody is inside, but I don't know Cyrus or what he is capable of. If he wants me dead, I'm sure he is the kind of man that will stop at nothing to get just what he wants. I grab my phone off the table, making sure it's on silent before I punch in Shady's number.

"Yeah?" This time, Shady must sense something is wrong because he is anxious.

"I got a problem," I whisper into the phone, and the sounds I hear on the other end tell me he is already on his way.

"Six minutes," he answers, and I hang up, putting the phone on the floor because there is nowhere else to put it considering I'm only wearing boxers. I hope like hell they don't kill me tonight. Mainly because of Saylor, but I damn sure don't want them to drop me wearing nothing but my fucking underwear, and I don't have the time to waste getting dressed.

The voices are now in the front parking lot instead of out back. I don't know how long I have, but I'm sure that within six minutes, someone is gonna be dead. A knock at the front door has me nearly jumping out of my skin and shooting out of impulse. The thought of being caught off guard is more terrifying than what's on the other side of the door.

I can hear my heart beating in my ears and I wonder why I'm so worked up. Maybe it's because I'm so wired. Maybe it's because Saylor is here. Or maybe it's because for the first time in my life, I'm scared of dying. A knock sounds again and this time I expect it. Unless Cyrus is stupid, or just don't give a fuck about respect, he isn't gonna shoot me as soon as I open the door. His street cred would go to shit for being such a pussy. Taking out a man like me should be done in a more brutal way. This will ensure you high respect and earn you the fear of other men. Shooting me at my door, well that just shows that you were too weak to take me on.

I think of Saylor and what they will do to her if they kill me. Then I think of Shady and how he is now only five minutes out and will likely be able to track them down and get her back, if they even take her. Fuck it.

I put the gun behind my back and open the door, making sure my facial expression tells whoever is on the other side that I'm fucking pissed. When I see Cyrus standing with his arms clasped in front of his waist, showing me that he isn't holding a gun, I immediately feel the fear of dying leave me. Then I get pissed that it was ever there in the first place.

There are four men standing around Cyrus, but none of them wear cuts. Even though Cyrus is proudly wearing his. I open the door wide, then walk backward to retrieve the phone from the floor, never taking my eyes off the five men crowding my doorway. I hit redial and put the phone to my ear.

"Two minutes." He must have taken a shortcut.

"No need," I respond, watching as the corner of Cyrus's lip turns up slightly.

"I'll be two blocks over. I'll have eyes on you; you'll have none on me." I hang up, knowing in two minutes, Shady will be in the shadows if any of these men try anything stupid. The knowledge is reassuring.

"We'll be in the parking lot across the street when you're ready." Cyrus turns to leave and I shut the door, watching his retreating back. I find Saylor still in the bathtub. This time, she is praying. Or asleep. When I say her name, her eyes open and prayer is confirmed.

"I'm going across the street to talk to some people. Shady is close and nothing is gonna happen, but I need you to stay in here until I get back. I'll only be ten minutes."

My words do nothing to ease her mind and I know she is fixing to fire off questions at me. I open the door wide and point to the alarm clock on the nightstand that is visible from where she is. "Ten minutes." I pull on some jeans and a shirt, tucking my gun in the back of my pants, and slip my boots on. I walk outside, lighting a smoke on my way over to where Cyrus and his men are standing. I position myself so that I can see the front of the apartment in case someone has balls big enough to try to go in.

"No one is gonna mess with your girl, Dirk." I remain silent, knowing that my ten minutes have already dwindled to eight. "I know that wasn't your call. I know Tick, the SA your man Shady shot, initiated the fight. You say he made it personal. I don't care. You know as well as any man that wears a patch that right and wrong goes out the window when it comes to your brothers. I didn't know the club had taken it upon themselves to seek out Saylor."

The mention of her name from his mouth makes me want to pull my gun out and end this all now. And I don't try to hide how I feel. He already knows Saylor is my weakness. And I know he is lying. He was fully aware of what they did.

"The twelve men I buried, their blood is on your hands. And their deaths will be avenged." He pauses, and I see his eyes flick to the pocket of my jeans. "I'm gonna ask you for a cigarette, Dirk. I don't want the men whose guns are trained on my head to fire when I reach for my own." He knew Shady was here. It doesn't make him good, it just makes him experienced. He would be stupid to think I would walk out here all alone.

I hand him a smoke and even light it for him, then offer one to his men, who refuse. I don't want a gunfight any more than they do. "But avenging my brothers' death is only worth it if I get something out of it. When Sinner's Creed offered your life in return for peace, they had one exception. They wanted me to give them six months. I refused, so they sweetened the deal. Not only are they giving me you, they're giving me five mil on top of it.

So, if you think about it, your club is actually paying me to take you out. I never thought Sinner's Creed was the type to turn on their own. I guess I was wrong. But killing you won't bring back my brothers. So I have a new demand. Your club has something I want. Something that can make this all go away."

I watch his eyes as they dance with pure fucking elation at the question that he thinks is running through my head. What the fuck could he possibly want? But I already know what they want. If he's waiting for me to ask, he'll be waiting all night. Or at least he would any other time. But I don't have all night. I have four minutes.

"What?" I ask, feigning boredom.

"I want Texas."

"Why?"

"Why is not important. All that you need to know is Texas belongs to Death Mob. If a Sinner's patch rolls through, he better have permission from me before he does."

"You already know that's not going to happen."

"I was asked to spare your life for six months. That was two months ago. Now I'm rethinking the negotiation. So it would be in your best interest to make this happen." Cyrus's suggestion sounds so simple coming from his mouth. And just like Jimbo predicted, he is going back on his word. But what he doesn't know is that I have something he wants too.

"I don't think you're in a position to negotiate," I say, unable to hold back my smirk as I watch the fear spread across his face.

"What the fuck does that mean?"

"It means that you made a deal. You gave your word. But, because we're aware of what a lying piece of shit you are, we collected something of yours." The monster inside me becomes ecstatic at the thought of his reaction when he finds out what it is I have.

But he surprises me when he laughs. "What the hell do you have that can be more important to me than Texas?"

I give him my best smile. One that wipes that shit-eating smirk right off of his face. Shady really was the best at what he did. And he found out a secret Cyrus never thought would ever surface.

"I have your daughter."

23

"**I PRAYED TODAY,**" I tell Saylor when we are back in bed. Her back is to my front and I feel her tense in my arms.

"What did you say?"

"I prayed today." She turns to face me, the light from the scent warmer on the dresser just enough for me to make out the unbelieving smile on her face. It makes her so happy that I elaborate. "I prayed for both of us," I tell her, and I see a glint of sadness in her eyes before she smiles wider.

"That's great, Dirk." She kisses me before snuggling in closer. But I want to tell her more.

"It worked," I say, still not believing that it did. I'm sure God did it for her, but the fact that I asked and he actually listened was enough. She pulls her head back, and this time confusion floods her face.

"I don't understand." Then I realize why she doesn't. She thinks I prayed she would get better. Maybe I should have. Maybe I will.

"I don't want to go into detail about it. I just needed something to go away for a while so I could concentrate on you. I know that no one will take care of you like I will, and I think God knows that too. So I asked on your behalf if he would give me a little more time before I had to deal with it. Tonight, I got confirmation that he did." Maybe that was a little too much information. Now Saylor is propped on her elbow, and I have her full, inquiring attention.

"Deal with what? Are you in trouble?" I laugh at her concern, even though it really isn't funny. She smiles, and I watch her eyes as they fall to my mouth. She likes when I laugh.

"No, baby. I'm not in trouble. It's just some club business I have to handle. I thought I was going to have to do it sooner rather than later, but it worked in my favor. Maybe it was just coincidence." This has her head shaking furiously.

"There is no such thing. If you asked and got it, then it was 'cause he gave it to you. Don't go looking for any other explanation than that." I can already tell she is fixing to go into a huge spill about God and how wonderful he is and how magnificent he is and all that, so I shut her up with a kiss. Then I do what I done last night. This time, I make sure that yesterday wasn't better, by making sure today is the best.

After Saylor is asleep, I walk outside and stare up at the sky, thanking God for the first time in my life. I called in my favor, and he gave it to me. Shady found the leverage we needed, Cyrus found something more valuable than Texas, and Death Mob would give me four months of life before getting their revenge. And it was all the time I needed.

Tuesday, I got the first taste of what the next six weeks would consist of. Saylor was fine one minute, drinking chocolate milk at the kitchen table. The next, she was vomiting all over the floor. There was no warning, it just hit her suddenly.

It stopped as suddenly as it started, but when she realized the mess she'd made, she began to get upset and insisted on cleaning it up herself. Because she begged me, I stepped outside and smoked while she did.

That night, she was laying in bed, sound asleep, then woke up vomiting. Before she could make it to the bathroom, the diarrhea started. This time when she tried to push me away, I refused to leave.

I helped her shower, then put her clothes and the sheets in the wash before remaking the bed. I placed a trash can by the bed, but since her sickness was so sudden, I wasn't sure it would work. We spent the next hour sitting up while she sipped a glass of Gatorade. I was sure it wasn't enough to hydrate her, but she said she couldn't stomach any more.

Wednesday morning, she got worse. When Donnawayne and Jeffery came over with doughnuts, she was only two bites in when the nausea hit her again. I expected them to freak out or be grossed out and make a scene, but they simply helped me clean up, ignoring her feeble attempts to do it herself and reassuring her it was okay every time she apologized.

By that night, her throat was so raw that every time she threw up what little bit she drank, tears would fall from her eyes from the pain. But she never complained. I called Dr. Zi on the cell number he gave me, and told him what was happening. He said it was normal, and that the steroids were wearing off, that was why she was experiencing the sickness now.

He told me a home health nurse would be over Thursday morning to give her an IV of fluids, so she wouldn't have to go out.

When the nurse arrived the next day, she gave Saylor two bags of fluid, and before she left, I could already tell a difference. That night, she managed to eat some applesauce and Jell-O. By the time we went to bed, she was in a much better mood, and had some of her strength back.

Friday morning, we had to be at the hospital for treatment by ten. Saylor ate some oatmeal, drank two glasses of water, and bathed me when we showered. I tried to stop her, but she told me she needed it.

When we arrived at the hospital, they did blood work first and found that Saylor was still dehydrated. They upped the dosage of steroids, administered two more bags of fluid, and this time, Saylor took the green bag of Skittles. While she was in treatment, I went out and brought back the Skittles you can eat, and she managed to eat ten or twelve with no problem.

She had lost three pounds, but it wasn't enough to notice. By the time her treatment was over, I was sure Saylor had put makeup on. The color was back in her cheeks, the life was back in her eyes, and she was laughing. It still sounded like she had a cold, but her laughter was heart wrenching in all forms.

After we said good-bye to everyone, Saylor and I were asked to go to the maintenance department. There, we found sixty new ceiling tiles that would replace the old ones in the room where she took her treatment. They were painted in bright colors consisting of different scenes. I wasn't surprised to find a sunset, a rainbow, and a clear blue sky. The maintenance man promised her that he would have them installed tomorrow.

Our weekend was good. Saturday, the high was in the sixties, which wasn't unusual for January in Mississippi, and I took Saylor out for a ride on the bike. Sunday, Donnawayne and Jeffery came over. I grilled, then they all sat down to watch chick flicks. I chose this time to go over to the clubhouse and hang out with Shady.

On Monday, Shady, Rookie, and Carrie came over and the guys drank beer while the women sat and gossiped, or did whatever in the hell it is women do. Saylor was doing so good that I figured the increased dosage on the steroids was enough to keep her body fighting against the medicine. But it's Tuesday morning and Saylor has been puking her guts up for the last ten minutes.

I know she doesn't have much dignity left and if it gets worse, she will lose it altogether, so I give her some space. She had said that the vomiting isn't as embarrassing as the diarrhea. It doesn't bother me though. I love her, and nothing she does could ever make me think less of her. I just see it as her body ridding itself of poison, no matter what orifice it chooses to come out of.

I fix Saylor a glass of water, grab the trash can and a bottle of Gatorade, and then head back to the bathroom. When I tap on the door, I get no response. So I open it. And my heart stops. Saylor is lying on the floor in her pajamas that are covered in vomit and feces, shaking and crying. Sobbing. And in her hand is a clump of her beautiful hair.

"It just keeps falling out." She cries, pulling another wad of loose hair from her head. I fall to my knees beside her and take her in my arms. Not knowing what do to. She wails so loud, it scares me. She hiccups in the back of her throat, and another round of vomiting begins. It's all over me before I have the chance to position her over the toilet, but I don't pay it any attention. My eyes are drawn to Saylor's scalp, which is visible through the large bald spot in the back of her head. "I'm so sorry," she manages, while trying to catch her breath.

"Baby, it's okay," I tell her, rubbing her back while her head rests on the side of the toilet. The scent of the room is off and I take notice of what's around me. This isn't vomit; it's bile. I'm glad I'm equipped with a wrought iron stomach; I just wish Saylor was too.

She continues to vomit until there is nothing left and the scent alone has her gagging and dry heaving. I struggle to pull her pajama top over her head, which is a task considering she lacks the strength to hold herself up. I sit her on the toilet and remove her pants, hiding them so she can't see what they're covered in. Not wanting to wash her hair for fear that it will fall out and add to her distress, I sit her in the tub and grab the glass beside the sink to bathe her.

When she is clean, I leave her sitting in the tub while I clean up the bathroom. Once her clothes are washing, the bathroom floor and toilet are clean, and the loose strands of hair are disposed of, I wrap her in a towel and carry her to the bedroom, propping her in the middle of the bed against the pillows.

"Saylor," I say and a piece of me dies at the sight of how sad she looks. I could beat around the bush, but I'm not. This is her and I'm me and she wants it straight. This shit might affect our daily lives, but it doesn't change who we are.

"Your hair is falling out pretty bad. I remember what you said to me the other week. And if you still want me to, I will." She cries a little harder, but nods her head. I leave her to get a chair from the kitchen, a towel, and the scissors. Then I position her in front of the floor-length bathroom mirror behind the door so she can watch.

"Will you take a picture?" she asks, and I leave to retrieve the camera and throw some sweats on in the process. I come back and take my first-ever bathroom mirror picture. She manages a smile and I give her a smirk before snapping a few more. I grab her hair in my hand, at the base of her neck, watching as some of the strands fall out with the slightest pull.

"You ready?" I ask, meeting her eyes in the mirror. She takes a deep, staccato breath and nods. I lean down to her ear, never taking my eyes off of hers. "You will still have your power, Saylor. It's in your heart, not in your hair. And you will still be you." A tear falls from her cheek and it causes a burning in the back of my own eyes.

I look away long enough to line up the scissors, then meet her gaze before making the first cut. She closes her eyes when the sound echoes in the bathroom, and I look down to finish cutting the ponytail in my hand away from her head. When it is gone, I hold the long locks out to her and she takes them from me.

While she strokes them, I concentrate on cutting the remaining long strands, then take the clippers and run them over her head until the only thing left is a short fuzz that I'm sure will wash off in the shower. I step in front of her, kneeling down and lifting her chin so she is looking at me. "You are beautiful." And she is. Her hair was something I found remarkable about her, but now I find that she is even more perfect without it. It allows me to see a part of her that I haven't seen, which is just as flawless as every other part of her body. "I like that I can see more of you. Too much of a good thing is a good thing, and I will never get too much of you."

When Saylor is asleep, I call Donnawayne and Jeffery and ask them to come over. It's only been ten minutes and they are at the front door. Judging by their disheveled looks, they came in a hurry with no regard to their appearance, which speaks volumes for them.

"I need a favor," I say while I pour my coffee. My back is to them because I can't look them in the eye. I know it's stupid. They care about Saylor too, but it's a blow to my pride to ask them for help when I should be able to handle everything.

"Whatever you need, Dirk." Donnawayne's voice catches me

off guard. I know he is doing this for Saylor but the fact that he is addressing me says we are making progress.

"I shaved Saylor's head this morning." This time, I meet their eyes and the room is filled with a silent sadness so thick you couldn't cut it with a knife. "I don't know much about fashion, so I was hoping y'all would go get her a wig or some head scarves and shit. Something to make her not so self-conscious. We all know how important her hair was to her."

"We will take care of it. Anything else she needs?" Jeffery asks, not bothering to wipe the tears from his face.

"Some more pajamas. Maybe some that button up." Diapers probably wouldn't be a bad idea either, but I don't want Saylor having to wear those. I could never ask her to do that. Cleaning her didn't bother me anyway.

They go to leave, and I have to force them to take the wad of cash. I don't know their financial situation. All I know is that she is mine and I will take care of her. When I tell them this, I might have growled it because they stopped arguing.

Wednesday, Saylor stayed in bed. She was so sick Tuesday night that her body was too physically exhausted to get up. I'd had to carry her to the bathroom, and even hold her head while she was sick. Her mouth was covered in sores, making it painful for her to talk and impossible for her to eat. Due to her condition, Dr. Zi sent over the home health nurse again to administer more fluids.

Donnawayne and Jeffery came over Wednesday evening, and I had never been more thankful to see them. They brought not only wigs, scarves, and pajamas, but large, cloth changing pads, new sheets, Pedialyte, Ensure, and a home spa kit. After the fluids, Saylor was marginally better and was able to drink a bottle of the grape-flavored Pedialyte.

I stood in the doorway and watched her smile through her cracked lips at the men as they modeled all of her new wigs. She chose the short purple one to wear to treatment to match her purple stage-three dose of Skittles. Saylor told me to get out of the house awhile, but I couldn't leave her. I didn't want the responsibility to fall on Donnawayne and Jeffery, but after thirty minutes of them convincing me that they could handle it, I finally gave in.

I was missing my bike, and was more than surprised to find it sitting at the clubhouse. Shady had pulled it on a trailer back with him when he brought our car. His kindness earned him a hug from me.

After only an hour of riding, I was anxious to get back to Saylor. I found her in bed, with green mud shit on her face and cucumbers on her eyes, wearing one of her new scarves and gowns. A straw sat in a half-empty bottle of Ensure, and an empty bottle sat beside it. The sight of her relaxed and not sick and in pain made me smile.

Then I noticed the two men who lay on either side of her. How had I not noticed them? They too were covered in green mud and cucumbers, wearing jogging pants and nothing else. Both of them held one of Saylor's hands in theirs, and even though it made me feel weird, I grabbed Saylor's camera and took a picture of them together. Either they were asleep, or they didn't know I was here. I was betting on the latter.

Thursday was more of the same. The vomiting and diarrhea were now pure liquid, and the mouth sores were so bad I called the doctor again. He called in a prescription for some kind of medicated mouthwash and told me to have her rinse with it every couple of hours. Because of the pain, we had only done it twice today.

Without my knowledge, Saylor had asked the guys to pick her up some of those adult pull-on diapers. I didn't realize it until I found her struggling to remove it. I helped her take it off, put on another one, and we never said a word about it. I just kissed her on her head, told her she was perfect, and was rewarded with a smile.

Carrie came over that night and painted her fingernails and toenails, then laid in the bed and watched *Sex and the City* until Saylor fell asleep. Before she left, she told me she was only a phone call away, which was reassuring considering she was a friend and a nurse.

Every day, Saylor managed to find the time and strength to write in her diary. And I always managed to find time for myself too. But, if it was pushups in the hallway or TV in the living room, I was always only a few steps away.

By Friday, Saylor was so sick I was afraid she was too sick for her treatment, but she managed to find the strength to tell me to help her get dressed, that she was going. So I did. And that included putting on her purple wig.

When we got to the hospital, the report from the doctor was good, even though Saylor was anything but. Since she hadn't been prone to any infection, or had yet to be hospitalized, they felt confident that her body was responding well to the treatment.

But it's Monday and we are at the emergency room at UMC. Saylor came down with a fever earlier today and when I called Dr. Zi, he said to bring her in. I'm watching her sleep and listening to the monitor around her beep while they pump her body with antibiotics and fluids. She's lost a total of fourteen pounds and it shows. She looks small and fragile, almost lifeless. And the good doctor just informed me that things are fixing to get worse.

We are moved to a room and they assure me she will be fine

while I run home to get clothes, toiletries and, of course, Saylor's diary. I call Donnawayne and Jeffery to let them know, giving them the doctor's orders that her visitors have to wear masks, gloves, and gowns. Then I call Shady and inform him of where I am and ask him to let Rookie and Carrie know.

I'm gone only an hour, but I can hear Saylor's cries when I step off the elevator. I'm down the hall and through the door in half a second, ignoring everyone in the room but the woman who is crying my name.

"I'm here," I say, and to confirm it, I push my lips against hers and rub her head. When she sees me, smells me, and tastes me, she instantly relaxes.

"I don't know what happened," a panicked orderly says. "I was just checking her vitals and she woke up and asked for you. I told her I didn't know where you were, but I'd see if we had your number. Then she became hysterical."

I'm listening to the woman, but I'm talking to Saylor. Telling her over and over that I'm here and I'm not leaving. I explain to her where I went and that I wasn't gone for long, and that I'll tell her before I ever step out of the room again.

"I didn't know where I was," she whispers, running her hands over my face and arms.

"You were out of it when we left the house. I should have told you." I lean over the bed, kissing her, whispering to her and rubbing her smooth head until she falls back to sleep. By the time I stand, I feel like I've been hit by a truck.

Dr. Zi comes in later and tells me that her white blood count is up and she has a yeast infection in her oral, vaginal, and anal areas, and that is what is causing most of her discomfort. I didn't know she had any discomfort because she hasn't complained. When I tell him this, he only nods in understanding and says that they will keep her until it is cleared up, but he can't promise that it won't come back.

It's Tuesday and I open my eyes to find someone dressed in a gown, mask, and gloves standing at the door. When I see his boots, I know it's Shady.

"Hey, you," I hear, and both our heads turn to find Saylor sitting up in bed, smiling. Her color is back, her voice is clearer than I've heard it in days, and her eyes are bright green and shining.

Shady walks up and kisses her head, but all I can do is lay here and stare at her. She looks incredible. When her eyes meet mine, her smile widens and for the first time in days, I'm smiling too. I go to the bed and kiss her good morning before going to take a shower. When I come back, she is eating. It's only Jell-O, but at least it's something.

"How come you don't have to wear this shit?" Shady asks, looking down at his ridiculous fucking wardrobe.

"I'm special," I say simply. He looks to Saylor and she nods in agreement.

"He's special."

The truth is that since I'm her primary caregiver, I'm exposed to her as much as she is to me. Dr. Zi seems to think that if I had anything, she would have caught it by now, and since I haven't left her side since she's been sick, I haven't had the chance to be exposed to anything that could potentially hurt her.

Then he tells me that Saylor said she wanted to see my face, that it was what kept her pushing on. I'm sure it was just a tactic she used to try and keep him from making me wear it, afraid of what I might say. She had nothing to worry about. I would've worn a fucking pink jumpsuit if it was required. Thank fuck it's not.

The rest of Tuesday was good. Wednesday, we had even more visitors including Donnawayne and Jeffery, who accessorized their gowns with jewelry and paper bows. Surprisingly, I found it funny.

Rookie and Carrie came, bringing in a big basket of junk food that I knew wouldn't last long with Shady around. But I had managed to salvage all the Skittles. After everyone left, Saylor asked me to lay with her. So I am.

"I didn't get a chance to write in my diary Monday. Will you do it for me?" she asks, laying on my arm while I flip channels on the TV.

"How about I tell you what happened and you write it?" I ask, hoping she agrees. She doesn't.

"I want you to." Reluctantly, I grab her diary from the side of the bed and open it up. I try not to glance at the pages, but I can't help but notice some of the pictures that are in it. There are pictures of her and our friends, some of just our friends, but most are of me and her. "Did you take a picture on Monday?" she asks, her look hopeful. I had promised Saylor to document every day for her. And of course, I kept good on my promise.

"I did."

"Okay. I'll add it when we get home." Home. Home was in Nevada, and it was a place I never thought I would long for, but now I do.

"How do you want me to start this? Dear diary?" I ask, thinking how stupid it already makes me feel.

"I want you to write it like you're writing me a letter. But wait till I'm asleep." I sigh and put the book back on the table. Saylor laughs at my reaction and I smile at the sound. I look down at her, noticing how bright her eyes shine now that her eyebrows and eyelashes aren't obstructing their view.

"You are so beautiful," I say, running my fingers across her face.

"You got a fetish for baldies?" she asks, blinking up at me.

"I got a fetish for you."

"You know, there is a plus side to losing my hair. I don't have to shave my legs." I laugh and have to agree with her. I kiss the top of her head and pull her closer. Today was a good day. Yesterday is gone and tomorrow doesn't matter. Only today, only this moment, and only me and her.

24

FRIDAY, SAYLOR IS strong enough to walk down for her treatment—stage-four blue Skittles. She is wearing a colorful head scarf, shorts to show off her smooth legs, and a hoodie. I brought a blanket with us just in case. The room is always cold, and considering Saylor's attire, she is probably going to need it.

It had become tradition for me to leave and get candy, and this time was no different. They had already done the blood work in her room and had it sent down, so we were able to bypass that part. I kiss her at the door and leave to go on my weekly store run. I'm in the parking lot when I get a call from the hospital.

"Hello."

"I need you to pick me up something else," Saylor says, and her voice is sad.

"What's wrong?" I ask, already making my way back inside to her.

"I'll tell you when you get back. Will you please pick up some markers and a poster board for me?" I pause in the lobby.

"Saylor, will you please tell me what is going on?"

"Dirk, will you please just pick it up? And bring extra Skittles," she adds, and the smile in her voice is enough to have me heading toward the car.

"I love you," I tell her, knowing she can't hear it enough and I can't say it enough.

"I love you too. Hurry up." She hangs up and I'm laughing.

I push open the door to find one of the reclining chairs empty. Someone has died, and the room is so melancholy, that even I feel depressed.

"Okay, guys," Saylor says, addressing everyone and taking over the show. The nurses are staring at her like she's lost her mind, and one is on the phone asking someone to come up. "The doctors here think that we shouldn't talk about our friends when they pass. Well, I think that's bullshit." All the patients take turns looking at one another, probably thinking that Saylor has lost her mind.

"Marcus would have wanted to be remembered. I'm not saying we have to mourn his death, I'm saying we should celebrate his life. So, my handsome lover Dirk has been kind enough to pick us up some things to help us do that."

I cross the room to Saylor, thinking that maybe she has lost her mind. No one says a word and all eyes are on me and Saylor and the bag in my hand.

"Ralph," Saylor says, addressing the old man to her left. He looks at her with raised eyebrows, or what were once eyebrows, and looks nervous that she called on him. "What was your favorite thing about Marcus?" Ralph stutters before answering.

"Um, well. He was a nice boy. Said he worked on his daddy's chicken farm. I like that he was a hard worker. He was respectful too."

Saylor writes on the poster board with one of the markers as

Ralph speaks. When I see her struggle with it in her lap, I locate a table next to the nurse's desk and bring it to her—shooting a look to the nurse when she starts to object.

"Thank you, baby." Baby. I like when she calls me that. "Hershel?" Saylor looks pointedly at the man to her right, and he looks around the room before answering.

"He had a good sense of humor. And he laughed at all my jokes, even the ones that ain't real funny." Saylor writes again, and so it goes until every patient in the room has said something they like about Marcus.

I take a minute to look behind me and find six nurses, some that I've never seen, and four doctors standing behind the desk. There are tears in the eyes of the nurses and curious stares on the faces of the doctors. Some are even smiling.

"Dirk?" I look back at Saylor, who is waiting for my thoughts on Marcus. Hell, I didn't even know the boy. All I knew was that he couldn't have been out of his teens, and always asked for extra Skittles.

But Saylor wants something, so even if I have to make it up, I'm going to give it to her. When determination steps in, she is impossible to argue with. But, I do remember something about Marcus, and it's not a lie.

"He always made you smile." I watch Saylor fall more in love with me. She nods, brushing her tears from her eyes and laughing before leaning down to write my answer.

"Yes, he did." When she looks back up, she is even more determined as she looks at the doctors and nurses. I move out of the way so she has a full view of them. "I don't care how long you say I have left. As long as I live, I will honor every person I share this room with if they leave here before I do. So, either you can jump on the celebration-of-life bandwagon, or you can be soul-sucking, coldhearted demons. It's your choice."

I feel my dick swell in my jeans. It's wrong. Fuck, it's wrong. But I can't help it. When Saylor takes on bitch mode, it makes me horny as hell.

Dr. Marks, who I haven't heard say one word ever since I've known him, walks up to Saylor and squats down at the side of her chair. "You, Saylor Samson, are an incredible young woman. The world needs more people like you." He kisses her cheek, then shares his favorite thing about Marcus.

By the time her treatment is finished, Saylor's poster board is full. On our way out, she stops to tape it to the wall for everyone to see. When I open the door for her, I glance up and see the signatures at the bottom, including my own, with a title above it that reads *In Loving Memory of Marcus*.

Saylor is sent home Saturday morning. When we arrive, the house is full of people waiting for us. Donnawayne, Jeffery, Shady, Rookie, and Carrie. Knowing that this might be the only good day she has this week, we take the time to do something she wants. And what she wants is to go bowling. So that's what we do.

Saylor wears another one of her head scarves and even puts makeup on. Donnawayne assists her in drawing on fake eyebrows and even though she is superthin, she looks like herself. I try to encourage her not to overdo it, but she stops me by saying, "The bad days are gonna be bad regardless, so I'm gonna enjoy the good while I can." So I just shut up and kiss her.

We bowl and eat, and I show Saylor how to shoot pool. I don't let her win, because she asked me not to. And by the fifth game, I'm trying like hell to beat her. When she lines up a perfect combination shot and puts just the right amount of English on it to sink the eight ball, I know I've been hustled. "My teenage years were spent in a pool hall. It's kinda my thing," she tells me. Little shit.

It's after midnight before we get home, and I'm more exhausted than Saylor is, although I don't let her see it. We shower together, then lay down, and I rub Saylor's back while she writes in her diary, trying to fight the heaviness of my eyelids.

"You want a back massage?" Saylor asks, and I'm reminded once again how unselfish she is.

"No, baby. But I'll massage yours," I offer, thinking that would wake me up and have me beating off in the bathroom.

"Turn over," she says, jumping out of bed and disappearing into the bathroom. She comes back holding a bottle of lotion and makes a motion with her finger for me to turn over. "Please?" she begs, poking her lip out, and I can't argue with that face.

I roll onto my stomach and Saylor climbs on top of me, her weight barely noticeable. When she digs her fingers deep into my shoulders, I can't help my moan of appreciation.

"I know you're exhausted. I know you're tired and sore and I know the sacrifices you are making for me. And I don't know if I've told you, but thank you." Her thanks aren't necessary, but it feels good to hear her say it.

"There is no place I'd rather be, and nothing else I'd rather do." I wish I could look at her when I say this, but she knows the sincerity of my words. And as I drift, not only do I feel her hands on me, but she is singing and her voice is the perfect ending to this perfect day.

Sunday morning I wake up to the bed shaking. I picture Saylor jumping on it, trying to get my attention, and smile. But then, I feel something hit my back. And again. And I turn over to find Saylor seizing beside me with white foam running out the side of her mouth.

I'm screaming, panicking, rolling her to her side, and holding her down. I'm lost. I'm desperate and I'm still screaming, but this time it's for help. I hear banging on the front door, but I can't leave her to answer it so I scream at whoever is there to call 911. And I scream it over and over again until I hear sirens in the distance.

Saylor's eyes are open, but they are lifeless. Her body is still jerking and she has wet herself. The movements are so violent that the only way for me to prevent her from hurting herself is to climb on top of her. My arms are holding down her arms. My legs pin her legs, and I'm fighting like hell to keep my weight off her tiny body. When I hear someone beat on the door, I order them to kick it down. When I'm not sure if they can, I wonder what the fuck I'm gonna do. Then I hear gunshots, and I'm afraid that whoever is coming in might not be who I think it is.

"Dirk!" I hear Shady scream from the kitchen and I'm so relieved I let out a sob.

"Shady! Shady, help me!" I'm screaming and my vision is fuzzy. When I blink and I feel wetness run down my cheeks, I realize I'm crying. But I'm not just crying. I'm hysterically sobbing and begging for help. I'm begging for someone to save her. I'm screaming for Shady, and I don't know why. "Help me!" I yell, and it's so loud and guttural it hurts my own ears and burns the back of my throat.

"Dirk." I look over to see Shady on his knees on the bed next to me, his hand on my shoulder. "Dirk, the paramedics are here. I need you to let Saylor go so they can take care of her." I look around the room and see two men staring at me wide eyed. I look down at Saylor, whose convulsions have diminished to erratic shakes.

I move off of her and out of the way of the paramedics, who immediately begin examining her. Shady has my phone and he is talking to someone, and giving orders to the paramedics. And I'm just standing here, thinking I'm in a bad dream.

When I hear one of the men tell the other one to get her shirt off, something inside me snaps. I'm not thinking rationally. The reasonable part of my brain is telling me that they are helping her, but the other part is telling me to kill. But, before I can get to them, I feel the darkness taking over. Suddenly, the floor is coming up to my face, and it's the last thing I see before it completely consumes me.

I wake up and rub my eyes, thinking how terrible this nightmare was compared to the ones I had growing up. When I reach over to feel for Saylor, my arm hits something hard and plastic. And then my senses kick in. I smell rubbing alcohol. I hear the steady beep of monitors, and when I open my eyes, I'm in a hospital room.

I sit up, cringing at the ache in the back of my head. I look over and in the hospital bed next to me lays Saylor, who is sound asleep. And very much alive. What the fuck? I go to stand, but something pulls at me and I look down to see an IV attached to my arm. I'm wearing a hospital gown. I search the room for a clock, but can't find one. Judging by the darkness outside the window, it's late at night. How long have I been out?

I look back over at Saylor, and let the memory of what was not a nightmare come back to life. She was seizing. Was she okay? I was gonna kill the paramedics. Did I? Shady was there. Where was he now? I hear the door open and one of my questions is answered. Shady is here.

"Hey, man. How ya feelin'?" Shady asks, stuffing his face with chips.

"What happened?" The room begins to spin so I lay back down, hoping it will still. It does.

"Saylor had a seizure. She's stable now." Shady takes a seat at the end of my bed and I want him to tell me everything, but because I can't stand smacking, I wait for him to finish eating.

"It was about eight this morning. I was on my way to the store and an ambulance passed me. I don't know why, but I had a feeling I needed to follow it. When it headed in your direction, I called you. When you didn't answer I knew something was wrong." Shady swallows hard and I watch his brow furrow as he relives the moment.

"I could hear you screaming, man. Begging for help. The neighbors were trying to get the door open but it wouldn't budge. I shot out the lock and . . ." He stops, running his hands through his hair and struggling to find the right words. "I've never seen you like that. It scared me."

I think back to how I'd let panic overcome me. The feeling of helplessness is still fresh and it still fucking hurts.

"I told the paramedics not to touch you. I didn't know what you would do. So I talked you into getting off her and then called Dr. Zi from your phone. He said for them to take her straight to the ER. When they tried to get her clothes off so they could take her vitals and hook to the port in her arm, I saw the look in your eyes. I knew you were going to do something you would regret. So, I hit you." I stare at him, unbelieving.

"You hit me?" I ask, needing him to confirm it.

"Yeah. Maybe a little too hard, but I figured you'd done something to me to justify it." He smirks and I reach back to feel the knot on the back of my head.

"You hit me?" I still can't believe it. Shady packed a powerful fucking punch if it knocked me out cold.

"Well, technically, the butt of my gun hit you."

"You motherfucker."

"What? You think I can take your big ass down with my fist? I'm barely one ninety and that's soaking wet." Bastard. "Look, I took care of everything, didn't I? I insisted that they put you two in the same room. At first, they refused, but when I told Dr. Zi that if you woke up after what you'd been through, and Saylor wasn't there that you'd lose your shit . . . well, let's just say he made it happen."

I look over at Saylor again, knowing Shady is right. There's no telling the damage I would have done. I want to thank Shady, but Dr. Zi walks in and smiles when he sees me.

"Well, Dirk. Looks like you took a pretty nasty hit to the back of the head. You want to press charges?" he asks, and I don't hesitate.

"Yes." The doctor laughs and takes a seat in the chair next to me. I don't like that he's getting so close. It tells me that what he is about to say is important.

"The treatment didn't work, Dirk." I just stare at him and he looks down, avoiding my gaze. "We ran an MRI on Saylor, and the seizure was caused because the tumor has grown." I think I'm going to puke, and reach over to grab the bottle of water Shady has between his fingers.

"We're stopping the treatment, and it will take about a week for the last of the chemo to get out of her system. After that, her hair will start growing back and the other side effects will stop too."

Hell, that's wonderful news. I don't understand why he looks so upset. I know they had a lot riding on this, hoping that it would work, but I can tell by the sadness in the doctor's eyes that this has nothing to do with the loss of funding for the new study.

"Give it to me straight, Doc. I can handle it." And I would. I wouldn't allow myself to panic anymore. I couldn't. It almost cost Saylor her life the last time I did.

He looks me dead in the eye, not bothering to hide the emotion in them. "If Saylor manages to live another two months, it will be a miracle, but not one we wish for. The position of the tumor is crucial, and if it grows any more, she will lose her eyesight. If it grows beyond that, she will lose her ability to communicate verbally. And beyond that, depending on which direction it spreads, it could affect her movement, her hearing, and possibly her memory."

The thought of Saylor not being able to see wouldn't affect me in the least. I would still get to look at her every day. If she couldn't see and couldn't talk, I could still talk to her and watch her smile and laugh. If she lost her mobility, I would carry her everywhere, but if she lost her memory, I would lose her.

"So, if we don't wish for a miracle, what do we wish for?" I'm asking for his answer because I can't bring myself to process my own.

"Judging by the rapid growth, and her health, my best guess would be two weeks before we start to notice a decline in her health." Two weeks. Fourteen days. Three hundred and thirty-six hours. That was all the time Saylor had left to live in her current condition. And one of those weeks, seven of those days, 113 of those hours, would be enduring the fading side effects of her last chemo treatment.

There was no positive outcome in this scenario. Either Saylor lived longer and suffered more, or lived less with minimal suffering. And there was no way for us to choose.

The doctor puts his hand on my shoulder, and I meet his eyes. Pain, sorrow, and pity are there. And this time, I don't mind it because it's well deserved. "I'm sorry, Dirk." He stands to leave and I can't help but cry out to him with one more desperate question.

"Is there anything we can do?" He offers me a sad smile and a one-word answer.

"Pray."

25

"SHADY, I NEED a minute," I say, only moments after the doctor left me alone with my thoughts. He nods and walks out. I feel the burn in my eyes and the sob building in my throat. It's just before escaping when I hear her sweet voice.

"You know, Samson lost his vision too." I turn to see Saylor on her side, her hand shoved under her cheek, studying me. Apparently, the anesthetic they gave her to help her rest wore off. And it did so just in time to hear the doctor tell me her fate.

"There's nothing to be scared of, Dirk," she says, and despite the circumstances, she smiles, bringing light to the darkness that is clouded around me. "If I can't see, it will heighten my other senses and I'll be able to appreciate more about you than your good looks."

I give her the smile she deserves, and listen as she continues to comfort me when it should be the other way around. "If I can't talk, you'll get to say all the things I never gave you time to say before." I laugh and shake my head, completely amazed that she has the ability to bring me joy when all I want to feel is sorrow.

"If I can't move, then I know you will carry me everywhere we go, and there is no place I would rather be than in your arms." I feel my smile fade, wondering what her solution is to the other problem. When she doesn't offer it, I ask.

"And what if you forget me?" This time, there is no smile on my face. There is no joy in my heart and there is nothing she could say to convince me that this loss has a positive outcome.

"Then you will find a way to make me fall in love with you all over again." And just like that, I'm convinced.

I'm signing my discharge papers from the hospital, but leaving is the last thing I plan to do. As long as Saylor is here, I will be too. Even the minutes I'm away from her to piss, or shower, are crucial minutes I've lost and will never get back. With that being said, I've cut my showering time down to about two minutes and leave the bathroom door open when I piss.

I've only left her side once, and it was to visit the chapel downstairs. I prayed, cried, and begged for a miracle from God, but I asked that it be in Saylor's favor. If he was a miracle worker, then maybe the tumor would shrink on its own and we could wake up from this bad dream. I didn't care if getting my hopes up was a bad idea or not. I was convinced that he was gonna pull through.

When I made it back upstairs, Saylor didn't ask where I'd been, but I suspected she already knew. Maybe it was God telling me that he was listening. Maybe Saylor was stronger than what we thought or maybe the medicine was weaker than they claimed it was. Whatever the reason, in two days' time, Saylor's side effects were nonexistent. When Dr. Zi came in to discuss her blood work, even he was amazed at how normal everything was.

Her red blood count was perfect. Her white even more perfect and her strength was back, as was her appetite. When she scarfed down the cheeseburger Rookie brought me for lunch, the doctor and I both watched in amazement. It was as if none of this had ever taken place.

When Dr. Zi asked if she would like to undergo another CT scan to check on the status of growth, she refused. She claimed it didn't matter one way or another. I guess she had a point.

He then informed her that she would need to come in weekly, and before he could explain why, she cut him off and thanked him for his service and that she would keep in touch, but it would be over the phone. He didn't argue and I found his decision very wise.

We visited the treatment center, where Saylor dropped off letters for all her fellow chemo patients. It was Tuesday, and Ralph and Hershel, who took treatments five days a week, were there to tell her good-bye in person.

The nurses promised to carry on Saylor's legacy and celebrate the life of the patients there. Dr. Marks had insisted that all the posters be framed with a gold plaque on the bottom, labeling their name, date of birth, and date of death. This seemed to please her and I felt proud knowing that this woman, my woman, had made a difference.

Before we left, she stood in the middle of the floor while everyone watched her close her eyes, extend her arms, inhale, and smile. And unbeknownst to her, I captured the moment.

We stopped at Dairy Queen, where we both got the Peanut Buster Parfaits and Saylor ate every bit of hers.

"I see you have your appetite back," I say, looking questioningly at her. Was it possible? I thought if you didn't eat, your stomach shrunk. I guess in Saylor's case, it didn't.

"I've always been a big eater. You know that. That's what I hated most about chemo, I couldn't eat. And I was always so hungry." I feel my face frown at the thought of Saylor going hungry all those nights. I'd never missed a meal, although she never saw me eat one. Now it made me feel guilty. Maybe that's why she never mentioned it. "But I plan to make up for it. I hope you like big girls because I'm fixing to pack on the pounds." This turns my frown into a laugh.

"First of all, you got a lot of eating to do if you want to be a big girl. And second, I probably shouldn't tell you this, but I've always had a thing for big girls." Just the thought of Saylor with a fat ass, wide hips, curves in all the right places, and tits that bulge out the top of her shirt has me nearly coming in my jeans.

"You know, there is a lot I don't know about you," she says, the mischievous smile on her face making the hair on the back of my neck stand up.

"Ask me anything." Hopefully, she would keep it G-rated.

"What is your last name?" Her question catches me completely off guard—more from the fact that she doesn't know it.

"Dixon."

"Dirk Dixon. I like it," she says, letting the name roll off her tongue again and again. In the MC, I was just Dirk. I never had a reason to use my last name. And when I did have to use one, it usually wasn't mine.

"If you weren't a Nomad, what would you be?" Nothing, I'm sure. Talk of the MC and my position in it is not something I want on my mind right now, so I give her an answer that is sure to avert her attention.

"A priest." She bursts out laughing, and it's a stomach-holding, eye-watering, lose-your-breath kind of laugh that has me taking a mental picture. It's a look I never want to forget.

"Okay, one more and you have to be honest." I agree, and wait for her to finish laughing. "Who was your first?" That one was easy and one I would never forget.

"Her name was Harper Sloan. I was sixteen and she was thirty. Her dream was to fuck on the back of a bike and I helped her fulfill it. You should thank her; she taught me everything I know." I wink at Saylor and she smiles at me.

"Maybe I will. Do you know where I can find her?"

"She lives in Georgia. Last I heard she was stripping at Magic City." I watch her fidget a minute and then ask the typical question all women ask when you talk about previous lovers.

"Was she better than me?" Any other time I would lie, but this is Saylor, so I don't have to. I grab her hand and kiss the back of it, then tell her the words I know she is expecting to hear.

"Nobody is better than you." And it's the fucking truth.

"I want to go home" are the words I woke to the next morning.

"Okay," I tell her simply. There is no place I'd rather be than in Jackpot with her. Home. "I'll call Shady and get him to book us a flight."

"What about our car?"

"We'll buy another one." She rolls her eyes at me and sits up, reaching to smooth out her long hair that isn't there anymore. I noticed she did this often. I guess old habits are hard to break.

"There isn't anything here I want to take with me. I just want to go." I know she wants to go home, but I can hear the sadness in her voice as she looks around the place that, until recently, has been her home. "I've been here for six years and the only happy memories I have here are with you, or have been made since I started treatment. Donnawayne and Jeffery always insisted I go to their place. It's a lot nicer." Silence fills the room and I know if I don't say something, she is likely to fall apart.

"I know this place in Jackpot, Nevada. It's beautiful. Like the woman who lives there. And the only happy memories I have of it are with her." She looks at me over her shoulder and smiles.

"Will you take me there?" she asks, that playfulness I've missed is back, and it's promising. I don't answer her, I just reach over and grab my phone from the couch.

"Shady, we want to go home."

26

WE FLEW FIRST class, surprise to Saylor, but not to me. I expected nothing less from Shady. When he picked us up, it didn't surprise me either. But the bike waiting did.

"I heard through the grapevine that someone wanted to ride." Saylor squeals next to me and throws her arms around Shady's neck. I glare at him when he returns the hug, and he gives me the finger.

It's cold here, in the thirties. But I can't deny Saylor something that makes her so happy. Shady hands her a bag and smiles. "A gift from Sinner's Creed." She squats down, opening the duffel and rummaging through the bag full of leathers and boots to keep her warm. I don't know how they got her sizes, but I'm sure Shady had Donnawayne or Jeffery's number laying around somewhere for times like this.

"I got you something too," he says to me, and I follow him to an SUV parked behind the bike. A Prospect sits inside and offers me a nod. I give him a salute, then turn to see Shady holding a leather vest in his hand. "We thought you might like to have this." My own cut is in the backpack on my shoulder. It goes everywhere I do. But this vest is too small so I know it's not a replica of mine, just in case I didn't have it. And where the triangle-shaped creed symbol with the openmouthed, fire-breathing skull was stitched on my cut, this was replaced with *PROPERTY OF SINNER'S CREED NATIONAL DIRK.*

I take the thick black leather vest from his hands and take a moment to run my fingers over the threads. When I turn it over, a patch consisting of angel wings is sewn on the left side, and on the right Saylor's name is stitched in white.

Before I met Saylor, I was just a Nomad. Now both of my worlds have collided and in my hand I hold the proof. Despite my attempts to shield Saylor from the violence of the club, she opened her heart and our home to Sinner's Creed.

She never asked why they did what they did. She never passed judgment on their lifestyle choice either. She accepted them for the men that they were, not the patch they wore.

That diamond-shaped 1% patch I wear stands for something. It signifies that I am a part of the 1 percent of bikers that are outlaws. The 1 percent that isn't afraid of breaking the rules. The 1 percent that serves as their own judge and jury. And that patch is worn over my heart, serving as the only thing that's kept me alive, even when I felt broken inside. Everyone good in this world has a heart that pumps blood, and mine pumped venom. Until now. Now it is full, whole, and completely filled with everything Saylor Samson.

I turn to Saylor, who is all smiles and now fully dressed in leather. She's beautiful. I want her to wear my patch, but more importantly, I want her to know what it means. And I want her to accept it as my vow to always protect her.

"I want to give you something," I say, fighting hard to keep my emotions in check. She walks closer, her eyes shining bright as they land on the cut I hold in my hands.

"I think I've loved you from the first moment I saw you all those years ago. I didn't know what love was, but you showed me. You saved me, Saylor. You're more than I ever could have hoped for in this life." Her eyes well up and I have to take a moment to fight my own tears.

"I can marry you. I can give you any ring your heart desires. But to me, this means so much more. In my world, Saylor, men like me don't find women like you. We're born as rejects, throwaways, and victims of society. You've given men like me hope. You've proven that we are capable of love. And in return, I want to give you something that proves my love to you.

"This is not just a token of my love, but my vow to always be your man. I'll protect you, take care of you, and devote my life to making you happy. Saylor Samson, will you do me the honor of being my ol' lady and wearing my patch?"

She walks closer, running her fingers over the threads, pausing to trace each stitch in my name, the angel wings that signify that, even in death, she will be my angel, always riding on the right shoulder of her man. I don't have to explain the significance of these patches; her knowing smile tells me she understands.

She turns and I slip the cut over her shoulders. She sighs at the feel of the heavy leather. When she turns to face me, tears fall down her cheeks, and her smile lights the world around us. I already know what she is going to say, but I long to hear the words.

"It's perfect."

The woman I love and the club I'm devoted to are no longer two different things. We are one. Her patches signify that she belongs to me, and that I belong to her. I am Dirk, Nomad National for

Sinner's Creed MC, and my soul mate is not just the woman I love or the light in my life, she is Saylor, property of Sinner's Creed Nomad National Dirk. And now, my life is complete.

Saylor loved the ride and even though she was frozen when we got home, she asked if we could go again. Regretfully, I had to decline. I don't know if Shady really forgot, or if he was just being a dickhead, but that bag didn't consist of any leathers for me.

Our first ride together with our colors on would definitely be memorable. Saylor fell in love with the cut, and now that we're home, she refuses to take it off. I'm still thawing out when she asks Shady to take our picture. She glares at me when I don't smile, and I want to explain to her that I can't, but she doesn't give me a chance.

So the picture shows her looking exceptionally hot in leather chaps, a jacket, her patch, knee-high boots, and a black head scarf, and I look constipated. Shady thinks it's a great picture. When my hands thaw out, I'm going to choke him.

Because Saylor is in such a good mood, I say yes to everything she asks that doesn't consist of riding in freezing temperatures. So when she asks if I will eat spaghetti for supper, I say yes. When she asks if I'll watch *I Love Lucy* with her, I say yes. When she asks if I'll shower with her, of course, I say yes. And when we are laying in bed and she asks me to make love to her, I say yes, but this time I don't tell her. I show her.

There is a candle flickering in the room, providing the perfect lighting for my plans. I want to give her what her body craves, what her words ask for, and what her heart desires. And I want to do it with an intimacy that neither one of us has ever experienced.

"You're sure?" I ask her, already knowing that she is. She

nods, her eyes wide and her breath ragged. It's like the first time all over again, but so much better. Saylor lays next to me in my T-shirt and a pair of panties that I've yet to uncover.

I kiss her forehead, cradling her face in my hands, then kiss her lips softly. She is already writhing beneath me and I know she shares the same thought I do; it's been too fucking long.

I kneel between her legs, lifting one up so I kiss the instep of her foot. My tongue trails its way up her right leg to the inside of her thigh, then across to the other and back down to her left foot. Her skin is satin beneath my tongue, the lack of hair making it smooth and responsive to my touch.

When I slide my hands to grip the sides of her underwear, I find lace. Having to see the way her body looks in it, I push her shirt up her stomach and look down to find the tiniest scrap of material covering the swollen lips of her pussy. "Fuck, baby."

I slowly pull them away from her, revealing the part of her my mouth and my cock crave. Her knees fall open further, and I now have a view of the soft, pink flesh that is wet and desperately awaiting my touch. My thumbs spread her wider, exposing her more as I run my finger up and down the length of her pussy. I can't even pull my eyes away from the sight of its perfection. Even when Saylor moans and calls out my name.

"You have the prettiest pussy," I tell her, and when she squirms, I know my words embarrass her, but they make her horny as hell too.

"Please, Dirk. Please." Even now, she still can't ask. And I still won't make her. I lower my head between her legs, putting my hands beneath her ass and lifting it so my tongue has access to all of her. She struggles slightly, but when I tell her to relax, my breath blows over all her most intimate and sensitive areas, and she stops fighting me. Nothing about this moment should embarrass her. There is not a part of Saylor's body I don't want to devour, and when I do, there won't be a moment where she don't enjoy it.

My tongue makes long, circular strokes between her lips—drinking the wetness of her arousal and replacing it with my saliva, which builds from its taste. She is the sweetest, most satisfying thing I have ever put in my mouth. When she sinks further into the mattress and I feel her pulsing, ready for release, I move my tongue further south—invading the forbidden area.

When she screams in pleasure and convulses around me, my tongue pushes deeper inside her, prolonging her orgasm and flooding my face with her sweet release. While she's still trembling with the aftershocks, I move my tongue to the entrance of her pussy, pausing to swirl it inside her before working my way up to her clit, then her stomach, until I reach the swollen peaks on her chest. I lift her up, removing my T-shirt from her body and placing a kiss on top of her head before lowering her back down and letting my gaze fall to her chest.

I torture her small, hard, pink nipples with my tongue until her hips buck in demand of my rock-hard cock that's pressed against her pussy. I balance my weight on my arms, covering her body with mine but not enough to hurt her.

"I love you, Saylor Samson," I tell her, fighting back the tears that I feel burning in the back of my eyes. This time, making love to Saylor—my heart, my reason, my property—has more meaning than any other time I've been with her. It's not because it might be the last. It's because this time, I feel like I'm making love to my wife. It's like that patch she wore so proudly today sealed some holy matrimony between us.

"I love you, Dirk Dixon," she tells me, and when she runs her hands up my arms and neck to curl her fingers in my hair, I feel the heat of fire in their wake. "I want you inside me," she says, lifting her hips to me once again.

I place a hand between us, positioning myself, then rest my forehead on top of hers. With a slow pace I didn't know I was capable of, I push inside the tight, hot confines of her pussy. Just the heat is almost enough to make me come, but I dig deep and find the control to give her what she asks for. I'm halfway in when her eyes close and her breathing becomes heavy.

"You okay, baby?" I ask, as breathless as she is. I start to back out of her, when her hands tighten in my hair.

"It's perfect. Don't stop." She pants against my lips, and I kiss her before I move deeper. When I'm buried deep, all the way inside her, I swivel my hips, catching her moan with my mouth until her hips jerk in anticipation for more.

I make love to Saylor for what could have been forever. Our bodies separated then joined again every time I drove slowly inside her. But my eyes never left hers. The feeling was too much. For both of us.

When Saylor's eyes fill with tears, I watch my own fall on her cheeks. I don't know why I'm crying. There is nothing sad about this moment. Some people cry because they're upset, some because they're happy, and I guess some cry when there is so much to say that you don't have words to say it.

"I want you to come with me, baby. I need you to," I tell her, because we have to stop. It's not the burning in my arms from holding myself over her. It's not the soreness of my stomach muscles from the countless strokes I've delivered. It's the overwhelming feeling of everything all at one time. Love, desire, want, need . . . It's a soul-shattering, heart-wrenching, burning passion that I can't stand to experience anymore. I've never had a feeling as intense as this one. It's just too fucking strong. And Saylor agrees.

I quicken my pace, slightly change my position, and drive harder into her. It's exactly what she needs. My name fills the room in a cry of passion, and I feel her walls as they clamp down hard on my cock. And then I'm filling her. The sound that rips through my chest echoes off the walls in the room, and soon Saylor is comforting me as I cling to her and weep.

The following Monday, Saylor sleeps well past noon. When I ask her if she is all right, she smiles that sleepy smile I love so much and just tells me she's tired. It's enough to worry me and I call Dr. Zi, who offers no support.

"Honestly, Dirk, I don't know what to say. She handled the treatments with fewer problems than I anticipated, and her miraculous recovery still has me confused. At this point, I don't know what to expect. It seems everything that happens is just so unpredictable. My advice is just to let her rest."

I promise the doctor that I will keep him informed and go back to lay with Saylor. The past week has been amazing. Mostly, we've just laid around the house and done nothing. We haven't made love again, but she asks me to hold her a lot, so I do.

I'm still processing my mental breakdown from our last episode of lovemaking. I would do it all over again if she asks, but it doesn't bother me that she hasn't. I just know that if she does, I can't let myself get that involved again.

It's well after two when Saylor decides she is hungry and wants to get up. She's not sluggish and doesn't complain about any pain or discomfort. She's perfectly fine. But it's barely nine o'clock when she starts nodding off on the couch. When I ask her if she wants to go to bed, she says no and forces a smile to assure me she is awake. Ten minutes later, she is out so I carry her to bed and she's too deep in sleep to protest.

Tuesday, Saylor tells me that she feels weak, and that she struggles to get her limbs moving to do what her brain tells them to. Losing her mobility wasn't supposed to happen until later, but she shows no sign of any other problems. I call Dr. Zi again and this time he offers something that is somewhat useful, but not what I want to hear.

"I can't give a full diagnosis without examining her, but if you want my professional opinion I'll give it to you. The only conclusion I can come up with is that another tumor has formed on a different part of her brain. That part being her parietal lobe, which affects her movement. Now, this is all in theory. If she wants to come in, I'll take a look and give you a better analysis."

I tell the doctor that I'm sure she doesn't want that, but I assure him I'll mention it. When I hang up, Saylor is standing behind me, leaning on the wall for support.

"I'm not going back," she says. Her movements might be weak, but her voice is strong and adamant. So I don't argue, I just tell her what she wants to hear.

"Whatever you want."

27

"I WANT TO have a sleepover Friday," Saylor tells me Wednesday night. I ask her who all she wants to come and her answer is simple.

"Everyone." I'm guessing everyone is Donnawayne, Jeffery, Rookie, Carrie, Shady, and me. When I ask her to confirm this, she says yes. So I call them all and they assure me they will be here Friday afternoon. My job is to make sure there is plenty of food and clean towels in the bathroom. I can do that.

Saylor's ability to walk has been diminished to only a few steps every day. And those have to be assisted. I haven't let her out of my sight for fear of her falling.

Her arm movement is better, but after dropping and shattering several glasses, she demanded I get her some cups with lids. Sometimes she gets frustrated at herself. Sometimes we make jokes about it and laugh. But I've yet to see it sadden her or get her down. She seems to have a solution to everything. An electric scooter inside the house is where I drew the line. Not that I minded her having it, I just didn't want her to break her neck.

No one has been informed of Saylor's current issues, and I wonder if I should tell them without her knowing. But she can still read my thoughts, so she answers my unspoken question.

"You can call Shady and let him know about me. Tell him to tell the others. I'm sure Donnawayne and Jeffery are gonna fuckin' lose it." It still makes me smile when I hear her cuss, but not as much as it does to call Shady and tell him he has to break the news to the drama queens.

Saylor's hair is starting to grow back. It's just a little blond fuzz on top of her head, but it's there. When I asked her if she wanted me to shave her legs, a peaceful look came over her face and she smiled.

"There's not any hair on my legs." Because I'm an insensitive idiot, not only do I ask why, but I do it in a condescending way as if the thought of her not having hair on her legs was ridiculous. I'm kicking myself, but Saylor is unaffected. She just laughs and shakes her head. Then gives me an explanation that I wasn't expecting.

"Because I prayed that it wouldn't."

It's finally Friday, and although there is no place I want to be than in Saylor's company, I can't help but feel a little excited about having some male company.

Shady walks in first, shooting me daggers before turning on that big-ass goofy grin for Saylor, who is sitting on the couch. While he says hello, I hug Rookie and Carrie, thanking them for coming.

When Donnawayne and Jeffery walk in hand in hand, I nod. But their red, swollen eyes tell me they didn't take the news well, and that has me saying fuck it and hugging them too. It's just a one-armed hug, but it's a milestone for me. The sad looks fade and smiles are replaced when they see Saylor.

Everyone is happy and nobody mentions or complains about the amount of time it takes Saylor's arms to embrace them in a hug. When I hear her laugh and watch her eyes light up at the faces she loves, I can't help but stand in line and patiently wait for a hug too.

"Hey, baby," Saylor calls to me from the pallet party in the living room. I'm popping popcorn in the kitchen, upholding my promise to be a good host. I go to her, leaning down over the couch so I'm in her line of sight. She yelps at my sudden appearance, then laughs and pokes her lips out for a kiss, which I give to her.

"What's up, beautiful?" I ask, and her eyes sparkle at my words. I've told her she was beautiful many times, but I've never addressed her as if her name defined the word. Maybe I should have.

"Um." Saylor smiles, forgetting what she was going to say. Her cheeks redden and she laughs, still stunned by my words. "I was wondering if I could borrow you a minute. You see, it seems that I have to pee." I give her my best smile, and I know if she could, she would reach out and touch me. So I take her hand and put it on my cheek.

"You know me too well," she says so only I can hear. I kiss her palm and shoot her a wink, then scoop her in my arms and lift her over the couch. "Well that was subtle." She laughs, her head falling back as I carry her down the hall.

This is something I've delighted in, carrying her in my arms, and something she enjoys too. After all we've been through, there is no more room for embarrassment or shame. I just do what has to be done and she lets me. There is no sacrifice on my part when it comes to her. It's my duty, and one I enjoy doing.

I deposit her back on the couch with a thud and Donnawayne frowns at me, but Saylor laughs.

"Oh, don't be so serious, hon. I'm sure if you asked nicely he would do the same to you," she tells him and everyone laughs. Everyone but me, of course.

I grab the popcorn, then lay on the couch between Saylor's legs and place her hand in my hair where I know she wants it. I hear the click of the camera and I look over to find Carrie snapping a picture of the two of us together. Soon, we are all piled on the couch and since I have the longest arms, I'm instructed to take the picture. It takes three tries but, eventually, the selfie is approved by Saylor.

Later that evening, I look out at the scattered bodies that cover the mattresses on my living room floor while Saylor painstakingly writes in her diary. She and I are on the couch, and on the floor next to us lay Donnawayne, Jeffery, Carrie, Rookie, and Shady, on the end.

I wish there were more days like this, but I doubt there would be. It was a special day, for a special girl, and although she was deserving of more days like this, men like me and my brothers were lucky beyond measure to just experience one.

It was no secret that I believed in God, and it was no secret that I didn't deem myself worthy of his love. But tonight, I tell him the words Saylor has longed for me to say. I tell him I know he exists because I see him in the eyes and feel him in the heart of my love. I tell him I'm sorry for all the things I've done and the people I've hurt. And then I thank him for giving me the gift of life. It didn't happen when I was born, it happened the day I met her. And even if this was the last day I had, it was way more than I ever deserved.

Before I fell asleep that night, I told Saylor I loved her. And she told me back. And then she smiled at me, closing her left eye on a wink. It was the perfect ending to a perfect day for me, and a perfect ending to a beautiful life for Saylor Samson.

28

WE BURIED SAYLOR the following Sunday. I arranged to have the service in the evening, just as the sun was setting in the Nevada sky. The funeral was small with only our closest friends present.

Hardly anyone spoke, but there was no silence. I could hear Saylor all around me. I could hear her laughter in the birds that nested in the trees surrounding her grave. I could feel her in the wind that carried the slightest scent of citrus from a source I had yet to find. She was everywhere.

Before I met Saylor, I felt empty inside. I was surrounded by nothing but hate, greed, and power. I never missed her, because I never knew she existed. But now that I've had her and she is gone forever from my life, the emptiness is back, and it's worse.

I'm void of any emotion. Nothing exists inside me. I feel no pain, no fear, no anger . . . nothing. It's like I'm just here being a waste of space and sucking up air that could be better used by anybody other than me.

Yesterday, after the last shovel of dirt was placed on her grave, I wondered how I would move on. Saylor once told me that I was her reason and now that she had me, she wasn't needed in this life anymore. So, if I was her purpose and she was mine, then why in the hell was I still here?

I can't keep the saying *the good die young* from invading my thoughts. If that's the case, I'll live forever. But what is worse? Living a life here on earth without her, or living an eternity in hell without her? It didn't matter. I knew my fate, and it was well deserved.

"We delivered Cyrus's daughter back to him this morning," Shady tells me Monday afternoon.

We're sitting on the couch—the last place I held Saylor in my arms. Shady hasn't let me out of his sight since the funeral. I know he is worried about me, but I couldn't offer him any reassurance that I'm okay. Because I'm not.

"That's good," I mumble, my thumbs rubbing over the leather-bound diary that was Saylor's most prized possession.

"Dirk . . ." Shady runs his hand through his hair. I know what's coming, and somehow I find the strength to help ease my brother's turmoil.

"I know, Shady. I know." My impending doom was quickly approaching. And I'd never welcomed death more than now. I couldn't feel like this any longer. Maybe there wasn't an afterlife for people like me. Maybe hell was just a myth. Could I be that lucky?

Standing, I cut my eyes to him. "Follow me." I lead him down the hall into Black's old room, which now belonged to Shady. Saylor had made it a point to tell him that this house was his home, too. After I'd told her he'd never had a place of his own or even his own bedroom, she'd insisted that we designated this room solely to him.

I open the safe in the closet, making sure he knows what the code is. I pull out a manila envelope, and hold it out to him. "Everything I own belongs to you. I had Cleft draw up the paperwork."

Immediately, Shady shakes his head. "Dirk, it doesn't have to be this way. We can hold them off. I'll help you leave. Hell, I'll fuckin' go with you."

Brotherhood.

My relationship with Shady was the definition of it.

I meet his eyes that are full of sorrow and regret. I feel something twist in my chest. I thought my heart died with Saylor, but apparently a piece of it still remained. And it beat for Shady.

"If there is a man in this world who will understand what I'm about to say, that man is you." Wrapping my hand around the back of his neck, I narrow my eyes on him. "I've never felt peace. She was the closest thing I ever had to it. But even with her, my mind raced with thoughts of when I would lose her, or how I could be a better man for my club. I don't want to be here anymore, Shady. There's nothing left for me."

Tightening my hold, I place my forehead against his and do the one thing I've never done in my life. I beg. "Please, Shady. Just let me go."

Without warning, he pulls me in. I welcome his embrace and tell him everything in this one moment that I've never said out loud. I want to remain silent. I want to hold tight to my dignity. But there is no pride where he is concerned—not anymore. Not after everything he's done for me. And if Saylor taught me anything, it was that sometimes words were needed.

"You're the greatest brother I've ever had," I say, my arms wrapped around him. "You're the only one I've ever fully trusted.

My love for you goes beyond the patch, Shady. You're not just my brother. You're my best fucking friend."

My heart is shattered. Everything I've ever held dear I'm saying good-bye to. I can't do it anymore. I'm mentally exhausted. I'm ready to leave. I'm ready to meet my fate. I'm ready to die.

Pulling away from him, I shove the envelope against his chest, forcing him to take it. In my other hand I hold the most precious thing to me. Only because it was the most precious thing to my love. I hand Shady Saylor's diary. "She loved you. She'd want you to have this."

He looks down at the diary, his eyes transfixed on the book of Saylor's life. Before he has a chance to say anything, I walk out of the room. I don't give a second glance to anything in the house. There is no need for me to look—I have all the good memories already memorized.

On my bike outside, I sit in the darkness. My eyes roam over the dirty patches on my vest. The years of blood, sweat, and tears in my threads blaze through my mind as the memories come flooding back. Everything I've done wrong. Everything I've worked so hard for. All the lives I've taken. They're all a constant reminder of my life as Sinner's Creed.

As I pull out of my driveway for the last time, I don't feel any regret. I don't wonder what my life might have been. I am who I am. I'll die as the same man. Sinner's Creed was my home, my life, and my legacy. This world could take everything it wanted to from me. But it couldn't take this. My Saylor was gone, but my club still thrived.

Sinner's Forever . . .

Forever Sinners . . .

In the end, I might lose the battle. But I've won the war.

Alive or dead, I am the victor.

I am Sinner's Creed Nomad National Dirk . . .

And that's the fucking truth.

I'm riding hard, void of feeling, void of emotion, void of her. All I have are her memories, but they're not enough. So I ride harder, letting the sound of the wind and pipes silence the screaming in my head. But there is another sound that can't be silenced. It's familiar.

The loud rumble of pipes behind me is powerful enough to vibrate the concrete beneath my tires. And then I see them. Countless headlights shine through the dark desert night, and roaring engines speed behind me, creating a perfect two-line formation.

My first thought is that it's my brothers, coming to support me, to let me know that I'm not alone. But as they gain on me with no intentions of slowing, I know they are not my brothers. They are my enemies.

I wait for the familiar feel of adrenaline to course through my veins. I anticipate the heavy beat of my heart against my chest. I rack my brain for the knowledge of what to do. I'm sure the will to survive and desire to fight is coming.

But it doesn't. Just like Saylor, everything fades. I can almost feel the weight of peace as it settles over me like a blanket.

I hear the sound of a bullet being forced from the barrel of a gun. I can hear it whistle as it travels through the air. I can even hear the sound of flesh tearing, splaying open my skin, as it rips through the thick leather of my cut and connects just behind my left shoulder.

But I feel nothing.

My eyes begin to close and the sound of screeching metal against concrete and the thud of my helmet against the road is loud in my ears.

Still, I feel nothing.

Then, there is silence.

My eyes focus on the lights that shine down the two-lane road in front of me. Heavy footsteps surround me and a dark figure blocks the beam of light from my view. I somehow find the strength to meet the eyes of the man who stands before me. Cyrus.

He says something, but I can't hear him. Before the darkness completely consumes me, my last vision is of the shiny, metal barrel of his gun.

Then, nothing.

I don't know how long it's been, but I begin to feel. I wait for the smoldering heat to be so intense that my body ignites in flames. I wait for the sound of painful cries and torture to fill my ears. I keep my eyes closed because I know that if I can feel and I can hear, then I can see. And I have an eternity to look at the misery before me.

But something isn't right. I feel warmth, but not an agonizing, flesh-burning heat. What I hear is loud, but not cries of repent or suffering screams. I crack open one eye, and a shining, blue sky looks back at me. I open the other and stare up into an endless sea of blue sky and puffy white clouds.

My hands move beside me, and the softest granules of sand sift through my fingers. I sit straight up, and miles of ocean water stretch as far as I can see. I can feel, hear, and see so much, but I only have one thought.

I'm dead. And someone fucked up.

There is no fire. There is no darkness. There is no Black. There is only me, the ocean, and the sky. The peacefulness is almost overwhelming, but it settles inside of me, infiltrating every part of my body.

Instead of panic, I feel comfort. Suddenly, I don't know my name. I don't know who I am or how I got here. I'm just here.

Everything that seemed wrong and foreign only minutes ago seems right, and I know I belong here.

I inhale deeply, letting the scent of salt water and fresh air invade my lungs. There is a hint of citrus in the air. I know I should recognize it, but I can't quite put my finger on it.

I pull my boots off and sink my toes into the sand at my feet. It feels like satin. I walk to the water, letting the tide cover the tops of my feet, and it feels warm and cool at the same time. The perfect temperature.

Then I feel *something*. Something magnetic pulling at me, causing me to turn my eyes back toward the tall palms that line the beach.

And I see her. She is a vision in white. Her hair is blond, curly, unruly, and sticks out over her head like she stuck her finger in a light socket. She is the most beautiful thing I've ever seen.

Her smile is wide, two full, pink lips framing a set of perfect white teeth. Her dress flows at her bare feet that she places one in front of the other, bringing her to me. She stops inches from my face, closes her mesmerizing emerald eyes, and holds her arms out to her sides. The light breeze from the ocean swirls her hair around her head and I have the overwhelming urge to close my eyes too. Her scent fills me as memories come flooding back.

I'm a child, crying in the back room of a house. There is a man there, Black.

I'm a man, confused and torn on the inside. There is a knife in my hand and an unrecognizable man laying dead at my feet.

I'm wearing a vest. Thick, black leather covered in patches. I'm a Nomad for Sinner's Creed.

Images of death, feelings of pain, memories of darkness, they overtake me and remind me of who I am.

Then there is her. She is scared. She is distracted. She is singing, dancing, crying, laughing, sick, hurt . . . Then there is me. I am angry. I am powerful. I am a monster. I am feeling, loving, caring, smiling, laughing, praying . . . I open my eyes and she is still in front of me. This angel. She looks shy, maybe even a little nervous. Then, she speaks.

"You're late."

"I'm Dirk."

"I'm Saylor."

"I know."

EPILOGUE

PINK FLOYD'S "WISH You Were Here" is blasting on my stereo. I hear the low rumble of motorcycles, riding at a slow pace. Beneath my feet, the concrete shakes with the vibrations of pipes. Hundreds of bikes ride behind me in two straight lines. And in front of me, in a glass custom-built trailer, lays the body of my brother.

And my best friend.

I've tried to imagine I was honoring someone else by leading the pack in a final ride. My mind flashes with images of Dirk riding beside me. I can almost feel the hate radiating off him—his mind spinning in a hundred different ways on how to bring hell to those who just earned revenge by the hands of Sinner's Creed's finest. His presence is so powerful that I turn and look to my left, expecting to see him wearing that pissed-off look he perfected. But I see nothing.

The reality hits me again, and it hurts just as bad now as it did when I first found out.

One phone call.

Two words.

"Dirk's dead."

He's gone.

Forever.

And all I have left are material things to remind me that he was real. His house. His money. What's left of his bike. And Saylor's diary—the most painful reminder of all.

He was her king.

She was his queen.

I hold the greatest love story of all time inside my cut—close to my heart. The story lives on, but their love will be buried today. Laid to rest with my brother, who's freshly dug grave lays next to the woman who saved him.

I wish this tragedy had ended differently. It should have been me they found dead on that highway. It should be Dirk riding behind my casket today. I pulled the trigger that night. But Dirk took the fall. If he was here, he'd tell me to quit feeling sorry for myself. He'd tell me he only had two reasons to live—Saylor and Sinner's Creed. One was already gone. The other he died for.

If he was here, he'd give me that look that made me feel stupid. Then he'd ask, "Do you really think I'd just lay down and die? I went out the way I wanted. They didn't kill me, Shady. I was already dead."

And he was.

He is.

Tears fill my eyes, but I force them back. Dirk doesn't want my tears. He wants my wrath. My tribute will be paid by slaughtering those who did this. It's more meaningful, and a fuck of a lot bloodier.

Inside, I'm screaming in agony. But no one can hear me. My eyes are filled with sorrow and loss. But no one can see it. My chest aches with a thousand flames from the fiery sea of hell. But no one can feel it. No one but me.

Shady.

The man who was born with nothing, lost everything, and has something he doesn't deserve. Life.

Whatever controls me, whether it is my instincts or my subconscious, leads me to a deep hole surrounded by men and a handful of shovels. These men are said to be my brothers, but the truth is only one ever really earned that title. And I watch as they lower his body into the ground.

Every patch holder strives to make the club prosper. Many will die trying. Dirk did it by just existing. His life stood for what the patch really means. And his death proved that he was willing to give it all for Sinner's Creed.

He will be remembered as the greatest Nomad that ever rode.

A man of power.

A leader.

A ruthless enforcer.

A fucking legend.

He's the most loyal man I ever knew. I never understood respect until I gained his. He's the greatest loss I've ever suffered. And in this moment, I struggle to find the strength to let him go.

I want to crawl into the six-foot hole and breathe life back into his body. I want the man who was too fucking mean to die to rise from this grave. But death was peace for Dirk. And now I have to be at peace too.

I grab a handful of dirt, letting it slowly sift through my fingers and fall reverently on my brother. The granules of sand drop silently, but I swear I can hear every particle land on the black box.

The other patch holders follow suit, taking turns to bury one of our own. The process is slow and torturous, but I beg for it to go on forever. I know that once the hole is filled, then it's over. It will be the end. Just like the last page in Saylor's diary.

This is the end. The end to a beautiful life for me, Saylor Samson.

Now it's the end of Dirk's life. The only beauty of it came from his time with Saylor. With her he found happiness. And when he found it, it was like I found it too. But just like Dirk, that happiness is now buried.

After everyone leaves, I kneel at his grave. My fingers dig into the soft dirt as I bow my head over the grave. Two tears escape me. It's all I allow myself. A tear for Dirk, and a tear for me. A part of me did die out on that highway with him. And today, that Shady is laid to rest. As I stand, I leave what's left of who I was.

I'm no longer the lost little boy who nobody wanted. I'm not a young man searching for his place in the world. I'm not the same man who ran his fingers over the threads of his new patch again and again.

My anger is fueled by all that's been lost. Fury blazes in my eyes. Rage consumes me. Revenge is my only thought. Killing is my ultimate goal. Death is the only justice.

Death Mob killed Dirk. Now they'll pay the price. Their blood will pour like rain from the sky. Their bodies will decompose in shallow graves. The smell of their fear will fill the air. Their days are limited. Their nights will be haunted. One by one, they'll die. Every death will send a message: I'm coming for them.

All of them.

But I'm not coming alone. I'm bringing hell with me.

In Loving Memory of Quinn "Dude" Jordan
12/8/1949–5/31/2015

"I'm tellin' you like God knows it . . ."

———————